HER ONE REGRET

HER ONE REGRET

DONNA FREITAS

Published by Soho Press, Inc.
227 W 17th Street
New York, NY 10011

Copyright © 2025 by Donna Freitas

This is a work of fiction. The characters, dialogue, and incidents depicted are a product of the author's imagination. Any resemblance to actual events or persons, living or dead, is entirely coincidental.

ISBN 978-1-64129-638-0

Interior design by Janine Agro, Soho Press, Inc.

Something is still profoundly missing from our public discourse about motherhood; something still waits to be said, as if on the tip of the tongue.

—ORNA DONATH

LUCY

A BABY CRIES, alone in a parking lot.

―――

Lucy unpacks groceries from her shopping cart, placing them into the trunk of her car on a sunny afternoon in September; a perfect, Narragansett Beach day. She holds the baby in one arm, safe and tight, as she shuttles bag after bag of eggs, milk, bunches of kale, baby gem lettuce, organic greens. The baby, Emma, leans into the top of her mother's bare shoulder, her mouth wide and blowing raspberries against Lucy's skin. Between bags Lucy runs her palm over her daughter's fuzzy head, presses her lips against her baby's skull.

"Momma is doing better, isn't she?" Lucy says to Emma. Even Lucy can hear the strain in her own voice.

"Hmmm, hmmm," Emma says, sucking away on her mother's shoulder.

Lucy fits everything side by side in the trunk so the bags won't fall over. She always ends up with eggs broken, milk cartons dented or spilled, stalks of rainbow chard snapped in half. Sam, her husband, says it's the way Lucy drives, not how she packs the trunk, but he's wrong. He's wrong about so many things, lately. Including the biggest one of all.

Lucy needs to shove the last canvas recyclable sack into the spot where it will keep the rest of her purchases snug, but she needs two hands. She sets Emma into the seat of the shopping cart, then wedges the wheel of it against the wheel of the car so Emma won't roll away across the lot of Belmont Market. She makes sure her baby is sitting just so, her body only a little slumped. Emma gets stronger and stronger by the day, back and neck. It does seem a miracle to watch.

"There," she says to her daughter, who appears delighted by this new experience of sitting in a shopping cart. She kicks her chubby legs, bare toes curling, arms flailing, a happy little bee.

For a moment, Lucy stops. She takes in the sun above, the bright round yellow disk of it beaming down on the two of them, the slightest breeze rushing across her skin and her long, red hair. The world stills. No one else hurries across the lot, no cars drive the aisles. There is only Lucy and there is only Emma, mother and daughter. She looks at her baby, Emma's mouth wide and smiling, so tiny and fragile and soft, eyes so big. She takes in the beauty of this perfect little being, and her heart breaks.

She turns away.

"Mommy loves you," Lucy whispers into the trunk and all those groceries.

PART 1
—
THE FIRST 48 HOURS

1
MICHELLE

"I KNOW THAT baby! That's Emma!"

Michelle Carvalho races across the parking lot yelling, trailing cartons of yogurt. They spill out of her bag and splat open on the steaming asphalt, white ooze on black tar. A protective crowd has formed around the little crying darling, all of them women. Sirens wail in the distance; someone must have dialed 911.

Which is, of course, what one does when a baby is found in a parking lot.

The trunk of a nearby car is open, full of grocery bags.

Lucy's car. Lucy's groceries. In Lucy's canvas recyclables.

Michelle reaches the crowd and dumps her shopping bags to the ground. She stretches out her arms toward Lucy's baby. "Emma, sweetheart, where is your Mommy? Where is Lucy?"

Emma is wide-eyed and quiet, settled against the body of one of the women. Older, gray-haired, maybe a grandmother. She watches Michelle with suspicion. She doesn't move to hand Emma over. "Who are you?" she asks Michelle.

The crowd of women tightens around this newest addition, grocery bags slung over shoulders, plopped onto asphalt, tipped over by feet. The sirens get closer. Another woman, blond-haired, tall, plucks a peach from the top of a bag and holds it to Emma's mouth. Emma leans forward to suck on it. Soon Emma is squealing and sucking the sweet flesh, slurping the juice. A few of the women chuckle. The scene would be adorable if not for the absent mother of the happy baby.

Michelle's eyes scan the group, trying to make contact, to convince them she is not a foe. "I'm Lucy's best friend. Lucy is this baby's mother."

The gray-haired woman nods but still doesn't offer Emma to Michelle. Michelle takes in the state of this body before her, this fit older woman in leggings and a tank top. Shame washes over Michelle. Maybe when her own two boys are older, she'll have the will to get back into shape.

A dark-haired woman with a worried look turns to Michelle. "Do you know where your friend is? Where she could have gone?"

This startles Michelle into action. She shakes her head. "Why don't I just call Lucy? That seems like the logical thing to do, right? Because I'm sure there is a logical explanation for this."

Fear unspools through Michelle for the first time since she came upon this strange situation that is her friend's baby abandoned in the parking lot of the local Belmont, surrounded by a huddle of random women in workout gear.

Where could Lucy be?

Hands shaking, Michelle pulls the phone from her overstuffed bag, stuffed not only with her wallet and car keys, tampons and used napkins and Ziplock bags of cheerios, but also a pound of coffee and a crackling package of strawberries that couldn't fit into her reusable shopping bags at the checkout. Plus a small carton of half-n-half wet on the bottom with milk. A jumble of needs piles up in her brain. She should call the babysitter to say she might be home late, she should call David to ask if he can come home early from work in case the sitter can't stay; shit, that half-n-half is going to get all over everything in her bag. The most urgent need wins out, which is Lucy. Michelle clicks on Lucy's info and calls her, something she hasn't done in a while. Usually they text—constantly, about everything. Recipes, comments about their day, random thoughts about the meaning of life or its lack thereof. Memories from college, from their life before getting married and having children. Frustrations and annoyances about their husbands, David and Sam.

The phone is hot against Michelle's ear. Everything is sticky and humid, the summer heat refusing to break even though it's September. Lucy's line rings and rings, but no answer. Only voicemail.

The women stare at Michelle.

"No luck?" one of them says.

Michelle shakes her head. "Let me try again."

She does. This time one of the women puts a finger to her lips to tell the group to *shush* even though no one is speaking. She bends forward and points under a nearby SUV.

That's when Michelle sees a small, flat object vibrating on the ground. "Oh my god, is that Lucy's . . . ?" Once more, Lucy's line goes to voicemail, and the phone under the SUV stills. Michelle takes a deep breath and hits send to restart it ringing.

The phone under the SUV jumps to life, a steady buzz.

"Oh god, oh no, no, no, no!" Something icy rushes across Michelle, despite the heat.

Another of the women heads toward the SUV. Soon she's flat on the ground and reaching. She stretches her arm and *there*, she's got it, the vibrating phone is in her hand. She crawls out again; gravel and sand cling to her loose black T-shirt dress. She holds up her prize, waves it at Michelle. "Is this it? Is this your friend's phone?" She hustles back to the group.

A hole opens in Michelle's middle. She glances at Emma.

"Hmmm, hmmm," Emma hums as she sucks on that dripping peach, face a mess of sticky, yellow flesh.

The phone case is unmistakably Lucy's. Michelle was with Lucy when Lucy bought it. "Will you be embarrassed if I buy something so girly?" Lucy had asked. Michelle laughed and said, "Of course not, get what you want. Who cares if it's pink and polka-dotted? I like pink. I like polka dots." But when Lucy offered to buy Michelle one so they could have matching phones like two best friends in middle school, Michelle shook her head. "I love you, Luz, but maybe not that much." Lucy had wrapped an arm around her friend's middle and squeezed, told Michelle, "I always knew I was the one who loved you more," and they laughed.

A fire truck screams into the parking lot, followed by another, followed by an ambulance, followed by a few police cars. Emergency vehicles galore, sirens wailing. Michelle thinks in passing, *Charlie would be in heaven, all his favorite trucks are here*, then pushes this thought aside.

Several women in the crowd jump up and down, flagging down the vehicles.

"I'm going to try Lucy's husband," Michelle informs the group, some of whom still look at her with suspicion. "I swear we're friends," she hisses as Sam's phone rings on the other end. "Lucy was over at my house for dinner two nights ago," she can't help adding, even though it's strange to discuss dinner at a moment like this.

Sam's line goes to voicemail.

"Come on, Sam," Michelle mutters. She shakes her head, annoyed, then remembers she has an audience. She tries Sam again. It rings and rings and she huffs. This time she leaves a voicemail: "Sam, call me NOW, this is an emergency."

Next, her thumbs go to work. *CODE RED, EMERGENCY*, she types, *Emma needs you, PLEASE CALL ME. ASAP!*

The ambulance, the fire trucks, the police cars pull to a stop nearby. Men, all men it seems, begin pouring out of these siren-topped vehicles, spilling forth and coming their way. Men in uniforms equipped with belts and pockets and hooks on which to hang the tools of their trade, guns and batons and hoses, crackling radios, frightening metal objects for puncturing tracheas and restarting hearts.

But there is no body to help or bring back to life.

There is only the absence of a body. Lucy's body.

And the presence of a baby.

One giddy, peach-covered baby.

A policeman walks up to the older woman holding Emma. "I'm Officer Fiske. Now tell me what's happened."

Oh, Michelle thinks, swallowing hard. *This is a crime scene.*

"Did someone take Lucy?" Michelle asks out loud. Until this moment, her brain has kept Lucy safe from this terrifying thought. From going to the most upsetting place of all.

Yet another of the women leans toward Michelle, puts a gentle hand on her arm. "I hate to say it, but it's looking like your friend might have been taken," she says. "I mean, I'm trying to think of other explanations, but . . . I just can't."

Michelle's legs give way and she collapses to the ground.

2
JULIA

JULIA GALLO IS sitting on the couch in her living room.

Screams come from upstairs. Incessant wails.

She doesn't move.

Her eyes remain steady on the front door, brain numb.

She wills Marcus, her husband, to walk through it.

It's almost 9 P.M.

Next to Julia is an open sketch pad and her pencils, but the smooth page is blank. It's impossible for Julia to draw, for there to be any inspiration. Maybe she will never draw again, maybe her career as an illustrator is over. Maybe her mind will never experience that spark of creativity like it used to, the excitement that drew her to the page and had her hand flying across all that white space. Maybe she will never again long to pore over the work by her favorite sketch artists, Egon Schiele, Cathy Riley, Monica Ahanonu, Laura Callaghan, Camila Rosa. She didn't know to cherish these urges, the need to feed her eyes with magnificent artworks, believing it would always be there. But it's as if her brain has no thoughts, no desires. No energy, no inspiration, no ideas. Just an endless fog, day after day. Flat and empty. Yet how could Julia have known it would all vanish the moment she had a baby? Everyone told her it would be fine.

Everyone lied.

Julia shifts her gaze to the couch cushions and the shiny outline of her phone. She wills it to light up with a message from her husband.

Theo's wails get louder.

Julia's eyes strain, her whole body strains. The cries from the second floor cause a physical effect on her body, she feels it in her torso, her breasts. If only she could walk out that door. If only she could go and never come back.

Still she doesn't move.

She can't.

She won't.

Tears roll down her face.

They drip off the edge of her jaw and onto her neck, her tank top, down along her aching self. The spit-up stain on the wide, left strap of her top grows wet with the moisture.

The evening is warm, not like September. In another life Julia would be out in town, maybe with Marcus, maybe with another illustrator, the one who does art for children's books who Julia was getting to know before she got pregnant. She used to love nights like these, stolen from summer and gifted to everyone during fall. She used to love to put on a strappy dress and sip cocktails by the water. The contrast of this before-Julia to the now-Julia—she can almost see these two women at once, splitting through time and going off in vastly different directions. She ended up in the wrong Julia's body.

The light has faded from the sky and she sits in near darkness.

But she can't seem to use her legs, not to go upstairs to tend to her baby, not to stand and turn on a single lamp.

When Julia got pregnant and put her due date on the calendar, she immediately saw it as the date her life would end. Beyond that moment there would be nothing else for her to live for—nothing she wanted or enjoyed, nothing to look forward to. No trips, no romance, no exciting new professional opportunities. Just empty space extending onward for eternity. Whereas Marcus saw it completely differently, as though the due date marked the true beginning of their lives. The time when everything good would suddenly befall them as a couple, when they'd finally find true purpose. Julia should have told Marcus the truth when she still had the chance, that the thought of becoming a mother almost made her want to die.

Her phone chimes. *Finally.*

She grabs it, assuming it will be Marcus.

But no, it's Maggie, her older sister.

Haven't heard from you in a while, you okay? Want to chat?

Theo shrieks from above.

The dreaded soundtrack of Julia's new existence.

If only she could shut it off and never hear it again . . .

Julia's mind forcibly turns down the noise.

No, Maggie, no, she thought.

She isn't okay, she'll never be okay again. She doesn't want to talk about it. What she wants is to draw, to go back to her coworking space and spend the day absorbed in sketching for some advertising campaign, or for the cover of a book, yet another avenue down which Julia was taking her career before everything changed: her body, her marriage, her being. She was just starting to get publishing houses interested in her art, which was so exciting, and then, and *then* . . .

The doorbell rings and Julia startles.

Who could it be? She imagines a police officer there to say that Marcus is three hours late because he is dead. That in the end, Marcus has the best excuse of all to have left his wife alone yet again with a screaming child, a child causing Julia to lose her will to live. Or maybe Marcus is in the hospital. She'll open the door and find out something terrible has happened to him—a car accident? a heart attack?—something to justify this abandonment. Because that's what this is. Wholesale abandonment of Julia ever since they took their baby home from the hospital. Marcus has carried on like nothing has changed, leaving Julia to do everything on her own. The fact that Julia needs to breastfeed coupled with his own inability to perform this function have become his excuse for every single goddam thing he cannot manage with Theo and that she must do instead.

The bell rings again.

Julia's gaze travels upstairs. She doesn't have time to get Theo and stop him from crying before she answers. She finally turns on a lamp and squints into the glare of it, trying to adjust her eyes to the shock of light.

She pads across the room and opens the door.

It's the woman from across the street who Julia sometimes sees gardening. Maia is her name, maybe? She's petite, with short dark hair, a friendly smile.

"Hi, I'm so sorry to bother you, but I was outside on my front porch enjoying the evening and I heard screaming and crying, and then, well." Maia's eyes travel behind Julia toward the staircase. "There weren't any lights on and I got worried something terrible had happened."

Theo's cries are so audible, even louder than Julia had realized.

Her face heats with shame.

Maia's gaze returns to Julia.

Does she notice the way Julia's skin flushes red?

"Is that your baby?" Maia asks. "Is he or she all right?"

Julia wipes her eyes, blinks a few times. "Sorry, we're sleep training our son and it's been hell," she lies. "Not being able to soothe him while he cries. The doctor convinced us this was a good idea."

At first the skepticism on her neighbor's face doesn't shift, but then understanding dawns in Maia's eyes and relief spreads through Julia.

"Oh, I remember that," she says. "It's hard to let them cry it out. One time my son cried for three hours straight and I practically had to lock myself in the basement to live through it."

Julia nods. "It's really upsetting."

"Hon, we've all been there, you know? New motherhood is so hard. But you'll get through it, and it will get so much easier. Just you wait."

Julia keeps nodding even though her brain itches to change the direction of her head to side to side. To no, no, *no* it won't, it will not get easier, it never will.

This is the moment Marcus finally comes home.

Of course.

At the sound of Marcus's car, the neighbor turns and looks toward the driveway. She waves enthusiastically at Julia's husband, while a cold rush goes through Julia. She suddenly notices the crickets, how loud they sing in the dark.

The car door slams, the hard sound of it ringing through the mild evening. Marcus comes toward the front of the house, crossing the yard. He eyes Julia head to toe, lingering over her bare feet, her ratty gym shorts, the spit up by her shoulder, before turning his attention to the neighbor. "Hello."

"Hi, I was just checking on your wife," Maia chimes. "I'll get out of your way, I know how hard this is, sleep training and all!" She glances at Julia sympathetically. "Good luck, and so glad everything is okay." Then she turns and heads back across the street.

Theo's cries become whimpers.

Marcus enters the house, shuts the door behind him, eyes traveling upstairs. "What was that woman talking about, sleep training? We're not sleep training! How long has Theo been like this, shouldn't you go to him?"

Fire and ice flow through Julia, equally burning. "Shouldn't *you*?"

Marcus looks at Julia in shock.

Is it shock that Julia wants him to take care of their baby, or is it shock that his wife could allow their son to wail and not go to him? Both?

He dumps his work bag to the floor and thumps his way upstairs, cooing as he goes.

Julia sits back down onto the couch.

She breathes. In and out. She must calm down. She stares into space.

Five minutes pass, maybe seven. Soon—too soon—Marcus descends to the first floor. He didn't truly soothe Theo. Theo will be howling again at any moment. Marcus would know this if he was around more, if he acted like they both had a baby nine months ago, not like just his wife did.

Julia forces herself to stand again. "You're late."

Marcus's face flashes with guilt. *Good. It should.* "I know, but there was a departmental event—"

"It's the third time this week you've come home after nine P.M. You didn't even text me."

"But Julia, you know I teach an evening class this semester—"

Her hands ball into fists. "Your evening class is on Mondays and Wednesdays, today is Thursday. And you never taught late classes before we had Theo. Why *now*? Couldn't you have argued you have a new baby at home and nine P.M. is too late to be getting back to your wife?"

Julia closes her eyes. She breathes through the anger coursing through her, trying to stop herself from saying all that wants out of her mouth, but so many thoughts are screaming to leap from her brain, all of them bottled up. How did she allow this to happen? How did Marcus allow this to happen? How did a single, tiny baby do this to them? To her?

She opens her eyes again.

Marcus stares at Julia like someone body-swapped his wife. "Julia, you know I'm going up for tenure this year," he says quietly. "I have to do what my colleagues tell me. There was a guest lecture tonight and if there's an event I have go. You are fully aware of this. We've talked about it."

"Well, you seem to go to these so-called events and happy hours and departmental dinners more now than before."

"That's not true. Don't you think I'd rather be here with you and Theo?"

"Honestly, no! If it were me, I would rather be at your university than here."

"You don't mean that."

"Oh, I do."

Shadows fall across Marcus's face. His expression shifts between horror and guilt. "You're not being fair. It's not my fault Theo's birth coincided with the year I go up for tenure."

"But isn't it? Isn't it *exactly* your fault? I told you, I *told* you the timing for a baby wasn't right—"

"—but the timing is *never* right for a baby, and it was never going to be right because you kept putting it off, you kept coming up with reasons for why this year wasn't a good time and next year wasn't either because of your work, when the timing shouldn't matter, because a baby matters more than anything else, career, money—"

"That's easy for you to say given that *your* career is flourishing! Whereas mine is sputtering and dying!"

Marcus turns on another lamp. "Julia, we discussed this. I'm the one with a steady salary so it's on me to make sure we can pay the mortgage and take care of Theo's needs! We agreed!"

Julia's fingers curl into claws. "Don't you dare, Marcus, don't you fucking dare try to tell me that your work is more important than mine! Don't you dare gaslight me like that! You do not—you *cannot*—understand what this is like for me, day in and day out. I am all alone in this! ALONE!"

Marcus lets out a heavy sigh. Julia can see him counting, trying to calm down. His face shifts again, filling with sympathy. "You are *not* alone. And you're obviously overtired. I'm sorry if I've contributed to that. Let's talk about everything tomorrow. It's always easier in the morning." Marcus's gaze travels into the kitchen, specifically to what's sitting on the island. His mouth parts, he rushes toward the container, stares at it like it might explode. "What is *this*?"

Julia watches him through the doorway. "You know exactly what it is."

He takes an exaggerated step away. "You haven't been giving this to Theo?"

"I have. And now you will too. Quit acting like it's poison."

"But this is *formula*, Julia. We agreed—"

"*We* never agreed. *You* decided. And now I've decided because it's my body, not yours, that I can't breastfeed any longer. I refuse."

"Breastmilk is the best for Theo, you know this! Everyone knows this!"

Julia's eyes narrow.

Weapons lie all around her. She assesses them, the small, kitschy glass figurine of a fish on a nearby shelf, bought on their honeymoon as a joke, to remember the fun they had, when everything was new and good and easy. There is her mother's blue ceramic vase that was the first thing Julia used when learning to draw as a kid, a precious heirloom of her life as an artist. The glass frame that holds the photo of Julia and her sister, Maggie, looking like movie stars on a beach in bikinis and sunglasses. But she doesn't take any of these in her hands to throw them, to smash them to smithereens, even though she wants to.

"And what about what's best for your *wife*, Marcus? Have you thought about *that*?"

"This is just a few months of sacrifice, Julia. We've talked about it a million times. A few crucial months in our son's life. I know it's hard—"

"No, you don't. You don't *actually* know how hard it is, because every day you walk out that door, a free man. Like you've never had a baby. That needs to change. Because if you recall, *you* are the one who wanted this baby, *you* are the one who promised me the moon if I'd just have one."

Marcus's eyes are wide.

But with what?

"Maybe you need help, Julia."

Julia steps into the archway of the kitchen entrance, reaches for the door frame so she doesn't do something else, something physical and violent. "I don't need 'help.' Don't even do that to me. What I need is my husband to take responsibility for the child he insisted we have and that he promised he'd share the responsibility of caring for."

"You know I can't breastfeed—"

"Which is exactly why we're turning to bottle feeding. Why I've been weaning Theo."

"But Julia—"

"No buts."

A cry pierces the brief silence between barbs.

Theo. Again.

Neither one of them turns, their eyes locked on each other.

Even as Julia's body reacts to the sound of her baby's cries, a response that makes her want to scream and break everything within reach, she stays completely still. "Your son needs you," is all she says in a cold, clear voice. Then, "I'm going to bed. I don't want to be woken for any reason. The instructions are on the side of the formula container. Good luck feeding Theo tonight."

Julia walks away.

She heads up the staircase and right past Theo's room, into the one she shares with Marcus, slamming the door behind her. As she gets into bed, Julia thinks about all she's just said, both the truths and the lies. How the real truth of how she feels about their baby she can't get out of her mouth. Sometimes she can't even allow this truth to enter her brain, and maybe she never will. Maybe this is her penance for as long as she continues to live, to choke on these forbidden words.

3
MICHELLE

"DO YOU WANT to talk about it?" David asks Michelle when they get into bed that night, the kids finally asleep.

Michelle's just settled in with her book to try and read, an attempt to distract herself from the awfulness of the day which includes the seemingly impossible—the disappearance of her best friend. She inhales a sharp breath. What if Lucy's already been . . .

"You know, about Lucy?" David goes on, voice hushed.

His face expresses concern, but Michelle detects the tiniest of thrills; that underneath his effort to show worry, there is also intrigue, even excitement, because suddenly they're living something ripped from a television series—a young and beautiful mother mysteriously disappears while out grocery shopping with her baby.

Michelle turns the page of her book in answer.

She adjusts the reading glasses on her face.

David rolls onto his side and watches his wife, waiting for her to say something. He props his head in his hand.

She draws the book closer, even though this makes it harder for her to read, the words on the page blurring. Lucy's husband, Sam, enters her mind for the thousandth time since this afternoon, the fact that she can't reach him, that he's not calling her back. Where is he? Why is he not returning her messages, texting, something, anything? She glances toward her phone on the bedside table yet again, but it's dark. She resists the urge to grab it to reread her text chain with Lucy, combing it for clues.

David runs a finger down her arm. "Michelle? Come on, I know you. You always complain I don't want to talk enough about what's going on with you, and I can't believe you wouldn't want to discuss Lucy. I'm trying to be a good husband here."

Michelle resists the urge to jerk away from his touch. It's true, she does complain that David doesn't ever want to talk about the things that are important to her, like when it will be time for her mother, Evelyn, to move in with them, or that article she read about the big tech founders who've forbidden the use of screens with their own kids. But those topics don't interest David. The one time Michelle doesn't want to discuss something is the time he wants to run through all the possibilities: Could Lucy really be kidnapped, and if so, by who? Had they seen anyone sniffing around, did Michelle notice anything strange? The sort of things the police officers asked her today. Was Lucy having an affair, could it be her lover? What will happen in the end? Will Lucy be found or will she be gone forever? Murdered? Questions that make Michelle want to sob. All she needs is a bit of peace and quiet, the chance to read a few pages of her novel. Anything to forget. She's allowed to need this, isn't she?

Michelle lets the book fall forward onto her chest. The ceiling fan spinning above the bed seems overly loud. "I appreciate the effort, David, but I don't feel like talking. It's been such a long and difficult day." Her stomach gurgles. She hasn't eaten since this afternoon. She can't ingest food, she's too sick, too nauseated. Every time she tries to lift an almond or a piece of cheese to her lips, she can only wonder, *Is Lucy eating? Is she hungry and scared? Is she . . .*

"I know you're worried," David says, dangling the statement in the air, pushing for his wife to say more. "I can see it on your face."

An angry wave rises inside Michelle at her husband's cluelessness, like the kind she sees on Narragansett Beach after a storm. She can feel his desire to dissect what might have happened to Lucy wafting off him, as though it might be a fun game for them as a couple. It's in the quickness of his breathing, his wide-open expression, he can't hide the intrigue in his gaze about this awful turn with Lucy—Lucy, with her loud laughter, her lack of fear, her sharp comments David often doesn't like—"David, are you *really* going to let your wife clean up all the dinner plates like that? Are your hands not working today?" Things Lucy will say to David with a smile, but her tone is always unmistakably cutting. Lucy is fierce and calculating when she doesn't trust you or like you. This is one reason Lucy's been so stellar at real estate, charming and sweet on the outside, yet with a killer instinct, a shark masquerading as a siren. But when Lucy loves you, she is the most loyal person on earth.

"I am worried, David," Michelle snaps. "Of course I am."

She turns her head and catches sight of the framed photo from their wedding on the wall. A candid shot from their outdoor dinner. In it, Michelle is leaning close to whisper in David's ear and David's mouth is wide open and laughing, a shining glass of wine clutched in his hand. This image evokes so much, the joy of their day, their playfulness with each other, their future sons. All the sex they'd have in those early years of marriage.

And then ... now ... well.

Michelle tears her gaze from the photo.

David is blinking at her, waiting for her to say more about Lucy, Emma, the police who interviewed his wife earlier in the day. "Michelle?"

It seems impossible how much can change between two people in only a few years.

"Come on, you can talk to me," David presses.

But can she?

Michelle gives in. "I'm terrified, all right? What if it's true and someone kidnapped Lucy? Some sociopath? What if she's right now ..." Michelle shudders, pain shooting through her middle, the book lying on her body jolting as she flinches.

David's brow furrows. "Wait, why wouldn't it be true that Lucy was taken? Where else could Lucy be?"

The secret Michelle has kept for Lucy burns in her mind, the flames of it rising. She wants to douse it with a bucket of water; no, an entire ocean. She wishes she could unknow it, that Lucy had never told Michelle a thing. That she could rewind to that night at Lucy's house and unhear all those words. Though maybe if Michelle could just repeat them out loud, the act of doing so would disarm what Lucy said, and Michelle would realize there is just no way.

But the look on David's face ...

No, she can't. She can't tell anyone.

Michelle shakes her head. "I'm not going to let myself think about what might be happening to Lucy. About where she might be right now." She closes her eyes.

For a moment she's grateful to be secure in the house she

shares with David and their two children, this comfortable bed with the soft but not too-soft pillows that she searched for until she found the perfect ones. She presses her head into them, lets her body sink into the smoothness of the sheets, the safeness of the room, her husband next to her, this man she fell in love with after college when she'd convinced herself there wasn't a man she'd be willing to marry and yet there was, and it was David. She relaxes into the thought of him watching over her, day and night, ensuring that she and their children are protected.

But then Michelle opens her eyes to find her husband still staring, still waiting, still wanting yet another thing. When did her husband become so like a third child in the house, another person who looks to her with need after need after need?

"I mean, it seems that way, Michelle," David says.

"What way?"

"That Lucy was taken. Right?"

Michelle nods. But now she is enraged again. She expands with this anger, it's uncontrollable, it's filling her up and she imagines floating above the bed on top of it, a poisonous cloud of gas suspending her there. She can't stop her emotions from careening, they've been careening all day. "I think we are going to wake up tomorrow and find out Lucy is fine," she says. "That this was all a misunderstanding, and today is going to seem like a dream. Lucy is going to show up at our door, we'll hug and end up laughing about the drama of today." She wants to believe this.

But David is not listening. "I mean, Lucy would never leave Emma on purpose. Can you imagine? Doing that to Charlie? To Aidan? Just up and leaving them screaming in some parking lot? Alone and vulnerable?" David's voice gets higher, more agitated as he paints this impossible and horrific scenario for his wife.

The truth is, David is right, and no, Michelle cannot imagine leaving a baby alone in a parking lot. She cannot bear the thought of leaving her children alone in a public place.

"Please, David, I don't want to talk about this anymore, I just can't." Before David can reach for her, needing yet another thing, she sets her unread book onto the nightstand and leans over to shut out the light.

Michelle pulls the covers up to her chin and rolls onto her side, facing the wall. She does her best to wipe away thoughts of Lucy, of unspeakable things happening to her friend, of Lucy stuffed into a trunk, bound and gagged, bruised and frightened and hungry. Or in some psycho's basement, chained to a wall. She can sense David still hovering, waiting. She pretends to sleep.

4
DIANA

DIANA GONZALEZ HASN'T slept all night.

The clock says 4 A.M.

The retired detective tosses and turns in bed next to her wife, Susana, who sleeps so peacefully. How does she do that? Diana hasn't slept that peacefully in years. Being a detective will do that to a woman.

She shifts in bed again and shivers even though it's hot. The air conditioner is limping along and needs to be replaced. The uneven groan of it is so loud Diana's tempted to get up and turn it off but then the bedroom will become stifling. Diana turns her pillow over seeking the cool side of it, but it's just as warm as the other one.

Maybe she should get up. Maybe tonight there will be no sleep. Maybe she should just accept this. It's not unusual for Diana to be unable to rest. For years, maybe even more so since she retired, whenever Diana closes her eyes and before dreams come to claim her—if they even do—she inevitably thinks about some of the worst cases in her many decades on the force.

There was the man who raped and killed three teenage girls in quick succession twenty years ago during three separate high school after-proms on the beach. He snatched girls stumbling around in the wee hours of the morning, drunk and vulnerable. He took advantage of the spring high school formals season, when half the teenagers in the state head down to the water for parties and plucked them right off the sand. By the third killing the governor of Rhode Island called off all after-proms unless they were held inside school gyms with tight security and guards posted at the entrances. Even though Diana and her partner, Joe, had found the killer before he could take the life of a fourth young woman, the dossiers of the three he did murder would haunt her forever, the devastation of their parents, all those friends and loved ones.

Then there was the man who held his wife in a locked room whenever she displeased him, even for an infraction as minor as breaking a dish. He would let her out after an amount of time he determined was commensurate with the violation, until one day he didn't let her out and her best friend—who'd been suspicious of the man for years—reported her friend missing. But it was too late. They found the poor woman dead inside.

Rhode Island is such a lovely place, a person might think that nothing bad ever happens here, but Diana knows better.

Bad things happen everywhere, and they usually happen to women and girls. Women, girls, and children. Accidental deaths because of guns and drugs, domestic violence a common disease that runs in the veins of the most average households. These cases stick with Diana too. But there is something about these men—because it's always men, isn't it?—who plan and prey and terrify a place, that have always obsessed Diana the most.

Maybe it's because she was on the force back when Craig Price, the notorious Rhode Island teenage serial killer, murdered four people, two women and two young children. Price began his killings at the age of thirteen. He mowed people's lawns, which is how he got access to his victims. He stabbed each of them dozens of times, so brutally the police found the knife handles splintered. Cold-blooded killings during middle school. Diana had just made detective and she was still far too green to catch such a high-profile case. But hearing her colleagues talk about the investigation as it unfolded had chilled her to the bone. They'd figured out the killer was the kid from down the street because one of the victims had bit off the tip of Price's finger and it was found inside the poor woman's stomach.

Diana turns again in the bed, so she faces her wife, who's still snoring peacefully.

No wonder Susana had been so happy when Diana retired.

There *were* happy endings during Diana's career.

Of course there were.

But it's always the unhappy ones that haunt a person. The random deaths by guns left lying around that could have been prevented, the ravages of drugs within a family. Having access to all the horrors one human will commit against another.

Against women. So many *women*.

Diana rolls onto her back and blinks her eyes open in the darkness.

Stares at the ceiling.

Maybe it's the sea air, the salt and tang of seaweed along the Rhode Island coast that sparks it. An occasionally deadly cocktail of beachgoers letting their guard down because the ocean and the surf relaxes them, combined with the reality that murderers and sociopaths live to take advantage of exactly those individuals who think nothing bad can happen in such a beautiful place. Families move to Rhode Island because they believe it's one big small town, beachy and quirky and safe. But while it's a tiny state, it also has four hundred miles of coastline. Four hundred is a lot. So many nooks and coves good for snatching someone and hiding a body afterward. The churn of ocean waves loud enough to cover someone's screams. The tide strong enough to suck remains into the deep blue sea forever.

Diana sits up in bed. She reaches for her phone on the table with her books, her pills, her reading light, and gives the screen her thumbprint. It lights up. She calls up the message that Joe, her ex-partner, sent before bed.

We've got another missing woman, D.

The Narragansett Belmont parking lot—baby left behind in a cart.

Young mother, beautiful.

Thought you'd want to know.

Her heartbeat skips.

Her eyes catch on three particular words.

Another missing woman.

Another.

She thinks of Joanna D'Angelo from three years ago.

Susana's steady breaths are loud in the dark.

Or is that Diana's guilt calling out?

She finally does what she knew she'd do all along when Joe's texts first came in. Her fingers tap against the screen.

Yes I do want to know, so keep me posted.

5
JULIA

JULIA WAKES TO Theo wailing and she groans.

The soundtrack of her every morning for the last nine months.

She turns her head to the left. Marcus's side of the bed is empty. Maybe he's already on his way to their son to quiet him, to pluck Theo from his crib and cradle him, to do whatever it takes to calm their baby. At least, this is the fantasy.

Julia waits.

The sunlight filters through the curtains. Last night, she slept like the dead. The kind of sleep that obliterates all thought, even dreams, the kind of sleep she hasn't had in ages. If only she didn't wake up to this life again, if only she'd woken up in a different house. If only she'd woken up as a different person. Unmarried, unmothered.

Can a woman do that, *unmother* herself?

Julia keeps waiting for the moment she'll feel bonded to her son, that miracle other women talk about when connection and unbelievable love will flood her person and overcome the dread, the sadness, the resistance. But it never happens. How could it, when all motherhood seems to involve is crying, feeding, changing on repeat, her every moment hijacked, a level of exhaustion she never understood was possible, plus a newly oblivious husband and a total erasure of her person. How do other women do it? Or is Julia just made wrong, an essential gene left out of her blueprint?

Theo's wailing continues.

Come on, Marcus.

She checks the clock. 6:03 A.M. She glances at her phone, sees a notification from the group text of friends from art school, surely yet again about Daphne's growing success, her star rising ever higher because of Instagram. Julia can't bear to watch Deke and Hans and Selene carrying on about Daphne, then Daphne pretending to be modest about everything. So Julia has stopped checking their messages. She had been rising once like Daphne too.

"Marcus?" She lifts her head from the pillow. "Marcus?" she yells again, louder.

She longs to hear Marcus calling back, reassuring her that he's taking care of things, trying to make up for the many months of consecutive nights of sleep his wife has lost due to breastfeeding. Speaking of, her breasts ache, though not as much as they did when she first turned to formula. What a mess, her body filling then leaking through the pads onto all her clothing, the worry she'll be walking around in public with wet spots on her chest, the shame of not even realizing it. But every day that passes her body feels better, more her own again. Yes, she was right to wean Theo. She should have never agreed to breastfeed in the first place.

Julia pulls her legs from under the covers and plants her feet on the floor.

Rubs her eyes.

She'd planned to tell Marcus she was weaning their son. She was going to do it when he came home in a good mood.

She had an entire argument prepared, to soften the blow because Marcus is obsessed with her breastfeeding Theo as long as possible to stave off allergies like the ones he suffers, believing he has them because his mother didn't breastfeed him. And maybe Marcus is right, that not being breastfed is why he has eczema and can't have pets, but it's easy for him to tell Julia she must breastfeed for at least a year because he isn't the one chaining himself to a baby hour after hour, day after day, feeding Theo from his own body, enduring the pain of cracked and bleeding nipples, the sheer agony of it.

Breastfeeding has been her undoing. Like an open invitation for everyone to ask her about Theo, how long will she continue breastfeeding, which leads to other questions Julia loathes, like is Theo crawling yet, has he tried to walk, what is he eating, does he have any words, has he tried *Mama, Papa? Dada?* It's as if by giving birth, Julia stopped being a person with a life separate from her child, as though all new mothers only want to talk endlessly about their babies. If one more person extols the gloriousness of the mother's body to be able to nurture a baby with milk from her own breasts, Julia might claw their eyes out. What it's done is imprison her in the house, deprive her of sanity by not allowing her to sleep for more than a few hours at a time, and cause her to feel like an animal. Not to mention making it impossible for Julia to sketch, to get back to work, like her brain will never function again, not the way it used to. She can't even bear to visit her favorite artist Instagram accounts. They only depress her and remind her of what she isn't doing for her own career. Then there's the fact that Julia seems to have stopped being a sexual being. She can no longer conceive that her breasts were once a source of pleasure, and can't imagine allowing her husband to ever touch them again. She doesn't think she could endure it.

She reaches for the hairband on the bedside table and pulls her hair into a ponytail.

"Mama's coming!" she calls over Theo's cries, attempting to be cheerful.

But Julia doesn't get up, instead she slumps forward, head in her hands.

She can't. She just can't. But she has to.

This is the deal she signed up for, isn't it?

So like every other morning since Theo came home from the hospital, Julia steels herself, pushes herself to standing, forces herself to take the steps that lead into Theo's room.

His face is red.

How long has he been crying?

"Mama's here," she coos, tone strange, like she's playing the part of someone else on a stage, pretending she's a real mother. If only she could go home after the show to an apartment she lives in alone. Julia scoops Theo up, kisses him all over his face, and he quiets, staring at her. She smells his bottom, checks his diaper to see if he's wet. He's just hungry.

"Let's get you fed," she sighs, and carries Theo downstairs into the kitchen, talking the entire way as he clings to her, quiet now, against her hip. "Where is your daddy, hmm? Where did he go so early? Did he flee his responsibilities as usual? Do you think he's got a made-up student meeting at school? Did he leave Mommy all alone with you as though he had no part in making you even though he promised Mommy they'd do this fifty-fifty? Is that what's happened *again*?" Julia turns on the kitchen faucet with her free hand, runs the water so she can prepare the formula. "Marcus!" Her voice is becoming shrill. "Are you home? Marcus!?"

When again there is no answer, her throat tightens. Tears sting her eyes. She avoids her baby's stare. Her guilt is immense, a vast wide country occupying her insides, uncrossable. She will never reach the end of it.

Julia shuts off the faucet and everything goes quiet.

A tear escapes her left eye, rolls down her cheek, the hours ahead in this day are many, so many, too many. If only her sister lived closer. If only Julia made more friends after they moved here and before Theo arrived. Been less of a loner. But then, her art has always been company enough. Until now.

"Where the *fuck* is your daddy," Julia whispers into the kitchen.

She buckles Theo into his high chair. Goes through the motions of mothering. But no matter how often she goes through these activities, it doesn't turn her into a person who adores having a baby. Marcus wants Julia to be this good woman, he waits for some perfect mother to show up in his wife's body. But Julia is never going to be that woman. How can Marcus not see that he didn't marry *that* woman? Can he not see Julia at all? Has he never seen her?

As she prepares the formula for her son something catches her eye.

A note on the countertop.

One of her graphite pencils lying next to it.

She picks up the little paper, the message on it written with her artist's tool. *I had to leave early—getting my teaching evaluated today, there was no way I could go in late. Hope you got some good sleep. Let's talk about everything tonight. I love you, Marcus.*

She stares at the words. The smoky texture of each graphite

letter. Egregious. Taunting. Thoughtless. Why couldn't he just open a drawer and take out a regular pen? The cup stuffed with different pencils—charcoal, graphite, colored—that Julia keeps in the corner of the kitchen catches her eye, the place where Marcus retrieved his writing utensil of choice. The placement of this pencil holder is left over from the days when Julia was constantly sketching, trying on different styles depending on the task. She hasn't touched a single pencil for months. But now her arm reaches toward it, fingers plucking the deepest black charcoal she can find. She grips it in her hand so tightly it hurts. Places the note back onto the counter. She moves the pencil across the tiny paper in lightning strokes until Marcus's words are blacked out completely.

Theo whimpers behind her.

Her hand stops moving.

She nearly forgot he was there.

She doesn't turn around.

Instead, she sends the pencil rolling across the countertop away from her and it comes to a stop against the wall with a weak *clink*. Then she crumples the note into her fist and lets out one long cry of anguish, one that matches her son's as he joins her in this concert of despair. But Julia's voice screeches out of her, high and desperate, like some kind of animal. Theo's shrieks grow louder too but she still can't face him. She goes to the sink, throws the paper into the drain and turns on the faucet full force, watches the little yellow square become wet, then begin to disintegrate into a pulp, evidence of her violent scratchings along with it.

Julia is trapped. This was always going to be a trap and she walked right into it. This thought emerges against the backdrop of her son's ever louder needs, which she will have to attend to because—like every other day since she gave birth to Theo—she has been left alone to do so. Marcus will always have an excuse to leave the house and not deal with their baby. If it's not his teaching being evaluated it will be a departmental event or a departmental happy hour or a conference where he must present, or it will be extra departmental service, yet another committee he'll sit on, or additional office hours to show how good he is as a professor. Or it will be student meetings or a meeting with his chair or a meeting with the dean or a meeting with the goddam president of the institution. Tenure is Marcus's excuse this year, but then it will be going up for full professor for the pay bump, then it will be the importance of maintaining good standing at his university because of the college benefits they offer faculty kids.

Meanwhile, Julia has no formal work structure, no boss, no colleagues pulling on her time, needing her presence. She's a freelancer, she can't even provide her own health insurance. She failed to see that the only person truly requiring her after having the baby *would be the baby*. But did Marcus see it? Did he calculate how this would play out like in some kind of chess game, anticipating future moves Julia could not yet predict? God, did he *plan* this, realizing he had a built-in escape hatch that would release him from the care of his own child? The child he begged Julia for, or else his life—their life—would be without true meaning?

The force of the water beating the metal of the sink is loud and it pulls her back to the present. She stares down at the decimated bits of Marcus's note in the drain. Shuts off the faucet, realizes that her son has grown quiet. She leaves the paper remnants clogging the sink, and finishes preparing Theo's bottle.

She turns to face him.

He looks at her with those wide dark eyes, cheeks wet with tears.

"You hungry?" she asks, like she's talking to an adult. She just can't muster that *other* voice, the mother's voice. Sympathy, really all emotion aside from anger, eludes her.

Theo reaches for the bottle, she sits down next to him, helps him hold the thing.

With her free hand she wrangles her laptop open to read her feeds. The thing everyone is posting about this morning startles her. The link that everyone is sharing, including Maggie. The same headline pops up over and over as she scrolls.

LOCAL MOTHER DISAPPEARS FROM NARRAGANSETT PARKING LOT.

Local, as in local to Julia.

She clicks on it and starts to read.

Not five minutes after the bottle is empty, Theo is full of protest and Julia is full of thoughts of women gone missing. She shuts her laptop and turns to him. Some babies fall asleep after they're fed, but not this one, not today.

Julia peers into his tear-stained face. "We're going out for coffee," she tells him, even though it's barely after 7 A.M.

What do other mothers do with so much time alone with an infant?

How do they fill the hours?

She packs Theo's squirming body into the stroller while he protests this too. She misses the quiet of the house before this baby arrived. The serenity of this kitchen. She used to love to be alone with her work.

"Extra blanket," Julia lists, talking as she goes, tucking Theo's favorite blanket around his arms and under his legs, looping the pom-poms bordering the soft fabric into the stroller's seat belt so the thing won't fall off when Theo kicks his little legs on their walk. Julia makes sure she has Theo's bottle in the pocket behind the stroller's handlebar, formula packets, a banana and yogurt for herself, the garish green vinyl bag she's grown to loathe full of diapers, burp cloths, spare onesies, pacifiers. It's like packing for Europe, except that Julia's not going to Europe. Maybe not ever again.

Did Lucy Mendoza do things like this just yesterday, bundle her baby and all this paraphernalia into her car to go off to the market? For an afternoon that would turn out to be anything but typical, because she wouldn't be coming back?

A shudder rolls up Julia's spine.

She shops at Belmont all the time.

Before she can convince herself that it's pointless, she goes to the shelf in the living room and slides out one of her favorite art theory books from school, and returns to the kitchen, tosses it into the basket on the bottom. Along with her newest sketchbook. Maybe she can find five minutes to get beyond the banal this morning.

Theo screams louder.

"I know, I know, you wish you had another mother too, I don't blame you," she says. But then she runs a hand along his chubby cheeks. Forces cheer into her voice. "You'll be happy in a sec, I promise. We're going outside and it's another beautiful day!"

For a second her son stops and blinks up at his mother.

Julia bends down, kisses him. She can't resist.

And there it is, right before her eyes:

Julia's potential.

To be a good mother.

She can see it there, sparkling in the air like dust.

But when she pulls back her son's cries resume.

"Okay, all set and we're off." She points the stroller toward the back door, opens it, gets Theo down to the walkway, turns the carriage so it's on the path between her house and the neighbor's. She maneuvers the carriage around a crater in their driveway, leftover from last year's bitter winter. Weeds poke up in the middle of it.

The stroller jolts over another pothole.

Then, a loud bump comes from the house next door.

Followed by a hollow-sounding thump.

What was that?

Julia halts the carriage.

A chill runs across her skin. She feels its tug along her scalp. Did the noise come from the window by her head on the first floor, or the one in the neighbor's basement? Whatever it was, there was something . . . *off* about it.

Lucy Mendoza fills her mind.

Imagine if . . .

Julia shifts her head right, toward the neighbor's house. She has never met the man, not formally. She sees him on occasion in the driveway or crossing the front yard. After he first moved in, Julia would wave, but he would only look at her, nod slightly. He never waved back, never smiled or registered any facial expression. Eventually Julia stopped trying to greet him. If she's honest, he gives her the creeps. His eyes are always so . . . empty. So grotesquely vacant. She even sketched them once, attempting to give life to their vacuity.

"Let's get out of here," she murmurs, shoving the carriage forward again. They reach the sidewalk and turn down the street, Julia chatting about the trees and the clouds and the color of the sky today, a Columbia blue if she were to sketch it. Anything to fill the quiet on their way to the café. She tries to banish her neighbor's eyes from her mind, but she can't. As she rambles on about the sweet French bulldog they pass, followed by a friendly golden retriever who noses Theo and makes him giggle, Julia wonders what in the world the man does in there all day.

6
MICHELLE

WHEN MICHELLE WAKES up, the sun is rising, the air is warm, the summer still claiming September for itself, hot and humid and bright. Cheerful, beachy, glorious. If it were any other day, Michelle would be planning an outing with her sons.

But it's not any other day.

Michelle's best friend is missing.

What if Lucy's not just missing but . . .

Michelle swallows hard.

The word *dead* whispers through her mind.

She forces air into her lungs, pushes this thought away, slips out of bed quietly to check on the kids.

First Charlie, the oldest, sleeping in his big boy bed with his Spiderman sheets, bought by his Spiderman-obsessed father. Charlie's skinny limbs are tossed about, half-in, half-out of the covers. Sometimes the sight of him, the slightest baby pudginess that remains on his body, the softness of it along his arms, his cheeks, makes Michelle want to weep. Her little boy is growing up, and soon the physical signs that Charlie was once a baby will disappear forever. Most days Michelle is thrilled Charlie's baby years are behind her, but there are moments she wishes it all back, that time when Charlie was just a blinking bundle she would scoot around in a carriage. Michelle had no idea how she'd feel when she had her first child, but she wasn't prepared for the intensity of this overpowering, blinding love. Sometimes the mere sight of this tiny, beautiful person she and David created steals her breath, knocks her over. It's first love all over again, but stronger. Overwhelming and beautiful and terrifying.

Michelle ducks out of Charlie's room and into Aidan's to see her little one, his round tummy rising and falling peacefully, his quiet breaths, his sweaty curls. His perfect rosy cheeks. That belly of his is what always gets her, the sweet sight of it. How she loves to pat it, how she adores his laughter when she does. Yet another child Michelle can't believe is shifting from baby to boy, pudgy arms and legs becoming longer and leaner by the day. How does a mother stop this from happening? Can Michelle just put her children on pause so she can take them in leisurely, witness their beauty, stand there and stare without moving, without attending, without worrying? Michelle tries to take in each small change as it happens, careful not to miss any of it.

When Aidan was just a solid little thing at three months, she and David joked he was their sack of flour. Dense, thick, growing heavier and heavier, their arms building muscles from holding him. How they marveled at each new pound on his body, the relief of Aidan becoming sturdier than when he was born. Aidan, always smiling and laughing, such a joy after the colicky trauma of Charlie's first year, when Michelle thought she'd never stop hearing his cries, or bouncing him around the house, or driving him in the car, or pushing him around in the stroller, anything to quiet him. She almost didn't want a second child, but she's glad they had one anyway, since Aidan helped to heal all her scars from Charlie's baby years.

Besides, Charlie has turned into such a love, and now Michelle has two sons she worships maniacally. Sure, they've changed her life. But who cares when a woman finds out that a love like this not only exists, but she now possesses it simply by becoming a mother?

After checking on her sons, Michelle goes downstairs to put on coffee and to guzzle at least one cup before the rest of the house wakes up. This is how Michelle manages the chaos, this one private cup of coffee all her own, a fifteen-minute gift she gives herself that she cannot live without. But as she's spooning grinds into the filter, closing the lid, flicking the machine's switch to *on*, reality hits her again like a terrible slap.

Lucy. Emma crying in the parking lot. The circle of worried women.

Where is Lucy now? Could she have come home in the night?

"Please, please have come home in the night," Michelle murmurs into the silent kitchen. She checks her phone for texts from Lucy, for messages from Sam, telling Michelle all is well, her best friend has returned and this was all a misunderstanding, even a funny story. Wait till Michelle hears.

Nothing from either of them.

She rings Sam again despite the early hour, but it goes straight to voicemail. Then she stares once again at the text chain between her and Lucy, rereads the last message Lucy sent yesterday morning:

I got a fancy bottle of wine from a client. Let's drink it together soon?

Michelle stares at Lucy's last words.

She wanted to see Michelle. Soon.

She scrolls higher. Reviews their back and forth, so much of it mundane. The two of them making plans, complaining about lack of sleep, bitching about husbands falling short, sending random photos, selfies from a dressing room trying to decide on a pair of pants, another of jeans, dumb videos, cats, bears, Minions GIFs because Lucy loves Minions, so much that Michelle got her a stuffed Bob. Michelle keeps scrolling—she can't stop—all the way to texts from months before, an entire line of champagne emojis from when Lucy sold her first house after Emma was born, followed by three words from Lucy, *Hooray for me!* Michelle goes back even farther on the text chain, closer to Emma's birth where there are big swaths of time when the conversation is one-sided, with Michelle trying to coax her friend to life again post-baby.

The coffee machine gurgles and gasps.

Michelle reaches for the pot, hand shaking. She splashes coffee onto the countertop, onto the floor, onto her hand, burning herself.

"Shit!"

She sets the pot back onto its warmer, makes herself breathe slowly, in and out.

Michelle can try to do all the normal things to start off this day, but she can't change the fact that her best friend is gone. All night her brain simmered with the knowledge of Lucy's disappearance, but she worked so hard to tamp it down. Yet here it is again with the morning, pressing on her, invading her mind, her house, their lives. Fear blooms and spreads like cancer.

She picks up her phone to google Lucy's name.

Michelle was walking across her college campus when she first saw Lucy, striding toward her, all legs and willowy limbs.

Michelle was struck by this fellow student, her glossy red hair, translucent skin, the way Lucy glowed, how she almost floated above the sidewalk that cut across the quad, like the earth couldn't hold her there. Then Michelle noticed the beautiful woman was crying.

She reached out an arm before Lucy could pass. "Are you okay?"

The woman stopped, clearly startled. But then she shook her head, blinked at Michelle, said with the slightest of accents, so slight Michelle couldn't place it, "Not really, no."

Michelle was surprised at herself, talking to a stranger. But it was their freshman year, the time a person does such things, becomes daring and different. Michelle was leaving her past behind, emerging new from the chrysalis of high school. "Do you want to sit and talk about it?"

The woman brushed a lock of hair from her face and nodded. "I'm Lucy," she said. "Luz, actually, but everyone here calls me Lucy."

"I'm Michelle. Just Michelle."

Lucy, or Luz—which one should Michelle use?—nodded. The tears streaming down Lucy's face caught the sunlight.

They walked over to a bench to sit in the shade of a big old maple tree. Michelle's first week on campus, she stumbled to this same bench with some sophomore guy whose name she no longer remembered, to kiss him for about thirty seconds. She shook off the memory and focused on the woman next to her.

At first Lucy cried, and Michelle handed her a napkin she dug out of her bag full of heavy textbooks. Michelle was still pre-med, though soon she'd change to anthropology, and eventually to advertising.

Lucy sniffled, dried her eyes and looked at Michelle. "Men are shit," she said.

Michelle laughed.

Then Lucy laughed too.

"They can be, yeah," Michelle said. "I kissed one that turned out to be a total shit on this bench a few weeks ago."

Lucy dabbed at the corners of her eyes. "Yeah?"

"Yeah. He seemed into me, and we started making out, then he abruptly pulled away, looked me in the face and said, 'You know what? Nah. I changed my mind,' and he just got up and left without another word."

"Wow. Seriously?"

Michelle raised her right hand. "I speak the truth."

"Well, fuck *him*," Lucy said.

Michelle caught her gaze. "And fuck your guy too."

The two college first years laughed again, then smiled at one another.

It was the beginning of a lifelong friendship that would involve traveling to each other's homes to meet each other's families, Lucy to Michelle's in New England, Michelle to Lucy's in Chile; a friendship that would outlast countless romances and outweigh even their marriages, that would traverse the birth of children and the tragedy of miscarriages along the way for Michelle. The beginning of the best kind of love story between women friends, the kind that surpasses all other types of love because it will endure even the darkest and most shocking of confessions, the most scandalous of whispered truths. Lucy was there for Michelle when she lost her dad and couldn't climb out of her grief, and Michelle coaxed Lucy through heartbreak after heartbreak during their twenties, before she met Sam.

Lucy and Michelle would be together, always, even if the men in their lives had moved on.

At least, until years later, when Lucy disappears from a parking lot in the middle of a sunny September afternoon and Michelle can't shake the fear that they may never see one another again.

7
JULIA

ON THE WAY to the café in town as she pushes a gurgling Theo along, Julia keeps getting waylaid by texts from Marcus about how he had to take off this morning. Yet again, like they do not have a baby—like *he* does not have a baby.

I was up all night with Theo even though today is important
Well, maybe my day is important too, but how would you even know?
Julia, it's my long teaching day, there's my evaluation too
Did it occur to you that *I* might have a meeting for my work?
But you're on maternity leave.
Did you realize Daphne has amassed nearly 50k followers?
Why are you talking to me about Daphne right now?

When the messages subside because Marcus has to go to class, Julia notices something wonderful:

Theo is out.

A flutter of excitement takes off in her chest.

She continues onward to the coffee shop, planning to treat herself to a latte and a few stolen moments while Theo sleeps. The thought of sitting at a café table on a blue-sky September morning, staring out the windows lazily, sketching and flipping through her book, is like the equivalent of a trip to Paris.

"Thank you!" Julia says brightly to the man who holds the

door for the mother pushing the baby, and she swerves the carriage inside.

She orders her coffee, then maneuvers the stroller through the maze of people and chairs toward a bench against the wall. She peeks to make sure Theo is still asleep. She smiles, and wonders what the other café patrons see—a mother who adores her sleeping child, or a woman celebrating a few minutes free from attending that child? Julia turns the stroller so it faces away, reasoning that Theo likes to people watch and if he wakes up this might keep him entertained, giving Julia a few more seconds of peace before he starts screaming about yet another dirty diaper or the need for a feeding or just because he craves reassurance after waking, the prosaic and constant demands that determine her life now on a minute-to-minute basis.

She plops onto the bench and fishes her sketchbook out of the stroller's basket as she waits for the barista to call her name. For a moment, Julia pretends she isn't here with a baby. That she never married Marcus. She loved Marcus before they became parents, but since then, she no longer loves anyone, really. Especially not herself. She doesn't love her days or her nights or food or drawing or even music. She tries to love Theo, she *does* love him, but she's not sure this love is enough to endure this new life. Maybe Julia has lost the capacity to love in any sustaining way. Maybe she will never love anyone or anything again.

Julia opens to a fresh, blank page, studies all that white space. Searches for the urges in her head that send signals to her hand and finds them dormant. She resists going to Daphne's Instagram on her phone, she needs to mute it. The monotony of motherhood has turned her into an obsessive lurker, a compulsive comparer to everyone else. She grabs the green diaper bag from the stroller and dumps her phone into it, zips the thing shut to stop herself from scrolling. Sets it onto the bench next to her. Then her gaze drifts to the empty table next to her own, at the discarded newspaper on the top of it. Today's headline:

POLICE SEARCH FOR LOCAL MOTHER CONTINUES

Lucy Mendoza again. The disappearance of this woman not even half a mile away from where Julia sits. She grabs the paper, scans the first paragraph of the article and can't help but think of Theo in this position, a baby crying outside of Belmont, alone, scared. The idea makes Julia physically nauseated. Just as quickly the nausea is replaced by the sharp knife of jealousy, but of a different sort than what she feels with Daphne. If only someone would take Julia. This thought is followed by shame, a tiny flickering candle of it.

Can she truly be jealous of a woman kidnapped?

Julia mulls this around in her mind a moment more.

Yes. Yes, she could. And she is.

"Julie? Latte with low-fat milk for Julie?"

Julia looks around. No one else is rising from their chairs. That must be for her. Julie, Jules, the workers say her name all sorts of ways here. She kind of likes being someone else for a bit, even if the difference is slight. The slightest deviation can change everything. The tiniest decision that doesn't seem to mean much can suddenly add up to a different life.

Julia squeezes by Theo's carriage to make the trek to the counter to retrieve the coffee. She considers whether to bring the stroller with her, since the barista is all the way on the other side of the café. She needs to travel at least fifteen yards, pass a sea of tables, patrons, people coming in and out. All it takes is a few seconds and a baby is taken. Julia keeps walking, decides Theo will be fine. Today is not the day when the million-in-one tragedy strikes.

But as she nears the coffee counter, she continues thinking of her young son alone in his carriage, so tiny and sleeping, how someone could just walk right up, the carriage already positioned so it's pointing toward the door. They could push it straight outside and down the street before Julia turns around and notices her baby is gone. Yesterday a mother taken down the road, today a baby right here, right now. How fast someone could slip behind the handlebar of the carriage as though they were the parent, stroll right into the neighborhood and onward, disappearing with Theo forever. Or get into a car and drive away to a place no one will find them, leaving Marcus and Julia to be alone again. As though they never became parents.

Julia lingers at the counter, trying to decide which of the fourteen coffees sitting there is hers, all with indecipherable names scribbled in black marker on the side.

This is not the first time Julia's imagined someone disappearing with her son, and it's not just Lucy Mendoza on the brain that's inspiring her fantasy. At night when Julia can't sleep, elaborate scenarios unfold in her mind. Sometimes it's a break-in during the dark hours of morning, Theo stolen from his crib, and she and Marcus wake to find him gone. Sometimes a man snatches Theo straight out of Julia's arms and makes a run for it, and Julia runs after him but he's too fast. Sometimes Theo is taken while Julia is shopping at the store or while Theo is playing in the park or because the babysitter Julia's hired turns out to be a baby-snatcher.

Julia picks up another coffee cup, not hers, for someone

named Peter, puts it back, picks up another, this one for Anastasia. *Anastasia, really?*

In all her fantasies, Julia gets to be the heroine, not the villain.

Because her baby is kidnapped, no one thinks Julia is a bad person. Instead, people revere Julia, hold her up as the tragic, grieving mother, wronged by the evil person who took her baby. In these fantasies, Theo ends up happy somewhere, he lives with a new family who wants a child so badly they go so far as to steal one. The upshot is always that Julia gets to no longer be a mother, while at the same time she is not maligned as a horrible woman for the rest of her life. Everyone understands why Julia doesn't have another baby because no one can replace Theo, even though some people will suggest she try this. And deep down only Julia knows the real reason she doesn't have another child: that she refuses to make the same mistake twice.

The latte with *Julie* written on the side is finally in her hands and she turns around, heading back to her table. As she walks, savoring each second alone, Julia wonders what she would do with all that freedom, returned like some miracle of fate.

Everything, she thinks.

At which point, she halts.

She raises the coffee to her lips, takes a small sip.

The door to the café catches her eye.

It occurs to her in an electric shock:

She could just . . . leave. Right now.

Abandon all of it, everything about her life, in a few, quick moments.

Her heart pounds in her ears. The coffee burns her palm

through the cup. She breathes, in and out. Her feet start moving again.

Toward the café door.

With her free hand she imagines reaching out, pulling on the handle.

Opening it wide, walking on through.

Not looking back. Not once.

The sun would shine down on Julia, she'd tilt her head toward it. All that big sky, blue and open and free. She would be free, bare of everything, her wallet, her book, her bag. Her baby. She would have left them all at the table.

Julia takes one more step.

But there is a tug. Like Julia is on a leash.

She turns back.

Sees Theo's carriage there at that table.

Her whole body slumps.

The woman sitting on the bench next to Julia's diaper bag gets up. She looks around, clearly concerned. She peers inside Theo's carriage. The woman's eyes slide to Julia's still-open sketchbook. Then back to the bright green diaper bag on the bench.

A book, a bag, a baby.

Yet no occupant. No mother.

The woman looks around again, searching the café.

Where is the mother to this baby?

Julia doesn't need to hear the woman say this to know these are the words in her head. Maybe she's also remembering Lucy Mendoza and thinking to herself, *It's happened again, and it's happened right next to me, while I was just drinking my coffee! Look everybody, another baby left alone in this very café! Call the police, NOW!* Maybe everyone in town is on high alert, watching for mysteriously abandoned babies, mothers suddenly gone, taken, kidnapped.

The woman places a hand protectively on the top of Theo's carriage.

Julia needs to move.

But which way?

She breathes, paralyzed.

Then she starts to walk.

Puts a bright smile on her face, brushes right by that nosy woman and peers lovingly into Theo's carriage, coos a little at her sleeping son, then slides onto the bench and sets her coffee next to the newspaper. Nothing to see here. Nothing at all.

Julia feels the woman's eyes burning into her.

Suspicious. Judgmental.

What kind of mother just leaves her baby alone at the table like that?

Julia bends over the paper, peering closer, though her mind is racing so it's not like she can read any of the words. Her face grows hot as she scolds herself for every single thought that has just gone through her head. Obviously, Julia is a horrible person to entertain the idea of actually abandoning Theo at this café, walking out the door and leaving him behind. Obviously, she is a monster, even she can see this. She's heard of women who have babies and experience sudden violent outbursts, the urge, say, to throw that baby down a staircase; she's even read the stories of women who kill their children in fits of madness. But whatever is going on inside of Julia doesn't manifest as violence toward Theo. The fantasies that plague Julia are the ones where Theo is lifted off her, safely yet permanently, where someone offers Julia a cure for this terrible affliction befallen her—the affliction of motherhood.

Theo screams, shattering the quiet of the café, and Julia jumps.

Her face changes, she feels caught.

The woman next to Julia is staring again.

Slowly, Julia gets up to attend to her son, who clearly needs them to be on their way. No more reading for Julia, no sketching, no more peace. Julia caresses Theo's unhappy face as the woman observes Julia mothering. She tucks his blanket tighter around him, runs a soothing hand over his soft head. Her emotions swing between worry for Theo's cries, and despair that Theo interrupted the only happiness of her day, as though to remind Julia she doesn't get to be happy anymore. What she gets is to be a mother and nothing will ever change this, because the motherhood is permanent.

She looks up from the carriage, says to the nosy woman still watching Julia over the top of it, "I guess this is my cue to go." She half-smiles, shrugs, *What's a mother to do?*

The woman nods, but the suspicion on her face lingers.

Julia leaves the newspaper, grabs the bag, stuffs her sketchbook inside it, shoves everything else into the basket at the bottom of the stroller, positions herself behind the handlebar. She leaves the coffee on the table too because what's the point? It's not like she can enjoy it now. The moment she pushes Theo forward his wails lessen. She doesn't look back at the woman, but knows she's being watched.

The mother is always watched.

Soon Julia is out of the café, the September sun big and round and bright. She moves the carriage down the sidewalk. Theo's cries eventually stop, but then Julia is the one who's crying. She thinks about all the decisions she's made to get herself here, how she had opportunities to choose differently but she didn't. She's arrived exactly where she is and there is no changing it. Theo gurgles happily as she pushes him along the street, reminding Julia yet again that he is there, that he is hers. Tears run down her face, one after the other, dripping along her chin and neck. But then another idea comes to her, one she can't resist once it blooms inside her.

So Julia turns the carriage in the opposite direction, heading away from the house she shares with Marcus and the neighborhood where they live, her steps faster and faster. Straight toward the scene of yesterday's crime, the same supermarket where Lucy Mendoza was taken.

8
MICHELLE

"THERE IS STILL no sign of Lucy Mendoza," the newscaster says on a video Michelle plays on her laptop, what must be the twentieth video she's watched this morning. "The local real estate agent disappeared from a supermarket parking lot yesterday in broad daylight. Police are searching for this married mother of a nine-month-old girl found alone in a shopping cart, asking anyone who might have information to come forward."

A deep, hollow ache pulses inside Michelle.

Along with a throbbing in her head.

Where in the world is Lucy?

Fear is a sea that wants to swallow her.

The phone next to her laptop doesn't light up with the messages or calls for which she longs—from Lucy or from Sam. It only lights up with worried texts from Michelle's mother and the occasional curious college friend she hasn't talked to since before she had Charlie.

This is happening, Michelle thinks.

Lucy is gone and no one can find her.

People from her and Lucy's past are already rubbernecking the drama.

Michelle takes another gulp of coffee and it goes down

like acid. Her third cup this morning already. Her whole body jumps with it.

David thumps down the stairs, a sleepy Aidan in his arms. "Is that a report about Lucy?"

Michelle shuts her laptop, ignoring David's question. She looks at her husband, or maybe it's more that she looks through him, realizing how late it is, nearly 9 A.M. David should be dressed and heading to work. God, Michelle has spent hours down the rabbit hole of online reports and social media commentary, people's stupid conspiracy theories, people claiming they saw something when of course they didn't. The ways everyone just makes things up and plasters it on their profiles enrages Michelle.

"Honey?" David approaches the kitchen table.

Aidan's little fists reach for his mother.

Michelle gets up and plants a noisy kiss on her baby's plump cheek and coos, "Good morning, button. You slept late today!"

David plops Aidan into his high chair and puts on his bib. "I thought you'd want me home longer this morning, given everything with Lucy. I called the office and told them I'd be late." He stops, he waits, he wants Michelle to give him the Lucy update. When she doesn't, he goes on. "Well, I'll just find out about Lucy myself, I guess." David sits next to their son at the table, pulls his phone out and starts to scroll; waits for his breakfast, she supposes.

David does this every day, he sits down in the kitchen waiting to be fed. For his wife to feed them all. Whether Lucy has disappeared or not, this is the drill.

He used to cook, but when they had Charlie it was like a switch went on inside him; he began assuming the kitchen, the house, were Michelle's domain. It's also true Michelle stopped working in advertising when Charlie was born, while David kept them afloat financially, heading off to the office each day, coming home tired at night. Michelle fell into the habit of doing everything at the house and David fell into the habit of allowing her to. But before the kids they'd shared the household duties, saw themselves as equals in all regards, both of them driven by their professions. Michelle sometimes wonders how they got here, but she knows the answer. She can see it like a well-lit path over their last few years. The real question is, *How can we get back to where we were?* And even more concerning, *What if we can't?*

Michelle uses breakfast to distract herself from thoughts about her marriage, and of course about Lucy. She puts bread into the toaster, cracks eggs into a pan, listens to them sizzle so she doesn't have to hear the words on the video David watches about Lucy's disappearance. She gets out applesauce for Aidan, who's obsessed with it. She thinks about Emma sucking on the peach, then pushes Emma out of her mind. When the eggs and toast are done, she puts them onto a plate and places them in front of David. She sits down next to Aidan to feed him.

The way Aidan looks at her makes her forget everything else, the gentle curve of his eyelashes, the soft pudge of his chin. She gives him another big wet kiss on his rosy cheek. "Momma loves you," she sings, and he laughs. There comes a different kind of ache in her chest.

How is it possible to love someone so much?

Whatever else is going on in the world, her life, her marriage, Michelle can't help smiling at this boy that is hers. She leans forward and touches her nose to Aidan's, so he giggles again. "Momma's lucky, isn't she?"

Aidan gives her a big grin, little stubs of white breaking through his gums, and her heart breaks for the millionth time. She gets ready to feed him the applesauce. The second Aidan sees what's coming he gets excited, bucks in his chair, mouth wide.

David's eyes are still on his phone, his finger scrolling across the screen in between spooning eggs onto his toast. All the videos David pulls up are reporting on Lucy's disappearance.

The current one talks of how the FBI is involved.

Michelle's heart sinks. *The FBI?*

David scrolls to another, presses play, a woman's voice booms into the kitchen.

"Unlike everyone else commenting on what happened yesterday, I was actually there at Belmont so I wanted to add my firsthand account so people get their facts straight. My name is Alice Chesterfield, and I'm the woman who found the baby and waited for emergency crews to arrive on the scene."

Michelle moves sideways so she can peer at the phone in David's hand and watch this homemade video that's already being shared and reshared. She recognizes the woman, who'd been in head-to-toe aqua and pink workout clothes. But now she's in a tight-fitting royal blue dress, like she's playing reporter. She stands in front of a house which looks about as nice as she is pretty. There's a riot of flowers on either side of the porch steps, the expensive kind of outdoor furniture, a blue painted door against the backdrop of dark gray shingles behind her. Someone films her as she speaks, but who? Her husband? A son or daughter of her own?

David crunches his toast, Aidan gums his applesauce, the three of them wait to hear whatever else Alice Chesterfield is about to say.

"I knew immediately something was wrong when I saw that baby. I'm a mother of two myself, both of them adults, married, with children of their own. I just hope the police can find Lucy Mendoza soon, because that little girl needs her mother. She is such a sweet baby. The ridiculous things people are posting about how they were there too—that they saw Lucy in Belmont buying strawberries or whatever, that they were part of the crowd of women who found that darling girl all alone—need to stop lying and saying they were there. You are interfering with a police investigation."

And you aren't? Michelle nearly wants to laugh despite her dread.

Aidan flaps his arms. Michelle is failing to feed him fast enough. The thought that they need to get Charlie up, that he's late for school floats through Michelle's mind, but in the jumble it disappears. "Here it comes, open," she says, but Aidan's mouth is already stretched wide.

Meanwhile, Alice Chesterfield is talking about Lucy like *she* is the best friend.

"Lucy Mendoza is extremely beautiful, and with that smile of hers, it's no wonder . . ."

Michelle grabs David's phone, hits pause, and places it face down on the table.

"Hey, why'd you do that?" he asks.

She spoons more food into Aidan's mouth. "I can't listen to that woman any longer."

"But don't you want to know—"

"—do I want to know what some random lady thinks about Lucy in a video she posted to her socials? No."

David reaches for his phone again, but she grabs it and holds it away.

Michelle knows she's acting childish, that she's picking a fight, but she's so annoyed at David, how he just expects her to do every goddam thing in the house, his failure to grasp that maybe he shouldn't listen to people talking about her friend's disappearance at the breakfast table. An unbelievable frustration builds in her belly.

David gets up to grab his phone but Michelle gets up too and moves farther away. Before he can reach for it once more, there is a loud knock on the front door.

"Who could be here this early?" David barks.

"Don't look at me, I have no idea," she barks back.

Aidan makes a confused face, his lip growing wobbly.

At the sight of her baby, Michelle's arm grows limp.

David plucks his phone from her hand and goes to answer the door.

Michelle returns to feeding Aidan and misses his mouth, smearing applesauce all over his face. "Oops, Mommy slipped," she sings, hoping he doesn't start to cry.

Are those walkie-talkies she hears crackling?

David returns. "It's for you. The police." He stands over her.

Michelle forces herself to get up. They switch places. David takes the spoon for the applesauce to continue feeding their son. Michelle glares at her husband. She apparently needs to be wanted by the police for him to help with Aidan's breakfast. God, the police are here to ask about Lucy and all Michelle can think about is how much she resents her husband. She walks into the living room before she can say something to David that she regrets.

Two men in tan pants and oxford shirts with blazers sit on her couch. One might be in his forties, medium height, with dark thick hair, a serious expression. The other is younger, a bit soft around his middle, but his eyes hold an even harder gaze than his partner's. Yesterday, the officer who questioned Michelle was wearing a uniform. The scene was so chaotic, people crawling everywhere, literally crawling under cars, looking for evidence, she supposes.

They both stand.

The older man says, "Good morning, Ms. Carvalho. I'm Detective Suarez."

"And I'm Detective Marist," the younger one says.

Michelle shakes their hands. "Please sit," she says, then takes the chair across from the couch. "So you're here to ask about Lucy?"

Detective Suarez pulls out a phone, holds it up to show Michelle he wants to record what they discuss. "Is it all right if we get this?" Suarez asks. "It's just procedure." The younger one, Marist, watches him closely, and Michelle wonders if he might be in training. She hopes they didn't put a trainee on finding Lucy.

The skin on Michelle's arms prickles. "Sure?"

Suarez nods, makes a show of pressing the red button. He places it on the coffee table.

"Are you with the FBI?" Michelle asks.

"No," Marist says. "We're local, so we're helping with interviews of people who knew Lucy."

Alarm shoots through her. "Knew?"

"I mean, know her, *know*," Marist says.

Detective Suarez gives his younger partner a look, then leans forward, elbows on his knees, hands clasped between them. "We understand you know Lucy well."

Michelle's heart pounds inside her chest. "She's my best friend."

"Can you think of anyone who might want to hurt her?"

She shakes her head. "No. I've been racking my brain ever since yesterday."

Detective Suarez wears a ring on his finger, and Michelle wonders if he has children of his own. "Has Lucy been acting strangely lately? Did she indicate she felt like someone was following her? Anything that seemed off or alarming? Someone at work giving her a hard time?"

Michelle finds herself wanting to please this man, to give him the right answer, if there is such a thing, but she shakes her head again.

"What about an affair, a boyfriend, someone outside her marriage?" Marist asks next.

"No, Lucy would never do that to Sam." Michelle thinks about some of the problems Lucy and Sam have had, but they still seem irrelevant. If there was an affair, she would know. Lucy would never keep it from her. "They are just normal married people, adjusting to life with a baby. That sort of thing." Michelle wonders if David is eavesdropping from the kitchen. So she adds, "Lucy loves Sam. I have no doubt about it." Which is the truth.

"There's no sense protecting her on this," Suarez says, in this way that makes Michelle wonder if these detectives know something about Lucy that she doesn't.

Could they?

No, Michelle decides. *Impossible*.

Suarez changes the clasp of his hands. "You mentioned Lucy was 'adjusting' to her life with her baby. Can you say a little more about that?"

Michelle again wonders if this man has children, if he knows what it's like on a marriage when a baby arrives.

She also reminds herself to breathe, to keep the air coming steadily. Her eyes flicker to the phone between them on the table. Recording every word. "You know, just regular stuff. Loss of sleep, all that change at once."

Suarez's thick eyebrows arch. "You were at Belmont yesterday shopping for groceries too."

"I was."

"Did you and Lucy go together?"

Michelle shakes her head. "No. Why?"

Suarez shrugs. "I just find it interesting that your best friend goes missing and you happen to be one of the women who finds her baby."

"That's just a coincidence!" Michelle's voice rises, she can't help it. "A *horrible* coincidence! I would never . . . I love Lucy with all my heart. How could you even suggest—"

"If Lucy *was* having an affair," Marist cuts in, "now is the time to tell us. This person could be a suspect in your friend's disappearance."

"Your *best* friend." Suarez lets these last words hang in the air.

Michelle stares at these two men on her couch, the dark blue canvas cushions beneath them, a fabric and color she picked out because it's durable, easy to clean, the inevitable stains of spit up, applesauce, drool and other bodily fluids remaining hidden. "I'm telling you the truth. Lucy didn't have a boyfriend or someone on the side. I promise. Or not that I know of," she quickly adds.

But Michelle would know, is the thing. Lucy would never not tell her something that big.

Right?

Detectives Suarez and Marist glance at each other, something passing between them.

Michelle gets the sense they're getting ready to leave.

Thinking, *This woman is no use to us after all.*

Suarez stares down at the braided rug under his feet a long moment. Then he looks back up at Michelle. "Is there anything else you can think of that we should know? Anything, even a small detail that seems off or that's stuck with you? The first forty-eight hours after a disappearance are crucial. The clock is ticking."

Michelle's heart thuds when she realizes what clock he means:

The clock keeping how much time is left on Lucy's life.

A jam of possible answers collides inside Michelle's body, a ninety-car pileup entering her throat provoked by all the things she's holding back. Michelle wonders again if she might choke on so many unsaid words. But instead of offering her thoughts, of telling them the truth about what she does know that might be very relevant, Michelle looks Detective Suarez in the eyes, then Detective Marist, and lies straight to their faces.

"No, not anything," she says. "Nothing at all."

9
MICHELLE & LUCY

Three months ago

MICHELLE HOLDS UP the wine bottle, ready to pour some into Lucy's glass. She waits for Lucy to give her the go-ahead, but Lucy's brain seems elsewhere. She nudges her friend. "Helloooo?"

Lucy startles. "Hey, sorry, sure I'll have more. I may as well."

The two best friends sit on the floor of Lucy's living room, cross-legged, backs against Lucy's couch, the coffee table littered with the stuff of their evening. Sam has taken Emma to his mother's, and David is home with the kids. There are moments when Lucy seems like Lucy, vibrant, laughing, talking about something she read in *The New Yorker*, the subscription she's kept since her college major in English, telling Michelle an anecdote about Sam, an annoying seller or an annoying buyer, asking Michelle if she'll consider going back to work after so many years away. But Lucy keeps drifting off, then snapping back.

Michelle studies her as she fills the glass. Something is going on, something more than the strain of sleeplessness, the discombobulated state of new motherhood. She sets the bottle back onto the table.

Lucy takes a slow sip of wine, turns to her best friend, debate in her eyes.

Something is wrong, Michelle thinks.

She reaches for Lucy's hand, squeezes it. "Whatever it is, Luz, you can tell me. You know that." Michelle remembers other times when Lucy has had something big to share. The extremely good ("I'm getting married to Sam!" and "I sold my first house!") and the awful ("My dad is sick, and the prognosis is bad."). Michelle hopes it's the former but she can tell it is not.

Lucy blinks, looks away.

Michelle follows Lucy's gaze to the photos on the wall of her and Sam, the two of them with Emma, of Emma, Emma, and Emma. Six framed photos of their daughter so far, one for each month of her life. Michelle keeps joking with Sam they are going to run out of walls soon.

Lucy's gaze returns to Michelle.

Michelle squeezes her hand again. "Please. Whatever it is, say it."

"I wish I could go back," Lucy whispers, then hangs her head, hair falling forward over her shoulders, eyes on the table. The remnants of their snacks, crackers and cheese, a bowl of chips, one lone stick of celery and the crusty dregs of hummus on a plate. Lucy reaches for the celery, then decides against it, hand falling heavy and empty into her lap.

Lucy's nails are bitten down to nothing. This is not like the Lucy Michelle knows, always so together, someone loud and observant who can convince anyone of anything, who will walk the world in a hot pink coat, wear skintight leather pants with a soft cashmere sweater, and who, even while very pregnant, was wearing string bikinis at the beach. Michelle's always admired her audacity. But this Lucy shrinks within herself, hides herself within enormous sacks of sweaters and sweatshirts.

Michelle leans closer. "Go back, Lucy? Go back *where?*"

"I wish I could go back and undo what I've done." Lucy's voice is barely audible.

Michelle's alarm glows red, her heart pumps hard. A pit forms in her stomach. "But what have you done?"

"I had a baby," she says, eyes still boring into the table. Then, "I should have told Sam I'm not cut out to be a mother." Lucy lifts her gaze finally, meets her friend's. "But I didn't and then I got pregnant and now . . . well, now I'm stuck."

"You don't mean that," Michelle says before she can think.

"I *do* mean it."

"You *don't*. You're a wonderful mother. These early months are the hardest but they will pass soon and you'll feel differently."

Lucy's face flashes. "Did you know seventy percent of couples go into crisis when they have a baby?"

"Where did you—"

"And even worse, that statistic goes up to ninety percent—*ninety percent, Michelle!*—when that baby is a girl?" Lucy shakes her head. "Apparently because in heterosexual couples, the men see a girl as more for their wives than for them. Isn't that horrific? Doesn't that make you want to scream?"

Michelle's mouth opens wide, but Lucy is not yet done.

"Can you believe I knew all that and still went ahead with the pregnancy? You know me, I had to go looking up all kinds of things when I got pregnant. As if I needed statistics to tell me what I already knew about myself." Lucy takes a long gulp of wine.

"Those statistics can't be right," Michelle says, even as she thinks of how her own marriage has been in crisis ever since the birth of their sons.

A flush comes over Lucy's cheeks. Anger fills her eyes. "You're not listening to me. You're not *hearing* me."

Michelle inhales sharply. "I am listening. But what am I not hearing? I'm trying to reassure you, that's all!"

Lucy grabs that celery stick and hurls it across the room. "I thought I could tell you, but I guess even my best friend can't handle the truth."

Michelle hears the hurt in Lucy's voice, but what else is she missing? She tries to think of what to say that won't upset Lucy further. "You're right, Luz, I'm sorry. Tell me more. I want to know," she says. But does she, given the preamble?

"I shouldn't have become a mother," Lucy repeats, slowly, each word pronounced carefully. Her gaze is fiery. "I should never have had Emma. I don't want this baby." These words spill from Lucy's mouth like a waterfall of marbles, loud and pounding, rolling every which way, reverberating through the living room. "I knew before I even got pregnant. Something in me didn't want to do it, something strong, a voice telling me not to. I should have listened. Because now Emma is here and there is no going backwards. She's stuck with me. And I don't know how much longer I can do this. I want to . . . undo it, Michelle." Lucy stops talking.

The couch seems to undulate behind Michelle's back, the room, the walls with their photos, the chair in the corner where Lucy likes to read. Maybe it's the wine. She can hear the insides of her body pulsing, the sound loud in her ears. She wants to turn the volume down. She wonders if she's going to be sick. "Okay," Michelle says carefully, like Lucy might suddenly be a bomb that could go off. "Okay. But . . . can I ask you a question?"

"What?"

Michelle can almost see the fire vacate Lucy's eyes, replaced by something else. Despair? Sadness? Uncertainty? "When you told me you were pregnant, you said you were happy."

Michelle remembers, because she was thrilled and thought, *Now we'll have this experience to share with each other!* For a few blissful months, they were pregnant together, Lucy with Emma, Michelle with Aidan. But maybe it was only blissful for Michelle. She shouldn't have simply assumed this was a happy moment for Lucy. After all, she'd listened to Lucy talk for years about how maybe she'd never become a mother. How she was already happy in her life, her job, her marriage with Sam, why would she go and change everything by having a kid? Take that kind of risk? Michelle should have prodded Lucy about whether this baby was more for Sam than herself. If it was for Sam, Michelle could have packed Lucy into the car and driven her to an abortion clinic. She would have. Right?

"I guess I lied," Lucy says. "To you. To everyone. Or, I didn't even know what I really felt. I kept thinking, plenty of women don't want children or aren't sure, then go ahead and have them and they're fine. Or, they tell everyone that," she adds, bitterly. "You know, fake it till you make it."

"But you love Emma so much," Michelle whispers. "You always talk about how much you love her. I see the way you look at her. A mother's love is in her eyes. It's in *your* eyes."

"I *do* love Emma. I'll never stop loving her." Tears drop down Lucy's cheeks. "But both things are true. I love Emma with all my heart, and I also wish I could go back and tell Sam

No, we shouldn't do this. This is not what I want or who I am. That probably doesn't make sense." Lucy's normally straight back starts to curve over again until she is hunched.

"I can understand how both things can be true," Michelle says.

And she does, to a point. She understands the mysterious love for a child as well as anything she's ever known. It isn't a choice, it happens unbidden, a tidal wave of emotion a mother will be drowning in for the rest of her days. It's immense and awesome and beautiful and terrible. A fate a woman can't shake no matter what, and some women take to it better than others. But eventually all mothers do figure it out. Some just take longer. Some need extra help getting there. Lucy will get there, Michelle decides, she simply needs more time to find her way.

"I think this happens a lot with new motherhood, Lucy," she tries. "You love your baby and your baby drives you crazy. You can't imagine your life without your child and yet you find yourself imagining going back to a time before they existed, when you had so much freedom but didn't appreciate it." She grips Lucy's hand tightly. "What you're feeling is normal. It happens to a million women when they become mothers. Especially in the beginning."

Lucy is shaking her head. "No. *No.* I *can* imagine a world without Emma. I do it all the time. I wish for a world without her so I can live the life I'm meant to have. As much as I love Emma, I *want* to live in a world without her. I feel like I'm living someone else's life and I don't know how much longer I can do it. I want to go back to before and undo . . . it." Lucy's eyes flash. "And don't tell me again that I don't mean it, Michelle. And don't you *dare* tell me I'm crazy or depressed or something. I'm as sane as I've ever been. Maybe I've never been saner."

Michelle shakes her head quickly. "I won't, I'm not. And, a lot of women experience this kind of ambivalence," she tries again. "A certain amount of ambivalence is normal."

A cold stillness passes over Lucy. "This is not ambivalence. This is something *else*."

Michelle sets her glass down onto the table and nearly topples it. "But Lucy, listen. That love you have for Emma is going to help you figure this out." Michelle knows this is true because her love for her sons is a constant light and she keeps her eyes trained on it. It never goes out, she can always see it, she's bathed in it, and it always eventually gets her through whatever darkness has fallen. It's a light that makes Michelle's life worth living, the greatest truth she's ever known. Aidan and Charlie, their smells, their little tummies, their delicate skin, their soft breathing, their voices, their silky hair that Michelle loves washing in the bathtub, combing it afterward with her fingers, her lips on their wet cheeks, their noses, their foreheads. Those two small boys are her heart; it's made of them now. Soon, Lucy's heart will be made of Emma too. Michelle's sure of this. "It's going to get easier. You're back at work and you'll see, things will balance themselves out. I promise."

Lucy guzzles her wine, puts her glass onto the table next to Michelle's with a sharp *clink*. "But what if they don't?"

"They will," Michelle insists—because she believes this, and also because the moment requires it. She can hear that this is not just Lucy overreacting or being insecure. She means what she says. "It's *going* to get better. It *will*."

Lucy's eyes blaze. She scrambles up from the floor until

she is standing. "But that is what everyone always says! Stick it out! It's hard now but eventually you will be fine and love being a mother! I don't love being a mother, Michelle!" She is practically screaming now. "I fucking hate it! This isn't me! I don't want to be a mother anymore! I want it all to stop! Why won't anyone just let me say it? Why isn't anyone willing to believe me?"

"Lucy, I—" Michelle tries, but Lucy is not done.

"Why is it so difficult to accept that maybe some women are not cut out for this? That no matter what they do it's not going to be enough to fix things? I'm just not cut out for this! I know I'm not! I want to go back and undo it all! I wish Emma never existed!"

Michelle rears back against the couch, eyes wider and wider still.

Lucy's yells echo through the quiet, her face blotchy, cheeks wet with tears. For a moment every muscle is taut and strong. But then she crumbles to the floor. Michelle crawls around the coffee table and reaches for her, rubs her friend's back as she weeps, circling her hand around and around like she would with Charlie and Aidan.

"Lucy, you are not alone. I'm here. I'm always going to be here, I promise." As these words emerge, she realizes they are the same words spoken time and again by her own mother, Evelyn, that it's her duty to pass them along to the only other woman she could love as much as that same mother loves Michelle. "There are people who can help and we are going to get you some help. I am going to get it for you, I'll be with you every step of the way."

Lucy cries harder. "I don't need that kind of help. No amount of therapy is going to change how I feel. I'm alone in this, and it's done. I agreed to have the baby, *I* did that, I could have said no but now I'm stuck. And this is *not* ambivalence, this is *not* about motherhood being hard." She looks up, suddenly still, stares into Michelle's eyes. "Michelle," she whispers.

"What, tell me?" Michelle whispers back.

"Emma," she says in a hush. "Agreeing to have her, it's my one regret."

The two women blink at each other as Lucy's words linger in the air.

Something deep and secret recoils in Michelle, and she uses all her strength to hide it from her friend, but what is it, exactly—disgust? shock? fear? some combination thereof? She promised Lucy she was safe to say anything. But what Lucy has said about regretting Emma, Michelle cannot understand. She and Lucy are categorically different in this way. She believes few mothers can truly understand what Lucy has just claimed. So maybe Lucy *is* alone in this. Michelle always wanted to be a mother, she wants it even now with every molecule within her; this desire is what always returns Michelle to the place she needs to be, the force that smooths over any remorse that rears up inside her about the changes in her life because she had a baby. She thinks of how women can be so different. Some will go to great lengths, even risk their lives, to get pregnant; some will grow up anticipating the moment when they will finally have a baby, fantasizing about one day holding the child that is theirs. Then there are women who feel no desire at all. And the women who are unsure, ambivalent, who could veer either way. But Michelle is one of those women who's always known motherhood is her destiny. That it would be her life's true joy. And it is.

Lucy wipes her face, holds her friend's gaze, eyes wild. "I even have a plan, Michelle."

"What kind of plan?" Michelle asks, afraid to hear Lucy's answer. She can already tell that whatever it is, it won't involve seeing a therapist for postpartum depression.

And for the first time since their conversation began this night, Lucy sounds hopeful.

10
JULIA

JULIA SEES THE sharp yellow lines of police tape flapping in the breeze. Her heart jumps, like someone's attached cables to it. She peeks down at Theo. If he wakes again she can always do a lap around the aisles of cars. She bends low and sniffs but doesn't smell anything, at least not powerful enough to require a diaper change. So she beelines across Belmont's lot toward all that undulating yellow plastic. As she does her phone vibrates in the pouch hanging from the carriage handlebar.

She picks up. "What."

"Hi," Marcus says.

"I'm busy," Julia snaps. She's so focused on the police tape she doesn't see the motorcycle blazing across the asphalt, about to hit her.

The driver swerves in time, but yells at Julia, "You nearly got your baby killed!"

"Sorry!" she calls back, but he just roars off.

"Julia, Julia, is everything okay?"

"Calm down, everything is fine."

"I called because I don't want to fight anymore," Marcus says.

"You left this morning without telling me. You do this

every day. Imagine if we both just took off without checking in about who was going to watch Theo."

"But you're on maternity leave."

She halts, mid-stride, jolting the carriage. Julia opens her mouth wide in a silent scream toward the sky. "Really, Marcus, how many times are you going to use that excuse on me? And maybe you should try some paternity leave yourself!"

"You're not being fair."

"*I'm* not being fair?"

"I didn't call to fight."

"Well then maybe you shouldn't have called."

An SUV passes in front of Julia, slowly, slowly. The driver catches Julia's eye—another man. Men watching her here, women watching her in the café, everyone always watching, watching.

"You don't seem to appreciate how important this year is for me at school," Marcus goes on. "How hard I'm working for *us*. If I don't get tenure, our family will be in financial trouble."

Another car passes carefully behind Julia and Theo, because the mother and son are still in the middle of the lot. The urge to sit down right on the steaming blacktop pulses inside of Julia. The fight in her comes and goes in spurts.

"And what about *my* work? What about the fact that my friends from art school are doing all kinds of things that I'm not? It makes me feel so bad about myself."

"But none of them have kids, Julia."

"Believe me, I know."

"I stayed up all night with Theo," Marcus goes on.

"What, so you're a martyr? I stay up every night with Theo, have you noticed?"

"But you're his—" he starts, then stops.

"What am I, Marcus? What were you about to say?"

"Nothing."

"Nothing? Right. You were about to say but I'm his *mother*. So what, it's *my* job to take care of Theo? You have a PhD and are always claiming to be some kind of feminist!" Julia's voice is rising, she can hear the shrill of it. "If this is what you really think, I wish we'd had this conversation before I got pregnant so I'd have known all your promises and feminist claims were total bullshit. God, what century am I fucking living in?" She sees a woman pushing a shopping cart toward the supermarket entrance in the next aisle glance her way.

"I'd never say that. And listen, I'm sorry. I'm *really* sorry if that's what you believe I'd say."

"Don't gaslight me. My day-to-day is living proof of what you believe."

A long sigh comes through the phone. "I don't know what's gotten into you, Julia, but let's finish this when I get home tonight. We can figure everything out together. We've always been able to talk things through. Haven't we? Because we love each other?"

The change in Marcus's tone causes something in Julia's chest to crack open and it hurts. Now she's on the verge of tears. "Yes. And I do know." Julia rocks the carriage slightly, back and forth, hoping Theo will stay asleep. "But I'm not sure we can talk through *this*."

"You are my person and that means we can get through anything."

The heart in Julia's chest aches even more. "You are my person too," she whispers, because it's something they've always said to each other and believed. But in that same, aching heart, Julia doubts they can get through this. All she sees in front of them is a wall she cannot scale. Because in the end, Marcus is not about to give his wife the boost she needs to get over the top. "Fine, we'll talk when you get home."

"Okay. I need to go teach class now anyway."

"You always do," Julia trills. Rage flares high again, uncontrollable and fierce. She ends the call before Marcus can say anything else—before *she* can say anything else.

Julia pushes the carriage across the lot until she reaches the police tape that marks the spot where Lucy Mendoza disappeared, not even twenty-four hours ago. It's a big swath of space, and Julia wonders why. A baby in a shopping cart is so small. What other evidence did the police find to make them clear an area so large? A suspicious van? A dropped receipt? Julia swallows hard, letting her mind go darker. Lucy's blood?

She hears the sound of yet another car, tires crunching over pebbles.

A few people have left flowers against one of the parking lot's light poles, a teddy bear, a couple of candles. Julia removes a hand from Theo's carriage and reaches for the police tape, closes the plastic yellow strip inside her palm. Tries to pray for Lucy's safe return.

But really, she's praying for herself.

One single night of sex and here she is, with a baby. A few seconds in time and it was done, her life turned completely at an angle she cannot shift because something irrevocable occurred. There is no undoing those few seconds. As she stares at the tape crushed in one fist, while she rocks the carriage in the other, once again she focuses on the different forces that can change the angle of a woman's life.

Death for one.

Or, say, a kidnapping.

Until today, until Lucy Mendoza, it never occurred to Julia to imagine being relieved of motherhood not because someone steals the baby but because someone steals the mother.

The yellow tape grows blurry under her gaze, the word *caution* warm and twisted in her hand. She hangs onto it tightly in the bright, safe sunlight of a September day in front of the market where she buys benign things to put into the fridge and kitchen cabinets. She waits and she waits. Because maybe the person who took Lucy will come back?

Take me too.

Take me.

"Do you know her?" a woman's voice asks.

Julia startles, a quick slash of fear knifing through her—she'd thought she was alone. She turns and sees a woman right next to her, not even a foot away. Older, gray hair, in baggy jeans and a loose short-sleeved top. Julia's fear loosens. She might be a grandmother. Julia shakes her head, finally releases the yellow police tape. "I don't. Do you?"

The woman also shakes her head. She studies Julia harder, with a pensive gaze. What, exactly, is this woman thinking about Julia? "What are you doing here then? Just curious?"

"I guess just hoping Lucy Mendoza is all right."

"Are *you* all right?" the woman asks.

For some reason, Julia can't simply answer yes. So she tells a total stranger, "I've had a difficult few days."

The woman's eyes travel to Theo's carriage then back to Julia. "Motherhood is hard."

"Everyone says that." Julia stares at the older woman, searching her face for a reaction but the gaze that meets her is unreadable. So she shrugs. "But I know, I know, it always gets easier."

"I wasn't going to say that," the woman says, "because I wasn't about to lie."

Julia blinks in surprise. "Thank you for that," she says slowly.

The woman stretches her arm out and pats Julia's hand, the one gripping the carriage. "But I do believe you'll find a way through." Her attention drifts back to the area of the lot marked out by the police. "And let's hope Lucy does as well."

Before Julia can respond, the older woman is walking away.

Her words echo awhile inside of Julia's chest.

A few minutes later, when Julia pushes Theo toward the lot's exit, she hears her name.

"Julia?"

She halts. There's a man by a pickup truck, loaded with long planks of wood that stick out from under a tarp. He's looking at her.

"Henry?"

She knows him from a prior life. They used to frequent the same coworking space. She'd rented it to get herself out of the house. She works on paper with pencils, so she technically doesn't need a studio like most of her artist friends. Her tools are compact and portable. It almost feels strange to see Henry outside of the coworking space. Like they've run into each other in another country. She raises her hand in a wave.

He strides toward her, smiling, like some shining mirage in the desert. Julia watches Henry walk, the lightness of his body, the sureness of his movements. She imagines the muscles of his back and shoulders rippling underneath his shirt. She imagines sketching the lines of his torso.

"Hey there," Henry says. "It's been so long since I've seen you at your desk." He doesn't glance at the carriage or make eyes at Theo like everyone else, he keeps his gaze on Julia's face.

Like someone finally remembers the real Julia exists. "Yeah, it must be what, a year?"

"At least. Are you still illustrating? Any new exciting drawings? Book covers under contract?"

Julia's heart dips. "I'm on vacation," she lies, adding a laugh. But she likes that he asked her about work and not about Theo. That he still sees her as an artist.

"God, I need a vacation," Henry says with an inviting smile. But an invitation to what, exactly? "Will you be back at your desk anytime soon? I need someone to help me procrastinate in the coffee room again."

Henry needs her? "Probably not, so you'd better find someone else." Julia hears a hiccupping sound, looks down and realizes Theo is fully awake, about to let out a wail. Of course he is, of course right now. He probably needs a diaper change. "I've got to go." She returns her gaze to Henry. *Is that disappointment on his face?*

Henry finally glances at Theo's carriage and nods. "See you around then, Julia?"

She smiles, she can't help it. "Sure. See you around, Henry."

He doesn't move, just stands there waiting, so Julia is the one to head off. The carriage's movement does the trick as usual with her son, and his whimpers grow quiet.

"I hope so," Henry calls softly to Julia's back.

But she hears it.

Something about Henry lodges within her.

Take me, her mind calls out yet again, and something inside her body ignites.

11
DIANA

DIANA GONZALEZ'S PHONE rings and she pulls it from her pocket. The retired detective stares over the top of her former partner's car. Joe's just arrived at Belmont; it's his lunch break. "Hang on, it's my daughter," she says.

Detective Joe Suarez nods. "Tell Clara hello."

Diana leans against the passenger side of Joe's police sedan, the metal hot from the sun. She swipes at the screen, smiling at the sight of her daughter's lovely face. "Hola, mi amor, I'm so glad you called."

"Hi, Mom," Clara replies, then hesitates.

"Is something wrong?" Diana asks automatically. She'll never stop worrying about Clara no matter how much her daughter complains that at forty-two, she's old enough to fend for herself. Susana is the same about her own two sons, both grown like Clara. It's one of the many things Diana and Susana bonded over when they met a decade ago at the party of a mutual friend. How they'd laughed at the eternal worry of the mother even when the children are happy.

"I'm fine, Mom," Clara says. "I called to talk about *you*."

Diana straightens. The metal of the sedan is so hot she's sweating through her top. She can guess what Clara wants to discuss, but plays along. "Eh, what's on your mind, querida?"

"You know exactly what."

"I can't talk long. I'm here with Joe."

"Mom, exactly! You're retired!"

"But another woman has gone missing, and Joe just wants to talk. He's on his break so we don't have forever." As these words unfurl on Diana's tongue, she feels the familiar urge to pull her daughter close, the need to physically ground Clara to the earth. The thought of something like this happening to Clara, someone taking Diana's baby, causes a beast to spring to life inside her.

"It's all over the place about Lucy Mendoza and I knew this would happen. Which is why I called." Clara goes silent a beat. Then, "You promised you were done."

"You don't have to worry about me, querida, it's my job to worry about you."

"Oh, Mom."

"It's just a chat with Joe, Clarita. It's important to me."

When Clara's father died fifteen years ago, it was Diana's detective work that saved her from her grief, kept her going, day by day, until she found her footing and life started to mean something again. Diana never expected to fall for Susana, but then they hit it off and it became so obvious Diana was in love she couldn't not see it. Somehow their children took everything in stride. Lucky for Diana, they now enjoy this beautiful blended family.

Joe and Diana's eyes lock across the top of the car and his brows arch.

"Mom?" Clara asks.

Joe walks around the back of the police sedan to join Diana.

"Clara, I'm sorry," Diana says, "but Joe's waiting, I love you!" She hangs up before her daughter can protest any further.

Together Diana and Joe move across the lot toward the police tape.

"I'm guessing Clara is not too thrilled with me," Joe says.

Diana watches a woman pushing a cart across the lot, the child next to her with ice cream dripping down his arm, smiling as he eats and walks. "She'll get over it. I want to help."

Joe puts on his sunglasses. "Good. I need your analytical brain, Dee. And Marist isn't you."

Diana glances over at her former partner, feeling odd to be dressed casually next to his detective attire, attire that was hers not that long ago. "So catch me up then."

As Joe starts down his list of updates, Diana takes mental notes as they walk: hairs found at the scene, some long and red, likely Lucy's, others too but it's a parking lot; they'll all be tested. Someone saw a van down here around the time of Lucy's disappearance, but they tracked it to a pair of surfers living down by Narragansett Beach. They've got Lucy's laptop from the house but there's nothing much of interest on it.

"Let's see, what else," he says, and trails off.

Diana wipes her brow, it shouldn't be this hot in September. "In your messages, you mentioned that Lucy Mendoza's friend—"

"Michelle," Joe supplies.

"Michelle, right, she seems convinced Lucy is not having an affair."

"But I got the sense she was holding back," Joe says. "I'm not sure about what."

"That doesn't mean this Michelle is right. Lucy may have secrets. Most people do."

A car comes roaring down the aisle then swerves to avoid hitting them.

Joe throws up a hand and the driver winces and slows down. "Yeah, and there's the weird coincidence that this friend was shopping inside Belmont while her friend was getting taken."

They reach the section of the lot cordoned off with yellow police tape.

"Well, that's an interesting coincidence."

"Yeah."

"Did you already speak to Lucy's coworkers?" Diana asks.

Joe raises an arm against the glare, but even with sunglasses the day is brilliant. "Yeah, but we didn't get much. Lucy was well-liked, she was good at her job, one of the top salespeople in the office. One of them did say that some of Lucy's clients would ask her out, god, even while she was pregnant apparently. So I've got Marist tracking down those guys. Lucy even fired one of the clients who was hitting on her—we're trying to find him too. But nothing on Lucy's laptop or her phone suggests an affair. The FBI has already swooped in and taken them from us, of course."

"Of course." Diana huffs. "So now you're on handling locals and passing along info?"

"Yup."

"Joanna D'Angelo?"

"Yup."

The candles and stuffed animals left in the spot where Lucy was taken are piling up, and the sight of a stuffed rabbit breaks Diana's heart a little. "Do you think there's a connection?"

Joe removes his sunglasses and rubs his eyes, puts them back on. "I don't know. Joanna D'Angelo was much older than Lucy, completely different features, different backgrounds. Different situations entirely. And Joanna D'Angelo was having an affair for sure, the husband knew it, everyone knew it. There were signs she took off."

"But she also had a child," Diana says.

"She did. But that's where their similarities end. And Dee, if someone did take Joanna, then we're looking for a body by this point. It's been three years."

After another car passes they resume walking.

Diana's cheeks burn hotter as she thinks about how what Joe says is true on every level, how they've failed Joanna and her family, how they continue to fail her even now. The press never cared about Joanna D'Angelo. No one did, not even on social media, not like they do with Lucy, posts already everywhere, people sharing updates about her disappearance, flooding her Instagram page and liking photos. But there was nothing sexy about Joanna D'Angelo—not her age, not her demeanor, not her social status, not her job down at a clam shack in Watch Hill. She didn't make for glamorous news photos and besides, her husband likely had Mafia connections. A lot of people in Rhode Island do. The Mafia still has an outsized presence here. On Atwells Avenue in Federal Hill, a person can pass by gray-haired men sitting in lawn chairs out on the sidewalk, as though they stepped off the set of *The Sopranos*.

"Well, it's probably Lucy Mendoza's husband anyway," she offers.

Joe ducks under the police tape to look at the stuffed animals and candles and other things people left in tribute. He glances back up at Diana. "We had the guy, Sam, all night at the station and he was the portrait of the distraught husband. His alibi is weak, though—he was at home working in the garage by himself."

"The FBI didn't find anything else of interest in the house?" Diana asks.

"Nothing of note so far, at least not that they've shared with the local force." Joe bends low and reads a notecard inked in bright blue marker. *We're praying for you, Lucy!* "It's early stages, maybe they missed something." He straightens again.

Diana and Joe begin a lap around the site. They used to do this, return to the scene of the crime after forensics had done their thing, to talk through what might have happened, imagine all possible scenarios, however outlandish, play them out, one by one. Once a detective, always a detective. Diana will still feel the urge at ninety.

"So I've been watching the lot for a while now," she admits. "I came early because I wanted to see who else might show up when the police aren't here."

Joe glances at her with a smirk. "Of course you did."

Diana takes his wry tone as a compliment. "Mostly it's been a lot of people looking over nervously as they come in and out of the market, or intentionally avoiding this place like they're afraid it might happen again if they come too close. Someone left another bunch flowers thirty minutes ago. A few people have spent some time here, though."

"Yeah?"

Diana nods, squints against the glare, still annoyed she forgot her own sunglasses. Maybe her daughter is right and she's getting too old for this. "One woman was here quite awhile. If I had to guess, Lucy's age, and with a baby carriage."

Joe gestures at the candles. "Was she praying or something?"

"Maybe. I don't know though."

Her old partner gives Diana a detailed tour of the scene,

where Lucy's car was parked, how the shopping cart with the baby was wedged against the tire, the exact location where Lucy's phone was found under an SUV across the way. Diana nods as she listens, eyes roaming between where Lucy's phone was found and the place where her car was parked, the baby in the cart beside it.

"No groceries were tipped in the trunk of Lucy's car," Joe goes on. "The bags were all perfectly upright. The shopping cart was neatly parked against the wheel, so it wouldn't go rolling away with the baby in it. No wallet on the ground, no signs of a scuffle. Really, the only thing out of place was Lucy's phone."

Diana inhales these details like she's starving. "That's a big thing out of place."

Joe's thumb taps the legs of his pants. "But nothing else."

"Exactly," Diana says and nods.

"So maybe Lucy knows whoever took her?" Joe asks.

Diana breathes deeply. "Or maybe Lucy went willingly? Maybe Lucy tossed the phone herself?"

Joe thinks about this. "See, this is why I called you, Dee."

Diana stares hard at the scene, once again picturing the car, the cart, the baby, the sun over their heads, the moment whatever happened began to happen, trying to imagine the how, the who, the why. Her pulse races, she wishes she wasn't retired. The sense that this is the kind of thing Diana was born to do surges through her like she never left the force, like it's still her job to try to find this woman. "Because why take a woman here with a baby?" Diana asks. "If you're planning on taking someone, you could obviously take someone unencumbered by a child. Because you'd want to eliminate any X factors, right? Any hiccups that might go wrong. The baby left behind seems risky." Diana's eyes return to the little stuffed rabbit. "With Joanna, the daughter had been with the husband at the time she disappeared."

"Those circumstances were so different," Joe reminds her. "She took off with her mystery man. Or *men*." Joe pauses, glances at Diana.

There was a time early in her police career when she would have balked at such a comment about a woman, its shaming implications, but now she knows better and nods for Joe to keep going.

"Or it was Joanna's husband's fault because of his . . . connections. You know how it goes."

"Still. What if Lucy isn't his first?"

"The FBI will already be on that," Joe says. "Not to mention the press is running with the story and I can tell it's going to be a shit show. It's already a shit show on everyone's goddam socials. Beautiful young mother taken from her equally beautiful baby. That photo the husband released of Lucy on his own socials makes her look like a model. Soon we'll have a fucking podcast." Joe checks the time on his phone. "I should go. Marist is going to think I'm cheating on him for sure."

Diana laughs, but something nags. "Before you head off . . ." *What is it, exactly?* Diana looks around the lot. "That woman I saw with the baby carriage who was here for a while?"

Joe nods. "Yeah?"

"Not too far off I noticed a man sitting in his truck, watching her. At first, I was suspicious, but then it seemed like they knew each other. When she started to head off, he got out of his truck, talked to her—yelled her name, she clearly recognized him. Seemed happy to see him." She pulls a note from the pocket of her jeans, the ones Susana calls her retirement jeans, and hands it to Joe. "I took down the license plate and the make and model."

Joe takes it from her. "It's good to have you back."

"It's probably nothing," she says. "And I'm not technically back."

"Right." Joe stares at the information Diana wrote down before tucking it away. "Maybe the guy was just getting up the nerve to talk to her and it took him awhile. Men can be cowardly."

Diana considers this. "Some can. Maybe."

12
MICHELLE

DOZENS OF REPORTERS crowd the edge of Lucy and Sam's yard under the beech trees by the driveway, in the street where the neighborhood children play. Big vans with satellites are parked on the road, one after the other.

"Oh wow," Michelle says to no one, slowing her car to a crawl.

What should she do? Should she turn around? Forge ahead?

Sam has not been answering Michelle's calls, so Michelle decided to show up at Lucy's house. But now Michelle sees the nightmare waiting for Sam if he tries to leave, and her feelings soften. Maybe Sam can barely move because he's besieged by reporters.

Between early morning and now, Michelle's already had quite a day. First she was on the phone to an old colleague from her time as an advertising exec. He connected her to one of his social media interns as a favor. Alejandra. With this young woman's help, in about thirty minutes they'd put together a MISSING flier for Lucy that's so professional and eye-catching that if this college grad had been working for Michelle, she'd immediately give Alejandra a promotion. Not only did she create the poster, Alejandra formatted and sized it for every possible social media post in existence. And now this magical intern is in the process of distributing this flier across platforms, getting people to tag others in an online campaign to search for Lucy, with a fund Michelle provided to create and purchase ads.

At least Michelle can do this much. At least she's doing something.

She presses harder on the brake to review the chaos in front of Lucy's house and so she doesn't accidentally run into anyone. "Poor Sam," she says, guilty now about her impatience that he hasn't texted. "Poor Emma," she adds, her frustration shifting to the reporters who don't seem to understand there's a frightened family inside that house, a husband searching for his wife and a baby who misses her mother.

Michelle glances at the clock on the dashboard.

Soon it will be twenty-four hours since Lucy disappeared.

Where are you, Lucy? Michelle wonders for the umpteenth time.

She parks on the street a couple houses away. There must be thirty, forty people out there. What, exactly, do they think is going to happen? Lucy's going to waltz up and greet them, offering interviews about her miraculous reappearance? Some of the media are forking takeout into their mouths, rice spilling onto asphalt, people biting into burritos, guacamole smeared on chins; a thin, coiffed woman daintily eating sushi with chopsticks in a folding chair set up on the sidewalk. Coffee cups and water bottles galore are scattered across a table, like it's a party.

Michelle feels like screaming, *This is not a fucking party!*

She tries to see a way into Lucy's house that doesn't involve wading through newscasters and true crime YouTubers sticking microphones in her face, but can't think of one. Before Sam and Lucy had Emma, they put up a fence around the backyard with a lock on the door. The neighbors have a pool and they didn't want Emma toddling over and falling in.

"Okay, just go on through," Michelle tells herself, opening the driver's side door and trying to shut it as softly as possible. "You can do this."

She takes a step, runs a hand through her hair. Shit. She should have anticipated the reporters, taken more care with her clothing and makeup. She thinks about the woman's video from earlier this morning in her electric blue dress, so put together and poised. Yoga pants and a sweatshirt are not exactly how Michelle wants the whole world to see her, looking like some stereotypical suburban mother. Which is exactly what she is. Michelle cringes.

"Remember this is about Lucy, not you," she mutters, and moves toward the front walk of Lucy's yard. Then she plunges into the crowd of reporters and their teams because she has no other choice. They're everywhere.

At first, they don't notice Michelle. It takes people a minute to realize a woman who is not a member of the media is pushing through them on her way to the front door of the house.

"Are you a relative of Lucy Mendoza?" someone shouts.

"How do you know Lucy Mendoza?" someone else tries.

The crowd erupts, everyone yelling at once.

Michelle imagines she's a linebacker, her job to shoulder on through, not caring who she bulldozes or who goes down. She imagines climbing over hips and backs and faces.

"Do you know what happened to Lucy?"

"Are you the husband's mistress?"

"Do you know where she is?"

"Who are you?"

"What are you?"

"Do you trust the husband? Do you think he's hiding something?"

"Do you think he's the killer?"

"Are you worried some psycho has Lucy?"

By the time Michelle reaches the door she's surrounded. These people are a malignant forcefield, she feels them behind her, ready to zap. She pushes the doorbell, pounds on the wood with her fist, the curtains closed tight across the windows. *Come on, Sam. Hurry. Please be here.* Everyone keeps shouting questions about Lucy, about Sam, about her, who she is, why she's here, what she knows.

"Do you think Lucy Mendoza is dead?" a woman yells.

Michelle's whole body goes cold. She turns around, she wants to reach out and push this woman over, scream in her face, *How dare you say such a thing!* The crowd goes quiet, they've got her attention, she might actually speak. Michelle sees how they gather in a huddle barely a foot away, so close but not touching. The way they hush, all eyes for her.

What, exactly, are they hoping she might say?

A woman raises a mic to Michelle's face. "Do you think Lucy Mendoza's dead?" she repeats.

Michelle wants to grab the mic out of this woman's hand and wield it like a club. She draws in a breath, angry, nasty words rising through her chest into her throat. But then she pulls herself together. She was once an accomplished professional who could handle anyone and anything. Michelle takes in a hoarse breath, tries to remember her best course of action is silence, that she did not come here to make a comment. She came here for Sam, for Emma, to make sure they know she'll do whatever she can to help, to show support, *something*.

The front door opens a crack.

Michelle hears it, the sucking sound of rubber against the kick of the door, leaving its frame.

"Come in," says a whisper. "Hurry."

Michelle turns back around and pushes inside Lucy's house, slams the door shut. She pants as she leans against the painted wood, and her eyes adjust to the dim lighting.

Sam stands in front of her. He takes in a sharp breath. "Hi, Michelle."

He's trying not to cry, Michelle realizes.

So is she, she realizes.

Sunbursts blot Michelle's eyes but the smell is what hits her hard. Potent, familiar, traces of cedar and other wood Michelle cannot begin to name, mingled with something sweet. The lingering scent of Lucy's perfume, the memory of her body moving through this house, proof of its existence. Lucy haunting this place. A pain shoots through Michelle's middle, she doesn't want to imagine Lucy haunting anything, because that would mean she is, already, dead.

"Hi, Sam," she says.

His eyes drop to the floor. His clothes are ratty—ratty T-shirt, ill-fitting sweatpants, bare feet. He rakes a hand through his tangled curly hair, looks like he hasn't showered. He probably hasn't. Michelle hasn't either.

"I'm sorry I haven't called you," he begins, "or messaged, or..."

She puts a hand on his shoulder. "It's okay, I get it now. Those reporters are..."

He looks up, wipes a hand across his face. "No, it's not just that. They took my phone. The FBI searched the house. The police kept me down at the station all night."

Michelle's gaze travels toward the living room, everything slightly crooked, piles of things stacked hastily onto tables, Lucy's precious collection of her father's poetry books falling over and splayed on their shelf. The place is a mess.

"They've taken everything else too," Sam goes on. "My laptop, Lucy's, boxes full of I don't know what. My mother and I have been trying to clean and organize the mess all morning. They think it's me, Michelle. They interrogated me for hours, like I'm some murderer."

Her eyes widen. "Oh." Of course they did. She should have known. Don't they always decide it's the husband? "Two detectives came to see me this morning too. They grilled me about why I was at Belmont at the time of Lucy's disappearance."

"Yeah." His gaze shifts sideways. *Is he wondering why as well?* Or maybe he's just looking at the photo from Lucy and Sam's wedding on the wall, or the one from their honeymoon, still crooked, all those photos of baby Emma, not quite righted either. "I'm not surprised. Wait till the FBI arrives on your doorstep. Like you could do something like that to Lucy. Like *I* could do something to my own wife."

"Sam, I'm so sorry," Michelle says, relieved that Sam has told her this. "They can't think that you would ... or that I ..."

His shoulders slump. "But they do. I've complied with everything they want, let them search, handed over the laptops willingly, even my own journal. I'm sure they'll be back any moment telling me they've found evidence that I killed her."

Their eyes meet, and when they do Michelle catches something unexpected, something she's never seen before on

Sam's face—a coldness, a flash of ice, of what . . . malice? For a second, Michelle lets herself wonder, *Could Sam have done something?* But then the thought disappears, and out loud she says, "Well, obviously they're not going to find any sign of that. You got a lawyer, I hope?"

He blinks, he shakes his head.

"Sam! You need a lawyer. I can help with that. I can help with other things too. In fact, this morning I started organizing online so people will search . . ." But Michelle trails off.

Sam turns toward the wall behind him. He runs a finger across the glass of the wedding photo right next to his head, leaving behind a streak right across Lucy's breasts, stopping when he reaches the bottom edge of Lucy's elegant mermaid gown. He stares at his smiling wife, so happy and beautiful, and Michelle wonders what might be going through his mind. "Their other theory is Lucy left me," he says. "That she packed her things and took off. They keep asking me if there are any suitcases missing, clothing missing, that kind of thing."

Michelle's knees become rubbery.

"All her things are here, right where she left them, of course they are!" Sam shakes his head, eyes still on his wife in a wedding dress. "I told the police, why in the world would my wife pack her things then leave our baby in a parking lot? That doesn't make any sense."

"It doesn't," she agrees, though privately Michelle wonders what the police might have encountered at the scene that wasn't so obvious. She decides not to ask Sam. She would consider this later, parse it out in her head. Go back over every detail.

Sam finally looks away from the photo, inhales a sharp breath. "My mother is with Emma upstairs. Do you want to see her?"

Michelle wonders if he means Emma, or his mother. She just says, "Yes."

Sam climbs the steps behind him, feet heavy, *thump, thump, thump*. Midway up, Sam teeters, loses his balance, and Michelle sees him flail above her in slow motion. Her arm shoots out, flat and sure on his back as he catches the banister.

"I'm here," she says.

Sam grips the railing and he pants. *This is pain*, Michelle thinks. *This is heartbreak*. The force of it, the gravity pulling him to the ground, doubling his weight, threatening to topple him. Steady now, Sam starts trudging upstairs again, *thump, thump*.

When they reach the top, they turn down the hall, also lined with photographs, including Michelle's favorite: Michelle and Lucy drinking wine and laughing at a café, from Michelle's first visit to Santiago, Chile, just after they graduated from college. She straightens it, then lingers in front of the image, remembers how much fun they had, how Lucy kept trying to set Michelle up with handsome waiters, long streams of Spanish flying from her friend's mouth, Michelle protesting, nudging Lucy, whispering for her to stop, the whole time Michelle giggling. She puts a finger to her lips, presses it to the glass over Lucy's smiling face. Aside from Lucy's late father, Michelle and Sam are the two people who love Lucy most. At least Lucy's father isn't alive to experience the trauma of his daughter having disappeared.

Through the doorway of the bedroom, Michelle sees Emma playing on the floor underneath Grandma Rachel's watchful eyes, loving hands tickling Emma's tummy until she laughs. Emma, blissfully unaware of Lucy's absence. How long will it be before Emma senses her mother is gone?

Michelle approaches her friend's baby, gets down on the floor next to Rachel, arranges herself on the blanket where Emma is scooting around, her little bum wiggling as she tries to crawl. She's almost there, she's almost got the hang of it. Emma stops squirming, manages to roll over, and reaches for a soft, bright butterfly, the wings crackling when Emma squeezes them. She puts the butterfly in her mouth. A gift from someone or other at Lucy's baby shower. Emma loves that butterfly.

"Michelle," Rachel says. The joy in her eyes for Emma transforms into darkness.

"What can I do?" Michelle asks. What she really means is *What can I do to help with Emma?* But Rachel takes it differently.

"You can tell us what you know." Rachel's voice is sharp and laced with suspicion.

Words choke Michelle, they are poison today, eating away at her insides, stuffing together in her throat until she can't breathe. "What I know?" Michelle repeats, stupidly.

"Yes." Rachel's eyes narrow. "You're her best friend. You must know *something*."

"I know as much as anyone," she says, adding yet another lie to the string that keeps on growing, like the construction paper chains she makes with Charlie at Christmas to hang around the house. "Only that Lucy was taken." Her eyes slide back to Emma, guilt striking like a bat. This seems to be her job now, to lie for Lucy, absorb the guilt of so much silence.

Emma sits up now, and she watches Michelle, eyes so big. Lucy's eyes.

"Oh, sweetheart." Michelle pulls Emma onto her lap. She kisses her head as Emma snuggles into Michelle's warm, soft chest. She catches Rachel's gaze over Emma's plump body. "What do *you* know?" Michelle shoots back, and wonders if Lucy would have told Rachel about her fantasy, her unhappiness. Her regret.

Something uncertain enters Rachel's eyes. But then it disappears, and Michelle decides there's no way Lucy would have told Sam's mother. She kisses Emma's head again, smells her sweet baby scent.

"All I know is that my daughter-in-law is missing," Rachel says, and bursts into tears.

Sam gets down on the floor with the three of them, puts an arm around his mother as she cries into her son's shoulder.

Michelle bounces Emma in her lap, amazed at Emma's sleepy face, her little sucking mouth, a tiny eye in a storm of sorrow, unaware of so much tragedy around her—a tragedy that's also hers.

"I just hoped," Rachel says between sobs, "that maybe there would be a different explanation? That this nightmare would turn out to be some kind of mistake?" Rachel looks at Michelle. "That you would tell us Lucy was having an affair and that's where she's been?"

"Mom!" Sam protests.

"Well, it's what those detectives keep wanting to know!"

"She wasn't having an affair." This is the one true thing Michelle can offer. Her eyes drift toward the walls of Emma's room, the flowers Sam and Lucy painted as they prepared for Emma's arrival, as Lucy's middle grew big and round. Michelle remembers how much it amused Lucy to see how she had to stretch to get to these walls, paint brush in hand, marveling at the growing distance between her feet and the baseboard because of her belly. There's the crib Sam put together four whole months before Lucy gave birth because he was so excited, the green chair in the corner meant to be Lucy's nursing chair, which Lucy never used because Emma wouldn't latch and she gave up.

Rachel wipes her face with a tissue and reaches out to take Emma back. She's nodding off peacefully and Michelle gives her up. The three of them watch Emma as her body relaxes, limbs going limp, breaths long and steady.

Michelle looks at Sam. "Emma has you so she will be all right," she says, another truth.

The stoic expression on Sam's face collapses. "What if they can't find Lucy?"

"But they *will*," Michelle says. "*We* will. There are so many things *we* can do—"

Rachel turns to them, eyes imploring. *No more in front of Emma.*

Michelle pulls herself up from the floor, pulls Sam up next, maneuvers him from the room into the hall. She knows what it's like to try to be strong for a child, when you don't allow yourself to feel so they don't have to be scared. When you can't manage to be strong for even one more second but then you do, you manage it. And then you manage it some more.

Sam's mother closes the door quietly behind them.

Michelle leads Sam down the hall toward the stairs, the softness of the rug familiar under her feet, the way it sometimes slips along the wood as she walks because Lucy never got around to buying a pad to go underneath it. The bright blue color of the walls, turquoise, the same hue as the front door. Everything in Lucy's house cheerful, a pink chair at a desk, a grass green dresser. Michelle wishes she too had the guts to paint a wall bright orange. But Lucy makes the color scheme work. If Michelle tried this, it would come out garish.

When they reach the kitchen, Michelle sees it's also a mess, all kinds of things pulled from the cupboards. Michelle wonders how it's legal for the police, the FBI, to leave things in such a state when the family living here is having the worst crisis of their lives. She picks her way carefully across the floor which is littered with pots and pans, unearths the kettle, fills it and puts it on the stove to heat, then grabs two mugs from a still-open cabinet.

Sam sinks heavily into one of the chairs at the breakfast table, which is piled high with dishes and peppered haphazardly with wine glasses. "What do you think happened, Michelle? I mean, you were there at the scene."

Michelle busies herself opening Lucy's jar full of tea bags, pulling out two of them and carefully hanging the tag over the lip of each mug. Then she leans against the counter to wait for the water to boil. A long silence follows as they both ponder this coincidence that Michelle was one of the women who found Emma outside Belmont. Only now does it occur to Michelle that David was nearby too. He'd met Michelle for lunch because he had business in the area, something about a new corporate client for his accounting firm who'd wanted to meet in person before signing on. That's what David told her, at least. She'd thought it was nice since usually David is chained to his desk all day. Huh. She makes a mental note to ask David his whereabouts around the time Lucy was taken when he gets home tonight. Then she physically shudders at this thought. God, soon she'll start suspecting even Charlie and Aidan.

Michelle's empty stomach gurgles. "I know. The timing of it all is weird."

The kettle shrieks and they both jump.

She shuts off the gas, absently pours water into the mugs. Plops a spoon into each one and carries them to the breakfast table, moves a stack of *New Yorker*s from the chair so she can sit down. Thinks of Lucy reading them in the mornings, then pushes the thought away.

Steam from the tea rises in front of Sam's face. "Did the police tell you anything new?"

"No," Michelle says.

His eyes drift above Michelle's head, maybe toward the windows that look onto the backyard. The maple whose leaves will soon turn a fiery red for fall, Lucy's favorite tree. "Is there anything else I should know, Michelle?"

There it is again—something in Sam's gaze that she can't quite name.

Lucy has hinted before that Sam can sometimes "disappear," emotionally sure, but also sometimes he'll literally disappear, leaving her alone with Emma, not picking up his phone, then reappearing out of nowhere. Michelle has chalked this up to Sam just needing a break from married life, from parenting, since David does the same thing; but then, David leaves everything to Michelle and Sam isn't like that. Or at least, she's never thought of him this way before.

Michelle composes herself, takes a slow sip of tea. "What do you mean, is there anything else you should know?"

"Upstairs with my mother, you said there was no one else. But *was* Lucy seeing someone? *Was* she having an affair? Could this person have taken her? Could she have run away with him? I mean, you and I both know that she had clients who hit on her all the time. Maybe one of them finally ... got to her?"

"Sam, no. I wasn't lying." She sees that Sam doesn't quite believe her. There's something going on with him that Michelle's missing. But what is it? Or is she imagining things? "I swear," she adds. Then guilt comes for Michelle again like a hawk, it swoops in and digs its talons into her shoulders, cutting through skin, through tendons. She feels Lucy's secret tearing at her. *Could Sam be holding something back too? Something the police said?* Michelle swallows. *Could Sam have found out about Lucy's plan?* But then she reminds herself: *No, it was just a fantasy, not an actual plan.*

"Whatever it is, you can tell me, Michelle," Sam says, "I can take it."

"I know," she says, but *can* she tell him? *Can* he take it? Can anyone? "When you were looking around the house for signs that Lucy left, you didn't find anything, right?"

"What, like Lucy emptied her underwear drawer and her closets?" Sam sounds defensive. "I told you, *no*, so why are you asking? Do you think Lucy was planning to leave me?" Sam's fingers keep opening wide over the top of the steaming mug, then curling tight. "What do you know about Lucy that you aren't saying, Michelle?"

I could ask you the same thing, she thinks.

Michelle blinks once, twice, stomach nauseated. She shakes her head, keeps shaking it. "Nothing," she lies for the third time today, because this is who Michelle is now, a liar. "Nothing I haven't told you already. Not you or the police," she adds for emphasis, as though this might make her words become true.

13
JULIA

THE HOURS OF Julia's afternoon are vast and unwieldy. There are too many as she waits for Marcus to come home; they hang like weights around her neck. Early on she buckles under them, hunched over as she cradles her son and bottle feeds him, as she puts him down for his nap, as she later fills the dishwasher, folds T-shirt after T-shirt of Marcus's, matches tiny socks for Theo, stacking everything on the couch, the detritus of a baby littered around her feet. The house is so quiet and Julia so alone. All her plans to force a pencil to paper today if only to draw a single line, have fallen apart. Futile.

She places another shirt on top of the stack.

The afternoon light filters through the curtains, innocent.

She again glances at the clock on the wall and sees the time.

Three o'clock.

She halts folding.

She thinks of Lucy Mendoza.

It's better than obsessing over Daphne's Instagram, she supposes. All her friends' applauding hands emojis on Daphne's every post.

Julia checks her phone to see if the woman has been found.

She hasn't.

Lucy's been gone for twenty-four hours.

Julia remembers the parking lot where Lucy was taken. The metrics of a disappearance, surprisingly large in a way, so much space blocked off in such a mundane area. But also so small when one thinks of what happened there—the disappearance of a person, a woman Julia's own age with a baby as little as Theo. A woman with a whole life ahead of her.

Thoughts of Lucy remind Julia about running into Henry, the pleasurable shock of it. Memories of seeing Henry at the coworking space unfold in her mind. Henry's big eyes, the tiny scar under his chin, the perpetual stubble on his cheeks, the shape of his hands, the sound of his voice. The way he'd look at Julia while they chatted in the coffee room, a fact she barely registered since back then things were still good with Marcus; they were still in love.

But now . . .

Something in Julia shifts.

Out of nowhere, a cry of *Oh* inside her, as she luxuriates in the image of Henry striding over to say hello, calling out her name. A roaring back, a feeling in her middle, the need to take her fingers and touch a man. Lose herself in the anonymity of someone who doesn't see Julia as just a mother.

She remembers the house Henry had told her he was renovating way back when she last saw him at the coworking space, imagines him working there, walls stripped bare around him, Henry shirtless, sweating as he hammers and saws.

A long lost feeling passes through Julia, followed by a tightening between her legs.

She sets the last set of matched socks onto the couch cushions and pads toward the staircase. She tiptoes to the second floor, hands curling around the railing, not wanting to wake Theo. Sometimes the slightest creak in the wood will do it. And right now she just *cannot*. There are so many things she just *cannot*, some as simple as turning on lights. She has also managed to avoid sex with Marcus, she's mastered the baby excuse—her breasts hurt, she's still recovering, she's too exhausted. The truth is that Julia doesn't desire her husband anymore. She's perpetually numb, as though getting pregnant and having a baby deadened this aspect of her to the point that she's wondered if the desiring part of her might be dead forever.

But maybe not?

"Women's desires are complicated," her older sister, Maggie, keeps telling Julia over the phone on the subject of sex with husbands, especially after a baby. "Whatever works," is Maggie's other adage. She means vibrators in secret drawers, clandestine crushes on neighbors. Maggie is all about getting it done like it's an errand, like running out for a carton of milk or filling the dishwasher. She literally schedules sex with Simon, her husband, twice a week.

She pops her head into Theo's room. He's still napping.

Then she continues down the hall and shuts herself in her bedroom. Slips between the sheets. She closes her eyes, lets those images of Henry flood her mind again. A flash of Henry's face, a few whispered words hurled at her back and *whoosh*. That spark is back. Julia feels it again, the shock of desire overpowering.

She pulls off her shirt, her bra, tosses them aside onto the floor.

Slips off her sweatpants.

Henry, Henry, chants her brain, heart pounding, body throbbing.

She reaches inside her underwear, imagines Henry's fingers stroking her, Henry's lips teasing her, his hands on her aching breasts, his mouth sucking her nipples. Julia moans. She imagines the feel of his skin, his eyes on her naked body, his tongue roaming all over, her back arching into him. In Julia's mind she returns to the coffee room at the coworking space, but this time she and Henry don't stop with casual chatting. He sets down his coffee onto the counter, desire filling his eyes, a desire he can't control and now, unlike then, Julia wants him too. He leads her toward the way back of the building that's always deserted, pulls her into one of the carrels where Henry will be free to kiss Julia, undress her, slide her underwear down her thighs until it falls onto the carpeted floor, where he can push Julia onto the desk and touch her until she begs for him inside her, desire winning out against reason, the risks of getting caught worth the reward of being together.

Pleasure builds between Julia's legs, and she moans again.

"Henry," she cries out, an orgasm ripping through her, a full-throated yell.

Julia lays there afterward, panting, the sheets hot beneath her, marveling at how easy that was. A switch suddenly flipped. The seemingly impossible instantly possible again.

But then Julia hears Theo's muffled cries beyond the closed door of the bedroom.

Reality returns like a slap. She remembers where she is, the life she has. That it's not a life where a man she barely knows undresses her in the middle of a workplace. Julia will not get to feel Henry's naked body, his skin on her skin, his fingers between her legs, Henry pushing up inside her, his breath on her neck, whispering in her ear, *Julia, Julia*. That is not her life.

It never was or will be. She bites her lip, draws blood, refuses to cry.

A breeze rushes through the curtains and across the bed.

Forceful, shocking, fabric buffeting high into the air.

Exposing her.

Julia's gaze snaps toward the window. She hadn't realized she left it open and there she is, half-naked and moaning for anyone to hear. She jumps out of bed to shut it. Right as she does, another gust of wind puffs the curtains wide, revealing Julia as she reaches up to close the window. She grabs for the curtain to cover her chest.

This is when she sees the man.

He's standing at his own window, smoking.

Her neighbor.

Listening. Watching. Staring.

Eyes expressionless. Unblinking.

Heart pounding, chest, neck, face burning, Julia slams the window down, draws the curtains closed and slides to the floor, lungs heaving. How much did he hear? How much did he see? What was he thinking, looking into Julia's bedroom window like that?

And how he stared at her!

God, maybe they have some sort of voyeur living next door. Maybe Julia should call the police. But then, the man has every right to be smoking at the window of his own house, Julia reasons, watching whatever's there. Today it happened to be his woman neighbor, naked. The first time she noticed him smoking at his window was shortly after he moved in, while she was pregnant. She should have thought about this before she took off her clothes, before she stood there topless, like some exhibitionist. She draws her arms over her breasts.

Did he hear her moaning, shouting out a name that isn't her husband's?

A memory from this morning floods her mind—that *bump* she heard coming from his house. His basement? What was that? The thing is, Julia's noticed how he comes and goes, especially in the night. She's always up in the wee hours—2 A.M., 3:30—when it's dark and quiet, sitting in the nursing chair by the window, trying to soothe Theo back to sleep. She'll see him come out of his house and into the yard, dressed in dark clothing, black gloves on. He'll emerge from the basement and head up the stairs, footsteps soundless, to retrieve something from the shed by the fence. Julia can never see what it is, it's always covered, wrapped in a cloth or hidden in a bag. Then he'll descend the basement steps again, and disappear inside.

"I wonder what that man keeps in his basement," Julia said to Marcus maybe a month ago. They were in the kitchen, Julia silently wondering how long it would be before Theo's cries would interrupt their dinner. They'd made it all the way to dessert, which involved a pint of ice cream.

"Why?" Marcus asked.

"I see him in the middle of the night, heading into his basement. It's strange."

Marcus spooned ice cream into his mouth. "He's probably just a night owl. Maybe he has a workshop down there."

But what would he be doing? Building furniture? Painting? A shudder went through her, followed by a chill, which had nothing to do with the ice cream in her bowl. Keeping people prisoner? "Whatever it is, he gives me the creeps."

Marcus swallowed another spoonful. "Maybe he's looking at old photo albums from when he was young. Going through boxes of keepsakes. Something sad."

"Or"—Julia stared at the melting mess at the bottom of her bowl—"perhaps he's a psychopath?"

"Or that," Marcus concurred, and then he laughed.

Julia didn't join in on the laughter. She was thinking about how she would catch her neighbor watching when she takes Theo for walks, or packs him into the car. How often he's in the windows staring. She'll see him out of the corner of her eye in the shadows, smoking.

The more it happens, the more unsettling it is. She keeps telling herself Marcus is probably right, their neighbor is just lonely, just interested in the baby next door. On the occasions when Julia manages to feel bad for him, she decides that soon she'll march up to his door and bring the man some cookies like a good neighbor, bring Theo with her. She'll introduce herself like she should have when he first moved in, provide him some company, give herself the chance to find out their neighbor is kind.

Something always holds her back. Some excuse always makes the visit impossible. There's no brown sugar in the cabinet, so cookies are out. There's no powdered sugar, so frosting for a cake would be impossible. There's the washing, the shopping, Julia's constant attempts to start work again, the failures followed by the new attempts to do some sketching. Always some excuse to not get around to doing the neighborly thing. And now that he's seen her naked, she'll never be able to convince herself to go next door.

Julia's eyes slide toward the window of her room again.

Surely this won't be the last time she catches him watching her. There's something else too, niggling at her brain, a connection her mind is longing to make. It's right there waiting to be joined together if she could only see it.

• • •

Theo's cries turn into wails.

Julia rushes to pull on a shirt, her sweatpants, she races to Theo's room. She lifts Theo from his crib and bounces him in her arms. She paces the room, patting Theo's back, hugging him to her, wanting to make up for the fact that she is his mother.

How can Julia ever make up for this?

Theo snuffles a little, wide eyes blinking up at her.

She whispers soothing words and peeks out the window of Theo's room, which is on the same side of the house as her and Marcus's bedroom.

The neighbor is gone.

She thinks of his expression when their eyes locked.

Empty. Like a dead man's.

14
MICHELLE

THE FAUCET OF the kitchen sink runs on high.

Michelle stands there, dazed. The water grows hotter until it is scalding. She gazes at the trees in the yard through the window, but doesn't see the soft green leaves, or the birds whizzing by, or the puffy clouds floating against so much blue.

The terrible knowledge Michelle carries about Lucy, her idea—her plan? It's rotting Michelle from the inside out. It slices at her organs, makes her wince in pain. Like broken glass scattered through her body. It clinks as she moves, the sharp shards of this secret threatening to puncture something vital. Michelle goes through the rest of her day taking care of Aidan while Charlie's at school, organizing life and paying bills while Aidan naps; texting Alejandra between the agonizingly ordinary movements of life, consoled by this young woman's reports about the MISSING poster already spreading across the internet, alerting people about Lucy's disappearance. Alejandra keeps sending Michelle screenshots of posts and ads already up, numbers of clicks, likes, hearts. Yet amid all this, Michelle still can't stop wondering if Sam has information he isn't sharing. That he's doing the same to her as she is to him.

The water has grown so hot that steam rises around

Michelle's face. She turns it off. The suds on her hands slide across the metal handle, slowly, like the tears running down her cheeks. She can't stop these dark thoughts, thoughts that the worst has already occurred. Michelle grabs her phone, not caring she'll get it wet. She squeezes it in her palm before she looks at it. "Come on, Lucy, just send me a message," Michelle prays, but to who she doesn't know. "Tell me you're all right."

Her fingers are too soapy to unlock it so she grabs a dishtowel, convinced this will be the moment Lucy sends word somehow. From a burner phone she bought as part of her plan? From a phone she grabs from a kind stranger? *I'm in Paris, don't worry about me. Santiago was the perfect place to escape for a while, Meesh. Went to Morocco but will be back soon. Love you so much.* Michelle scours her hands until they are dry, and this time when she touches the screen it lights up.

But there's nothing.

Michelle swallows when she notices the time, throat dry.

Lucy's been gone for more than twenty-four hours.

She tosses the thing onto the kitchen table and it lands with a clatter.

Is Lucy's heart still beating?

This thought is like a punch to her chest.

If only Sam had his phone, if only he could just call her with new information, with news that the worst has not occurred and Lucy has been found alive. Sometimes she dials his number because she doesn't know what else to do, even though she knows he can't answer. Soon she'll have to brave the press outside his door again, but not yet.

Michelle slides down along the wall in her kitchen until she is sitting, thighs pulled tight against her, the tile hard underneath her. She rests her forehead on her knees and tries to breathe. She wishes she could go back to the day in the hospital when Emma was born. She relives it in her mind, what she might have done differently.

Emma arrived a few months after Aidan. Michelle was with Lucy in the room and when the birth turned the corner of thirty hours, Lucy's birth plan suddenly turned into an emergency C-section.

"No, no, no!" Lucy had cried. She'd held on to Michelle's hand so hard Michelle thought it would break.

"It's going to be okay, Lucy, it will, I promise," Michelle kept saying in her friend's ear, murmuring that she knew how scary this was, but once Emma was in her arms, Lucy would barely remember the pain and the fear. Michelle remembers the look in Lucy's eyes afterward. Vacant. Shocked. Full of despair.

After Emma was cleaned up, Sam proudly walked his newborn up and down the hallway outside, upon Lucy's request. "Just give me a moment, please!" Lucy kept shrieking, tears running down her cheeks. When the doctor put Emma on her chest, Lucy turned toward the darkened window. "Take her away, I can't."

"She's beautiful, Luz," Michelle kept saying. She remembers brushing the sweaty hair off Lucy's forehead, combing through Lucy's wet locks with her fingers, telling Lucy all kinds of things. "You're going to forget how hard this was before you know it, you're going to look at Emma and think all of this was just a dream."

Lucy tore her eyes from the window and looked at Michelle. "How am I ever going to forget this, Michelle?" The tone of her question was accusatory.

Michelle had actually laughed. "Well, because, *Emma!*"

Now Michelle realizes how her own love of mothering Charlie and Aidan made her blind, how it had supplanted the delivery in her mind. Her experience of giving birth the first time was beyond painful too, barbaric even, but once Charlie arrived it seemed like magic—natural and mysterious and empowering that somehow she, Michelle, had brought this tiny bundle of beauty into the world. Miraculous that her body had endured such shocking agony and exhaustion, only to be presented with this baby to be laid on her chest. She'd assumed this jagged seesaw of emotion was true for every woman, at least eventually.

But tears kept streaming down Lucy's cheeks as she lay there, despondent.

"You just need some sleep," Michelle had said, as though this would cure everything.

Looking back, Michelle realizes her gigantic mistake.

Lucy wasn't fine, she was trying to tell Michelle she wasn't okay, and Michelle did the thing everybody does with mothers: dismiss their feelings as not real. Michelle gaslit Lucy, kept gaslighting her. She hadn't meant to. After their night of wine and Lucy's confession, Lucy never mentioned regret again. Neither one of them said that verboten word in each other's presence. Then Lucy started attending a local postpartum moms group, going twice, sometimes three times per week, and Michelle's worry lessened. Eventually Michelle wondered if she might have dreamed that night. If only she could know for sure.

She pulls herself to standing and looks at the clock. If she doesn't get Aidan up soon then he'll be awke all night so she heads upstairs to retrieve him.

She leans over the rail of his crib, lifting him gently. He

sighs and snorts, those funny snores a relief. She holds him, he's getting so big. She loves the solid feeling of Aidan against her body, the substance of him. As much as Michelle has loved when her babies are tiny, the soft lightness of their torsos, their skinny limbs, their tender heads, she loves it more when they become plump babies who can knock around the room. Dragging themselves on the floor by their arms and elbows, bumping into things, tumbling over when a limb unexpectedly gives way, even though each time worry slices through Michelle. But then they get up and continue forward, unfazed, like they're made of rubber, stumbling, falling, always bouncing back.

Michelle carries Aidan downstairs, her big and ever bigger baby, and sits on the couch, cradling him, listening to him breathe, kissing his head and his cheeks and his nose, whispering to him. Michelle often marvels how her children can be a storm of chaos and also her tranquility. Her stress and also her peace. Even when they are thunder and lightning, she is grateful they are near, their tiny hearts beating close. Soon she'll have to go pick up Charlie from school and both her babies will be with her again, distracting her from the darkness. How she needs them so.

Aidan opens a sleepy eye. Closes it again.

She draws him to her, inhales his scent.

"How could anyone regret a little thing like you?" Michelle gazes down at her younger son. These words are out of her mouth before she can catch them, before she realizes what she's said, her judgment of Lucy laced throughout. The darkness comes rushing back.

Later that evening, Michelle stands in the doorway of the house, glass of wine in hand. David sits in a chair on the front porch, a beer on the table next to him. The clock ticks past more minutes that Lucy is gone. The children are in bed, the light seeps from the sky, the evening mild and summery. Nice enough that a woman could almost forget her best friend has disappeared.

"David, I don't know what to think," she blurts.

He doesn't look up from his phone.

Michelle gulps down some red, a wild feeling inside her. "I don't know what to think about *Lucy*."

David glances up. "I know, everyone is worried." His eyes drop back to the screen in his hand.

Michelle's heart and mind race. Maybe if she speaks Lucy's secret out loud, the toxins of this knowledge will release her, the poison draining from her body. The pile of lies that keeps choking her throat will be dislodged and she'll be able to breathe again. Yes, Michelle should confide in David. He's her husband. She can trust him. Right?

She takes another gulp of wine.

A firefly, stolen from the end of summer, lights up in their front yard.

She takes this as a sign. "Lucy told me something, David. I can't keep it to myself any longer. I need to tell someone else," she adds, as though David is a random person on the street and not the man with whom she shares a house, two children, and drinks on the porch in the evening.

David looks up. "Tell someone what?"

"That it was her one regret." The moment Michelle says this, there is relief in having it outside her body. Of no longer carrying it alone.

David's brow furrows. "Wait—what are you talking about? What did Lucy regret?"

"Having Emma. Having a baby," Michelle whispers, almost

afraid as the words form in her throat and rumble out of her mouth. Will Michelle be struck down by God for speaking this? For betraying Lucy's trust? Will she be punished in some future time? "Lucy told me a few months ago. That she regretted her decision to get pregnant. To become a mother." She swallows, her throat so dry. She's not done yet, she needs to get out the most important part, the part destroying her insides. "Lucy said she sometimes fantasized about faking her own kidnapping. You know, so she can get away from her life and being a mother. She told me she wanted to start over where no one knows who she is."

There it is. *There.*

The knowledge that's been suffocating Michelle since the parking lot and Emma and the circle of women, the police and ambulances arriving. That maybe Lucy wasn't taken, because maybe Lucy made it look like she'd been kidnapped. Because maybe Lucy's disappearance was planned by Lucy herself. It sounded so outrageous when Lucy told this to Michelle that she brushed it off. But now Lucy is missing, so how can she brush it off as fantasy any longer?

It's reality.

Sometimes I feel like the only way I could leave is to make it look like I was kidnapped, Lucy said to Michelle that night. *That's the only way for a mother to avoid seeming like a monster. Because mothers never leave. We expect the men to go but not the mothers. We would never forgive them.* Lucy's eyes had blazed. *I don't want to be a monster, but I don't think I can do this any longer. Be a mother to Emma. I think about it all the time. Just going. Going and never coming back. Having my life to myself again, somewhere else. Somewhere far. Changing my name, starting over, the world leaving me for dead.*

Michelle remembers Lucy's every word and each one haunts her. She never considered her friend might actually do it. That it could be a real plan. If she'd thought Lucy was serious, she would have watched Lucy like a hawk. She would have done everything differently. She would have prevented Lucy from taking steps in this direction. She would have found a way.

David's mouth is hanging open. "I don't believe you."

Michelle thinks, *You're not the only one. I didn't believe Lucy, either.*

"Michelle," David says sharply.

But she stares out onto the grass, the flowers in their beds, gazes into some other dimension where she gets to tell the truth and have it be okay. The growing darkness of evening feels like protection. "I just can't stop thinking about my conversation with Lucy and what she said, David. Given what's happened," she adds, with a big release of air from her lungs. "Her disappearance." Michelle finally looks at her husband directly.

The expression on his face causes her relief to falter. She has David's full attention, and her husband's staring, eyes wide. "Are you actually *serious* about all of this?"

A shaky feeling runs across her, a pot of anger simmering dangerously underneath it. "Yes. Why would I tell you otherwise?" Her voice wobbles. "How could I make a thing like this up?"

David shakes his head. "I don't believe you. Lucy would never say something so horrible. That she regrets having her baby? Who *says* that?"

Michelle feels her body heating up; a flush rushes across her face. Is it worry? Shame? It was stupid and reckless to talk to David. How long did her relief last? A few seconds? Meanwhile, she risked Lucy's secret, her friend along with it. Lucy's deepest vulnerability now in the open. Michelle is falling into a pit of sand and it swallows her.

She breathes purposefully. "I heard Lucy say it from her own mouth." What is she doing? Why can't she stop? "I keep wondering if she's run off somewhere. I'd be *thrilled* if that's what happened. All I want is for her to be okay. Isn't that all you care about, David? Finding out Lucy's all right?" Her voice is a temperature gauge, speeding toward peril. "Who cares about anything else right now, regret or whatever!"

David's eyes shift to the wide wood planks beneath his feet, painted gray. "And what did the police say when you told them, Michelle?" The way he says this, it's an accusation.

Her face grows hotter. She's no longer covered in sand but instead is a bonfire, threatening to burn down everything around them, her husband, her marriage, their family, their life. She grips the back of a chair. With her other hand she tips more wine into her mouth, swallows.

"I didn't tell the police."

David is silent.

Michelle can't stay upright. She sits down in the front doorway and starts to sob. She's tried so hard to remain strong but she can't anymore. She just can't. She cries for Lucy, for their friendship, for Emma, for herself. For her marriage, for how she and David have been faltering. She cries because the world is suddenly terrifying and impossible and cruel.

David gets up from his chair, Michelle hears the scrape of it, his body moving, feet shuffling against the floor of the porch.

Michelle assumes he's coming to console her, to sit and put

an arm around his wife, press his lips to her hair, rub his hand along her back. Tell Michelle she's not alone, that everything is okay, that they'll be okay, that Lucy is going to be okay, that he understands why she didn't tell the police, why she couldn't betray Lucy like that. Why Lucy is not a monster, why he'd never think that about her friend. How no matter what, he loves Michelle and always will.

But David doesn't do any of this.

Instead, he steps around her and goes back inside their house.

The front door creaks shut.

The sound of the latch clicks.

15
DIANA

"THERE!" SUSANA SAYS, fitting the puzzle piece where it belongs. She leans over the coffee table, hair falling across the side of her face, strands of wild gray dancing all over. She looks up at Diana across the vast blue-sky image between them and smiles. Both women sit on the floor.

But Diana shifts her eyes to the gaping holes dotting the puzzle. Oddly shaped blue pieces are scattered around its border. Together they amount to a uniformly colored sky, a gift from Diana's coworkers at her retirement party a year ago, a joke about Diana's future. Her golden years filled with puzzle nights, evenings on the front porch sipping orujo, days full of gardening. So unlike her decades as a detective, when every single thing is always urgent.

She tries to see a piece that fits the edges of the only cloud in the image.

Susana wants Diana to enjoy this, and Diana knows Susana is enjoying this.

But she can't focus. Her mind is on Lucy Mendoza.

A wine glass is held aloft in Susana's hand. "Where are you, Dee?"

Diana forces her brain to the present and her gaze to the waiting eyes of her wife. "I'm here." A pale blue puzzle piece comes into sharp focus; the moment she spots it she knows where it fits. She takes it into her hand, secures it in the right place. So satisfying, but not as satisfying as finding how other pieces fit into a different kind of puzzle. "Look at that!"

"Where did you go earlier today?" Susana presses.

"I told you, to Belmont."

The *clink* of Susana's glass against the table as she sets it down is sharp. "You didn't come home with any groceries."

Diana looks away, at the gray reading chair with its matching ottoman, another retirement gift, this one from Susana. Thoughtful, heartfelt, like everything else Susana has ever given Diana, this woman who knows her so completely, who made Diana's world good again after the loss of her husband threatened to undo her. Yet another item in Diana's life guiding her toward stillness, because apparently as she approaches seventy she's only good for sitting in chairs with books, for planting flowers in the yard, for mastering baking recipes, for weekends away in the mountains and all-inclusive beach vacations with those bracelets announcing permission for unlimited drinks and food. Now her gaze shifts to a photo on the sideboard of herself in uniform. It was taken decades ago when she first graduated from the academy, just starting out on what would become a long and decorated career. Next to it is a framed candid shot of Diana and Joe in front of a police sedan. Diana initially thought Joe would be a burden as a partner, given how much younger he was and so green as a detective. Diana had been pissed at her chief, thought he was punishing Diana for being a woman on the force even after paying her dues and proving herself to everyone. But it didn't take long for Joe and Diana to become friends. It was a good professional match. A great one.

She's trying to be retired, she really is. But her whole being is restless. Lucy Mendoza needs her. Joe needs her. She can feel it to her marrow.

"Dee?"

"I got all the way to Belmont and realized I forgot my wallet, Suse."

"Don't lie to me," Susana snaps and Diana startles. "I know what happened in that parking lot too. I live in this town like everyone else."

Diana bites her lip hard, lets it go. "You're right. I went to check out the scene where Lucy Mendoza was taken."

Susana leans into the couch behind her, gaze darkening. "I knew it."

"Joe called. I . . . couldn't tell him no."

"Joe called or you called Joe?"

"He called me! Well, he messaged first, then he called. I swear."

Susana shakes her head. "But if he hadn't, you would have messaged him eventually."

"Maybe," Diana admits.

Susana's the one to look off into the distance now, but at what? The photo on the far wall of their three children at a dinner party to celebrate their mothers' engagement, holding up glasses in a toast? Their wedding picture, both women in long white gowns? How delighted Clara had been to take Diana shopping for a dress, then Susana, not allowing either bride to see what the other was wearing on their big day.

"I'm sorry," Diana says, meaning it. She reaches for Susana's hand.

Susana doesn't move, doesn't look at Diana when she says, "Promise me you won't do anything stupid, Dee. Promise me you won't take any unnecessary risks. Please."

"I love you," Diana says instead.

"I love you too," Susana says, her voice soft, quiet. Sad?

"It's just me and Joe talking."

"No, it's not. I told you, don't lie to me. You went to Belmont to study the crime scene. That's beyond talk. Let the FBI do their thing. Let your old colleagues do their thing. I know how this works too." Susana huffs. "I know more than you think."

Diana doesn't speak. There's no point.

Susana shifts position onto her knees. She scans all those tiny blue pieces on the table. "Just go and call Joe. I know that's what you're dying to do. Go before I get more upset." Susana lets slip a murmured *yes*, then fits another piece into the middle. "Go. *Go*," she commands, reaching for yet another cutout of blue. "Get your update. Vete!" she nearly shouts.

Diana inhales, hurt, but she has no right, she knows this. She rises from the floor, then moves through their house, grabbing her phone from the kitchen island on her way to the screened-in porch out back.

The crickets are screaming tonight.

The moon is huge and gleaming.

Diana wants to cover her ears and eyes against the sensory overload.

She swipes at the screen of her phone.

"Dee?" Joe's voice is on the other end nearly immediately.

"Talk to me," she says.

Joe hesitates. "Do you really want to know?"

"I want to know it all. When haven't I?" Diana sits down onto a wicker chair, the cushion spongy, old. The screeching of the crickets fades, Diana's brain forcing all else aside.

Joe starts to talk, about FBI agents holding back; a connection to the D'Angelo case not being ruled out; the officers charged with combing the woods, the Rhode Island beaches, canvasing from house to house; about interviewing more of Lucy's colleagues, of the risky nature of being a real estate agent, all that time alone in vacant homes with strangers, and of trying to find the client Lucy had fired yet he was proving difficult to locate; about bikini photos posted online and how this shouldn't matter but yet, it does, how could it not?

Diana listens, rapt. Then she says, "Well, maybe I can consult? You know, off the books?" Then there's Susana again, suddenly eyeing Diana from the doorway of the porch.

Did Susana hear that?

She blinks at her wife, knowing what Susana is thinking, the moment she hears Diana say consult. *The trip to Vermont this weekend, canceled.*

"Let me call you back," she says to Joe. "Don't go anywhere. Five minutes."

"Sure, Dee. I'm at the station all night anyway. You know how it is."

She does. That's exactly the problem. Diana wishes she were there, pulling an all-nighter. Diana ends the call, sets the phone aside on the glass-topped table where they eat dinner sometimes on beautiful nights like these. Deceptively lovely evenings, especially when a woman has disappeared down the street. *Another woman.*

"I want to help," Diana says to her wife. "You know I can."

Susana nods, one quick bob of her head. Then she disappears into the house again, leaving Diana alone with the screaming crickets and the glare of the moon lighting up the dark.

16
JULIA

THERE JULIA IS, sitting on the couch. Again.

Darkness falling. Again.

Theo upstairs sleeping in bed. Again.

Waiting for Marcus. Again.

Where is he?

She texts, she calls, he doesn't pick up. Again.

I was in a meeting, I had a student in my office, I was with the chair of my department, I ran into the dean and couldn't pick up. Julia can already hear the excuses that will drop from his mouth.

Julia tries her sister, Maggie.

It rings and rings, but Maggie doesn't pick up.

"Maggie, call me," she says into the voicemail. "I need you."

She scrolls to Daphne's Instagram page, hating the inevitability of this online destination. *Daphne R* is her handle, just the initial of her last name, Reed.

A new post has gone up, the second Julia sees it, jealously and rage flood her body. All Daphne draws lately are self-portraits, herself in black and white, with only a single feature in color—her lips, her eyes, her hair, which she dyes a different hue each month like they are still in art school. Derivative in Julia's opinion, but apparently also clickbait. It surely helps that Daphne is beautiful. There are already 2,312 likes. Julia knows she should just heart it, but shame takes over. She and Daphne used to be good friends, they used to be on the same level—two aspiring women artists, toiling in oblivion. She finally does what she should have months ago: She mutes Daphne's page, and next she mutes the notifications on their group chat.

The urge to call Marcus is equally compulsive and yet again, he fails to pick up. Julia and Theo could be dying and he wouldn't find out for hours.

Now what?

A flash of Henry enters Julia's mind. He keeps doing that, filling her brain. If she had his number, she'd text him. She closes her eyes, pictures him, tall and handsome, shirt open at his beautiful neck as he talked to Julia in the Belmont lot. Imagines him leaning down to kiss her. *This is what you get*, she imagines saying to Marcus, *for abandoning your wife after having a baby. You get a wife who strays. How's that for a consequence?*

She tries to google Henry, putting search terms related to things she knows about him: Henry + design, Henry + architect, Henry + house flipping, Henry + all of the above terms, and then all of the above terms + the name of the coworking space. Nothing comes of it.

"Fuck."

She scrolls around some more and comes across the MISSING flier for Lucy Mendoza. She's seen it a few times, people posting and reposting it, tagging one another. Lucy is so beautiful in the photo, her eyes kind, her smile infectious. Her face is so perfectly symmetrical. Anyone who sees it would want to find her, to know her.

Julia leans her head onto the back of the couch. The living room is dark, Theo's blanket spread out and glowing across the floor, his soft little toys strewn about.

The phone is warm in her hand, she swipes her finger across it until a soft glow falls across her face. She returns to scrolling, eyes skipping over the daily newsletter she gets about motherhood from Melody Cho, which she rarely reads because it reminds her how far away she is from the lives of her art school friends, none of whom are even married. Cho is a professor who writes articles for parents, a woman researcher who's become a guru for all things pregnancy and having and raising kids. Maggie gifted Julia a subscription as soon as Julia told her she was pregnant. Normally Julia skips reading it, she can't take yet another conversation about the ins and outs of having a baby. *Should you formula feed? Will my baby self-wean? Should my baby wear a helmet while learning to stand and walk?* Only the rare article interests her, like the one from a month ago, *How do I convince my husband to get a vasectomy?* But usually the subject lines have titles that send her eyes rolling, or that even cause her to become enraged.

Today she clicks because the title pins her.

When a mother goes missing.

Could this be about Lucy Mendoza?

Her eyes scan the screen, picking up tidbits . . . *the way we fetishize mothers . . . Lucy Mendoza is a missing person, not just a missing woman and certainly not simply a missing mother . . . concern for Lucy via her baby as opposed to straightforward concern for her . . . we don't simply need to find Lucy Mendoza because her baby needs her, we need to find Lucy because she deserves to be found in her own right . . . we are still reducing women to this role of mother, even when they've been kidnapped.*

Something fills Julia, her lungs, her body.

Relief? In a place she didn't expect to find it?

Someone else is tired of how the world diminshes women to their reproductive function.

She looks up from her phone through the darkness of the room.

Her eyes catch on a streak of moonlight through the window. A memory of something, cold and brash and beautiful. Making love to Marcus on the front porch late one evening, the two of them wanting each other so much they didn't care about the neighbors, trying their best to be quiet, and giggling when they couldn't. Her eyes shift to the green diaper bag dumped onto the floor by the kitchen entrance, spilling open with junk, all of it alien, a symbol of her terrible now. Julia wonders if a woman's body can reject motherhood, like it might an organ transplant of the wrong blood type.

Her eyes slide to the front door of the house, that sharp slice of moonlight.

How the outside calls to her.

She gets up from the couch, moves across the living room, the door a magnet yanking at her chest. Out of the corner of her eye she sees a shadow in the window. Or does she? She turns. No. It's just her imagination. There is nothing.

Her chest heaves.

She needs air. Fresh air.

A little walk. A tiny one.

So short, barely a blink.

No one will know if she leaves and goes around the block, no one but Julia. Her eyes move toward the staircase to the second floor, the pulse of her son's heartbeat seeming to come through the wood planks. *Thump, thump.* She covers her ears. She has an idea.

Julia runs up to her bedroom and grabs the baby monitor.

How far can she take it? She tries to remember what Marcus said, something like 1,500 feet. "Just to be extra safe," he'd told her proudly after buying the best one on the market. For once, she's happy about Marcus's obsessive research on behalf of Theo. She does the math, that's more than a quarter of a mile. She could probably reach the little neighborhood park.

Before she can think better of it, she's tumbling down the stairs again, slipping her feet into flip-flops, twisting the doorknob. She's outside on the front porch. Gasping great gulps of evening air, like she's been choking. She hurries across the yard, baby monitor clutched harder and harder in her fist. The farther she gets from the house, the more alive and refreshed she is, like taking the coldest shower on the hottest day of a heat wave. The breeze on the bare skin of her arms and legs, the thwack of her flip-flops on pavement like music, the scrape of them against the grit of the sidewalk.

She halts.

She sees it in her mind, her phone tossed onto the couch cushions.

Shit.

But no. *No.* She won't go back for it. If she does . . .

It's just a little walk.

She studies the monitor in her hand.

There. Look. Theo is fine, Julia can see him right there, sleeping. She keeps on going, a little farther. She looks again, there he is. Still fine. Julia doesn't have to go far to realize there's an inverse relationship between her energy and happiness and the proximity of her son. The closer they are to each other the more she is sapped, drained, exhausted. The farther she gets the more likely she smiles, a wilted flower unfurling, stretching toward the sky. A mother shedding her motherhood. Finally free.

If only she had Henry's number—and her phone—she might dare to call him. She might dare to do anything right now. She could see if he wants to join her on a park bench within range of the baby monitor. She'd leave the part about the baby monitor out though.

The heart in her chest pounds and pounds.

She turns the corner, sees the little park. She glances down at the monitor. Still fine, everything's fine. Theo's fine. She forges ahead, she deserves this small indulgence, a few minutes alone. The lack of a stroller in front of her is intoxicating, that freedom from needing to push and maneuver, like a boulder constantly pressing against her. She heaves it to the side, watches it smash to bits in the ravine of her mind, throws her arms wide and submits.

Julia startles awake. She swallows.

The crickets sing so loud, so high tonight they almost hurt Julia's ears.

Oh my god. She fell asleep on the bench. That's how exhausted she is.

The first flicker of fear pulses.

The first flicker of motherhood returns.

Is Theo okay? How could she be so stupid?

She looks around, frantic. *Where's the monitor?* Then she sees it, it must have fallen from her hand onto the ground. She picks it up, but there's nothing—no sound, no video, she's certain she's within range because when she sat down on this bench she could still see Theo, sleeping soundly. Did it break when it fell from her hand? Did it just run out of battery?

How long has she been gone?

She can't even check her phone because she doesn't have it. "Oh my god."

Julia stands up, starts to run home, but it's hard in flip-flops. She needs to go faster, she needs to get back and make sure Theo's okay. What was she thinking? It's only a few blocks but it feels like miles and her body fills with dread. She knows—she knows deep, deep down—that a simple walk alone is an unforgivable sin. Her flip-flops scuffle along on the gravel, the night air cold against her skin, clammy and causing her to shiver. Responsibility rushes over Julia like a weighted blanket, motherhood cloaking her again.

She turns the corner of the block and halts.

Police cars, lights flashing.

An ambulance, fire trucks.

In front of her house.

"Theo," Julia yelps, picking up her pace, monitor gripped so hard in her hand she worries she might break it. *What has she done?* "Fuck. Fuck, fuck."

A crowd of curious neighbors flank the sidewalk in front of her yard.

The possible punishments for being so reckless slide over her like an avalanche. That something happened to Theo in his crib, that Theo is sick, no, he is dying? Could someone have broken into the house while she was gone, while Theo was sleeping and so helpless? Her ugliest fantasies come true? The closer she gets, the more gruesome and outlandish Julia's thinking becomes. She curses herself for going out at all, worse still in a holey T-shirt covered in spit-up, a pair of tiny gym shorts, her backside practically hanging down below their hems, seeming to scream to everyone, *Just look at this woman, what a mess! She can't take care of herself, never mind an innocent baby!*

But there's Marcus on the lawn, holding little Theo in his arms!

They both look fine. *They're fine.*

Julia stops at the edge of the crowd, tries to catch her breath. Two men are talking to Marcus, her husband gesticulating.

Police officers?

She clutches the monitor to her rib cage, she feels like everyone will be able to see through her clothing to her body, see into her mind, the mother laid bare for all to judge. For one tiny mistake. She straightens her shorts, pulls them as low down her thighs as she can. Then she rushes forward through the crowd. "Marcus, Marcus! What's the matter? Is everything all right?" she cries. What else can she do?

Everyone turns in her direction.

Marcus's eyes brighten with relief. "Julia, oh my god. You're okay."

"I'm fine, everything's fine," she says, reaching her husband, who immediately crushes her to him. Theo starts to cry, squashed between his two parents.

Marcus squeezes Julia harder, she feels Theo's fist twisting in her hair. "I thought someone took you, like that woman!" Marcus is breathing hard. "I was calling and calling, trying to reach you, and then I got home and saw your phone on the couch and immediately thought the worst so I called the police. I was sure something terrible had happened."

Prison walls take shape around her, tightening, opaque.

So this is what Julia gets for walking a couple of blocks—the police called. She wiggles out of her husband's arms, extracts Theo's fingers from her hair.

The crowd of neighbors dissipates. The ambulance and the fire truck pull away down the street. The absent mother found so everyone can go. *Are they disappointed?* She turns to the two officers, who don't seem to be leaving. Julia meets the eyes of the older one and her cheeks flame.

"I'm Detective Joe Suarez," he says, extending his hand, eyes flitting across her disheveled state. "This is my partner, Detective Marist, we're very glad to see you."

The other man nods at Julia. "As you can imagine, given recent events, your husband was frightened when no one could reach you."

Julia pulls Theo into her arms and bounces him, kissing his cheek. She smells his head instinctively, her nose pressing into his soft, fuzzy scalp, an impulse she can't resist. His little whimpers clamp around her heart. She made a mistake. A terrible mistake. "I'm sorry you got called for nothing, how awful. I'm mortified." She glances at her husband, presses her cheek to her son's, then turns back to the two detectives. She swallows, glances at Marcus. *This is your fault*, her expression tells him. She holds up the baby monitor. "There was an emergency," she lies. "I needed to go to the pharmacy down the street, and my husband was unreachable, late from work, and not returning my messages." She sees Marcus out of the corner of her eye. "I got all the way to the store, then realized I'd taken the baby monitor, but left my phone, which has my credit cards on it."

Detective Marist is watching her. "You left your baby alone," is all he says.

Julia lowers her gaze to the grass. "I know. I shouldn't have. But I was desperate," she adds, this part all true. She *was* desperate. She is.

"It didn't occur to you to text your husband and tell him where you were headed?" Marist asks.

"I told you, my husband was unreachable. He always is. It never matters how many times I message him, he never responds." Julia can taste the sharp bitterness of these words on her tongue. "So what's a mother to do?"

"Julia," Marcus hisses.

Detective Suarez steps between this husband and wife. Meets the eyes of Marcus first, then Julia next. "Given recent events, it might be helpful to let someone know where you'll be in case of emergencies. We're all on high alert. And we're glad to know you're safe and that your son is too."

"Thank you," Julia says, and swallows hard.

Detective Suarez raises his brows. "You'll be hearing from social services of course."

"What?" Marcus cries out.

Something in Julia's stomach plummets. "I'm so sorry. This will never happen again. And I took the monitor, I was careful, I—"

"I know, and I'm sure," the detective says. "But it's procedure in situations like this."

"We understand," Marcus answers, before Julia can say anything more.

Julia watches as the two detectives amble off toward their car. Her heart pounds while shame rages. This is when Julia notices something else. All the neighbors have left, save one, the man who lives next door, who hangs at the edge of his lawn. Face blank, eyes wide, staring straight at her. *Why is he still here?* She swallows, something inside her at sea. She turns and races up the front steps and into the house and straight to the place in the kitchen where they keep the alcohol. She slams the monitor onto the counter and pours herself a glass of Marcus's bourbon, drinks it down, the burn of it in her throat a shock.

Marcus appears at the kitchen island. "How could you *do* that, Julia! You *left our son alone* and now we have social services to deal with! And then you blame *me*!"

A fire rages through her. "You are to blame! YOU left our son alone! You leave our son alone every goddam day! You've left me alone every goddam day! This is what YOU get! Social services coming is *your* fault! You've fucking abandoned me to this, Marcus!"

The more Julia's voice rises the more Marcus's eyes widen. "I was sure something terrible had happened to you! That some psycho took you like that other woman!"

Julia meets her husband's eyes and her own are hard. "If only, Marcus," she seethes. "If only someone would take me from this life!"

Marcus stares back, like he doesn't recognize his wife. "You don't mean that."

Unease crawls up her spine. But doesn't she?

17
MICHELLE

DAVID APPEARS IN the kitchen where Michelle is sipping her coffee, the world still dark with the early morning. She's been reading through the texts Alejandra sent her in the night about how many people have already reposted the MISSING flier.

"You have to go to the police," he says.

Michelle looks up wearily from her mug, bleary-eyed. "What?"

David looms over her. "You have to tell the police about Lucy. You know I'm right."

"I can never tell anyone, David. I promised Lucy I wouldn't," she replies, even though she's already broken her vow and now her husband has hold of this priceless information. How stupid could she be? Michelle gazes down at her milky swirl of coffee. She should have gotten the kids out of bed early so they could run interference between their parents. She wants to forget last night, and focus on her friend—finding Lucy alive and well.

David pulls out one of the chairs at the breakfast table and sits. "You have important information about Lucy's disappearance." When Michelle doesn't speak, he continues. "The fact that Lucy possibly planned her own kidnapping? I know you know this, Michelle. I'll drive you to the police station. I'll get the kids up and we can all get in the car together. I'll watch them while you talk to the detectives."

Michelle is shaking her head. "No, David. I won't do it."

"Well, if you don't tell the police, I will," David says.

Michelle heart jump-starts, pounding. "Don't you dare."

David's mouth tightens into a long, hard line, and Michelle senses this is about to become not even a fight, but a battle. "It's the right thing." He leans back in his chair as though this matter is settled. He crosses his arms against his chest. "You should have done it the moment Lucy disappeared. The very first time you spoke to the police two days ago."

"No," she pleads. If she tells the police, what if they soften their search and Lucy winds up dead? This fear, plus the reminder that it's been two whole nights that Lucy's been gone, guts her. They're barreling toward the forty-eight-hour mark, that all-important window after which hope of a happy ending plummets. "Sam can't ever find out."

"You're withholding information," David seethes.

"She's my best friend and I can't betray her!"

"Sam should know who he married!"

"Why are you so angry at her?" Michelle shoots back. "What did she ever do to you, other than be a good friend to your wife?"

"Lucy doesn't deserve your protection!"

Michelle's heart comes to a stop. She stares at David. Before Lucy disappeared, Michelle never understood what people meant about veins turning to ice, but now she understands this viscerally, it keeps happening, this feeling of her whole body going cold in an instant. "What do you mean, Lucy doesn't deserve it?"

"You know what I mean," David says.

"I don't. Explain it to me."

"You shouldn't be protecting a woman who regrets her child. Enough not only to leave, but to fake her own kidnapping so she doesn't have to bear the consequences of her decision!"

Michelle tries to keep breathing. She has felt so many things about her husband these last years—resentment, exasperation, frustration, despair, amid all the good things, the love and the laughter and the gratitude, the results of a long, shared history. But never all-out rage. Not before this. But as she looks at the man she married, behaving so callously toward her missing friend, a chasm opens between them. Lucy entrusted Michelle with her feelings instead of choosing to live in silence, and here David is, ready to let Lucy die because she told the truth.

"You have no idea, do you," she says.

"What I know is you have to tell the police."

"What do you have against Lucy that you're not telling me?"

"What are you talking about? Nothing!"

"There's something David, I can hear it in your voice!"

"Michelle, the police need to stop treating this like it's a kidnapping!"

Michelle jumps up from her chair, knocking over her mug in the process. "No, no, no!" Coffee spills everywhere, streaming off the edge of the table and onto the floor. Neither one of them moves to catch it. "We don't know where Lucy is! She hasn't reached out to me. If she'd run she would have texted by now, I'm certain of it!"

"Are you *really*, Michelle?"

"I'm not going to the police, and promise you won't go either, David!"

He doesn't respond.

"Promise me!" Michelle shrieks.

"Mommy?" Charlie's voice floats down the stairs into the kitchen.

David's hands ball into fists, his eyes drift to the toppled mug, the pond of coffee on the tiles next to his shoes. "Or what, Michelle?"

Michelle shakes her head. Suspicion blooms. She calls to Charlie. "Little bug, I'll be there in a minute." How has their marriage arrived at this point? One that feels like war? "If you go to the police, David, I will pack my bags and take the boys to my mother's."

David gets up, pushing the table out, violently. "You would not do that."

"I would and I will." Michelle imagines she is in a trench, mud flying as she digs deeper, readying for whatever's ahead, to protect herself and her sons at any cost. Lucy too. "Try me."

"Mommy?" Charlie's voice again, louder.

Michelle's heart, her soul, are torn in two. Her body is ripping into separate halves, moving in two different directions.

David shoves the table back in place, and it shudders with the force of it. He walks into the living room, grabs his keys from the peg by the door. Michelle runs after him, glancing up the staircase, worried for Charlie, panicking that David is headed to see the police. She grabs for the keys in his hand, but David snatches them away, holds them too high for her to reach.

"Where are you going?" she cries.

"Out."

"Promise me, David," she pleads. "Promise!"

He hesitates.

Then, "I promise," he growls, and storms through the door.

Later that morning, after too many cups of coffee that do nothing to calm Michelle's nerves, after soothing Charlie and getting him off to school, Michelle is in a big-box store. She pushes Aidan in his carriage along one of its wide aisles, trying to forget her morning, trying to forget these last few days, all their horrors. Just for a few moments. She is doing something ordinary, something banal, searching for a dingle. A dongle? Dangle? What is that stupid-sounding thing David needs for his ancient laptop? Could they make it sound any more masculine and sexual? Michelle is doing this errand for her husband out of guilt for their fight. Out of guilt for what she said. Maybe she was too harsh, maybe her threats to leave and go to her mother's were too much.

Her stomach roils.

The fluorescent lights above glare down over her, making her feel sicker.

She pushes Aidan toward a store clerk and tries to smile. "Do you have something called a . . . dingle? It's for my husband's old laptop."

The young man working—he looks eighteen—smiles back and laughs. "A dongle. Yes, of course, follow me."

He winds her and Aidan through the gigantic store, careful to give Michelle time to maneuver the carriage down the wide aisles that seem designed more for cars than people. On their way, he takes her through the television department. The news flashes on every single screen, same channel, same report, one after the other in ultra-high-definition color.

Michelle halts, jerking the carriage so Aidan nearly wakes. "Hey, hang on a sec," she calls to the store clerk. "Wait!"

Alejandra's MISSING poster for Lucy stares back from those screens. But the ticker across the bottom of those televisions reads, *Missing Mother Lucy Mendoza—Did she abandon her baby?* The poster disappears, replaced by two women and one man at a half-moon table, mouths moving, presumably to discuss the question in bold below. But all the TVs are on mute.

"Can you turn on the sound, please?" Michelle asks, voice trembling, pointing to one of the many televisions. Her hand is shaking.

The clerk picks up a remote from the shelf and hits a button.

"—but men abandon their children and no one thinks anything of it," one of the women says. She glares at the man across the table. "Why is it unforgivable if a woman leaves?"

"No mother regrets her child," the man says. "Maybe they have postpartum depression, but regret? No. I don't believe it. That's extreme."

The other woman on the panel chimes, "I agree. Motherhood is the hardest job you'll ever have, I'm not one to claim it isn't, and I've certainly talked to my friends about this, but regret? No, just *no*. I can't even believe we're talking about this. No mother in her right mind can imagine doing what this woman did—faking a kidnapping so she doesn't have to face societal judgment for being a bad mother?"

"Well, obviously we're not talking about someone in her right mind!"

Michelle's legs wobble. She kneels down on the floor next to Aidan's carriage in the middle of the television aisle, startling a few shoppers. They move around the woman and her baby, this woman who is now saying, over and over, "Oh my god, oh my god."

Has Sam seen this?

The store clerk bends down to Michelle's level. "Ma'am, are you all right?"

She takes a hand from her head and uses it to grab for the phone in her bag. She does a search for "Lucy Mendoza." What comes up causes Michelle to groan, to grab her stomach. LUCY MENDOZA—KIDNAPPED MOTHER OR ESCAPED MOTHER? is the first. There are more. She clicks on the top story. She's going to be sick. She's going to be sick right on the shoes of this store clerk.

"I'm going to be sick," she says out loud as she reads.

New information has come to light about the disappearance of Lucy Mendoza, which indicates she may have orchestrated her own kidnapping in an attempt to avoid the consequences of abandoning her nine-month-old baby.

PART 2
—
ALL THE HOURS AFTERWARD

18
JULIA

"I NEVER WOULD have pegged Lucy Mendoza as someone who'd abandon her family," the woman next to Julia says. "Things are really hard right now, if I'm honest, but—"

"That's why we're here, though, right?" says someone else. "So we can be brutally honest?"

Julia's body tenses in her chair, rapt at the mention of Lucy. She sits among a circle of women in a house down the street as they wait for the meeting to begin—a postpartum moms group. Maggie had been trying to get Julia to attend for weeks, but put her foot down after she learned what happened with the police last night, plus the looming visit from social services. The two of them had texted into the wee hours of the morning.

Maggie: *It's time you get help.*

Julia: *I don't need help. I'm not crazy.*

Maggie: *You left Theo alone in the house, Julia.*

Julia: *And where was Marcus? Why isn't he the one who needs help?*

Maggie: *But he was at work!*

Julia: *He was late—again—as though he doesn't have a baby. No one called the police on him!*

Maggie: *It doesn't matter. Social services is coming, Julia. You need to show them you're getting help.*

At this, Maggie sent the link to this group where Julia now sits, which conveniently meets three times per week—an "intensive" for postpartum moms. It even offers a babysitting service so the moms can attend. Julia went down a rabbit hole of research about the therapist who runs it and discovered that Lucy Mendoza attended it herself until she disappeared. A tingling shimmered across Julia's body at this, a siren's call. She'd go. Now here she is. But what was this about Lucy and abandonment? After the chaos of yesterday, Julia hadn't yet managed to catch up on the latest news about her disappearance.

The women next to Julia go on talking to one another and she eavesdrops.

"Still, Lucy never mentioned anything so outlandish when she was here."

"I mean, I fantasize about things too. But this? I can't imagine going that far. Or making myself a spectacle."

Lucy, a spectacle? What kind of spectacle?

Julia wishes she could get a better look to her left, but she doesn't want to be caught listening in on other people's conversations, so she stares at the woman across from her, willowy, freckled, a blond who does not look like she recently gave birth. She's too thin, bony like a dancer. Briefly, Julia counts the chairs, *one, two, three.* Eighteen in all, more than she expected. Maybe they won't fill. Or maybe they will? Maybe there are dozens of local new mothers like Julia. She's been at this group for postpartum moms for only five minutes and it's already more interesting than she expected.

The women next to Julia grow quiet, then one of them

says, "I don't know, Ani, I sometimes think about something terrible happening, something that would take me away from everything. Something out of my control that would just put a stop to all this."

Julia stares into her satiny lap, at the skirt she forced herself to wear, in lapis blue if she were to draw it, with a prim white blouse. She used to dress like this all the time before the baby. Nicely, carefully, down to her underwear, something Marcus always loved about her, something she loved about herself. This woman's words wash over Julia's body; they fill her up because they resonate.

Out of the corner of her eye she sees one woman touch the other's hand.

"Don't say that. You don't mean it."

There is a pause.

"But I do," the recipient of this comment says, under her breath.

Julia's eyes are steady on all that shiny, shimmery blue encasing her thighs. She wants to reach for this woman's hand too, tell her, "I feel the same way." Finally, she turns her head to the left. Heart fluttering, she inhales. "I'm sorry to interrupt." The women turn to Julia and she keeps going. "I'm new to this group. Were you just discussing Lucy Mendoza? Did something happen? Did they find her?"

One of the women, dirty blond hair and rings under eyes, nods. She extends a hand. "I'm Ani."

"Noor," the second one says, a woman with dark hair and striking eyes, extending hers too.

Julia returns the gestures. "I'm Julia."

Ani leans across Noor and asks, "You haven't heard the latest?"

Something roils in Julia's gut. What had she missed? "I guess not. I've had . . . a lot going on since yesterday."

Ani glances at Noor, and Noor inhales to speak. "So we all know Lucy here—"

"She was part of this group," Ani interrupts.

Julia nods.

Noor meets Julia's eyes. "Apparently, Lucy might not have been kidnapped—"

"—not only that, she may have *planned* her own kidnapping," Ani finishes.

Before Julia can respond, an older woman walks down the staircase on her way into the room and everyone quiets, schoolchildren before a teacher they both adore and fear.

This must be Naomi Bresler.

Julia read all about her online when she couldn't sleep, this therapist who's been working with postpartum moms for years. She read about this group's excellent reputation, women driving from two, even three hours away to participate. For Julia this place is so close she can walk. It seems meant to be, the proximity of it in relation to her particular motherly affliction. She uncurls her fingers from her skirt, palms sweaty, joints aching.

The circle parts for Naomi, chairs opening with shrieks and scrapes before it closes again. Naomi is commanding, authoritative, a general entering the room. There is an elegance to her person, a knowledge evident in the expression on her face. Calm, certain, wise.

Julia immediately wants it—her wisdom.

This woman's approval.

There's something about her. What?

Naomi takes up space, she's tall, abundant. But her shoes

barely make a sound as her feet move across the floor of this old Victorian where she has her office. A tiny wooden placard announces her name and her degrees out front. Her dress is a simple black tent, the kind Julia admires yet can't wear because she is the opposite, too skinny to fill it out, even after having Theo. A long gray braid trails down the therapist's back. She takes a seat next to a redhead.

Everyone waits while Naomi fixes her dress around her.

How old is she? Julia wonders. *Ageless?*

All the seats in the circle are taken, she realizes.

Naomi looks directly at Julia, all sharp, flashing eyes. "Hello, everyone, I'm Naomi for those of you who are new." Her gaze travels around the circle. "I want to remind you, especially given the news today, that what we say here is private. It's protected. What's discussed in this room stays in this room, no exception." Naomi's eyes go from person to person again, not missing a single woman, and lingering on Julia. "This is a safe space, and for this to stay a safe space everyone needs to respect everyone else's privacy. Is that understood?" Naomi's stare becomes a weight on the collective conscience of the circle.

There are nods and murmurs of *yes* in a wave across the circle, widened eyes, solemn expressions. A little fear?

Apparently satisfied, Naomi continues. "Now that this is settled, let's begin with the topic I'm certain is on everyone's mind. Who would like to start the conversation today?"

An almost unbearable electricity crackles into the air.

How much time passes—one whole minute? Two?

Then, "I feel betrayed by Lucy," someone says.

Everyone turns their head toward a woman in sweats, a milk stain at her left breast.

"Say more," Naomi prompts.

"Because Lucy gave up."

Naomi's silent, waiting. A quiet, *And?*

The woman looks around the room. "And we're all still here. Toiling."

Another woman drops her face into her hands.

A tiny nod from Naomi. This time declarative, encouraging: *Go on.*

"I don't feel betrayed," from Julia's left.

Noor.

"I feel . . . relieved. Like maybe this means something horrible hasn't happened to Lucy, because she did what she finally needed to do, she just up and left." Noor closes her lush-lashed eyes. "I would feel happy for her. I would feel . . . envious."

"Don't say that," someone else snaps.

Naomi turns toward the new voice. "Why not?"

This woman, brown-haired, brown-skinned, in sandals, shorts, wearing an old concert T-shirt. "Because."

Arched eyebrows from Naomi. *Because?*

"Because it's *wrong* obviously," says yet another woman.

Julia's gaze bounces from one person to the next, riveted, engaged for the first time in what feels like months. A feeling of . . . *belonging* approaching after so much isolation.

"You don't get to change your mind."

"Men do."

"But *we* don't. We're different."

"Why?"

"We just are. Everyone knows that."

"That's such a sexist thing to say."

"Maybe, but it's still true."

"I envy Lucy too. I wish . . . I could."

"But you haven't, you're still here. And you won't. Because you would *never*."

"Because I'm not that *brave*."

"What Lucy did is not brave. It's too extreme."

"We don't know anything about what happened to Lucy and what she did or didn't do."

"But don't we? I mean, I remember what she used to say in our group."

"Maybe what Lucy did was finally be honest with herself. With the world. Truly honest."

"About what, exactly? Honest about what?"

The circle grows silent.

Julia puts a hand to her chest, palm pulsing from her heart, a rushing in her ears.

"Let's talk about this more directly," Naomi says, and something shifts. "There's a word we don't discuss in relation to motherhood. Some of you know what I mean but are afraid to say it."

No one moves. No one speaks.

The syllables, though, the two of them, they whisper through Julia's mind. She knows the answer but Naomi is right, she's too afraid to speak it.

But then Naomi says it for all of them:

"Regret."

Just like that, spoken like it's so ordinary.

But everyone knows it isn't.

It's a lightning bolt streaking through the room, flashing across faces, searing, burning.

Leaving its marks.

People shift in their seats, an uncomfortable rustling.

Some women look away. At the floorboards of the old house, the ceiling, the crown molding circling the light fixture.

But Julia leans forward, toward the word, toward Naomi, like this therapist is a waterfall on the hottest of days, beckoning. Julia lets this forbidden word rush over her skin, soothing her, releasing her. From something.

"No one regrets their child," a woman tries.

"But don't they?" Naomi says. "Are you so sure?"

Julia looks hard across the circle at this therapist.

There is the strongest sensation.

It floods her to the tips of her being.

Finally. She is home.

19
DIANA

THE ATTIC OF Diana's house is cluttered, dusty, creaky. Hot.

The second she saw the news about Lucy, her brain began to churn.

Not about Joanna D'Angelo this time. Someone else.

Where is that box?

She has to bend in order to move about, the eaves angled and low, wood beams a constant threat, the single bare bulb giving off too little light. The movement causes the left side of her lower back to protest. Diana shifts the corner of a heavy trunk so she can get past it. Her arm raises to grip the splintered edges of a wooden beam so she doesn't bump into it. She stops, surveying the floor, searching. *Where is it?* she wonders again.

There.

The file boxes Diana took home, not exactly stolen, but it wasn't like she'd been invited to remove them from the station, either.

She moves through the maze of junk at her feet, the detritus of combining two households when she and Susana married. Mother's Day gifts decades old, drawings and report cards and mementos from another time, favorite stuffed animals landing here in this creaky attic. She positions herself on the hard floor, legs crossed. Leans forward, wipes her brow. It's hot up here, the summer still stealing from September and fall. When will it finally release them from its grip this year?

The box Diana seeks is bent and ripped, all that's left of a case she caught long ago, one of her first. The notion that Lucy faked her disappearance is what made Diana think of it. She lifts the lid, the rough scrape of cardboard loud in the musty attic silence, dust puffing into the stuffy air. Diana stares at the fat file, plunges her hands into the box, gripping the whole of it, the final remains of yet another local woman's life. She hefts it out, bits of paper slipping from the folder, fluttering to the floor, notes scrawled from phone calls. The sight of her own handwriting from a lifetime ago, putting pieces together or trying to, getting nowhere.

Diana sorts through the mess until she finds the photo she seeks. She'll always remember this image, burned as it is into her brain. She holds it up amid the dust and swelter, takes it in for the first time in so many years.

Maeve O'Neil.

The young woman stands on Narragansett Beach in a bright green bathing suit, long hair taken by the wind. Maeve is turning back to look at the person snapping the picture, smiling at the camera, expression broken wide, bright, happy. The cold blue waves of the ocean frame her body, children play behind her on the sand, a perfect Rhode Island summer's day. It was taken two full years before Maeve disappeared from that same beach on a similarly perfect summer's day, with families and sun worshippers all around when it happened.

The best friend—Rebecca Abrams, called Becca to her family and her friends—gave them this photo to use in their search.

That smile, the joy in Maeve's expression, made everyone who saw it want to find Maeve O'Neil, this beautiful girl, this beautiful new mother with the gorgeous little baby to match.

Maeve was only twenty-four, married to her boyfriend right out of college. Probably she was pregnant when they got married—probably they got married because she was pregnant. But Diana could never get a straight answer from anyone, certainly not the husband, Trey.

She sets the photo onto the floor, but still Maeve smiles up at her.

Today, with the press screaming from west to east that Lucy Mendoza ran, Diana couldn't help but think of Maeve. The two cases, so many decades apart, so seemingly different in certain ways. But if there's any truth to what came out earlier this afternoon, the connection between Lucy and Maeve is almost eerie.

It was August that long ago summer, the temperature straining into the nineties, the Atlantic at its warmest for the season, topping seventy degrees and convincing just about anyone to go for a swim. The heat wave gifted them a stretch of unbearable days and this was one of them. Narragansett Beach was teeming with mothers and kids, college students, people playing hooky from work.

Maeve had been there with her eleven-month-old, Bridget, her tiny daughter dressed in a pink and white polka-dotted bathing suit, ruffles everywhere, adorable matching sun hat, even a tiny pink frilly umbrella to protect the baby's tender skin from the sun. It was knifed into the sand at an angle just so, to provide adequate shade to the infant beach chair where Bridget sat, buckled in, drooling watermelon juice onto the tray table, bits of it cut up and streaking pink and watery across the plastic. Mother and baby spending an afternoon by the sea, seeking relief from the heat, an occasional swim like the rest of the parents with children of every possible age. Bridget was a gorgeous little thing, chubby, laughing.

And, well, Maeve was at the beach that Thursday with Bridget—until she wasn't.

Until suddenly the people near her setup realized Bridget was alone. Sitting there, smiling and buckled into the chair under the baby umbrella, no mother in sight.

Diana sifts through the notes from the file until she comes up with what she's looking for, transcriptions from the taped interviews they did as they searched for Maeve's whereabouts, fearing the worst as one day led to the next and there was still no sign of her.

"I was just sitting there, thinking of going for a swim," one of the bystanders had reported, "when I realized that little baby was alone. The thing is, I'd been admiring her, she was such a cute thing, and her mother stunning, it was difficult not to stare. But the mother was there one moment, then the next I couldn't see her anywhere. And believe me, I looked, because I didn't want to make a fuss for nothing. But she wasn't down by the water, or talking to anyone on the sand, at least not that I could tell. I just didn't see her anymore and I didn't see her take off or anything, either. So I waited maybe five minutes, searching the waves the whole time, hoping to spot her? While keeping an eye on the little one just in case, and eventually I just thought to myself, something must be wrong here and I told my own kids to stay put and I went over to make sure that baby was all right while another man went off to find a lifeguard."

"There was a group of us who got worried the woman had

drowned, you know?" said another of the interviewees. "We were gathered around the baby and she was just smiling at everyone, poor little thing, no idea that her mother was just gone, gone! We were scanning the water, searching. A few people went with the lifeguards into all those waves, they'd gotten the rafts out and everything, and a few others went looking for the mother around the beach. I don't know who said it first, but somebody went to the boardwalk to use the pay phone and call the police. The surf was so big but people were braving it because it was so hot. The lifeguards had been waving people into shallower water all morning. But then, she wouldn't have gone to swim and left her baby alone like that, right?"

Sweat trickles down Diana's stomach as she sits on the attic floor. She should go downstairs to finish sorting through this, but something stops her—what? The worry Susana will come home from babysitting her grandson, Kiko, to find out that Diana squirreled away police files among their keepsakes? Or the fear they might have another Maeve on their hands?

After her colleagues and the lifeguards searched the water for a body and came up with nothing, it felt like Diana had interviewed the entire beach. Did Maeve drown or did someone take her? No one could be sure. The husband, Trey, was so young and distraught and ill-prepared to take care of Bridget on his own. Initially, he was the prime suspect, but then was ruled out since he was working all day at the garage where he fixed cars. Every coworker verified he'd never left, not even for lunch. The FBI got involved, Diana's first real missing persons case as a detective and all the stress and hoopla that come with such things. Search parties, Maeve's best friend, Becca, canvasing house to house across the town, putting up fliers.

Maeve's face had been impossible to miss if a person went to the supermarket, out for pizza—if they left their house at all.

A week passed, and everyone feared the worst.

Maeve O'Neil was likely never coming back.

Because likely she was dead.

But then Maeve's story had a happy ending—or seemed to. She appeared eight days later at the house she shared with Trey, just walked right in and shouted, "I'm home!" He'd been sitting there at the kitchen table, staring at nothing, a zombie after so many sleepless nights and agonizing days. As Trey told it, he just looked up and there was Maeve, suddenly home, in good health, perfectly fine. Not a hair touched on her head. Safe and sound.

Diana sorts through the file until she finds that newspaper clipping, the one that was everywhere in town the next day, held up in coffee shops, spread wide on tables.

MISSING LOCAL MOTHER FOUND ALIVE

This was the headline in *The Providence Journal*, a photo of Maeve holding Bridget in front of their Narragansett bungalow underneath it, Trey standing protectively beside them. But the upshot was that Maeve had run. Decided she couldn't do another day—another minute—of taking care of Bridget on her own while Trey was at work. Her plan had been to never return. But then Maeve couldn't quite go through with leaving for good—in the end she'd missed Bridget and came back for her. She went straight into treatment too, even though it wasn't like it is today, when postpartum depression is something doctors watch out for, and a woman can find lots of support; and she's told there's no shame in seeking help. Back then it was a scandal for a mother to struggle like that.

Luckily, this part of Maeve's story never made it into the

press. This was still a time when a person, a family, a detective could keep things private. Not like today where everything comes out, where everything is fair game, where everyone feels a right to dissect every single thing on social media and on podcasts, even the worst tragedies a person suffers.

Diana slides the yellowed newspaper clipping inside the file.

Lucy Mendoza is not so lucky. And Lucy and Maeve probably have nothing to do with each other. Maybe Lucy was taken and all the press is doing is distracting people from caring enough to find her. Now they'll spend all their time judging her instead.

Should she call Joe about Maeve?

Or should she wait?

She doesn't want to send him down a rabbit hole.

Diana gathers the rest of the documents and notes into the file and pulls herself up to standing, careful to avoid bumping her head on the eaves. She'll take it downstairs anyway and hide it in her desk drawer. She'll keep it to herself for now, so she'll be the one to go down the rabbit hole. After all, she has the time. Once again, she maneuvers among the keepsakes and the old furniture they'll likely never use again, then descends the attic steps. Maybe she can steal another hour to read and review before Susana gets back from babysitting Kiko. As she heads to the first floor and into the kitchen, the rest of Maeve's story floods her. Wherever Lucy is, Diana hopes her story doesn't turn out like Maeve's.

Diana went to see Maeve three times after she returned from treatment, to check on how she was faring and if the little family was doing better—they were. Or they had been. Maeve had gotten help, that friend of hers, Becca, finding Maeve every possible resource available at the time. Diana had felt satisfied by this. All ended well for Maeve and Bridget and Trey. Until it didn't.

Almost exactly one year later, on another hot summer's day at Narragansett Beach, a terrible summer storm had come through and the waves were as enormous as ever, the surfers out in full force to catch them, red flags flying all over, planted in the sand by desperate lifeguards, but the temperature so blazing that people went swimming anyway.

The worst tragedy of all occurred:

A mother and her toddler drowned.

Maeve and Bridget.

Gone into the water for relief in the sweltering heat despite all the warnings. But they never came out.

Diana had been called to the scene, in part because her colleagues knew she'd worked Maeve's case like her life depended on it. She broke down and sobbed when she saw that tiny body bag, and the bigger one next to it laid out in the sand.

It was deemed an accident.

But deep inside Diana had always wondered.

Was it really an accident? Or was it Maeve taking matters into her own hands yet again? A desperate mother fleeing her life, but this time taking her baby with her?

20
MICHELLE

"I ASKED YOU a question, ma'am," Detective Marist says.

He stares at Michelle from the other side of the table.

Detective Suarez is next to him, expression serious.

Michelle drove straight from the electronics store down to the police station. She barely remembers maneuvering Aidan through that aisle of blaring televisions, getting him out into the parking lot and buckling him into the car seat. Now a napping Aidan is being watched by the officer out front, so his mother can be grilled as an accomplice who helped Lucy escape her life. The table in this dank, ugly interview room where she sits, facing the detectives, has loops bolted into the top of it, presumably to handcuff a person.

At least Michelle isn't in handcuffs. Maybe that's next? "Sorry, can you repeat that?"

Detective Marist raps his knuckles on a pile of papers in front of him. Printouts it looks like. But of what? "I asked why you didn't tell us about your conversation with Lucy when we spoke to you the first time? The one the press seems to have gotten ahold of details about today."

Michelle looks first to Marist, with his dark eyes and muscular physique, then at Suarez, with his thick graying hair and weathered face. She drops her gaze to the table. She can feel herself sweating and sticky in these stupidly tight yoga pants. "You guys haven't been listening. Yes, Lucy did tell me all of that, but things were also getting better, she was getting help, attending a postpartum group like, three times per week." Michelle keeps trying to remember all her last moments with Lucy—the coffee they'd gotten with Emma and Aidan while Charlie was at school, the way they were trying to convince each other to join a gym, then finally reckoning with the fact that they weren't ever going to do it. Such benign, mundane talk. "You want to know the last thing Lucy asked me before she disappeared?"

Marist exchanges a look with Suarez, then says, "Yes, tell us."

"Lucy," Michelle begins, then pauses a beat, "had gotten a fancy bottle of wine from a client and wanted to plan a time for us to drink it together. Why would a woman planning her own kidnapping be exchanging texts with her best friend about getting together on the day she disappears?" Sweat trickles down her back. It's so hot in here. "If Lucy ran, I would have heard from her. Lucy would never go this long without being in touch with me . . ." She trails off.

Suarez shifts in his chair. "Listen, it's good you came to us today, because we can tell the FBI you're cooperating. But I don't really buy that you didn't think to tell us Lucy was having such difficulties adjusting to being a mom."

Michelle examines Suarez's question. Why are people so quick to condemn Lucy now that they know she was having a hard time? To assume she took off rather than that someone took her against her will? Her chest tightens and she says nothing.

Apparently it's Marist's turn to grill her again. "So did you also know about the time Lucy's husband came in the door to find Lucy had smashed half the dishes in their kitchen against the wall?"

Michelle inhales loudly. "What?"

Marist straightens the stack of papers in front of him, makes a show of gathering them into his hands. He bangs them against the table a few times until they become a neat stack. "Well, I guess Lucy didn't tell you everything. Sam described that particular episode when we had him on the night of her disappearance, how just a few weeks ago he was in his workshop in the garage and heard a commotion from the house, and rushed inside to find his wife screaming and breaking things, glass and china everywhere. At least the husband's been forthcoming about Lucy's recent . . . difficulties."

Oh Lucy, why wouldn't you tell me this?

Michelle wants to weep, but not here. Definitely not here.

"Michelle?" Detective Suarez tries, as though using Michelle's name instead of *ma'am* is going to open her up. "You can talk to us. You can *trust* us. Lucy needs you."

Regardless of what these detectives imply, anyone who saw Lucy with Emma could tell she loved her baby. *Loves.* The issue has never been love, though. It's about Lucy grieving her old life. But what woman who becomes a mother doesn't grieve at least a little? Michelle did. She still does sometimes. This is not a crime. Fantasizing about leaving one's family isn't a crime either.

"I didn't think my conversation with Lucy that night was relevant," Michelle says, repeating herself yet again. Realizing how weak this sounds each time she says it. Of course it's relevant! How could it not be? "It was just a discussion between friends over wine and cheese. Please. You need to keep searching for Lucy. She's *missing*."

Detective Marist narrows his eyes. "I don't buy it, that you thought the info you had on Lucy wasn't relevant."

Michelle doesn't either. But she's not about to admit this. Her gaze finds that stack of printouts.

Are they ever going to tell her what's on them? Are they just meant to be a prop to drive her out of her mind?

Detective Suarez places a hand flat on the table, ring finger shiny with a gold band, nails clipped neat and short. "You thought it was relevant enough to mention it to your husband." Lines crinkle around his eyes. "Who went and told the press what he knew."

"Speaking of your husband"—Marist slaps his hand on top of all that paper and Michelle jumps—"how are things between the two of you?"

"Why would you ask me that?" Are they watching her, have they bugged her house? Do the police do that sort of thing? Are those printouts somehow about David? She sees the detectives give each other a look. Suarez shakes his head ever so slightly at Marist, *no*. No, what? What do they know about her marriage that they're not going to tell her? Why would her marriage have anything to do with Lucy's disappearance? Michelle's throat goes dry.

Suarez runs a hand through his gray hair. "This sort of situation can put a strain on a couple. It's normal to be struggling." He studies Michelle with the sympathetic gaze of having been married himself. "So you and your husband agreed this morning that your husband should come forward to the press?"

Michelle wonders whether this man can read her mind. "Yes, David and I did agree," she lies. She wants the subject to move away from her marriage. "You're still looking for Lucy, right? You're looking at this as a kidnapping?" A terrible cold pierces her gut.

"We're still working with the Bureau, exploring all possible avenues, and we've got officers out combing the area and beyond. And we're handling the local interviews like this one." Suarez searches Michelle's face, waits for Michelle to say something else.

What Michelle hears in "exploring all possible avenues" is that they've stopped believing Lucy might have been kidnapped. They think she abandoned her family. That this is shifting from a missing person's search to a runaway woman special interest story. This is Michelle's fault. This is exactly what she was afraid would happen. She should have taken Lucy's secret to the grave.

"You're sure Lucy wasn't seeing anyone?" Marist asks.

Michelle shakes her head. "She wasn't. I'd know if she was."

"Like you knew about those plates she smashed?" Marist snaps. "Maybe you don't know your friend as well as you think."

"No!" Alarm rings through Michelle. *No, no, no! Not possible!* "I know her better than anyone. And I just want you to find my friend," Michelle cries out. "Please."

Michelle goes into the police station bathroom and locks the door. She turns on the faucet to splash her face, says to herself in the mirror, "This is just right now."

It was Lucy's mantra. *Is* her mantra. She said it whenever Michelle was struggling, or grieving, like when the college boyfriend dumped her out of the blue, or when Michelle's father died. Lucy would sleep in Michelle's bed, feed her, make her take a shower and get dressed, drag her into the sunlight and offer her coffee and breakfast and even do Michelle's laundry. All the while repeating, *This is just right now, Michelle.*

She shuts off the water. Grabs a paper towel from the dispenser. It's rough, like sandpaper, but she does her best to pat her face dry.

"This is just right now," Michelle whispers out loud again to the mirror.

A crack runs across the glass, jagged, spiderwebbed along one side. Maybe someone punched it. After sitting in that awful room, she can imagine someone coming in here and smashing their fist into it in a rage. Michelle stares into the broken thing. Sees the streak of new tears running down her cheeks. Bloodshot eyes, bags underneath them. Emptiness. She can hear Lucy whispering, "You are going to get through this, you are *already* getting through this. There is another side to this darkness," she'd say. And Lucy has always been right.

Michelle rips another towel from the dispenser and dries the new tears that have fallen. That night when Lucy confessed her regret, Michelle wrapped her arms around her friend and whispered, "This is just right now, I promise."

But this is Michelle's other secret. Those words from Michelle's mouth were hollow. She knew, or thought she knew, this wasn't *just right now* because motherhood is for always. Lucy could hear it in her voice too that Michelle was lying.

Pain shoots across her belly.

What if that's why Michelle hasn't heard from Lucy?

She tosses the crumpled towels into the trash. Pushes through the bathroom door and walks the gray painted hall, unable to bear the thought of Lucy watching the news stories and hearing what people are saying, understanding that it's her best friend's fault. The only thing worse than Lucy witnessing this betrayal is Lucy not being out there at all. Of Lucy being . . .

The detectives look up when Michelle reenters the interview room.

"You were gone a long time," Marist says.

She doesn't move to sit. "I'm leaving," she informs them.

Suarez inhales deeply. "We're not done yet."

"Unless you're going to arrest me, I'm heading home."

The two detectives stare quietly at the mother of two in the doorway.

"Can I go or not?" Michelle presses. "My son has been with your officer long enough. I need to pick up my other son from school."

Suarez's gaze is steady on her. "How about you tell us what you're still holding back, and we'll tell you something we know in return."

"Speaking of home . . ." Marist dangles.

Speaking of home? What the fuck?

Marist curls an arm around that stack of paper. Glances down. Then back up. "Your husband hasn't said anything?"

Michelle looks at him hard. "What, that he went to the press?"

Marist shrugs.

"What aren't you telling me?"

"What aren't you telling *us*?" he shoots back.

"I'm not playing this game with you," Michelle snaps. "A woman is missing." She turns to go but Marist halts her.

"Wait!"

She hears the scrape of a chair, and suddenly he is behind her, nudging her with something. What? She's frozen, afraid to know what's next.

He maneuvers around her in the hall. In his hands is that stack of printouts. He offers them to her. "For your evening reading. Make sure you ask David how his interview went with us."

Michelle gasps.

Marist blinks quickly, his face the portrait of innocence. "He didn't mention that we questioned him?"

She wants to slap this man.

He pushes the papers toward her.

She takes them, he gives her no choice. As she does, she slices the pad of her pointer finger, and hisses from the sting. Her eyes flicker to the top of the stack, reads a single text from Lucy to David that makes her want to vomit, a drop of blood seeping onto the clean white page from the cut.

David, wtf, are you cheating?

Heart pounding, she shoves the papers into her purse and hurries away. She practically runs, but from what? Information about David she doesn't want to know? Texts between Lucy and her husband? When she's nearly to the end of the hall, the words of Detective Marist come hurtling at her back, as though to underscore her worst thoughts.

"Make sure to ask David what else he and Lucy were fighting about!"

When David gets home from work, Michelle is waiting for him on the porch.

"How could you?" she barks toward the car as he is getting out, meaning so many things at once.

Where does she even start? With the texts between David and Lucy that show they were fighting about whether he was cheating? The part where her husband promised not to call the police and called the press instead?

Michelle drove straight from the station to pick up Charlie at school, got the boys home, gave Charlie a snack, fed Aidan. One task after the other in a daze, all with the soundtrack of people dissecting Lucy like she's some kind of monster on the news. Even Alejandra has stopped texting Michelle back. Now Melody Cho, the writer of the newsletter Michelle has read since she first got pregnant is weighing in, talking to NPR this afternoon for a segment on mothers who leave. What a nightmare. But worse is the idea David could have something to do with Lucy, that he has motive for people to think she ran. The idea breaks her already broken brain.

David crosses the lawn and stops a few feet away from the front porch, right next to the flower bed Michelle tried to cultivate but gave up on eventually. Michelle is better at raising children than tulips and magnolias. She feels the stress of her children alone in the house, a mother separated from her sons by thick walls. Before David was due home she strapped Aidan into his bouncy chair and sat Charlie in front of his favorite show on the iPad. Got them occupied so their parents can fight.

The work bag slung on David's shoulder falls to the ground with a loud *thump*. "I did what was right and you know it, Michelle." His silhouette is outlined by a gray sky, and the small green one-story house across the street. Such an unassuming setting for such a catastrophic evening in a marriage.

She breathes fire. "Oh did you? Or did you do what was convenient?"

"What are you talking about? You're really going to hold this against me?"

Those printouts Marist gave her flash in her mind. The incomplete conversation between David and Lucy that cuts off at the worst place, that bastard detective clearly omitting pages from the stack. Or maybe that's where the back and forth ended because Lucy was taken? One thing at a time, and first things first. "You promised me. And it's not just this." She feels words, long stuck, loosening inside her throat, unexpectedly spilling from her in this awful moment. "You've promised me so many things and not come through!"

"What are you talking about, Michelle?"

Here it comes. "You promised we would be equal. That you wouldn't let all the childcare fall to me. That you wouldn't let all the housework fall to me."

David's eyes find Michelle's. "But you wanted—"

"—to spend my life doing laundry? Cooking? Waiting on you?" Michelle's knees, her legs, they shake. How long can she hang on without collapsing? She reaches for the back of a chair. Stands in front of a house that is hers, with children inside that she bore with her own body, that she loves more than her own self, yet she is utterly lost. At any moment the wooden boards where Michelle stands will break away like some iceberg, leaving Michelle to drift without direction, destined to be alone, far from her family. This isn't the time to have this conversation, she knows, but maybe this is the fate of all marriages when they fall apart, when some unexpected tragedy chips away at whatever is left like some terrible pickax.

"That's not true," David protests.

"But it is. You've let this happen to me, to us."

"You let it happen too."

Michelle has sensed this showdown coming, lingering underneath their every morning, especially when they go to bed. But she thought she'd have more time to prepare, that she'd be able to run to Lucy. Together, Lucy and Michelle have always joined forces to help each other fix the other's broken thing. "Are you having an affair?"

"What?" he shouts.

She grabs the stack of printouts from the table on the porch and holds them out in her hand. Sees her husband's gaze flicker to them, then away. Watches the skin of his entire face, his neck, flush red. "God, you already know what these are, don't you," she says.

David looks away, toward the old oak in their yard that sprawls into the sky, beautiful and ancient. "I can explain."

Michelle descends to the bottom step, closing in on David. "Explain *what*? That Lucy found out you were house hunting with another agent, and fought with you about whether or not you're cheating?"

"I'm not! It was all a misunderstanding!"

"You've been lying to me this whole time!"

"Oh, right, and you haven't been withholding information about Lucy from me?"

"The detectives interviewed you as a suspect and you didn't tell me!"

"I didn't because I knew it would cause a fight! That you would take Lucy's side!"

"Well, congratulations, you were right," she spits. "Honestly, I'm not even sure I care if you're having an affair, David."

"What are you really saying, Michelle?"

Michelle's lungs are heaving. "I feel like we're living two

different lives, side by side. That we keep betraying the vows we made. And now, with Lucy, it's all just so poisonous."

David crosses his arms over his chest. She hates when he takes this posture with her. "You mean *I* betrayed the vows we made. That's what you're really saying isn't it?"

"Well *did* you?" she shrieks.

"No!"

"Did you have something to do with Lucy's disappearance, David? Is that why you told the press, so they'll turn their attention elsewhere?"

"I can't even believe you'd ask me that!"

"I can't even believe I'm asking!"

David comes closer, and Michelle scrambles backwards up the porch steps, the printouts crinkling in her hand. "I swear I'm not cheating! And I need you to believe me when I say that I had nothing to do with Lucy's disappearance!"

A neighbor walks by on the sidewalk, the man down the street with the grandkids. His steps are leisurely. He raises an arm to wave at Michelle and David, then seems to realize he's come upon a fight between husband and wife. He picks up his pace, hurrying onward. Michelle's eyes follow him down the street until he is out of sight.

Tears roll down her cheeks. "I don't know what I believe anymore."

"I love you, Michelle. We can figure this out. I want to."

Something flickers inside her. "That's because you're the one who benefits most from this marriage. You go off to work while your wife takes care of everything at home. Then you walk in the door and play Daddy with two sleepy children. I used to have a job, if you recall. I had a career before this. I was good at it. I loved it."

"But Michelle, you wanted it this way. You quit working, you took everything on at home yourself. I never asked you to. I work my ass off for this family too, every day."

Michelle is shaking her head. "You *let* this happen. You *let* me take it on."

"That's not fair. That's not *true*."

"Because of you, someone I love is being tried in the press."

"How can you defend her?" David shouts. He starts up the steps. "This person you love took off and abandoned you along with her family! Jesus Christ, she *planned her own kidnapping*, Michelle!"

"You don't know that!" Michelle cries, stepping backwards onto the porch and planting herself between David and the door of their house. "Nobody knows that! Not the stupid press, not the police, no one!"

David's eyes widen. "But that's not true, *you* do! *You* know, Michelle. You've known ever since Lucy disappeared from that parking lot! Talk about withholding the truth."

"I do not know. I do *not*. Something terrible has happened. I feel it right in here." Michelle slams a fist against the center of her rib cage. She does feel it. A cold emptiness, a gaping absence. Her bones ache with it, her teeth chatter.

"The only reason you told me Lucy fantasized about faking her own kidnapping is because it's haunting you, Michelle. *That* is the truth," David says.

Something sinks in her. A great block of cement falling to the bottom of her body, smashing straight through her feet and the floorboards of their porch. She stares at her husband. "And what haven't *you* said, David? What do *you* know about Lucy that I don't? If you love me then tell me!"

"I know nothing! And stop letting someone like Lucy wreck everything!"

"Someone like Lucy?! Lucy *is* everything!" With a giant swing of her arm, Michelle flings those printouts. They fan out into the air in an arc of white, scatter across the porch, down the stairs into the yard. She bursts into tears. Uncontrollable sobs. She turns away from David, covers her face with her hands, afraid. For herself, for her marriage, for her sons, but mostly for Lucy.

After a while, she feels a hand on her back and she looks up.

"I'm sorry you're in so much pain, Michelle." David's voice cracks. "And I'm sorry to be part of it."

"But you won't tell me how, will you," she cries.

"There's nothing to tell."

"You're lying!"

This is it, the crossroads of their marriage. She can go one way or the other. Left and maybe the marriage stands a chance. Right and, well... A part of her wants to sink against David's body like she has so many times before. But David's barely the man who made her fall in love with him. That man seems to be gone, replaced by this one. How lonely she's been, how little he sees her, all that she does for their life, what a trap it's become. She meant what she said before too, she doesn't believe him. She doesn't believe in anything anymore. If her marriage was a seam, she imagines it unraveling, the thread unpicked at one end, fingers pulling the fabric of it apart. Stitches widening. "I need to take a walk," she whispers and pulls away.

David reaches for her again. "Michelle, don't go. We can figure this out."

Without looking at him, she brushes by and descends the

porch stairs. She crosses the yard, the seam opening further. She tugs at the thread, stretches it to the breaking point. David's eyes burn into her. Michelle gets to the sidewalk and when she has the choice to go left or right, she turns right.

21
JULIA

JULIA CAN'T SLEEP. Not after their disastrous evening.

But Marcus snores away next to her. It used to make her laugh, listening to her husband snore. Sometimes it was soft and nonintrusive, but often it was loud, like a truck or a monster. In the mornings she'd joke about her restless night and she and Marcus would kiss and start their day; a missed night of sleep no big deal. But now it's yet another thing she has to tolerate about marriage, life, motherhood. The stakes are higher, it's so hard to sleep with a baby in the house, a baby who needs to be fed at all hours. Ever since Theo, Julia sleeps more fitfully, waking up at the slightest sound. Like Theo's existence tugs at her, even in her dreams.

Marcus never wakes up. Why?

Sometimes Julia wants to scream in his ear until he startles awake. Then she'd shrug and say, "Now you know what it's like, but for me it's times a thousand."

Can a woman exorcise this anxiousness of motherhood out of herself?

Julia throws back the sheets and gets up, pads down the hall. Leaves her phone on the bedside table so she isn't tempted to obsess about what's happening in the lives of others that isn't happening in her own.

Theo's night-light gives his room a soft blue glow. His crib, the mobile above it, the elephants and giraffes dancing in circles, the cozy chair by the windows. Julia peers down at her son, watches him lying there. She can't help but admire the slope of his puffy cheeks, the way his eyes are shut tight, the tiny lids, his feathery lashes, the movement of his puckered lips. She resists picking him up and squeezing him to her while he's too sleepy to wriggle out of her arms. She knows just how he'd snuggle into her.

Love fills her. She is suddenly glad to be a mother.

What would her life be without Theo?

In this moment she can't imagine, she doesn't want to. How can she ever want to? Why does she try and banish these feelings away? She wishes she could bottle this, drink it every morning, let it change her, make her permanently drunk. Sometimes the bad thoughts seem far from her brain, like she imagined them. She runs a finger lightly along Theo's soft cheek and smiles. Her beautiful, sweet son.

Julia's eyes drift toward the drawing theory book she keeps managing not to read on the chair. Maybe she'll try to page through it until she gets tired. She grabs it, sits down and leans back, tries to train her mind on the lovely moment that just passed between her and Theo. To bask in this moment of love and certainty. But then her mind inevitably drifts back to the failures of the evening—her failures.

Julia arrived home from the postpartum group to find candles lit on the dining table. A bottle of wine uncorked and breathing. Smells from the kitchen—roasting, frying. Marcus not only came back early from his university, he'd made her dinner. There he was, taking her hands and speaking words she'd longed to hear for months.

"Julia," he began. "I know things have been hard on you, and last night didn't help. *I* didn't help. You've been angry and you have a right to be." He stopped a moment, waited, searched her face—for what? Signs of forgiveness? He went on, "I've been late every night. I shouldn't have taken on that evening class. I *have* been making excuses. And here you are, trying to raise our son on your own. Giving up so much, and I know it's been hard for you to not be working." He paused again, squeezed her hands. "What happened last night was my fault, social services getting called, all of it. I've been putting you in one impossible position after another and so you acted out, I get it. Maybe I would have too, in your position. But we'll show social services we are a team whenever they come—because we're in this together." He drew her left hand to his chest, right over his heart. "I love you, Julia, with all my heart. I promise to be better, starting now. Can you ever forgive me?"

Something like relief shot through her at these words. She softened. She agreed with Marcus that they should try. As he stood there, eyes pleading, Julia allowed herself to remember the night they first met at Marcus's university where Julia was taking her Foundations for Modern Design class and they literally bumped into each other in the hallway. The happy hour dates when they were falling in love, introducing Marcus to her sister and how those two immediately hit it off. Plus, Marcus had loved that Julia was an artist, and promised her that his steady job could provide her financial security while she took a chance on her talents. So many memories cascaded through her. She'd fallen so hard for Marcus that she ignored how different she was becoming from her artist friends, all stubbornly single, or prone to short affairs.

Their meal tonight had started out so promising.

After Marcus put Theo to bed, Julia poured them each a glass of wine, and they sat down before the feast he'd cooked. They toasted to the promise of new beginnings, of getting a fresh start. They ate and talked. Julia asked him about work, and he told her more than he had in months. She thought about her own day but decided against bringing up the postpartum group. She didn't want to remind them both about last night. She could tell him in the morning. When he asked about Deke and Selene and her other old friends and whether it had been a long time since she'd heard from them, she changed the subject.

Julia reached across the table to take Marcus's hand. "I love you," she said. "The food, and what you said to me earlier, everything is perfect. Thank you. I've needed this. We've needed this."

He smiled at her, face full of emotion. "I wanted to recreate the best night of our lives."

Julia racked her brain, wondering what he was referring to. From when they were dating? From their engagement? From just after they married? "And which one is that?"

Marcus gazed at Julia from across the table. "I cooked the exact same meal from the night we made Theo." He pointed across the living room toward the rug, next to the coffee table.

Her gaze followed the direction of his finger. "Oh."

This jogged Julia's memory—but not in a good way. For her, that dinner and all that followed had not been the beginning of something but an end. The end of Julia. If only she had known where it would lead maybe she could have stopped it. It *had* been wonderful. Like tonight, they ate, they drank wine, they talked. But then they'd slid to the floor, eager for each other. Julia hadn't been thinking about anything other than Marcus, his body, his hands. Running her fingers through his thick, curly hair. Feeling the muscles in his back, his shoulders. She'd marveled at how she could love a man this much, how intensely she desired him, she couldn't imagine ever not wanting him. Theo was conceived out of all that love, which is beautiful—in theory. But conceiving Theo had been an accident.

When Julia's period was late, she took a test. "I'm pregnant," she'd told Marcus, emerging from the bathroom that morning, gut roiling. Questions about whether she'd keep the baby popped into her mind. No, she thought, *no*.

Marcus was making the bed. He looked up at his wife, face alight. "We're pregnant?" He went to her, gathered her into his arms. Then he whispered, chuckling, "I bet it was *that* night."

"What night?"

"The one when we made love on the floor in the living room," he said, and laughed.

This knowledge sent Julia spiraling. That night had been special. Lustful, frenzied. Adult. Hers, Marcus's, *theirs*. But the pregnancy immediately rewound it, changed it into something else. No longer theirs alone, but now also the baby's inside her. A baby should be made methodically, she'd thought, like in a doctor's office, intentionally and under harsh fluorescent lights. As her pregnancy wore on, that night seemed even more disconnected from all the sickness that followed, the aching muscles, the changes in her body. It disarmed the heat of her love for Marcus, turned what once felt illicit and thrilling into something involving diaper bags and breast pumps and strollers. Her desire for sex fizzled and sputtered and flared out. She kept striking matches, trying to light it, but the wind blowing against the spark was too strong. The flame always went out again. Poof.

Now Julia saw the look on Marcus's face from across the dinner table.

"I thought—" he began, then stopped. Began again. "I thought maybe tonight we could try?"

At this, Julia plucked the bottle of wine from the table, poured herself a very full glass and drained nearly half of it. She imagined Maggie's voice in her head, *Just get it over with. At some point you're going to have to, Julia.* She imagined Daphne's blond eyebrows arching in judgment that this was what sex had become for Julia, who had gone a little wild during art school, before she met Marcus. She forced herself to meet her husband's gaze.

"Will you come over here?" he asked, hopeful.

So she did. She got up and went to his chair. She let him pull her low, close enough to kiss. Julia gave in to it, she tried to lose herself.

"Julia," Marcus had sighed, running his hands along her legs until they were sliding up underneath her skirt. "I've missed you so much. I want you."

She let him pull her onto his lap. She told herself that at any moment, their spark would return, flare high like a fire. Julia would return, that woman she lost the moment the stick said PREGNANT. He kissed her neck and she let him. He reached for the top button of her blouse and she let him. Julia let him undo all the buttons and take off her shirt, throw it to the floor, followed by the silky camisole underneath it, letting him lift it over her head. She let him fondle her naked breasts and when he lowered his mouth to a nipple she didn't stop him, even though all she could think of was Theo, how her brain couldn't seem to switch back to experiencing Marcus's lips attached to her nipple as sexy.

How do other women do this? she wondered desperately.

Then Marcus pulled them from the chair onto the floor and got on top of her.

Now, all she could think was how good it was that she'd restarted her birth control. About that tiny pill she took this morning, grateful for the small, miraculous tablets as he pressed his hips into hers. She thought of the pamphlets hidden inside her bag, their message, *1 in 9 New Mothers Suffer from Postpartum Depression*, in bold black letters. She even thought of Henry.

She turned her head to the side, studied the legs of the chairs, the runaway potato that had fallen onto the carpet, as other thoughts found her. How Julia had known motherhood wasn't right for her. It had come to her like a premonition the moment she saw that the test was positive. She should have listened to her gut, told Marcus she wasn't ready, that maybe there'd never be a right time. But she didn't say a word and now here she was, staring at the crumbs on the floor that fell from the table during dinner.

Marcus moved on top of her groaning her name, "Julia."

Her gaze shifted until she was staring into the flames on top of the candles, until the light became sunbursts across her eyes. She tried to feel something, anything. She thought about the deadness in her neighbor's eyes and wondered if her eyes held that same vacant expression. It was like Julia had swum too far out from shore, she was deep in the water, she could see Marcus but only from a great distance. No matter how hard she paddled, she couldn't make it back to him. So she let herself sink. Julia's body was filled with rocks underneath Marcus's body. The life in her was going out. She felt it draining.

Tears rolled down Julia's cheeks, one after the other.

Marcus stopped moving above her. He looked down at his wife, whose face was turned away. She felt his eyes on her. "Where are you, Julia? Where did you go?"

Julia stared through the kitchen door into all that glaring light, at the detritus scattered across the tile from his efforts to cook. She couldn't look at her husband.

"I don't know," she told him, unable to lie.

Julia hears a noise coming from outside and startles.

From the yard, maybe?

The creak of a door opening, followed by the soft thud of it shutting.

Her neighbor's house.

Julia's heart speeds up in her chest. She welcomes the distraction. Does she dare go to the window? See what the man is up to at . . . she checks the time on the clock on Theo's dresser: 3:17 A.M. Julia glances at the night-light. She can't shut it off since her neighbor might notice, realize someone next door is awake. She doesn't want to draw his attention because she wants to do the watching this time.

Slowly, she slides off the armchair and onto her knees, crawls toward the window. She peers over the edge of the sill through the narrow gap in the curtains.

The second floor of her neighbor's house is dark.

She shifts her gaze to his yard. Where is he?

Julia's certain she heard a door opening and closing.

She waits, eyes scanning the ground.

Nothing.

Did she imagine it?

But then, movement.

The basement door swinging wide, the man emerging up the steps into his yard.

Julia squints.

What's that in his hands?

Is that a . . . bowl? A spoon inside of it?

A chill rushes over Julia's bare shoulders.

Why would he go down to his basement to eat? In the middle of the night?

The man halts. Stays completely still.

Julia holds her breath. Did he catch her moving in the window above him? Does he sense himself being watched? Does he see Julia's shadow in the glow of the night-light?

A minute passes. At least a minute. Maybe longer.

Shit. He knows she's there, he knows somehow, she's sure of it.

But then without looking up, he takes the steps to his back door and goes inside.

Julia waits to see his lights go on, but they don't.

His house remains in darkness.

Julia crawls away from the gap in the curtains.

What is he doing in that house?

She wants to know. And she also doesn't.

She gets up from the floor, checks on Theo one more time, and pads back to her room, thinking, wondering, then trying not to think at all. She slips into bed with Marcus, who's still snoring peacefully, like everything is completely fine, like their marriage isn't flailing dangerously, like their evening went perfectly and his wife isn't up in the night, peering out at their neighbor, haunting their house in the dark, thinking of depressing things, terrifying things, frightening men, women chained in basements. She rolls onto her side, away from the window that faces their neighbor's house, forces her mind back to the precious moments when the love she feels for Theo suddenly eclipses all else; how she wishes those moments never ended. But then they always do.

22

MICHELLE

MELODY CHO'S ARTICLE appears in the wee hours of morning.

Michelle's been up all night, sitting in the kitchen, laptop open as she reads all of the things people are saying about Lucy online. She can't make herself stop. It's keeping her from focusing too hard on her fight with David, that he might be cheating, that he's hiding something about Lucy, that he's a suspect in her disappearance and he kept this from her. It's like someone plugged her body into an electric socket and her brain can't stop churning.

Her finger scrolls and scrolls, eyes dry and tired as she reads the endless drivel people post. The worst is not even the death wishes, but the comments about Lucy from women like Michelle—mothers of little children, grandmothers, people who maintain normal social media accounts like her own, where they post cute photos of their kids, and the occasional selfie.

There's no such thing as a mother who regrets, I don't buy it.

Do you think the husband knew he married a monster?

I hope they find Lucy and she rots in jail for the rest of her life.

The comments go on and on as Michelle toggles between platforms. Even though it's futile, she keeps responding. It's as though she's back at work and her job is massive damage control for an advertising campaign that caused some kind of unforeseen public outcry that threatened the existence of the brand itself. But this campaign is the most important Michelle has ever worked, because the brand is Lucy.

Just because a woman questions becoming a mother doesn't make her a monster.

Is everyone forgetting that Lucy was kidnapped?

Does anyone remember that Lucy is a real person?

Do you really think a woman deserves to go to jail for regret?

On and on she scrolls, reading people's posts, getting sucked further and further down a rabbit hole of poison. Defending Lucy's regret, defending Lucy as a person, a mother, as the very best of friends. Prior to the obsessive scrolling and responding, she fired off a long missive to Sam over email, trying to explain—why she didn't mention her conversation with Lucy, that despite what everyone is saying, Lucy loves Emma, loves Sam, that this is all a tragic misunderstanding, that she's sorry, so sorry, that she's never been more sorry in her life. She checks her email again, even though it's still the middle of the night and it's likely that Sam will not respond at all because he's mortified and enraged and it's all Michelle's fault.

Right then, Melody Cho's article pops up in Michelle's email like a beacon.

Cho's articles often post early, at 5 A.M., sometimes 6. Michelle will wake up to find one waiting at the top of her inbox, with some appealing subject line or other. Sometimes her topics are mundane, like DOES MY BABY NEED TO WEAR SOCKS? or SKIN CARE DURING PREGNANCY. Or sometimes they're more complicated: CAN I REALLY NOT DRINK WHILE PREGNANT? or WHAT TO DO WHEN IN-LAWS TRY TO PARENT? No matter what, Michelle reads them all.

When she sees the subject line for today, she gasps. Then clicks on the email.

Regret: The Last Taboo of Motherhood?

Dear Readers:

I've been up all night. Ever since I appeared on NPR yesterday, so much has been bothering me about Lucy Mendoza. So much was **not asked** during that interview. As you know, I am a researcher, a statistician, a believer in the carefully crafted question, designed to be unbiased. Yet all the questions I was asked about Lucy were biased to the extreme—the negative extreme. They were conceived with a built-in prejudice about a mother who regrets.

Given the firestorm that has erupted with the latest news about Lucy's disappearance—the fact that she said out loud that she regretted becoming a mother, as well as her fantasies about running away—as a culture it seems we are struggling with a much larger, and more complicated question:

Is there a limitation on the range of emotions mothers are permitted to feel? Do we believe that regret is outside the purview of a mother's experience?

Let me back up.

As I often discuss in this newsletter, mothers today are allowed to openly admit how hard it is to mother. We are encouraged to seek treatment for postpartum depression. We even celebrate one another for revealing our hardships and our darkest mothering moments on our socials. We cheer each other on, we offer sympathy and understanding.

We're empowered enough to demand that we should not be judged for such admissions, but instead be supported.

This is all good. This is all progress.

But regret. Regret. Shhhhhhh. This word, we still cannot say it out loud. We cannot bear it said aloud by another mother. We silence this word from our own mouths and we silence it in the mouths of others before it can be spoken. We deny the possibility of its existence.

Why? Why are we, mothers and women ourselves, openly judging—even condemning—a mother for saying she wishes she did not have a baby? We are still a culture that tells a woman she is wrong to *not* want a baby, that she will regret *not* having one. So why are we so surprised—to the point of claiming it's impossible—that when a woman goes ahead and has the baby she didn't want in the first place, she might regret it? First we tell her she's wrong to *not* want the baby, then we tell her she's also wrong if she confirms it was a mistake. We gaslight her twice.

Do we truly believe that this woman, *a regretful mother*, does not exist? That she isn't *allowed* to exist? What do we fear might happen if we find out sometimes women really do regret becoming mothers?

Lucy Mendoza has brought this topic into the open. Are we going to continue to pretend that Lucy's regret simply cannot be?

I've been writing this newsletter for more than 10 years, speaking to you, my subscribers, as we navigate this journey that is parenting together. I've done national studies, I've written academic papers, I've appeared on countless radio programs and news hours and podcasts to discuss my research, because I've wanted all of you to have the facts, the data, the best findings available about the subjects you—that we all—worry about.

But I am a person, a mother myself. I'd be lying if I claimed I've never experienced regret in relation to my children or motherhood. There. I've said it out loud and to all of you. My bet is that you could say the same about your own lives as mothers. Have I experienced enough regret to consider running away, as Lucy apparently did? No. But I'd bet there are also mothers out there reading this newsletter who feel exactly as Lucy does, maybe strongly enough to conjure their own fantasies of disappearing and never coming back.

Do I have statistics to back any of these claims up? No. But you know why I don't? Because we don't ask mothers questions about regret. We do not speak the word, not even within our motherhood research. The topic itself is verboten, taboo, even among my colleagues and I.

I plan to change this, starting now. I want to forge a path for us to talk about this topic with openness, not judgment, with generosity and compassion, not malice. And my first question to all of you is this:

Are you Lucy too?

Were you Lucy in some moment, however brief? Do you relate to her, even a little? Can you recall even a few minutes in your life where you regretted having a baby? Have you ever wished to go back and undo what you've done? Do you wish that right now?

I want to know. If you have—and also if you haven't. I want to hear from my readers. I've been following Lucy Mendoza's story since it broke, and I plan to keep writing about her until she is found.

In fact, I'm planning on doing a live video recording of my podcast today, from noon – 2 p.m., so my readers can call in to ask their questions and engage in the discussion at hand: regretting motherhood.

None of us knows what happened to Lucy. The police don't know, the FBI doesn't know. The only information we have about Lucy Mendoza is that she was suffering gravely. Let's all agree to take a step back from this rush to judgment, and dismantle together what I see as **the last taboo of motherhood.** I believe we can make a difference for each other, and for Lucy. Let's find the courage to speak the unspeakable, for her sake and for ours.

Sincerely,
Melody Cho

Michelle wipes the tears from her cheeks.
She looks at the clock, eyes bleary. It's 4:30 A.M.
Below Melody Cho's article is a link to a survey, and Michelle clicks on it.

Has regret even been part of your experience as a mother?
YES / NO

Michelle moves the cursor of her laptop toward the NO, but then shifts it toward the YES and hovers there. She's almost afraid to click this answer, but then she does it. She wants to see what happens afterward.

A new survey page appears that has a single question:

Tell me the story of your regret in as many or as few words as you like. Feel free to include specific examples, ranges of time, to discuss if it is an ongoing experience or if it was as brief as a minute. All answers are welcome and will be kept confidential.

Below is an empty box for people to write. Michelle clicks away from the survey and goes to Melody Cho's Instagram. She types out a DM.

Melody, I'm Lucy's best friend. I'm certain she didn't run. I'm the person to whom Lucy confessed her regret. That was me. Thank you for writing this morning's article. Can we talk?

Michelle hits return so it sends.

She stares at the message box, hoping for an immediate response, until her eyes grow blurry, as though Melody Cho herself might be sitting at her own laptop, waiting for Lucy's best friend to DM her, both women up all night and thinking about Lucy Mendoza. The clock ticks by the seconds, the minutes. Michelle sits there, hunched over her laptop, still staring, until it's 5 A.M., then 5:30. Melody Cho isn't going to get her message, she thinks, never mind read it and respond immediately. She probably receives dozens, even hundreds of DMs and employs interns to respond. Or maybe she ignores them. Michelle is about to close her laptop and make some more coffee when the notifications bar shows one new message.

The breath in her chest leaves her when she reads it.

She has her answer in Melody's very first word:

Yes.

23
JULIA

BREAKFAST THAT MORNING with Marcus is silent.

Julia sips her coffee, pretending everything is normal. She scrolls the news on her phone avoiding the usual minefields while Marcus prepares formula for Theo. He's quietly acquiesced to this shift in feeding their son. She wishes he'd leave for work, wishes she could erase the events of their prior evening, wishes she could forget the man next door. She opens her email and one subject line from Melody Cho leaps out:

REGRET: THE LAST TABOO OF MOTHERHOOD?

Her heart rate quickens. She glances at Marcus testing the temperature of the formula on his wrist. Then she looks at Theo waiting to be fed in his chair, watching his father. Her desire to read what Cho wrote burns through her. But then Marcus joins Julia at the table, helps Theo hold the bottle, the sound of their baby's sucking conspicuous in the awkward quiet.

"I was thinking," Marcus begins.

Julia swallows and looks up.

Marcus shifts the bottle higher. "I was thinking I'd take Theo with me to work today. To give you some time."

This, Julia is not expecting. "Oh. And do what with him?"

Marcus's shoulders lift slightly, he has clearly not thought this through. "I guess, if he's napping I can bring him to class, I can watch him in my office. Maybe I can get one of the grad students to watch him for a bit as well. I'd pay her of course."

"Or him?"

"Or him," he corrects quickly.

Julia's brain zigs and zags between two poles, one that signals disaster ahead for Marcus, who's completely unprepared for how needy a baby is, and another that signals sheer joy at the thought of a whole nine hours free from the burden of caring for their son. Freedom wins. Let Marcus find out how hard Julia's hours are every day.

"Okay," she agrees.

"All right," Marcus says, and looks away.

The conversation ends there.

When it's time for Marcus to go, Julia watches him open the door and leave the house and walk away, pushing their son in his baby carriage. She examines her feelings, searching for signals that she is a good mother, an ache in her heart, a desperation to take Theo back into her arms, to not be separated from him even for a short while. All she feels is numb.

Once she's certain Marcus and Theo are gone, she sits down to read Cho's article, and clicks on the link for the survey. She scrolls the cursor over to that all caps YES under the question about whether she's felt regret. That Cho asked the question feels like forgiveness. But then Julia can't bring herself to do it—she can't seem to press down to click it.

Does she really regret Theo? Or is this just postpartum?

Julia gets up and goes to the sink, turns on the water to rinse what's there and fill the dishwasher, thinks of how Theo's eyes follow his mother whenever she's in the room because that's what babies do; how on most days this makes her crazy, but in her best moments, the way Theo seeks her, needs her, makes Julia feel seen. Loved. That because of Theo, Julia's existence means something important. Before him she was insignificant. With him her life has new meaning.

A plate slips through Julia's wet fingers and shatters in the sink.

"Dammit!" She slams her palm against the faucet handle and the water shuts off. She stands there, ignoring the broken pieces in the basin, staring into the emptiness of the yard, thinking of how it reflects the hollowness in her chest. During the night she felt such love for her son, so whole and full, but now devastation swallows her, followed by the sense that she is trapped.

She grabs a dish towel to dry her hands.

As she does, something possesses her—something she hasn't felt for a long time. Something she thought was gone, maybe for good. She rushes to grab one of the pencils from the cupholder on the counter, then her sketchbook. She sits down, opens it onto the kitchen table. Her hand flies across the page in lavish strokes.

An image begins to emerge.

Hulking. Hairy. Grotesque.

A self-portrait.

Nearly as wide and tall as the page itself.

The Anti-Mother.

She sketches these words with rudimentary, jagged letters in the tiny corner of white space that remains. Then she turns the page and quickly sketches another image, this one she titles, Monster-Mother. She keeps going until she's filled two more pages, experiencing a kind of madness, the good sort that takes over her brain. But what's coming out disturbs even Julia, she could never allow anyone else to see what she's drawn. Her deepest darkness, her most shocking secrets made visible. She thinks of Cho's question about regret, and almost wishes she could submit one of these self-portraits as her answer.

Julia sets the pencil down and leans back in her chair.

She stares up at the ceiling, tries to calm her breathing, her heart.

Is this how Lucy Mendoza felt before she ran? Lost in this strange land of maternity leave, this time when a woman is meant to become this thing called mother? Did Lucy feel like a failure—to her husband, her baby, herself most of all? Did she feel as monstrous as Julia?

What if Lucy didn't run?

This question floats across Julia's mind like a tangled piece of seaweed in the bay.

Then she hears a car rumble to life next door. She goes to the window in time to see her neighbor pulling out of his driveway. She watches his car disappear around the corner.

An idea percolates.

It tugs at her.

The timing of him leaving seems almost preordained.

What if she just sneaks a tiny peek?

Before Julia can decide otherwise, she rushes to the back door, pulls it open, spills into the yard on this gray morning. The cooler air greets her and she sucks it into her lungs. Stands there, still and listening.

Everything is quiet.

She turns toward her neighbor's house. Her feet move of their own volition, taking her across that line in the grass between yards. She glances sideways at the street. No one else is walking by to see Julia trespassing. She keeps on going. The gray from the clouds is like a cloak shielding her. The neighbor's yard is neat enough that it doesn't attract notice. Julia glances at the wooden shed by the fence and hesitates.

No, not the shed, she decides, and moves toward the stairs that lead up to the man's back door, footsteps soft against the ground, flat shoes brushing along the matted grass. Julia grabs the staircase railing, the metal sharp and cold against her palm. Her breaths are quick puffs from her lungs, nerves like static across her scalp and down her spine. Why is it that the only time Julia feels alive is when she's doing things she shouldn't, like snooping at her neighbor's? When she's portraying herself just now as a monster? Are she and this man somehow the same, is that why she's so drawn to him?

She hears movement, tiny but there, so she turns.

A bird flies by, wings flapping, nearly grazing Julia, and she jumps.

It's just a bird, it's just a bird.

She puts a hand over her heart and nearly laughs.

She's safe, she's okay, everything is okay.

The bird swoops into another low arc before settling onto the branch of a nearby tree. Cocks its head at the woman on the back steps. Julia stands there, chest heaving, listening again—for cars approaching, for people talking, a dog barking, anything really, but there's only silence. She lets out a stream of air, then cups her hands against the window in the door.

The light is too dim to see much inside.

When her eyes adjust, she realizes she's looking into a kitchen, much like her own. A big L of cabinets along two walls, an island at the center. Dishes piled on the countertop, a recycling bin on the floor, a bulletin board on the far wall covered in notes and newspaper clippings, each thing papering over the other. A bowl sits on the kitchen island, the kind Julia would fill with fruit, apples, oranges, bananas, but this one is piled with junk. There's a box next to it, maybe of mac-n-cheese, and next to this, a television remote maybe? What looks like an electric drill sticks up on the other side of the box, beside it a half-empty plastic package of napkins. Julia scans the doorway that likely leads to her neighbor's living room as it does in her own house. The same builders must have constructed both places, like most of the houses in this neighborhood. Her gaze sweeps across the kitchen floor and they catch on something.

Something pink? Or is it purple?

Her stomach drops.

A woman's hair band?

Julia squints, tries to make out what's there through the glass, but it's dirty from the rain. She resists wiping the window with her shirt. It's too far for her to get a clear look, and for all she knows it's nothing, just her imagination inventing evidence where there is none.

Shame floods her.

What is she doing? This is just a lonely man's kitchen. She shouldn't be prying.

Instead, she should be bringing him cookies, brownies, a cake. Something to cheer him up, to brighten this dank place. He probably goes to visit his mother every day. And here Julia is, thinking such terrible things because he lives alone, because he's a night owl, because his expression is blank.

She needs to go.

She's in the midst of pulling her hands from the glass, turning around at the top of the steps to return to her own house.

When she hears a bump.

A kind of muffled *thump*.

Or did she?

Maybe she imagined it.

It seemed to come from below. The basement?

But the sound of it is familiar to Julia. It's the same one she heard the other day when she and Theo were headed down the driveway on their way to the café.

The morning after Lucy Mendoza went missing.

What if it's Lucy Mendoza? What if she's in this house right now?

Julia's brain lights up again, flashing: DANGER. Adrenaline sends stars bursting through her vision. She remembers the way her neighbor stares, the way his eyes watch Julia through her bedroom window. Now his gaze seems less sad and lonely, more sinister.

She listens harder.

Maybe it was a dog? Or a cat? Maybe he has a cat and it knocked something over? Yes, that's probably it. Julia's never seen a cat in the widow, though. She's never seen the man walk a dog, or with any pet whatsoever.

What did she just hear in the basement then? Something? Someone? Nothing? No one?

The heart in Julia's chest skips and stutters. Goose bumps rise all over her arms. She gets the sense she is being watched, even though she knows her neighbor's out. She saw his car disappear with her own eyes.

He's just a lonely old man.

Julia stands there, waiting, listening for another *thump*, a *bump*, anything.

There is nothing. Only silence.

She lets out a long breath, and nearly laughs.

Lucy Mendoza is not in this house!

But as she descends the neighbor's steps toward her own yard, she hears a car coming down the street and halts. She waits for it to pass but it doesn't. Instead, it slows. There is the sound of gravel, rocks popping under wheels, a car pulling up a driveway.

Fear prickles her skin.

Her neighbor is home.

What am I going to do?

She hears the car door open, slam, feet on the front steps, a key entering a lock. The moment the front door squeaks open, Julia runs, darting between this man's house and her own, flying through his backyard hoping to catch that moment when he's entering his living room, hoping he doesn't hear Julia's own kitchen door opening or notice his neighbor rushing into her house like she's been caught doing something she shouldn't.

Julia glances back to make sure he isn't there, nearly expecting to see him in his dark hoody, running toward her, coming to grab her, take her down to the basement where he's also keeping Lucy Mendoza. Her toes catch as she's crossing the driveway, her left foot tripping the right one. She goes tumbling to the ground, hands flying out to break her fall. They smack the concrete hard, a painful shudder moving through her arms, her shoulders.

"Ouch!" she shouts, then slaps a hand across her mouth.

Julia struggles to get up from the ground, takes a few slow, unsteady steps forward.

She hears a noise behind her, from next door.

A rustle in the grass.

Thump, swish, thump, swish.

Cold washes over her.

The noise stops. She resists the temptation to turn her head and look at her neighbor. Instead, she walks toward her back door, unhurried, *Nothing to see here*. Soon she is shutting herself inside. Safe and sound.

But then, out of the corner of her eye, a flutter through the kitchen window.

She swivels toward it.

Her neighbor standing outside, watching her?

Or . . . nothing?

Her imagination playing tricks again?

She waits.

Not a shiver, not a glimmer. Nothing.

"Fuck!"

She slides down against the kitchen cabinets and onto the floor, tries to catch her breath, pulls her knees to her chest. Checks the time on the microwave clock. Soon, Melody Cho's podcast will begin. Soon Julia's focus will be pulled elsewhere, thank god. Maybe she can sketch some more first to keep herself busy. But her left palm is bleeding, both hands have pebbles embedded in the skin. She picks out the tiny rocks and the grit, brushes the dirt from them, from her pants, her knees. Examines the damage, takes in the full range of consequences from her adventure next door.

She shakes her head and somehow she starts to laugh.

What was she thinking?

Julia wipes the tears from her eyes, trying to calm herself.

This is the first and last time she plays detective, she decides.

24
MICHELLE

AT 11:53 A.M., Michelle opens her computer.

A part of her wishes Aidan was in her lap and not down the street at the babysitter's where she dropped him off. His fluttering heartbeat against her chest calms her, his sturdy bottom nestled along her legs always so soothing.

She writes one final note onto the index card she's been filling up with things she doesn't want to forget to say, glances at her email for the thousandth time in case there's something from Sam, then logs on to the podcaster link Melody Cho sent. Suddenly there she is on screen, this person whose work Michelle has been reading for years. Cho's expression is friendly, her hair cropped short; she's wearing a plain black top, nothing fancy. She could be any other mother Michelle met on the playground. She suddenly wishes they were friends.

"Hi, Michelle," Melody says, "it's good to meet you."

"It's nice to meet you too. I've been following you for years. Ever since I had my first."

Melody nods. "I'm glad you reached out. I'm sorry the occasion for our conversation is such a sad one."

Michelle blinks quickly, she will not cry. "Thank you for inviting me to participate. I would do anything for Lucy, to help find her, to . . ."

"Speak on her behalf when she can't speak for herself?"

"Yes." Her gaze drifts to the participant count climbing on the right of the screen, adding up the people waiting to be let into the session. The number has already risen higher than she expected. She curls her fingers around the handle of her coffee mug. *How high will it go?*

Melody must guess what's caught Michelle's attention. "I'm expecting a lot of people today because the topic is so controversial. But the only people who can attend live are my paying subscribers. Hopefully we won't get awful remarks in the chat box, but prepare yourself."

"I am," Michelle says. "I've seen what people are saying about Lucy."

Melody looks down, shuffles some papers in front of her. "Here's how it's going to go. I'll start things off by speaking about Lucy and the piece I sent out this morning, and I'll feature some of the things people have already written about regret from the survey. Then I'm going to explain that Lucy's best friend is here, and that's when I'll turn on your video so everyone can see you. People are going to be able to chat their questions once I open the comments. Are you okay with that? Obviously, I'll screen out anything inappropriate, but you'll be able to read what people post to the chat box."

Something shifts inside Michelle's stomach. "I'll be fine."

"Then after you and I finish our conversation, I'll introduce my next guest. She's local to you, and she's an important expert on postpartum. She's written for me before actually, so I'm guessing you know of her not only because she's local but because of Lucy. Naomi Bresler?"

Michelle startles at the name. "Yes, of course. Lucy was

attending her group. But isn't that . . . I don't know, against the rules for a therapist to speak about her client?"

Melody shakes her head. "She's just going to speak on the topic, not on Lucy specifically." Cho's eyes shift briefly. "Is there anything else you want to ask before we start?"

The clock on Michelle's computer changes to 11:59 A.M. "I'm good."

Melody turns off Michelle's camera, then smiles warmly through the screen. "Alrighty, I'm going to let people in. This is going to be a good conversation."

Then they are live.

"Hello, everyone," Melody begins, "I'm glad you could make it for this impromptu episode. Thank you to my subscribers who are here, and my listeners who'll join us later for the recording. Please bear with me since this is unscripted, but I wanted to allow you to participate with your questions about this very important topic. You can type them into the chat when I open it later, and remember to keep everything civil. We have two special guests joining us, and I want them to feel safe and supported during our conversation." Melody pauses, drawing her hair back behind her ears.

Michelle has been holding her breath. She releases her lungs in a loud *whoosh*.

Melody picks up a pair of eyeglasses and puts them on. "I wanted to start by reading a few answers I've received from the survey I posted this morning about regret." She holds up a printout in her hands. "I'll preface this by expressing my gratitude for the incredible honesty in what people have written. It shows how desperately we need to have this conversation, and how clear it is that Lucy Mendoza is not alone in her feelings of regret." She starts to read.

"I made three fatal errors in my life: one was choosing my former partner; the second was having children with him, and the third was having children at all."

"Even though my children are amazing and lovely and their generosity is incredible . . . If I could go back without feeling guilt and all of these strings attached? I wouldn't choose this path."

"I can't stand it, being a mother. Can't stand this role. I can say with certainty that yes, if I knew what I know now three years ago? I wouldn't have a child."

"I thought I wanted to be a mother and I don't . . . It's very difficult to know until you're in that position, very difficult to know how I would react—and you can't try it out."

Between each answer, Melody pauses, allowing these secret feelings to settle with everyone before moving forward with yet another.

Michelle is struck by how many women seem to wish to go back in time so they can choose a different path, one that doesn't involve having had a baby. It feels like Lucy speaking to Michelle all over again. Until this moment, it never occurred to her that there might be other women experiencing the same thing. Never mind how many.

A flush creeps over her, heating her cheeks.

When Melody finally stops reading the survey answers, Michelle is relieved.

Melody sits in silence, looking at all of them through the camera, letting these women's words echo onward. After what must be a full minute but feels like ten to Michelle, Melody takes off her glasses and inhales deeply. "Before I turn to our first guest, there's something else I wanted to say about Lucy Mendoza. Something that's really been bothering me. As you all are aware, we live in a country where certain states are eliminating abortion even in cases where a mother's life is in danger, which I know outrages my readership since it's been a frequent topic in my newsletter and on this podcast." Melody stops another long moment. "But societal pressures for women to have children aside, I want us to really think about why—in a country that forces women who want an abortion to have a child, even in cases of rape—are we so shocked and outraged that there might exist women who've had a baby and regret it? And I can certainly imagine a world where a woman desperately *wants* a baby, then decides later on she's made a mistake, which is exactly what some women commented in the survey." Melody stops and stares at everyone through the camera again.

Michelle's mind spins, so forcefully that as Melody continues speaking, it takes her a moment to realize she's just been introduced and Melody's turned on her camera.

There Michelle is on screen. Could Sam be out there, watching? She swallows. "Hi, Melody, thanks for having me. And for holding this forum."

Melody nods. "I'm happy you're here, Michelle. I was glad you messaged this morning. Let's start by talking about what made you reach out."

A swell of hope rises inside Michelle. Finally, a chance to speak for Lucy. She lifts the hand curled around her mug and sees that it's shaking. She drops it into her lap. *Just breathe.* Michelle opens her mouth. "Well, I wrote to you because I was grateful someone would defend my friend. I wish Lucy was with us now to hear everything you just relayed from the survey. I think it would have made Lucy feel . . . not alone." A flow of air releases through her lips as she forces air from her lungs. "But there are two different issues and I want to make sure we talk about both. One is Lucy's disappearance, the other is her regret. One is not necessarily connected to the other, even though everyone seems to assume they are." Michelle stops. She takes a sip of the coffee in her mug, tries not to wince when she accidentally slurps it. It's bitter going down her throat and she has the urge to wince again.

Melody looks at Michelle through the camera. "What do *you* think happened to Lucy?"

Michelle feels a drop of sweat roll down her stomach. "I don't think she ran." Her voice cracks but she clears her throat. "I believe someone took her."

"Tell us why," Melody prompts.

"Because I know Lucy as well as I know myself, and she would have been in touch with me if she was in a position to be. She would find a way to contact me. I'm certain of this."

"You're a mother yourself."

Michelle shifts the cross of her legs under the table, tries to keep her back straight. She stares into the green light at the top of her computer screen. "Yes."

"Can you tell us what went through your mind when Lucy told you that she regretted her daughter?"

Michelle is so hot she wonders if her makeup is melting down her face. She remembers Lucy's expression as she told Michelle what she was feeling. "Truthfully, I was horrified."

Melody nods. "I probably would have been too if it was my friend telling me this. I don't know how I might have responded, and this kind of subject is my full-time job."

This gesture of forgiveness washes over Michelle and allows her to continue. "I'm not proud of how I reacted. My immediate response was to judge Lucy. No"—Michelle backtracks—"that's not right either. My immediate response was disbelief. I told Lucy it couldn't be true, that she did not—could not—regret her child. I denied Lucy what she wanted to say. It was like a reflex or something. When a mother says something we don't like or want to hear, we tell her it cannot be. That it's impossible." Michelle adds in a whisper, "And I wish I could take it back with all my heart."

Melody doesn't speak. She waits for Michelle to go on.

So she does. "But that night Lucy did something uncharacteristic of her as my friend: She got angry at me for not believing she was speaking the truth. That's when I realized it wasn't fair of me to behave this way, that if she could muster the courage to be so honest, the least I could do was listen and try to understand." Michelle remembers the notecard with all the things she scribbled down that she didn't want to forget to say. She studies it a moment, before looking up again into the camera. "I want it to be clear: Even as Lucy spoke of her regret, she also spoke of her love for her daughter." Michelle's heart pounds in her ears. "Ever since she disappeared, I can't stop thinking about how both things can be true. A woman can wish to go back to her life from before, *and* she can still love her children. Maybe the only way to get to the other side of this pain is to speak it out loud and still be loved by the people around you." Michelle's voice falls to a hoarse whisper. "Lucy needed to know I wouldn't abandon her. And I worry I failed her." Tears stream down Michelle's face. She glances down at her notes once more before continuing. "She deserves our admiration. She found the courage to say what so few people do. I admire everyone brave enough to share their own similar thoughts on Melody's survey. You're telling the truth about a forbidden topic, one that brings women shame. I wish that kind of courage for any woman feeling the way Lucy was." Michelle backtracks. "*Is*. The way Lucy *is*."

When she meets Melody's eyes again, she's surprised to find them glassy.

Melody wipes her cheek. "As you've been speaking, I've been thinking about how the real failure here is that our culture doesn't make room for the word regret. It doesn't prepare us to hear a woman say such a word. That's why I wrote my article this morning, that's why I was up all night thinking about Lucy Mendoza too, and that's why I wanted to be here with all of you today. On that note, I'm going to turn on the chat so people can ask their questions and add their thoughts in the comments that will be scrolling to the right of everyone's screens."

The chat box opens, and nearly immediately fills with comments, so many Michelle can barely catch them.

Melody puts on her glasses again as she reads what people are posting. "Michelle, there's one question I've seen a version of three times here already, and I think we should just get it out of the way." She squints a little as she reviews whatever it is. "This is from Mimi in San Diego: Michelle, don't you agree that the coincidence of Lucy's disappearance is a bit too convenient? Lucy Mendoza tells you a few months ago she's planning her own fake-kidnapping, then suddenly she vanishes?"

Michelle shakes her head. "No, you've got it wrong. Lucy wasn't *planning* her own kidnapping, she told me she *sometimes thinks about it*. We all fantasize about things we'd never do, don't we? People imagine affairs with the neighbor, or ramming their car into the person who cut them off on the highway. But very few of us ever follow through and do them."

The chat is going crazy, but the theme is similar enough that Michelle gets the gist.

But what about the fact that Lucy is gone?
Come on, Michelle, wake up
Lucy's disappeared, isn't that proof enough?

Her heart sinks as she contemplates the idea that Lucy really did plan this. Then she imagines her friend on a beach, somewhere beautiful. She imagines getting on a plane and going to see Lucy, how they would hug and talk about every last detail of all that has happened since she went missing. Michelle would do anything to take that trip, to have one more hour with Lucy, to experience the unconditional love forged between women friends. She imagines her own body floating upward into the sky, imagines sacrificing herself, how she'd do anything to get Lucy back. If only she could undo all that's happened since Lucy disappeared, unravel time.

"Okay," she continues. "To everyone writing in the chat, I just spent these last few seconds fantasizing that Lucy did plan her own disappearance, because then I could see her again. I would be sure of her safety, of a future that's still hers to live. So I *wish* that's what I believed. I *wish* Lucy was in some faraway place, hiding out, biding her time. But I know she isn't." Michelle's voice gets louder, sharper. "I meant it when I said that if Lucy could reach out, she would. She *would*. But the fact that she hasn't makes me believe that someone took her. Or worse . . ." Michelle trails off.

She just can't say it out loud. *Murdered.*

She glances at the chat.

A comment from someone named Julia catches her attention.

I believe you, that Lucy was taken. I hope you find her, and I appreciate everything you and Melody have discussed. I agree that Lucy is not alone in how she was feeling.

Michelle rubs her eyes. "Thank you for saying that, Julia."

Melody nods. "Yes, I'm sure so many people here feel similarly to Lucy, even if they're too nervous to say it out loud or type it into the comments section.

For a few seconds the chat goes still.

But then it erupts with comment after comment.

I am Lucy too
I'm Lucy
stop judging mothers
mothering is hard
sometimes I want to disappear too
I am Lucy

"I wish Lucy could see this," Michelle says, heart lifting, her voice getting stronger, surer with every new comment appearing on the screen. "How not alone she is."

Melody looks straight into the camera, and Michelle knows Melody is looking directly at her when she says, so full of feeling, "You never know, Michelle, maybe she can."

25
DIANA

DIANA CROSSES THE lot in front of the sandwich shop in town. She pulls open the door and heads inside. The man behind the counter looks up from chopping onions.

He smiles broadly. "Well, hello, Detective!"

Diana smiles back. No matter how many times she tells Paco she's retired he'll always call her Detective. It makes her feel good. "Paco, how are you these days?"

"I'm always doing all right, Detective. Lo de siempre?"

Diana nods. "Por supuesto. For here."

While Paco gets to work making her sandwich, Diana waits against the wall. She considers calling her daughter, but her mind automatically spins to that old box she unearthed yesterday. The similarities between Maeve O'Neil's situation and Lucy Mendoza's are plaguing her. Enough that she tracked down Trey online, Maeve's former husband, who now lives two hours away. From his socials, she can see he eventually moved on after losing his wife and daughter so tragically. He's remarried now, has two grown kids, and grandkids. His socials are full of photos of himself as grandpa, of Trey and his wife dancing at their son's wedding, of Trey walking his daughter down the aisle. Diana is pleased he not only recovered from so much loss, but that he's thriving. It all could have gone very differently for him.

The person Diana can't find, however, is Maeve's best friend, Becca Abrams. There's only dead ends on that front. This woman seems to have disappeared off the face of the earth. Diana's searched Becca's name in every which way and cannot find her. No housing records, phone records, no socials, no jobs, no anything. Diana can't find a marriage certificate or evidence of a name change. Something's eating at her about this. But she can't quite figure out what, exactly. Yet.

Then there is the unsolved Joanna D'Angelo case—missing for three years now, her situation similar to Lucy's but also different in—

"Hey Detective, tu almuerzo está listo," Paco calls out, and interrupts her thoughts.

Diana goes to retrieve her lunch. The whiff of her sandwich makes her stomach growl. "See you again, tomorrow?" she asks Paco.

He laughs. "Eat it while it's hot."

She takes the paper plate and sandwich from his hand. "Always."

Diana makes her way to a vacant table by the window and sits, glances at her watch. Joe should be here any minute. She unwraps her sandwich and bites into it, but her mind is still on Joanna. Is Diana wrong to fixate on Maeve O'Neil when Joanna D'Angelo is still a missing person—a missing mother? She is staring out the window, lost in thought, by the time Joe arrives.

He takes a seat on the other side of the table. "Dee, good to see you."

She pulls her gaze from the street. "You going to eat with me today?"

Joe leans his elbows onto the table, eyeing Diana's sandwich.

"How about I'll help you finish your lunch. Eggplant and peppers, right?"

Laughter erupts at the table next to them, two teenage girls cackling, and Diana thinks it's appropriate, given Joe's suggestion. "Yeah. Get your own."

"I'm glad to see you haven't changed," Joe says.

"Of course not." Diana wipes her greasy hands on a napkin. "Tell me your update and then I'll tell you mine."

Joe leans closer. "Why don't we start with yours?"

Diana shakes her head. "I'm probably way off. And for now, let's stick to the angle that someone took Lucy."

Joe looks longingly at the sandwich before he leans back in his chair. "Okay, I'll give you the rundown of what we've got, though the FBI likely isn't sharing everything they've got." He crosses his arms over his chest. The sounds of people coming in and out of Paco's shop, and Paco yelling out sandwich orders, pepper their conversation. "So far, the search has turned up nothing, not on the beach, not in the woods. Lucy Mendoza seems to have vanished without a trace. As far as local interviews go, as you know, she'd returned to real estate recently, and we do have a list of men who sent Lucy messages that are of interest—some of them clients, one of them the best friend's husband, David Carvalho."

Diana's eyebrows arch. "Oh?"

"Yeah. There's a whole series of text messages from the week Lucy disappeared between them. They were arguing."

"About?"

"Selling his house. Their back and forth got pretty heated. Lucy found out David was looking to sell from another agent friend he'd spoken to about representing him, and the agent told Lucy when she realized it was Lucy's friend's husband. Lucy confronted David about going behind Michelle's back since Michelle was clearly in the dark about it, whether he was cheating on Michelle, that kind of thing. Their messages cut off right in the middle of their argument." Joe reaches across the table and grabs the second half of Diana's sandwich. Before she can protest, he takes a giant bite, chews and swallows. "We had him in for questioning, but his main concern was his wife not finding out."

Diana shakes her head, then gives in and lets him have it. "Well, that's interesting."

Joe swallows another bite. "He gave us some story about how it was meant to be a surprise for Michelle, that he was planning to buy them a bigger house."

"Do you believe him?"

"I'm not sure I believe anyone right now, given what just came out about Lucy."

"What else?" Diana prompts, ignoring Joe's dip into the theory that Lucy ran.

"We have Sam Rosen, the husband, who told us of an incident at home when Lucy melted down, more or less, which could support the theory that she took off. All the flirty messages from Lucy's former clients asking her out. So far these guys are dead ends, except for the most persistent one, of course, who we can't seem to track down, but we're still trying. Then there's the best friend, Michelle Carvalho, who's spread her missing posters far and wide. We've interviewed her several times, both before and after the press got hold of this story about Lucy planning her kidnapping. If we take her word for it, though, she'd have heard from Lucy by now if Lucy was able to communicate. I don't know what I think on that front."

Paco appears at their table. "Joe, you're really only going to eat your friend's leftovers?"

Joe smiles up at him. "Paco." They shake hands. "Why don't you pick among my favorites so it'll be a surprise?"

Paco nods. "You got it, Detective," he says, and takes off.

"I'm eating half of whatever it is," Diana informs Joe.

"Whatever you say," he agrees. "So, we've interviewed the therapist from the postpartum moms group that Lucy was attending, but there's confidentiality issues."

"Is that everything?"

Joe's eyes travel to the counter, and he watches Paco make his sandwich. "We are looking into Lucy being stalked, without her knowledge. Maybe one of those former clients, maybe a stranger but as you are well aware it's most likely someone Lucy knows." Joe pauses, meets Diana's eyes. "But let's face it, Dee, we still have a scene in a parking lot that occurred in broad daylight, where—aside from Lucy's phone under that SUV—nothing seems to indicate a struggle."

Diana gives Joe a stern look. "We're not entertaining that version of the story at the moment, remember? Besides, the phone under the car is enough to indicate a struggle."

"Or that Lucy tossed it to make it look like a struggle," Joe says.

"Come on, Joe."

"We need to look at all angles and that is definitely one of them. You know this."

Paco delivers Joe's sandwich, and Joe unwraps one half.

"Anything come up related to Joanna D'Angelo?" Diana asks.

Joe shakes his head. "Aside from Lucy and Joanna both being missing persons who are also mothers, not yet. But a connection hasn't been ruled out either. Your turn to tell me what you've got," he adds, then takes a bite of his grinder.

The door of the shop opens and closes, opens and closes again, each time the bell on top ringing. Diana studies her former partner, remembering how much younger he is. "You probably won't remember this because it was before your time. But there was a case I caught when I first became a detective. It ended in tragedy. I hadn't thought of it for years until yesterday, when the press got hold of the story about Lucy's regret."

Joe's eyebrows arch. "Say more."

So Diana tells the story of Maeve O'Neil while her former partner eats. Joe remains silent until she gets to the part where Maeve and her baby drowned on Narragansett Beach.

"Wow," Joe says, dabbing his mouth with a napkin. "That's awful."

Diana nods. "It was."

"I'm not sure it connects to Lucy Mendoza, though."

"I'm not sure either, but Joe, I can't find the best friend, Rebecca Abrams. Went by Becca. It's like she's fallen off the face of the earth."

Joe balls up his napkin and tosses it onto his paper plate. "I'll run the name and see what comes up." He types it into his phone. "But Dee?"

"Yeah?"

"Don't do anything stupid, okay? Before you talk to anyone on your own, promise you'll call me first."

The air-conditioning is on too high in Paco's shop and Diana shivers. "There's probably nothing there anyway."

Joe's eyes widen. "Dee, do *not*."

"I'll call you if I find something."

"But will you? Don't forget, I know what you do when that nagging something finally makes itself known."

Diana leans forward. "Oh?"

"You take off on your own."

"We're not talking about criminals here, Joe."

Joe stares at her hard. "It doesn't matter. Promise me."

Diana stares back just as hard, thinking. Of Susana. Of her retirement. Of the ways even Joe underestimates her now. "I promise," she lies.

26
JULIA

"DO YOU THINK Lucy ran?" Julia calls out. She stands in the yard of the Victorian where Naomi Bresler has her office.

The therapist sits on the porch, drinking coffee. Maybe she's unwinding after the appearance on Melody Cho's podcast. All Julia knows is that after listening to it, her feet took her here. When she saw Naomi outside, her feet walked themselves right up the brick path to the front steps.

Naomi seems unphased, like women from her group show up unannounced all the time. "Hello. You came to the session yesterday, you're new." She pauses. "Julia, is it?"

"Hi. Yes. Julia Gallo. I know the group meets tomorrow but I was out for a walk and I saw you there . . ."

"It's all right. Do you want to come and sit? You seem . . . anxious."

Julia takes the steps to the porch and parks herself in a chair across from Naomi. It's true, she can't sit still.

Naomi sips from her mug, watches Julia but says nothing.

"You were on Melody Cho's podcast."

"I was."

"I heard you. Lucy attended your group."

"And?"

"Do you think someone took her?" Julia asks.

Naomi's eyes are steady. "Why, do you?"

Julia leans forward, palms pressed against her knees. "I think she was kidnapped."

Naomi's thick, dark eyebrows arch. *Oh?*

"I think . . ." she starts, but then can't get the words from her mouth about the neighbor. So she says something else. "I think that if someone stole me from this life, I might be grateful."

Naomi's posture intensifies, though she barely moves. "Tell me more."

So Julia does. Words spill from her mouth, a waterfall of confessions, the unspeakable finally spoken. She doesn't know how long she talks, but it is long enough for Naomi to drain her coffee. About how sometimes she's so full of despair she can't even turn on the lights, how maternity leave has been the most destructive time in her life, how her husband is always working, how it's like they suddenly dwell in two different universes, how she thinks about other men and how she went out and left the baby sleeping at home alone, so now she must contend with social services. The more she says, the more a door opens within her body, a slight shaft of light shining through and illuminating something of her old self. She pauses for a breath. Then, "Do you have children?" she asks the therapist.

Naomi blinks. "Yes. I did. Once."

Julia's gasp is tiny, but it's audible. "I'm sorry, I shouldn't have—"

"It's all right. You didn't know. And I'd like to keep talking but I have a patient coming soon," Naomi says, "so I'm going to have to go."

Julia's neck, her entire face flushes red. "Of course. I can't believe I arrived here like this and took up all your break. And then asked . . . something I shouldn't."

Naomi places her hand flat on the table between them and meets Julia's eyes. "Don't shame yourself. I'm glad we talked. It's okay that you came. It's okay that you asked."

Julia sighs and nods. "All right. All right. Thank you."

"Will I see you at the group?" Naomi asks.

"Yes. I'll come every day it meets. I'll do anything to . . . no longer be alone."

Naomi sets her empty mug onto the table. "Before you leave, tell me, what does your husband think of what you're going through?"

Julia shrugs. She searches for how to answer, then does the best she can. "My husband is perplexed, I guess. I think he would say he gives me everything, dotes on me and our son, works hard to provide for us. And that I should be happy with what I have. That a lot of women would be thrilled to stay home after having a baby."

Naomi stands and straightens her dress. "And what would you say to that?"

Julia watches as Naomi moves toward the front door of the house. "That I never asked for someone else to give me everything. That the everything he gives is not the everything I've wanted." A weight presses down on her stomach. "I never wanted children for example."

Naomi looks at Julia one last time. "So why did you have a baby then?"

"Doesn't every woman, whether she wants to or not?"

Julia hasn't had this much free time since Theo was born. She walks from the house where Naomi sees clients onward into town, arms swinging, marveling at the looseness of her limbs. She's needed Marcus to take Theo; this one day makes such a difference. Maybe, with a break now and then, Julia can do this, be a mother. Maybe to do it she needs a father in the picture too.

She passes the ice cream shop, the café where she sometimes brings Theo, the pizza place she and Marcus haven't been to since she was pregnant, the little bar where they used to sit outside and watch the ocean beyond the Narragansett Sea Wall. Every step, every lift of her knees is easier because she's alone. The stuff of motherhood so heavy to carry, all the bags, the carriage she must push down the road, up the steps, over the grass, up this curb and down from that one—she never gets used to the weight of it. Now she wonders if her body might float. She turns left toward the beach. She wants to feel the sand underneath her feet.

Julia's phone buzzes in her purse and she digs it out.

It's Maggie.

Julia picks up. "Hi," she says, guilt biting at her.

"Finally! I've been trying to reach you," Maggie says.

The beach entrance appears ahead. "I'm sorry, Mags. But today I'm better. Marcus took Theo to work and it's given me a break. I just . . . I really needed a break."

She can hear Maggie thinking on the other end. She's always been able to sense what's going in her sister's mind. "It's about time Marcus did his share."

Hearing this sends relief and gratitude through her. "It is. It's been hard. I keep fucking up, Maggie. I fucked up really badly when I left Theo alone in the house. But I only . . . I only went a couple of blocks, I had the baby monitor, I couldn't reach Marcus . . ."

"The whole first year is hard, Jules," Maggie says. "We all mess up. But you can't mess up like that again. Leaving Theo alone . . ."

Julia slips off her sandals. "I know, Mags. Trust me, I know."

"Where are you right now?"

"I'm about to take a walk on the beach."

"Call me later then?" Maggie sounds like she cares. "Promise? I want you to enjoy this time while you have it. I don't want you to waste it listening to your older sister's worry."

The waves up ahead call to her. "Okay. I'll be better about calling, I promise."

"I'm here for you," Maggie says. "I'm just a plane ride away."

"All right. We're due a visit."

"I love you. So much, Julia."

Her throat tightens. "You know I love you too."

They hang up.

Julia stops a moment before the high tide line, absorbs the warmth of the sun on her skin, in her sister's words and voice, breathes it in. Allows the light to enter her body. The skirt of her dress swirls around her legs. The tall grasses of the dunes rise high behind her. There's something about the sea that always reminds her of bigger things than herself, her worries, her humble life. The ocean helps her forget the stresses of the everyday, gifts her much-needed moments of beauty. She thinks of sketching earlier, how even though what she drew was about her darkness, it still felt good; she's proud of herself for trying. Julia cups a hand over her eyes to protect against the sun's glare, scanning the horizon. A wave crashes onto the beach, followed by the sizzle of it reaching for the shore. Julia watches this endless cycle. She imagines walking up to the water and laying the burdens of her mind onto the wet sand, placing them into her arms as though into a basket, bending toward the water and letting a wave wash over them, taking them far out to sea. Returning home liberated. Ready for a fresh start.

Julia walks toward the water, wanting to feel it rushing across her toes, inhaling the briny scent. She imagines baptizing herself. She's almost there.

"Julia!"

She halts, turns away from the water toward the sound of her name on the wind. She squints into the bright light, shoes dangling in one hand. "Henry?" For the second time in practically as many days he's right there, a tall shadowy silhouette. "Hi," she calls back, a bit off kilter from the strangeness of the coincidence.

Henry grins, shouting, moving toward her. "So nice to run into you again!" His wild bangs lift off his forehead in the wind. "Another gorgeous day, isn't it?"

The sea recedes as she heads in his direction, wondering if she might break apart in the breeze, atoms going everywhere. Nothing feels quite real in this moment, every single thing she once thought solid, now suddenly strange. The sand is warm on the bottoms of her feet, slippery and moving. Julia reaches up to catch a lock of hair that twists in front of her eyes in the wind, tries to put it back into place but it is only taken up into the air again. *Maybe Henry is a mirage.* When she's barely an arm's length from him, she stumbles and starts to fall.

Henry reaches out and his long arms catch her. "I've got you," he says, before righting her again, casual and unbothered. His hands linger on her body, at her side, her hip. "I guess we had the same thought."

"What thought is that?"

His hand tightens along her hip. "That it's a nice day for a walk on the beach."

Julia steps back, and his hand falls away. "It is, yes."

"How about we walk together?" Henry suggests.

What does Julia want, what does she feel? "Okay?"

Side by side, they start down the sand, the ocean blue and sparkling.

At first, Julia avoids looking at the man next to her. But then she steals a glance.

Meanwhile, Henry talks. He tells Julia about a falling-down barn in a beautiful copse of trees that he bought a few months ago with plans to redo it, about the endless challenges of restoration work, the effort to preserve and yet to also update. Eventually they approach the end of the beach, and Julia wonders what will happen when they arrive at the rocks. A seagull rushes overhead and Julia's gaze follows it. The sky is so clear, the breeze so light. A part of her enjoys how Henry keeps looking at her as he speaks. They reach the rocks and turn to face the water. Julia draws arcs in the sand with her toes, one after the other. She needs to do something as she tries to think of how to fill the silence.

But then Henry asks, "Do you want to sit for a while?" and nods toward the rocks at the end of the cove. "You still haven't caught me up on you yet."

It's true, she's been quiet. It's also been so long since another adult has asked Julia how she is, what she's been up to. The breeze buffets Julia's back and it feels like a push. Maybe what Julia needs is a friend. Maybe that's all she's needed. Not a lover, not an affair, just someone outside the life that goes on in her house. Here's Henry, offering himself.

"Okay," she agrees.

He smiles.

After talking the entire afternoon with Henry, and exchanging numbers before saying goodbye, Julia winds her way back home. She checks her phone for the first time in a long while and her stomach drops. She has a missed call from Daphne. She probably wants to regale Julia with her latest successes. Then Daphne will probe about Julia's depressing new life as a mother so she can feel good about her own choices. No, Julia will not call her back—she won't call anyone from her old life until she's fixed her current one. She continues to stare at Daphne's name on the screen, when her phone pings with a text. It's Marcus.

I'll be home early! Theo misses his mother!

Something in Julia caves, it simmers. Of course, Marcus will be home early, the one day he takes Theo to work. It's already back to reality for Julia, back to family life.

When Julia arrives at the house and turns down her driveway, she nearly startles again.

Her neighbor is standing outside in his yard, smoking.

She'd almost forgotten about him. She hurries along, refusing to turn her head, but then she can't resist—her gaze sweeps left, wondering if he's staring.

Their eyes meet.

She swallows hard. Raises a hand in a wave.

He raises one back.

Does he know she's been snooping through his kitchen window?

Julia hurries toward the steps, sand clinging to her calves and the soft skin on the back of her knees from sitting on the beach with Henry. Grains of guilt. She closes herself inside the front door, locks it behind her.

An image of her neighbor's eyes just now comes alive in Julia's mind.

She heads straight up to her bedroom and into the bathroom, pulls off her dress, turns on the shower, steps inside the tub. The hot water runs across her skin, washing away the sand, but the tiniest specks are so stubborn. They shimmer across her feet, her calves, even her thighs. Julia scrubs harder and harder until every one of them is gone.

27
MICHELLE

#ISUPPORTLUCY.

#IAmLucy.

It's yet another morning, and hashtags like these have started populating the comments section on Melody Cho's article about regret. Alejandra messages Michelle, offering help if she still needs it, which makes her wonder if she was imagining that the intern was taking some kind of stand against Lucy. The young woman was probably just busy, she's doing this for Michelle as a favor after all. Reporters and journalists have found Michelle too, seeking her comments on Lucy. The only request she accepts is the invitation from Melody to write a guest post that will go out with the newsletter. As Michelle pulls out her laptop to write, she pushes away the image of the news van she noticed across the street from her house.

"I cannot believe you did an interview without telling me!" That's what David said—hissed—once the boys were down last night.

She was sitting on the edge of their bed, waiting for the evening's inevitable rematch before they parted ways again— him to the guest room. "I had to do it. You went to the press, now so did I." *We're even.* "Be happy it was just a podcast for mothers and not, I don't know. *The Today Show.*"

David threw his shirt into the laundry basket with far more force than necessary. "Don't be this way. Don't do this to us. Don't do this to *me*."

Michelle stood. "And what exactly am I doing to you? You're the one who started this! These are the consequences for what *you* did. What *you* began. *You* did this to me. *You* did this to us. To Lucy and Sam and to Emma! You should have thought harder before you did it! All of it!"

He opened a drawer, pulled out one of the T-shirts he always wears to sleep, slammed it shut. "Michelle, I thought I was doing the right thing. I'm sorry, okay?"

Those stupid printouts flashed again in her mind. "I don't trust you anymore! Are you involved in Lucy's disappearance?"

David stopped moving. "Of course not! Stop asking me that!"

"The detectives questioned you as a suspect!"

"Don't let them drive us apart. And I told you, it was a misunderstanding with Lucy!"

Michelle's heart thumped in her chest as she thought back to the day of Lucy's disappearance. "You were right near Belmont. We'd just gone to lunch."

David tugged the T-shirt over his torso. He met her eyes. "I swear on our children that I had nothing to do with Lucy. And I'm not having an affair either."

Michelle's body started to shake. She stood in the middle of their bedroom, her reflection caught in the mirror on the wall. "Then how do you explain those messages?"

"You won't believe me if I try to explain because you've decided I'm a villain."

"I won't believe you about what?"

"I don't know, Michelle," David snapped. "Just forget it."

"David—" she shrieked.

But she was too late, David was already in the hall. He slipped inside the guest room and locked the door. She heard the click.

Michelle stares at the blank document on her laptop, still typing nothing. Her mind is full of venomous thoughts about David and what he might be hiding. She can't let this go.

She notices the date in the top corner of the screen.

Lucy's been gone for four days.

Is she okay? Is she alive?

I am Lucy Mendoza's best friend, Michelle types. *I'm certain she didn't run.* What else can Michelle say that will make people believe Lucy didn't leave on purpose, that she does love Emma, how Lucy is a good mother. That a woman is missing. Her fingers travel across the keys quickly now. Eventually she stops, rereads what she's written, rereads it again, then inserts a photo of Lucy from college, beaming and beautiful. She adds another hashtag to the mix:

#FindLucy.

After sending it off to Melody Cho, Michelle writes another missive to Sam. She sends him the link to the podcast recording, hoping he might listen. Michelle pulls out her phone to message the detectives. They've been calling her since the podcast, but all she writes are questions: *Any updates on Lucy? Any news on who might have taken her?*

"Mommy?"

Michelle looks up. Charlie is out of bed, hair tousled, eyes sleepy, staggering toward her in the kitchen. "Yes, Peanut?"

"Where is Tía Lucy?"

Michelle blinks, trying to figure out how to answer. "She's gone away for a while."

"Like on a train?"

"Maybe, Peanut."

Charlie brightens at this and snuggles into his mother's side.

Michelle closes her eyes, pulls Charlie onto her lap so his feet dangle above the floor. She loves his string bean body. "Are you cold?"

He shakes his head, silky hair against her cheek. "Can we take a train to see Tía Lucy too?"

"I wish we could." Michelle rests her chin on Charlie's head, breathes in his smell. Tears pool in her eyes as she tightens her arms around him, thinks of the simple pleasure of holding a beloved child, experiences she wants for Lucy with Emma. She sniffles.

Charlie looks up. "What's wrong, Mommy?"

"I'm just thinking of taking that train to see Tía Lucy." Michelle wipes a hand across her eyes. "I hope we'll get to see her again soon. Now let's get you some breakfast."

Later on when Michelle peeks through the curtains of the living room her stomach drops. One van in the dark of morning has turned into a sea of vehicles on the street beyond their yard. Her attention shifts to her babies on the living room floor, Charlie lining up his cars and Aidan watching his brother intently, doing his best to wiggle his way across his bunny blanket.

Michelle bends to Charlie's level. He's too busy parking his cars and trucks in rows to look up. "Stringbean, you are not to go near the windows today, okay?"

Aidan's eyes shift to his mother, wide, unblinking.

Her heart squeezes.

"Okay," Charlie murmurs, hand gripped around a tiny ambulance.

The phone rings, and she hurries into the kitchen to grab it. "Hi, Michelle."

A rush goes through her. "Sam! How are you? I'm so sorry about—"

"—I'm outside your house, parked down the street. Can I come in so we can talk?"

"Oh! Oh, of course, but there's—"

"Press everywhere. I know, I can see them. I'll come around to the back."

Two long minutes later, Michelle lets Sam inside. She regards Lucy's husband, standing in her kitchen, leaning against the cabinets. He looks like hell. Michelle throws her arms around him and they cling to each other. "I'm sorry for everything," she whispers into his shoulder. "I'll never stop being sorry."

They pull apart. Sam looks up at the kitchen ceiling, at the pale blue ceramic lights hanging over the island. Lights Michelle carefully picked out when details like this used to matter. "I know," he says. "I also get that there's no rule book for this."

Michelle wipes her eyes and moves around the kitchen, fixing them coffee. "Any updates on Lucy?" She glances at him as she opens the canister, begins scooping coffee into the filter.

He shrugs. "Not that I know of. Besides, I'm still the prime suspect."

Michelle pours water into the back of the coffee machine. "Aren't we all."

Sam picks up one of the little Beatrix Potter bowls Charlie loves from the countertop, leftover from his breakfast, a gift from his grandmother's childhood. He inspects the bunny rabbits running along the edge. "The longer this goes on with Lucy . . . gone . . . you know the deal, right?"

Michelle focuses on the gurgle of the coffee maker. She has prayed that her appearance on Melody Cho's podcast might cause Lucy to reach out if she did run. The fact that Lucy hasn't gives Michelle the most awful, sinking feeling. That her attempts to maintain some hope that Lucy's all right is just magical thinking. But she refuses to lose hope. The alternative is too awful to consider. The plate underneath the coffee pot sizzles loudly. "How's Emma doing?"

"She's her happy little self." Sam's voice cracks. "I'm glad she's too young to remember."

Remember. This word hangs in the air. What, exactly, will there be for everyone to remember? Will it be a Lucy found, alive and well, or . . .

The machine sputters, then stops. Michelle pours coffee into mugs, three sugars for Sam, no cream. She knows so much about this man who is her best friend's husband—how he likes his eggs, that he eats his steak rare, that he snores and sometimes suffers from insomnia, that he used to be an engineer before he changed his life and became an artisan of beautiful frames and began working out of their garage. Lucy's always pulled in so much money in real estate he's been able to devote himself to his craft.

Michelle holds out a mug to him, sees that her hand is shaking.

Sam takes it, slurps some coffee.

Michelle does the same. "Listen, I know the press is awful,

but the conversation about Lucy is changing. If people care about her, they'll search. We need them to search."

The rings under Sam's eyes are even darker than when she saw him last. "I wish there was something more that I could do to help. That we could do."

Michelle watches Sam standing there, sounding so hopeless. "Well, I had a thought."

Sam's expression shifts from desperate, to curious, to hopeful. His eyebrows arch. *What?*

"Hear me out," she starts, slowly. "It involves enlisting the press."

28
JULIA

#ISUPPORTLUCY.

#IAmLucy.

Julia is at the postpartum moms group, where Naomi Bresler is holding court again, her hair pulled into a tight bun today. Everyone is talking about Cho's podcast from yesterday and the hashtags that have multiplied since. About the survey Cho put out into the world for mothers to share their deepest secrets.

That word, *regret*, suddenly everywhere.

Noor is three women away from Julia in the circle. "Does anyone think people really mean what they're saying about Lucy? That they are her, or support her? I think..."

Naomi's gaze lands heavy on Noor. "You think what?"

"I think"—Noor's eyes seek the floor—"that like everything else online, it's just a performance."

Hearing Noor say this crushes Julia, and the hope that if she's open about her own true feelings about motherhood that she won't be met with hatred, or dismissed as not knowing her own mind.

The thin, freckled redhead in the group inhales sharply. "Well, let's be real about this." Her long fingers fly as she speaks. "Two conversations are happening about Lucy—the one sparked by Cho's newsletter, and the one taking off in the wider press about how mothers are all monsters no matter what we do, and blah, blah, blah, but Lucy is the most monstrous of us all."

"And?" Naomi prompts.

"Noor's right," the redhead goes on. "In the end, anything anyone says in support of Lucy at this point is bullshit. Lucy's secret is out, and whether she's alive or dead, she'll never live it down. She confessed that she regretted her baby and one day her baby will grow up and know the truth about her mother and that, simply, is a tragedy."

Murmurs ripple across the room.

The vertebrae in Julia's back are disintegrating, her torso collapsing in on itself. She thinks of Theo in the daycare room on the other side of the house, where the babies and toddlers are watched so the women of this group can all talk in peace. When Julia woke this morning she wondered if Marcus would take Theo to school again, but it didn't seem to occur to him, and Julia wondered if yesterday was just an aberration. A personal day for his wife, but as with so many jobs she only gets two per calendar year, one of them already used up.

"There is no escaping this," Julia finds herself saying out loud. "Not ever. Is there?"

The women in the group turn their gazes to her, this circle's newest member.

"No escaping what, Julia?" Naomi presses.

The therapist's expression beckons truth from Julia's deepest center. "Motherhood."

Naomi's gaze intensifies. *Say more.*

"I will never be released from what I've done. *I* did it. I could have stopped it yet I did not. I went ahead and had the baby and motherhood is the price I must pay. That I will continue paying forever. I will never be anything other than a mother from now on..." Julia's words trail off and she realizes the room has gone completely quiet. "I wonder if this is what Lucy felt too. This sense of finality."

A few women shift uncomfortably in their chairs.

Another clears her throat loudly.

Then the redhead says, "I know exactly what you mean when you talk about the inevitability of motherhood, which can be daunting, but that's not the same as *regret*."

But isn't it? Julia thinks. And she didn't say inevitability, she said *finality*.

As in, like a death.

Julia chooses not to clarify—she just nods once at the redhead, a quick bob of her head. When her eyes return to Naomi, she wonders if the therapist can see the truth behind her eyes.

"*Uh-uh-uh-uhhhhh.*"

Julia bounces Theo on her knee at the kitchen table while he experiments with sound, his voice vibrating in his mouth. Soon he will be talking, forming actual words. What will Theo say to Julia? She holds him steady with one arm.

In her other hand a pencil moves across a page of her sketchbook. Another Monster-Mother, this one with a pair of detached eyes that float in the upper corner, as though they look down from the sky. Familiar eyes—her neighbor's eyes.

"*Uhhhhh-uh-bahhhhh.*"

Julia feels she owes Lucy a debt. She can't pry Lucy from her mind. Well, Lucy or... She tightens her arm around Theo's middle. "You agree with me, bug? You think there's something going on with the man next door? That he's been watching us? That if there's the slightest chance Lucy's in our neighbor's basement, we owe it to her to find out, after she's given so much to so many women?" Theo continues to warble, Julia's knee bobbing to prolong his little game. "Let's get you fed. You hungry?"

Julia sets down her pencil and gets up, hoists Theo onto her hip and prepares his bottle.

He stares at her, blinking.

"What are you thinking, huh? What's going on in your little brain?"

The bottle turns on the glass dish inside the microwave, Julia listens to the noise of it whirring. She gives Theo a quick kiss and he giggles. The microwave beeps, the bottle is just warm enough, so she settles Theo into the special pillow Maggie sent her for feedings, so he's able to hold the bottle himself.

Her phone pings and she grabs it from the table.

A message from Daphne—she sees the first couple lines of it on the screen:

You didn't call me back and it's been too long. I wanted to see how motherhood's treating you, catch up, tell you about my upcoming show . . .

Julia swipes it away from view. She just can't.

But then a sadness sweeps over her, at how a good friendship can suddenly be so marred by jealousy. No, Julia corrects herself—it's a good friendship marred by *motherhood*. Yet another loss to add to the rest. Her gaze returns to the open sketchbook on the table, but these feelings have chased away her energy to draw, Daphne's sheer existence like poison to her now. What's the point of trying?

Theo watches her as he sucks on the bottle.

Julia forces herself to brighten. Her inspiration to sketch may have disappeared but there's something else she can do, she realizes. "You know what? Today you and Mama are going to bake a cake!"

She gets to work like a person possessed, moving around the kitchen, telling Theo about each of the things she's doing. Julia puts a stick of butter into a hot patch of sunlight that pours through the open window, then pulls out her baking things, cake pan, flour, sugar, eggs, vanilla. She sifts the ingredients together into a bowl. She opens cabinets until she finds the electric beater which has sat untouched for months, decides the butter is soft enough. Soon she pours batter into a pan and puts it into the oven to bake. Sets a timer on her phone.

Meanwhile, another text has come in from someone unexpected:

Henry.

It was nice to bump into you again. Let's do it next time on purpose?

A whoosh goes through Julia. She stares at Henry's words, debates a response, wondering about Henry's intentions and trying to figure out her own. Julia takes the nearly empty bottle from Theo and plucks him from the pillow so she can burp him. She glances out the kitchen windows as she pats his back. Today she has activities other than Henry on her agenda.

When the timer sounds, she pulls on the oven door to check the cake, sticks a knife into the center. Almost done.

"We're going to meet the neighbor today," she tells her son. "Isn't that exciting?"

• • •

An hour later, Julia rings the neighbor's bell with the tip of her elbow. Her heart pumps faster, adrenaline floods her. Like she's watching a scary movie, but finds herself inside it.

Theo gurgles and smiles at her hip.

Julia balances a red velvet cake in her other hand. It's slathered with cream cheese frosting. Julia spread it all over with a knife, then licked the knife clean. At one point Julia put a tiny dot of frosting on the end of her finger and let Theo taste it, even though she knows she shouldn't give him sugar, that sugar is akin to baby poison. At first Theo was skeptical, but then he opened his mouth, his little tongue darting out to lick. The way his eyes lit up!

He practically bit off her finger.

She gave him a little more, his reaction too delightful to resist, the animal desire it provoked in him. Maybe these small pleasures will eventually add up to Julia enjoying motherhood. Maybe motherhood is about weathering this early part until it gives way to something more manageable, maybe even something she could love. Maybe everything is going to be okay one day.

Julia moves her elbow toward the bell, rings it again, arms aching. She shifts her weight to the other foot. *Where is this man?* His car is in the driveway.

She adjusts Theo higher on her side, the cake heavier and heavier. She's about to give up, when she hears footsteps.

Thump. Thump, thump.

The drawing back of a curtain.

Then again, *thump. Thump. Thump.*

Julia's heart jumps back and forth, in and out of her chest.

The door opens with a creak.

Julia puts a bright smile on her face.

There he is. Her neighbor, not even two feet away.

Look at those eyes.

Yes, yes. Now she has it. She has *him*.

"Hello," she chokes out, cheerfully. "I'm Julia, your neighbor? I've been meaning to come over for ages to introduce myself, and bring you something sweet. I love to bake." She's lying, she almost never bakes. Her eyes dart from Theo to the cake back to her neighbor. His empty expression is even more frightening up close—but his eyes are also strangely beautiful, a cold, bright blue. The next time she sketches them, she'll get them right.

"Hello," the man says. His face changes, like he's trying to smile. *Is he?* "I'm Richard. You didn't have to do this." He lifts the cake from her forearm, relieving her of its weight. He turns, places the cake somewhere inside the house, doesn't invite her in.

Julia shifts Theo to her other hip. She gives him a kiss on the forehead. "This is your other neighbor, Theo," she trills.

For the first time, the man, Richard, smiles. "Hello there," he says, and bends forward, puts both hands over his own eyes then moves them away, *peekaboo*.

Theo laughs. Then buries his face in Julia's shoulder.

The man is still smiling. Genuine this time. His eyes soften.

Julia's relief is immediate. Look at this, he's a nice man. How can she have suspected him to be some kidnapping psychopath? He's obviously just lonely, not used to talking to strangers, but easily charmed by a baby. Babies are like that, Julia's learned, they make strangers talk to you, bring smiles to the faces of the grumpiest men. People grow kinder around babies.

"How old is he?" Richard asks.

"A little over nine months."

"That's a nice age," he says.

"Oh, do you have any children?"

He shakes his head. From the look in his eyes, there's a sad story behind this.

A wave of guilt crashes over her—for snooping, for imagining terrible things.

Poor lonely man.

"Why don't I cut you a piece of the cake?" Julia suggests.

The man hesitates, then opens the door and moves aside so Julia can head into the house. She plunges forward across the doorstep and into the living room, the layout exactly the same as hers. Everything is neat at least, if modest and spare. Nothing to be afraid of. But then the door shuts behind Julia, the light eclipsed with it. The room is dark—darker than is comfortable. Something inside Julia swoops and dips, crashes through her body. Her heart rate picks up faster. She remembers the middle of the night, this man emerging from his basement with dishes, spoons. She imagines a woman trapped in the basement, this very moment, Lucy Mendoza beneath Julia's feet, listening, hoping that whoever is here might realize she's only a few feet away. Chained to a wall? Starving?

Julia swallows. *Already dead?*

She forces herself to remember the smile the man gave to Theo. *Poor man.*

Richard picks the cake up from a side table, carries it as Julia hustles into the kitchen, Theo bumping against her hip. It's cleaner than when she was snooping through the windows. She opens cabinets, searching for a plate, searching, searching.

Her eyes sweep across the floor, scanning everything. *For what?* The hair tie she thought she saw the other day? Julia can feel her neighbor standing behind her, watching her look for dishes, and as she plucks a knife from the big block on the countertop. She talks the entire time.

"Marcus is my husband, I'm sure you've seen him coming and going. He works as a professor at URI. I'm an illustrator, or at least I was until I had this little one"—she plants another loud kiss on Theo's head. "It's been hard to work lately. Having a baby is a big adjustment." She swivels around, moves toward her neighbor. "Trade?" she asks, then laughs. She means the baby for the cake. "Do you mind holding Theo?"

Her neighbor's face registers surprise. "All right," he says.

She hands her son over.

What am I doing?

The man she's been watching do strange things at night, who's been surveilling her through windows, takes Theo into his arms. Her baby goes completely quiet—eerily still. Unease creeps up her spine. She shoos it off, places the cake onto the island, slices into it, the knife long and sharp. She cuts a big piece and places it on the plate she pulled from the cabinet. She rests a fork she found in a drawer alongside it. The color of the cake's insides is bloody. What was she thinking, making red velvet? Her eyes dart all around again, but there is nothing of note. Maybe she imagined that hair tie. Probably she did. She reaches for her son, who reaches back—is he relieved to no longer be held by this man? Can Theo sense something—danger? "Thank you for holding him."

Richard passes the baby to his mother. "He seems like a good little boy."

Julia is about to respond, *Yes, he is,* smiling wide. But then she sees something in her peripheral vision. Or does she? Is it a mirage? Another hallucination? A woman's dangly earring. Lying against the baseboards near a door. The *basement* door. Maybe a sister's? A mother's?

Lucy Mendoza's?

She shifts her head slightly.

No, she's not imagining it.

She sees it with her own eyes.

The curving hook of it to pierce through the ear is clear as day. But the earring itself is impossible to make out, the way it's wedged along the edge of the wall.

How long has it been there—years, or just a couple of days?

Julia feels Theo squirming in her arms.

She moves her head slowly away from this piece of women's jewelry.

Did Richard see Julia seeing it?

He clears his throat—loudly.

An unpleasant static rolls all the way up the back of Julia's neck.

She's afraid to meet the man's gaze.

Out of nowhere, Theo bursts into tears, followed by loud wails, a high-pitched scream, bloodcurdling, then shrieking.

Inconsolable shrieking.

"I'm so sorry," she says to Richard. Then, "Little bug, what's the matter?" She presses Theo to her chest. She plants a few kisses on top of his head, whispering for him to *shhhh*. She looks at her neighbor apologetically. "I'd better go, this one obviously needs his nap. I hope you enjoy the cake! The frosting is cream cheese!" She pushes past the man and heads through the living room, nearly in a run, calling back over Theo's cries, "Please stop by any time, really, don't be a stranger! My husband and I really would love to have you over for dinner!"

Julia's free hand reaches for the doorknob. For one horrible second, it occurs to her, *What if he locked it? What if I'm locked in?* But then she twists it and the door is opening and Julia is walking outside into the day again, bathed in light and breathing in the fresh air, lungs heaving, gulping it down. The moment she crosses from her neighbor's yard into her own Theo grows quiet, as though he senses they are back on safe ground. Home sweet home.

29
DIANA

DIANA IS JUST going to take a little ride. She wants to say hello to Joanna D'Angelo's husband, Luca, at the clam shack he owns down in Watch Hill. See if he's around to tell her how things are going these days. Rule out a connection. Or the opposite?

When she's near the fork for Route 1 and 1A, a call from Susana sounds over the Bluetooth. Today's the day Susana babysits her grandkids after school since neither parent can get home from work in time. Diana debates whether to pick up but she gives in. "Hola, mi amor."

"Are you near the house?"

"No, why? Did you forget something?"

"I meant to turn on the Crock-Pot before I left and didn't. So we'll have dinner later?"

Diana pulls onto the windy road that will eventually give way to some of the most beautiful ocean views in Rhode Island, not to mention the nicest houses in the state, some of them nicer even than the oldest ones in Newport. "Oh. I'll do it when I get home."

"And when will that be?"

"Not sure yet."

A sigh from Susana. "Amor, por favor, tell me you aren't doing anything stupid."

"Definitely not." A gorgeous New England beachfront house on a rocky bluff comes up on the left, owned by one of the most famous musicians in the world. "I won't be long. Give Kiko and Esperanza kisses for me. I've gotta go, amor," Diana adds, and hangs up.

This village by the sea appears ahead and Diana finds parking. She gets out, takes a big inhale of the briny air. Once September is over and the nicer weather slips away, all these little shops selling swimsuits and cover-ups and seashells and ice cream will shutter for the winter and this place will be a ghost town. Only the year-round residents remain, subsisting on a couple of diners and one coffee place until spring. Not even Narragansett gets as quiet as Watch Hill.

Diana heads along the sidewalk, the ocean on her right. Soon Jo's Clam Shack appears near the old carousel—Jo's as in Joanna's. Joanna D'Angelo grew up and took over the family business her parents had named after her, which is now run solely by her husband, Luca. There isn't a line at the shack, the season already pretty much over. A good time to talk to the man if he's here. He used to always be working when Diana was making regular trips to talk to him.

A MISSING flier for Joanna is tacked to an otherwise empty bulletin board near the shack. It flaps in the breeze, tattered and faded. The photo is from the day Joanna disappeared: a selfie she'd posted to one of her accounts. Joanna stares into the camera like a ghost from the past, her too bright pink lipstick garish against her overly tan face, her dyed blond hair, her too much makeup in general. Elaborate chandelier earrings dangle halfway to her shoulders, and a white tank top shines against her weathered bronzed arms and neck, Joanna a sun worshipper according to her friends and family. "A total townie," one of her girlfriends had told Diana once. But the smile Joanna wears is big and open; it reaches her eyes and those eyes are kind. It upsets Diana to think about how much a woman's appearance, her level of affluence, her race, will determine whether the public and press rally around her or dismiss her as unworthy of their interest. Then again, that interest can quickly turn into a feeding frenzy, as Lucy Mendoza's friends and family are figuring out.

Diana walks up to the window of the clam shack.

There's Luca, dark circles under his eyes.

He startles when he sees Diana. "Detective. I wasn't expecting you today."

"I wondered if you could talk a few minutes."

He adjusts the visor of his *Jo's* baseball hat. "You and everyone else lately."

"I'm sure."

"The only good thing about this Lucy Mendoza situation is that it's got people looking for my wife again."

A seagull waits near Diana, sensing a possible lunch. "I bet it's been hard."

"Every goddam day is hard, I'm lucky I've got my mother to watch Franny." Luca puts a cardboard sign in the window that says BE RIGHT BACK. "Hang on, I'll come around."

Soon Luca appears, holding a greasy paper bag. Diana's stomach growls at the thought of clam cakes. Luca points toward a bench, with a view of the clam shack. "Let's talk there." He hands her the bag and a thick pile of napkins. "I remember how much you like these."

"I do, that's nice of you." Diana reaches inside for a clam cake as they walk toward the bench. She holds the open bag toward him. "You want one?"

Luca makes a face that tells her *no way*. "I can barely look at the things."

They sit down. Diana splits the clam cake down the middle to let out some of the steam. Before she can ask Luca a question he starts talking. She eats as she listens.

"Here's what I told the FBI," he says. "I'm glad they're looking into Joanna again and all that, and maybe this Lucy Mendoza does give them new leads and blah, blah, but the more I learn about her, the more I believe their situations are different."

"Oh? Why is that?" She tears open another clam cake and waits for it to cool. A seagull squawks nearby on the edge of the dock, hoping for leftovers.

"Yeah. I mean, first, Joanna adored Franny and she couldn't have been a better mother. Sure, she wasn't the greatest wife. Sure, she cheated once upon a time, I get it, but we were working through that, as you know. By the time she disappeared, things were a lot better. Franny was the direct result of that, as you also know."

Diana takes in the state of Luca, his greasy shirt, his tired face. "You still don't believe Joanna took off."

He shakes his head. "I don't. I really don't."

"Lots of people don't think Lucy Mendoza ran either."

Luca shrugs. He reaches into the bag in Diana's hands and pulls out a clam cake, tears it into pieces and tosses it toward the seagulls that have gathered like it's a party. They dive for it and he tosses another. "Maybe she did, maybe she didn't, but I swear to you, Joanna never would have run because she never would have left Franny behind. No way. No. Fucking. Way."

"What about the other boyfriends we discovered when Joanna disappeared?" Diana asks, trying to be gentle, though knowing there's really no gentle way to raise such a subject. So much unwelcome information came out about Joanna because of the investigation. When Luca doesn't answer she continues, "Plus there are your . . . cousins." She turns her head, their gazes meet.

Unspeaking, they study each other.

In Luca's eyes, she sees beyond the exhaustion, the frustration, the shame he's lived like everyone else who finds themselves on the wrong side of a disappearance, forced to go through the tragedy of suspicion, followed by the humiliation of having one's most private and personal pains hung out for public consumption by not only journalists but everyone else with a social media account—which is basically everyone. Not to mention the unfortunate associations of some of Luca's family members, which complicated everything about Joanna's disappearance. Beneath his stare is a man with nothing left to hide, someone who's telling her the truth, who believes to his soul—despite his wife's affairs, despite having a child so late in life, despite the maybe-mafia part of their story—that Joanna did not run.

For a long, ugly moment, Diana wonders how badly she's failed him. How badly they all have, by assumptions made and searches given up too soon.

The clam cakes in the paper bag are growing cool and hard, soon they'll be like rocks. They need to be eaten immediately or not at all.

"Detective," Luca says, holding her gaze hard, unwilling to let it go. "I know Joanna is not Lucy Mendoza. That Joanna is, or *was*, Rhode Island working class, that she didn't post bikini photos looking like a model that people could pick apart, or lust after, that she didn't even go to college, never mind the fancy one Lucy Mendoza went to. I know she had . . . *boyfriends* and I know about all the other extenuating circumstances related to my family. But I promise you, she's either missing because someone took her or because she's dead."

Diana is the first one to blink. "I know you believe that."

Luca stands abruptly. "I don't just believe it, Detective. Have a good rest of your day."

She watches him walk away, back to the clam shack, watches him remove the cardboard sign to invite the customers that aren't coming. She sits there on the bench a long time before she stands up and ambles back to the car. She drops the paper bag still half-full of clam cakes into the trash; they're already stale. Even if they were piping hot, she couldn't stomach another one.

On the ride home Diana turns on the talk radio station. Clara makes fun of her for listening to it, since apparently nobody listens to such things anymore. But at Diana's age, old habits are hard to break, plus the younger generations don't know what they're missing. She's been listening to these Rhode Island guys ramble on about every single thing for decades. From Buddy Cianci's multiple runs at the mayor's office to his multiple stints in jail for multiple felonies, to discussions about the Patriots' latest game to, god, all the way back when the Claus von Bülow trial was in full swing, the husband who put his heiress wife, Sunny, into a coma.

Not surprisingly, today the subject is Lucy Mendoza.

"The announcement about our local missing mother is

imminent," Ron Valenti is saying. Diana recognizes his voice as clearly as she recognizes Susana's. "And apparently we should begin in around five, ten minutes."

"What's about to begin, Ron?" Diana asks into the car.

She turns the volume up as she pulls onto Route 1.

30
MICHELLE

SAM AND MICHELLE are about to step outside Sam's house, *Lucy's* house, to begin the impromptu press conference they called today.

"Are you all right?" she asks him.

Cradled in Sam's arm is a framed photo of Lucy, smiling at their wedding, radiant, gorgeous, and oh-so-Lucy. Michelle's pulse races, each hour that passes feels more urgent. She wishes she could stop time for her friend's sake.

He nods. "I'm just glad . . . I'm just glad to finally do something."

"Me too," Michelle agrees.

"Are you ready?"

Michelle's heart beats inside her throat. "I hope so." She reaches out to open the door, but then Sam's mother calls down to them. "Sam, honey, can you come here a sec?"

"Hang on, sorry," he tells Michelle, and runs up the stairs to see what Rachel wants—probably to try to convince her son one last time not to do this.

Michelle takes a deep breath. She straightens her dress, smooths it down over her body. A thrill goes through her about what lies ahead, an excitement she hasn't experienced in a long while—not since she had Charlie, and she's nearly forgotten what it's like.

Being a mother has made Michelle feel important in so many ways. She had no idea how consumed she could become with a single, tiny person. Then it was two tiny people, filling up her heart, tugging at her soul. Her being shifted—sideways into a different track, the Michelle-as-Mother track. An easy shift, so seamless she almost didn't notice how her professional concerns, the people at work, had faded like they never mattered. One day, while she was still nursing Charlie, she became acutely aware of the weight of him cradled in her arms, his little feet pressing into her thighs, the sound of his sucking. Despite the all-nighters, the lack of sleep, at the center of it all was a stillness Michelle had never known. She didn't want to ever leave this peace. She had never been happier. This was when she determined she wouldn't go back to work. That if she and David could swing it financially, she would quit. Before Charlie arrived, she'd even prepared herself for the postpartum depression that might come from the loss of her previous life, from the professional cost of motherhood. What Michelle hadn't prepared for was the pure joy. The wonderful contentment. The wholeness. The lack for nothing else.

But there is another kind of feeling important, and Michelle has recently begun to remember its contours, what it is like to be needed, but not by a child.

Michelle tugs at the fabric at her hips, trying to give herself a bit more room, self-conscious about the bulges where, in theory, there should not be bulges. When she was getting dressed for this press conference, she avoided her reflection in the mirror across her bedroom. She'd quickly headed into the bathroom to put on lipstick and do something with her mess of hair. As she fluffed and brushed, she conjured Lucy; imagined her sitting along the edge of the bathtub while Michelle got ready to defend her on camera.

"You need a haircut, cariña, let's get you one," Lucy said in Michelle's mind. "And let's update your wardrobe, get a manicure too. I know, let's give you a makeover!" She could hear Lucy's voice rising, getting carried away with her plans for Michelle.

Michelle had turned and sought out the spot on the tub's edge where Lucy always sits, a perch she's occupied countless times when they've been getting ready for dinner or drinks. Michelle said out loud to her imagined friend, "I'm too old for makeovers, Luz."

"You and I will be eighty and still getting makeovers," she pictured Lucy saying back.

"Oh Lucy," she'd said to the empty bathroom. "How I miss you."

The image of Lucy vanished. But the memory buoyed Michelle.

She hears footsteps and sees Sam descending the stairs. "Are we good?"

"Yeah, let's go," he says.

Then Sam is next to her, reaching for the doorknob.

Michelle manages to feel a little hopeful. They are going to find Lucy, and this is how. Michelle is how.

The afternoon light is a shock to her eyes.

A sea of press awaits them.

Click, click, click go the cameras.

"Did you kill your wife?"

"Did you help her run away?"

"Is there an update on Lucy?"

"Did you know your wife regretted your baby?"

"Is that why you killed her?"

Michelle steels herself. Shields her eyes, her body from their cameras, the shouted demands, the ugly questions. Tries not to flinch. A part of her marvels at how—with a single phone call from Sam—a podium has materialized on his front steps, a microphone. Who put them there?

Sam steps up, inhales, opens his mouth.

Everyone quiets.

The framed photo of Lucy is held high in his hands. "This is my wife, Lucy Mendoza. And regardless of how you dissect her in public, she's a wonderful mother."

Click, click, click go the cameras.

As Sam talks, Michelle's eyes scan the crowd of reporters, podcasters, YouTubers. She wonders what they are thinking, if they are buying Sam's praise for his wife as a mother of Emma. Michelle cannot tell if their skepticism is too great, if once Lucy's confession was let out it took on such a life of its own that it will be impossible for her to live down.

Maybe even if she's no longer living at all.

Michelle clutches her middle at this awful thought, then banishes it.

Besides, now it's her turn.

Sam moves aside.

She steps up to the mic.

Click, click, click.

"Hello, I'm Michelle. Lucy is my best friend. I've known her since college," she says, speaking the words she practiced in front of the long mirror in Lucy's room upstairs. "Everything that Sam said about Lucy as a person, a mother, is true, but I'm not here to vouch for why Sam and I think—why we know—someone took Lucy. She and I have not gone more than twenty-four hours without being in touch in nearly two decades of friendship." *Click, click, click.* She stops for a breath and catches one of the reporters, another woman, rolling her eyes. But she needs to keep going. "I'm also here to tell you about the monetary reward for any information that leads to finding Lucy."

Murmurs ripple across the crowd on the lawn and spilling into the street.

Then the shouts resume.

"What reward?"

"Is this reward sanctioned by the police?"

"Do the police even know you're here?"

Click, click, click.

"Who's funding this?"

"Sam, are you doing this out of guilt?"

Michelle licks her lips. "Some of you watching may be familiar with Melody Cho of the newsletter *Demystifying Motherhood*, and her podcast, where I was a recent guest. If you want to know more about what I think of Lucy, you can listen to my conversation with Melody or read the article I wrote for that same newsletter." The shouts die down as Michelle continues to talk. "Melody Cho has generously agreed to sponsor a GoFundMe campaign to raise money for this reward and Lucy's safe return. Sam and I are each donating five thousand dollars. I know there are other people who support Lucy and want to see her found. If you go to Melody Cho's website, you'll find more information about the campaign, plus the link to donate on behalf of Lucy." A swirl of feelings churn within her and she wonders if she might faint. "Please, we need your help. A woman is missing."

Michelle can see it: the faces of these people have changed with this new information. A thrill goes through her. Maybe this is the moment that everything shifts for the better, that begins Lucy's return home.

"I want to thank Melody Cho for her support, and that is all," she finishes.

Once again, everyone erupts into shouts, cameras clicking.

But Michelle can hear something else beyond the din before her eyes.

Sirens fill the air, blaring, screaming over the reporter's yells.

Police cars screech to a halt in front of Sam's.

Well, Michelle supposes, *at least now they've got the police's attention.*

31
JULIA

JULIA IS SITTING on the floor of her living room in front of the coffee table, sketching.

She draws jagged, skeletal letters along the slope of a woman's enormous head, face obscured by matted hair. MONSTERHOOD. In each corner is a pair of eyes. One belongs to Marcus, one to Theo, one to Naomi Bresler and the last to the man next door. The pencil in her hand digs hard into the page, scraping out the *D*, so absorbed in this work she can nearly block out Theo's wails as he sits there, inconsolable on his blanket.

He just won't stop.

She won't either.

Not until she's done.

There's no way she'll give up this motivation after so long fearing she's dried up.

The letter *D* finished, she eyes the front door. Wonders if the woman across the street is listening again for babies crying, gearing up to make another house call. Julia finally looks at her son's tear-stained face. "What is wrong, huh? Why won't you stop crying? I fed you, changed you, what else could you need? Are you mad at me for taking you next door? Are you worried the neighbor is a serial killer too? Did he frighten you? Did I?"

Theo only shrieks louder.

What would Maggie do?

Her sister has the magic touch, she got all the genes in the kids department. Maggie would probably tell Julia to get in the car and drive Theo around, or get him into the carriage for a walk, but she's already done those things today.

Theo screams and Julia jumps.

"You've got a lot to say today, don't you."

Julia is about to scream too. But instead she closes her sketchbook and gets up, goes over to the speaker in the corner of the room. She's not sure what possesses her. She tells it to play the '90s playlist she and Marcus used to love.

"Groove Is in the Heart" pours into the room, and Theo's cries stutter. Soon they quiet.

Julia wipes the tears from his cheeks. "You like that? Do you want to dance?" She studies her son, his eyes wide, blinking, watching her like always, just like in Julia's sketch. He deserves more than Julia, she wishes he had a better mother. He turns toward the sounds coming from the speaker. "So that's a yes, you would like to dance?" She picks Theo up and takes his chubby little fist in her own, bounces him to the beat of the song, sings the lyrics loud and off-key. A tiny smile appears on her son's face. She plants a big wet kiss on his forehead. "You like dancing with Momma? You have good music taste too?"

Theo laughs.

She tells the speaker to raise the volume.

Thank god, she thinks to herself as they dance away.

And also, *This is nice*.

She dances even more goofily, and Theo giggles and shrieks.

Julia takes in the joy on her son's face as the song changes.

Another upbeat tune floods the living room, and she finds herself laughing. For a moment, she forgets how hard her days have been, and she can see the tiniest of lights at the end of a long, dark tunnel. Faint, but there.

After Theo is down for his nap, Julia still glows from their dance session, voice hoarse from singing so loudly. She slides onto the bench against the wall in the kitchen and pats her cheeks. They're red and hot from all the exertion. "Wow," she says to no one, and chuckles. She hasn't laughed this hard in ages. In fact, she can't remember the last time she laughed so much.

Maybe motherhood isn't all bad. Maybe it can even be . . . Wonderful?

Julia puts a hand over her heart, feels the happy pound of it.

A bubbling inside her chest, an energetic fizzing.

A different, lighter kind of inspiration than that of her latest artwork.

She smiles even though there's no one here to see.

The phone on the corner of the table comes to life, vibrating.

Julia reaches for it and sees that she's missed quite a few messages.

Henry: *Are you free for coffee this week?*
Maggie: *Have you seen this?*

She doesn't click on Henry's text.

A half hour of fun with her son is potent, it works like a barrier, rising tall between Julia and the temptation of Henry. She wants that wall to grow, get strong enough to keep her on the side of her best impulses rather than the worst.

Julia clicks on the message from her sister instead.

Can you believe this woman was from your town? Did you ever see her around? Your babies are practically the same age.

It's followed by a link to a video of a press conference.

Something about the phrasing of Maggie's message stops her heart.

It's Maggie's use of the past tense in relation to Lucy Mendoza.

Julia rubs a hand across the back of her neck, clicks on the link. Watches the video until the friend, Michelle, gets to the part about the reward, then hits *pause*. A hotline phone number glares red at the bottom of the video. She moves the cursor back and replays that part, not because she wants the money, but because . . .

What if Julia actually knows something about what happened to Lucy?

Her eyes want to go to the windows of the kitchen, her body wants to get up and move toward the side of her house that faces her neighbor's yard, to go out the door and dare to peer inside the basement. But then Julia clicks on the link beneath the video, and it takes her to the guest post written by Lucy's best friend for Cho's website. The link for the GoFundMe page is right at the top of it. Julia starts to read.

Why is it so terrible when one of us admits she made a mistake? Michelle writes. *We're raised as though motherhood is our primary purpose in life. We're brought up to bear children without questioning if it's for us or not. Then some of us realize it's not, actually, for us.*

A swell of something expands in Julia's chest. Relief? Companionship? Hope? That wall built by thirty minutes of fun with her son grows higher. Maybe Julia can find her way through this hell, to a place where she isn't in hell. Maybe it's a world where she's happy being a mother, a world where she isn't a monster. Could that world exist for Julia?

Julia rereads all the things the friend, Michelle, writes about Lucy. If only Julia and Michelle were friends too, she could tell Michelle her most shameful thoughts, and Michelle would still love her. Maybe all Julia needs is to say out loud what she's going through and find that still, she is loved. Can getting through this moment be that simple? Can it be solved by love?

Maybe.

But then Julia scrolls to that big phone number on the screen, glaring red.

The plea for information.

Could that earring Julia saw on her neighbor's kitchen floor be Lucy's? Is it crazy for her to even wonder? Or is it the sanest thought she could have? Really, what if that earring *is* Lucy's and Julia does nothing? And what if she *did* see a woman's hair band on the floor that day she went snooping into the kitchen? But no, Richard *cannot* be the man that kidnapped Lucy Mendoza. *What are the chances? Seriously, what are they?* If Julia isn't crazy already, not knowing for sure is going to drive her there.

Julia opens her laptop and the screen comes to life. She tries to think of every term that might bring up the information she seeks and puts those words into the search bar on her laptop.

Lucy Mendoza jewelry parking lot
Earrings disappeared woman
Regretful mother wearing hair band
Lucy Mendoza style

Photo of Lucy Mendoza when she disappeared
Lucy Mendoza, last seen wearing what?
Lucy Mendoza accessories
Mendoza Lucy woman regret mother gone outfit
Mendoza vanished baby parking lot accessories ponytail

It doesn't matter what Julia types into the search bar, nothing comes up. Well, plenty comes up, just nothing helpful. Should Julia call that hotline? Leave an anonymous message: *Did your friend Lucy typically wear earrings? Do you think she was wearing them the day she disappeared? I'm pretty sure I saw a woman's earring on my neighbor's kitchen floor. Maybe also a hair band a while back? And this man lives alone. I know that probably sounds like nothing, but you have to understand—there's something about this man.*

Julia moves the cursor of her laptop to the search bar again.

"What are you doing?"

Julia jumps. Marcus is standing beside the kitchen table. She slams her laptop shut. She can't look at him. They still haven't really talked about what's going on in their marriage. "I didn't hear you come in."

In her peripheral vision, Marcus crosses his arms. "What were you doing on your laptop that you need to hide from me?"

"Nothing." She dreads Marcus finding out she's been searching for information about Lucy Mendoza, even though half the country is interested in this woman's disappearance. She worries talk of Lucy will lead to talk of Julia.

Marcus isn't budging. "Julia."

So she scoots over on the bench, makes room for him to sit, opens her laptop. Luckily the last thing she'd clicked on was Michelle's article from Lucy's website.

Marcus's eyes flick back and forth as he reads.

Julia rests one of her elbows on the table, head in her palm. "I've been following the story, okay? Is that a crime?" She hopes Marcus doesn't put the cursor into the search bar and see the list of her previous searches about outfits and style and accessories. She watches her husband scan the rest of the article, sees how his body relaxes.

The suspicion clears from Marcus's eyes, replaced by something else. But what?

"People have been talking about her at work in the faculty room," he says. "It's awful."

"It is awful," Julia agrees. Suddenly she sees the possibility of connecting with Marcus on this subject and all sorts of things sprout in Julia's mind. Like a door opening that would allow her to tell Marcus the truth about how she's feeling, all because of Lucy Mendoza's disappearance. Marcus will hear her finally, tell her they'll get through this as a couple. Then they'll spend time with their son, have some fun, and Julia's hope will grow until this period of her life is so obscured she'll barely remember she went through it. Yes. She looks her husband in the eyes. "I hope Lucy Mendoza is okay. I want them to find her. People are saying such terrible things, all because she was struggling. The poor woman." Julia waits for Marcus to agree, for this conversation to go where she longs it to.

Marcus's face registers surprise, then disagreement. "Poor woman?"

"Well, yes—"

"She abandoned her own child. She *planned* her own kidnapping, she *left* her infant daughter in a parking lot!"

The air goes out of Julia's body, her back curves like the bowl of a spoon. "We don't know that Lucy Mendoza ran away," she says quietly. "She could be anywhere." *She could be right next door.*

"I think she ran." Marcus states this like he would somehow know this truth.

"But why do you think that?"

"I just do."

"You aren't being fair."

"How so? Explain it to me. Explain it all, Julia. I've been waiting for you to."

They are no longer talking about the missing woman, Julia realizes. They're finally talking about each other, their marriage. Memories flash to a time when Julia was—when they were—happy. When she believed her love for Marcus was solid. Julia places a hand on the edge of her laptop screen, pulls it down until the light blinks off, the article gone from view. "I think it's brave that this woman's friend is defending her."

Marcus is working his jaw, Julia sees the way it clenches. "Once you have a baby, you have to live with the consequences. There are no easy outs. That's just the deal."

"It's more complicated than that and you know it, Marcus."

"No, it isn't," her husband says quietly. "I can't believe social services got called on us."

Julia's insides are calcifying. If she tries to get up, or move at all, she will crack and break. Her lungs, her organs, turning to pieces. Her whole body, falling to dust on the kitchen floor. She stares at the oven, the stovetop above it, the pot sitting on one of the burners ready for her to cook pasta. "Sometimes women don't realize they should have ended a pregnancy until they've already become a mother," Julia says deliberately slowly.

A long silence stretches between them.

When Julia looks at Marcus again, she sees that his eyes are full of horror.

Then, "What are you really trying to tell me, Julia?" he asks.

"I could ask the same of you, Marcus."

Marcus's gaze narrows. "I don't understand how you can be so forgiving of this woman."

"I don't understand how you can be so unforgiving of her."

"Why are you fighting me on every single thing, Julia?"

"I'm not."

"You are."

"You don't see me anymore." These words are whispered from Julia's lips, but she hears the truth as though she screamed them.

Marcus jerks backward. "What are you talking about?"

"You only see me as Theo's mother. The mother of your son."

His lips part. "Of course I see you as more than *that*."

That.

Julia is boxed-in on the bench, this corner of the kitchen, the table jutting into her middle, Marcus to her left. She considers sliding to the floor, crawling underneath the wood top and between the legs out the other side, but the monster inside her, the one she keeps sketching, is too big. It's taking over. "You leave everything to me. Taking Theo one day to your university doesn't count, Marcus. You have no idea what my life has been like. I'm in this all alone." She dares to look at him. "Maybe we should wait to talk about this."

"What, exactly, is *this*, Julia, that we shouldn't talk about?" Marcus asks.

Julia closes her eyes, hoping for something to save her. For Theo to wake up and start crying so one of them will have to go and soothe him, for something, anything, to stop this conversation from moving forward to its inevitable conclusion. Thunder, lightning, an act of god. Yet nothing is coming, so she readies her words, tries to gather them to answer.

The front doorbell rings, two loud chimes cutting through the tension.

Marcus gets up. "Are you expecting someone?"

Julia shakes her head. "No."

"Who do you think it could be?"

"I have no idea." She takes advantage of the moment to get up and out of this corner. She stands in the kitchen's entrance and watches as Marcus opens the door. But there is no one there.

He bends down to pick something up. "What's this?"

He brings the object back to his wife.

Julia recognizes what's in his hands and her heart speeds up. "It's a cake plate."

"Why would someone leave a cake plate on our doorstep?"

Julia stares at the empty dish. "I brought our neighbor a cake, the old man next door? He's just being polite and returning the dish." *He ate it awfully fast*, she thinks.

For some reason, Marcus laughs. "You made him a cake? That's so sweet. We probably should have done that a long time ago. God, you were pregnant when he moved in. That feels like a lifetime ago, doesn't it?" Julia sees the relief on his face, how he likes that his wife made a cake for the man next door, a sure sign there's still a good little woman living deep inside her. "He left you a note," Marcus says.

She takes the plate, a wedding gift from someone or other. Taped across the center of it is a torn piece of notebook paper, a bulge underneath it. Curiosity, sharp and clear, cuts across

Julia's mind. She lifts the edge of the tape, peels back the paper.

"Is that a little wooden duck?" Marcus picks it up. "It looks homemade."

"It does," Julia says.

"Well, that's very nice of him."

The duck is small, carved, the lines of the feathers, the eyes, carefully etched into the grains of the wood. The blue-green of the feathers, the black of the head also clearly hand-painted. Admiration for the work that went into it fills Julia. It's such a lovely object, the kind of toy that no longer exists, that can only be found in an antique shop, or stored in the attic of someone's grandmother. A relic of a past era. *Could it have been Richard's when he was a baby?* As she studies the beauty of the artisanship, she wonders if he made it himself. *Could this be what Richard's doing in his basement at night? Carving children's toys?* Yes. That would make sense. The possibility consoles her.

Marcus inspects the underside of the paper, the handwritten note. "Thank you for the delicious cake. Richard." He takes the duck from Julia's hand to inspect it more closely himself. "Really, this is so thoughtful. He's probably lonely."

"He probably is," she agrees.

Marcus looks like he wants to cry. "You're a good person, Julia. I'm sorry about before."

"It's okay," she says quickly, even though it's not. Not really. Not yet.

Marcus's eyes drop to the toy again. "I love that he gave us a gift for Theo."

"Yes." *No.*

As Marcus turns the wooden toy around in his hands, Julia

notices something on the bottom of it, letters etched into the base? Worn away and difficult to read.

"Look," Julia says, plucking it from his palm. "Maybe it's a name?"

They bend closer. "I can't quite make out the letters. Maybe that first letter is an *E*? Even an *R*? I can't tell if that's an *m* or maybe an *n*? They're too worn away."

"Or maybe . . ." Julia halts, nausea ripping through her. *E* and *m* for *Emma*? Isn't that the name of Lucy Mendoza's baby? She tries to swallow, her throat too thick. Where did she hear that, the friend on the Melody Cho podcast? Dark thoughts return to Julia.

"Maybe it's his mother's? A sister's?" Marcus suggests. "This could be pretty old."

Now all Julia can think about is the baby of Lucy Mendoza. She's sure she read that the daughter's name is Emma. What if this duck is that baby's? What if Lucy had it in her pocket when she was taken?

First the maybe-hair-band, then the earring, now this?

A shiver runs down her spine, Julia worries she might faint. And where did that cake go so quickly? Could her neighbor have thrown it out? Did he share it with someone else? Down there under his house? No, no. No.

"It's probably an *R* and an *e*. And maybe that's an *n*? For Rene?" Julia guesses.

What if the red velvet cake is all Lucy Mendoza has been given to eat in that basement, what if she isn't given any fruit or vegetables, only sugar and flour and butter? Julia should have brought over a salad instead of a cake, or a stew full of protein and vitamins.

She needs to see into that basement. Doesn't she?

Marcus is still smiling at the wooden duck. "I'm going to go and put this on the shelf in Theo's room," he says. But before he trots off with it on his way upstairs, he turns back a moment. "When social services shows up, we're going to be ready, Julia. We'll deal with it together."

Julia watches him, helpless. She tries to stop her suspicions and doubts from circling, but she can't forget the stupid earring. She can't be sure about the hair band, but that earring was definitely there. Now all sorts of other ideas spring to life in Julia's mind about the man next door and the missing mother the whole world is talking about. Lucy Mendoza. They are always coming back, she realizes. No wall is high enough to keep them out.

32
MICHELLE

MICHELLE IS IN Lucy's home office, sitting at Lucy's green painted desk. Surrounded by the sunny yellow walls, her sky blue bookshelves. A pink upholstered chair in the corner by the window. As usual, Lucy's world is a riot of happy color, such a contrast to the darkness of the present.

Lucy is going to be found alive.
Lucy is going to be all right.
Lucy is going to find her way back to us.
Lucy is going to live a long and happy life.

Michelle pens these wishes one by one in purple ink on a notepad from Lucy's desk. Lucy's name is bolded at the top of it in bright green lettering, the same green lettering on her business cards. In one of the longer emails Michelle received in response to her article, the writer told her she needs to send out positive messages to the universe about Lucy. Normally, Michelle doesn't believe in such things, but right now she'll try anything.

Lucy is going to fill this house with her laughter again.

She puts down the pen and stretches out her aching fingers.

A framed photo of Emma sits on the corner of Lucy's desk. She picks it up. Emma is only days old. So tiny, delicate, eyes shut tight, fists shut tight, perfect little nose and lips, swaddled in a soft white blanket. So beautiful, her whole life ahead. As Michelle waits for the detectives downstairs to finish admonishing Sam for the press conference so they can turn to scolding her, she wonders why Lucy chose this photo for her office. It marks Lucy's beginning as a mother, doesn't it?

She returns the frame to its place and leans back in Lucy's chair. Stares at the photo of Lucy's father hanging on the wall, a black and white from when he was a child, maybe six or seven, standing in front of the tiny house where she grew up on the outskirts of Santiago, Chile. Lucy's always loved this picture. Hanging next to it are several others: a photo of Lucy's parents at their wedding, a hand-drawn sign made by her dad for his house-painting business, a photo of Lucy's mother holding Lucy as a baby, before her mother died of a stroke when Lucy was still a child. As Michelle takes in the collage of keepsakes that decorate this office, she realizes that collectively they all represent beginnings.

"Why, Lucy?" Michelle asks aloud, as though Lucy were here to give an answer.

Maybe Lucy's losing her mother so young has something to do with why she'd surround herself with the evidence of lives only just beginning. If only Michelle had asked this question of Lucy sooner, she might have gotten to know her friend in new ways.

Will she still have that chance?

The detectives made Michelle leave her phone on the kitchen table downstairs, "To make sure you don't take any more matters into your own hands in the next sixty minutes," Detective Suarez had said. Without it she can't see what people are saying on their socials in response to the press conference, which she supposes is the point of taking it away. She can't check their GoFundMe campaign for the reward either. She wonders if it's climbing. She hopes it is.

The drawers in Lucy's desk beckon. She opens them, one after another. They're vacant except for a stray paperclip or two, a tuft of dust, a torn scrap of paper. Whether emptied by the police investigators or the FBI, Michelle isn't sure, but someone has taken nearly everything. Aside from the photo of Emma, the keepsakes on the walls, and the furniture, there's barely anything left of Lucy in here. Not her work laptop, not her accolades from her real estate successes. How in the world could a pointy glass trophy have anything to do with Lucy being taken, or Lucy running away? Even Lucy's framed photo of herself and Michelle, each one holding the other's new baby, both of them grinning madly, is gone. Why would the investigators take it—because Michelle's a suspect? The idea sends a shiver through her. She looks around the office again, this place where people systematically removed nearly all signs of Lucy in the name of an investigation. The notion that some of her most precious keepsakes, the symbols of her professional success, are boxed up in some dank evidence locker makes Michelle queasy. As though someone packed up and stored away Lucy's things because they already know she won't be coming back to claim them.

No. *No.* Stop it. Michelle looks at that hopeful list she's made on the notepad. "Everything will be okay," she says to the universe.

She gets up from Lucy's desk chair.

Whoever tore this office apart left behind Lucy's books. They clearly went through them and put them back out of their usual order. Thick real estate tomes are hastily stacked, mixed in with Lucy's textbooks from when she took her first course to become an agent, her guidebooks to the area packed with information about the different counties and their specific sites and restaurants that might interest new buyers. She loved having hard copies to open up and show people, so they could flip through a book with their own hands. One shelf is lined with the real estate portfolios Lucy offers prospective clients searching for an agent, boasting Lucy's accomplishments and accolades from former clients. Michelle helped her design them. Dozens of the thin volumes stand on the shelf, side by side.

Michelle goes to the bookcase. Why would the detectives not also take these? Or maybe they only took a couple and left the rest? She slides one of the portfolios out from the long row of identical copies. The hardcover binding is simple—a plain light, shiny blue—but the insides are full color, glossy, sturdy pages. Thick. Expensive. She opens the little volume to the beginning, the binding cracking. She pages through it until she arrives at Lucy's bio.

"Hi, Lucy," Michelle says. "I see you there. I miss you."

The photo Lucy chose to accompany her bio is purposefully casual, unlike her colleagues and their formal, school-like portraits. Michelle remembers talking through the choices with Lucy before she selected this one. Here, Lucy's walking through the tall grass of the dunes way down Narragansett Beach, smiling, a knitted scarf around her neck, thick brown sweater over jeans and ankle-high rainboots. Her eyes are bright, her hair long and glowing red in the sun. The background is slightly blurry, the focus all Lucy. Approachable, friendly, smart, successful, this photo says all this of Lucy and more. Beautiful, it says too. Of course it does.

Michelle runs a hand across the image. "You look so good

here, Lucy. So alive." She looks around the room as though Lucy might be listening. "Please still be alive, Lucy?"

She shuts the book, unable to bear reading through the accolades, see the magazine-ready images of Lucy's favorite houses, the materials that Michelle helped Lucy conceive and edit once upon a time. She returns the book to the shelf among the rest.

Then she notices something strange.

She bends forward, peering at the tops of all those bindings. "Huh."

One of them is different. On the outside it looks the same, but Michelle can tell the pages inside are plain, they lack the evidence of color photos marking the edges, lines of glossy black, slivers of blue and green. The paper itself for this one is thinner.

A mock-up maybe? The draft copy Lucy received before she ordered the rest? Michelle thinks harder, then it comes to her: the blank book she'd ordered when they were deciding on the binding, its color and design.

Michelle's breaths are audible.

It would be easy to miss if you didn't look closely enough.

If a person just assumed these books were all the same.

Her heart beats faster. Her fingers reach for it, grip it, slide it out. She opens the book, she swallows, starts to read. As she does, a lightbulb flickers on in her mind. A memory— the start of one, surfacing. Followed by a full-body chill. She clutches the book against her body, feet taking her across the room before she realizes they're moving. She flings open Lucy's office door.

"Somebody come!" she shouts. "Come quick! I've found something!"

• • •

The thirty seconds it takes the detectives to come upstairs feel like hours.

Somebody else knew, Michelle's mind pulses as she waits in the hallway.

"Somebody else knew!" she says the moment the detectives round the banister for the second floor. *And it wasn't David*, she adds in her mind.

Suarez is the first to enter Lucy's office. "Somebody else knew what?" Marist is close behind him.

The book that looks like one of Lucy's real estate portfolios lies open wide on Lucy's desk. Because it isn't one of her real estate portfolios. Michelle points at its pages which are filled with writing—in two different hands. "Somebody else knew about Lucy's regret. Someone other than me." She tilts the book at an angle, presses a finger into the paper. "Look." She watches the two detectives as they read. Shifts from one foot to the other. "Where's Sam?"

"Downstairs doing what he's been told for once," Marist says.

Suarez looks up from the book at Michelle. "Start from the beginning and take us through everything step by step, okay? How did you find this?"

Michelle explains how she came across the different portfolio and holds it out to Suarez. "It's one of the mock-ups from when Lucy and I were designing her portfolio. She was using it as a kind of journal, it looks like. And see?" Michelle points to a few lines of script. "This is Lucy's handwriting," she says. "But this"—Michelle moves her finger higher on the page—"this writing is from somebody else."

Suarez takes a pair of rubber gloves from his pocket, puts them on, reaches for the book. "And you don't recognize this script?"

Michelle passes it to him. "I don't."

Suarez flips through the pages. Quiet. He brings the book closer to his face, reading. "This is almost written like a Q&A, like someone was prompting Lucy to give specific answers about her . . . 'regret.'" He looks up from the book at Michelle. "But who was asking the questions?"

She immediately thinks of Melody Cho. "I have someone you can contact to ask. She might have ideas." A cold anxiety rushes through Michelle after she suggest this. *Could Melody Cho be a suspect? The way she's involved herself in the investigation from the beginning . . . isn't that what killers do?*

Something else inside Michelle unlocks—she hears the click of it, a door swinging open. Appearing in the light of her mind. The memory in full. It fills her throat and moves out of her. "There's something else . . . something relevant maybe. I can't believe I didn't think of it until now."

It was a few days before Lucy disappeared.

Can you come over? I need you.

Michelle read this message from her friend after she finished putting the kids to bed. "David, I'm going to Lucy's. You okay with the boys?"

The television was on in the living room, but David was scrolling on his phone. He looked over at his wife and shrugged. "Sure. Tell Sam hello."

The car keys jangled loudly from the way Michelle grabbed them off the hook on the wall. "Love you," she said, and hurried out the door.

On the way to Lucy's, Michelle wondered what was wrong and why Lucy needed her so urgently. Lucy had seemed better, going back to work had done wonders for her mood. She'd been watching Lucy carefully and what she saw was Lucy finding her footing, little by little. But what if Lucy's toehold was slipping again? She pulled up in front of Lucy's and got out of the car, thinking the worst as she rang the bell. The door opened.

Lucy stood there amid the light of the living room behind her. "Hey! Thanks for driving over so fast."

The muscles in Michelle's body immediately relaxed. "You're okay."

Lucy glanced behind Michelle, left then right, all around, as though she was expecting someone else to arrive. "Yeah, come in," she finally said.

Michelle followed Lucy inside the house.

Lucy dropped onto the couch and patted the spot next to her. "I'm sorry I worried you. I didn't mean to." She curled her feet underneath her.

Michelle sat down and grabbed one of the colorful throw pillows, hugged it to her chest. A tiny bead of worry returned. "Are things okay with Emma?"

Lucy nodded. "She's fine. It's just . . ." For a second, Lucy's expression faltered. "Sam is going to be late tonight. And I . . . I didn't want to be alone."

"Any particular reason?" Michelle was fishing.

Lucy's eyes darted to the coffee table then bounced away. On it was a thin blue book, Michelle recognized it as one of the portfolios Lucy gave out to prospective clients. Beside it was torn brown paper, like it had been wrapped up and sent in the mail.

Lucy shrugged. "I don't know. I . . . well, sometimes I just feel vulnerable lately."

Michelle nodded even as she wondered what, exactly, Lucy meant by vulnerable. About something to do with Emma? Or about something at work? Michelle's gaze landed on the portfolio book again and she guessed that maybe Lucy was doubting herself. But then, why the wrapping paper? Had someone mailed back to Lucy her own marketing materials? A disgruntled client? Was this what had her so unsettled? "It takes time to get back into the swing of things after a baby, but soon you'll be your top real estate agent self again," Michelle reassured her. "You've been doing so great already. You need to be kind to yourself right now."

Lucy's brow furrowed. She inhaled a big breath, lips parted like she was about to say something else, but the words never emerged. Instead, she closed her mouth again. Then after another beat, Lucy reached for Michelle's hand and squeezed it. "I'm just glad you're here," was all she said.

33

DIANA

THE TWO-HOUR DRIVE to Trey O'Neil's workplace takes three hours. Even though Diana slipped from the bed this morning long before Susana would stir, the traffic on I-95 is awful. Diana inches along the highway, thoughts of her conversation with Luca about his wife still lingering.

She wonders if she should call Joe and mention where she is headed.

But then, what really does she have to tell him? She'll try him after she sees Trey. Besides, he'll be dealing with the fallout of the press conference from yesterday on the investigation. Surely, everyone is calling in dead-end tips about Lucy, sending the police scrambling to see if anything is a real lead. This is always the problem with monetary rewards.

Diana switches between listening to podcasts and news shows dedicated to Lucy Mendoza and her disappearance—or her self-planned kidnapping, depending on who's talking.

The car rolls to a stop again on the highway. Diana picks up her phone from the passenger seat and hits play on a show she'd paused earlier to take a call from Clara.

"—Lucy Mendoza is probably sitting in some far away bar picking up men, while the whole country searches for her, and this baby cries for her mother," a man is saying.

Diana rolls her eyes, the car crawling forward slightly. She stares at the tractor trailer that's been in front of her for thirty minutes, blocking her view of everything else.

"Or," a woman's voice says from the speakers, "what if Lucy's friend Michelle is right, and the woman is locked up in some psychopath's shed while we wonder if she's in Paris and malign her suffering? Which, by the way, has implications for every mother in America!"

Diana presses harder on the gas. Maybe the traffic is finally loosening.

"Anna," says the man. "I don't care what the best friend or some mommy podcaster—Melanie? Melody?—says. We likely have someone who planned her escape to get out of *a choice she made for herself* instead of weathering a few play dates and Mommy and Me music hours like everyone else."

The car picks up speed, the traffic definitely starting to break up.

"Oh?" responds the woman named Anna. "How many Daddy and Me music hours have you been to, Richard? Or does your *wife* weather those?"

"Anna," says another voice, the host maybe. "Let's not make this personal."

"How is this *not* personal? This is the most personal topic there is! We have a missing woman whose life may be at stake and all anyone can do is condemn her and debate whether or not her feelings are real!"

"I think Lucy Mendoza—"

Diana presses pause on her phone and the voices fade.

Trey's exit comes into view and Diana takes it, glad to be off the highway. GPS guides her through the streets of this small town. Soon she turns into the parking lot of the garage

Trey owns. She hopes he'll be there or else she'll have driven all this distance for nothing. But the best way to get information out of someone is to show up unannounced.

She gets out of the car.

The lot is packed, the place booming. She counts five garage doors spanning the shop, all wide open, all with cars in various states of repair and readiness, a black sports car raised high with a worker staring up at its engine. There must be what—ten, twelve?—mechanics bustling about. Feet stick out from underneath an SUV, a pickup truck.

Despite Diana's reason for being here, she's happy to see Trey's business is thriving; that he's made his way beyond so much early tragedy in his life.

A man in navy blue coveralls nods at Diana when he notices her, points toward the office so she shifts direction. She heads inside.

Another man typing behind a computer looks up. "Hello, how can we help you today?"

Diana shakes her head. "Actually, I'm looking for Trey, the owner. Is he around?"

The man hesitates, maybe trying to suss out whether she's a disgruntled customer.

"I'm an old friend from when Trey lived in Rhode Island," she explains. "I was in the neighborhood and thought I'd stop in and say hello. I'm glad to see that he's faring so well."

The man's shoulders visibly relax. "Sure, I'll go get him. What's your name?"

She decides to just tell him. "Diana González. He'll know who I am."

Then she eyes one of the visitor's chairs and sits down to wait.

• • •

Ten minutes pass, maybe more, before the man returns to the office.

Diana stands up.

"You can head on back," he says. "Trey was just finishing a call. He remembers you," he adds, but doesn't elaborate.

Diana walks through the door behind the check-in desk and down the narrow hallway. Another door stands at the end of it, open wide. She pokes her head inside. "Trey?"

He's sitting behind a desk stacked with papers, printed-out receipts, a model of an old Corvette Stingray displayed on the corner. There's a streak of grease across his cheek and another up his arm. He wears the same navy blue coveralls as his workers, the name Trey stitched across a patch on the left breast pocket. He eyes Diana but doesn't say a word.

She takes a step inside. "I know this must be a surprise."

Trey doesn't move, doesn't nod. But then, slowly, he moves his head up and down. Places his hands on the arms of his chair and pushes himself to standing. "I'm sorry, I'm being rude. But I . . . I don't know. Hearing your name again, it conjures ghosts. And I try not to think back . . . I mean I wasn't expecting this today and . . ."

"I know," she says. "I'm sorry to show up like this. But can I sit?"

"Of course. I should have already asked." Trey gestures toward one of the two chairs on the other side of the desk.

Diana parks herself and watches as Trey lowers himself back to sitting.

"You weren't just in the neighborhood like Manny told me, right, Detective?"

She shakes her head. "No. Though it's just Diana now. I retired."

Trey's eyebrows arch. "Oh? Congratulations then. Good for you," he says.

"I was hoping you could help me with something."

"I figured. But ever since Manny came and told me you were out front, I've been racking my brain about why you'd want to speak to me. Our business was over a long time ago. Wasn't it?"

Diana thought so too. "Have you heard about the missing woman in your old hometown?"

Something dawns in Trey's eyes. "Oh. Yeah. I mean, hasn't everyone?"

"Given some of the more recent twists in her case, it reminded me"—Diana pauses, she hates to open old wounds but she keeps going—"well, the situation reminded me of Maeve's."

Trey blinks. Then he nods slowly. "I guess I could see why. How someone who knew about what . . . Maeve went through. But I still don't understand how I could be of help."

Diana leans forward, runs a finger across that shiny red Corvette. "I'm trying to get my head around something from back then and honestly, I don't know if it's related or not to Lucy Mendoza's case. There's something I can't figure out no matter how I search on Google and people's socials."

"And what's that?"

"I wanted to talk about Rebecca Abrams. Becca?"

Trey whistles softly. "There's another name I haven't thought of in a long while."

"I'm sure," Diana says. "But do you know where she is? What happened to her?"

Trey wipes his hands across the thighs of his coveralls. Then he does it again.

Is he nervous? What?

He sits up in his chair, takes off his hat, and runs a hand through his dark hair. "It's funny you should ask. There's a bit of a strange story there."

Something in Diana's middle flips.

She pulls out a pen and notebook from her purse.

"Tell me everything," she says.

34
JULIA

LUCY MENDOZA'S FRIEND Michelle is getting out of her car a few feet away from Julia.

Julia's pushing a fussing Theo in the carriage toward the café downtown while talking on the phone with Maggie, when she notices Michelle there. Julia's heart nearly leaps from her chest.

"You and Marcus need to get on the same page for social services," Maggie is saying. "This is serious—"

"I need to call you back, I love you," she says, and hangs up. Drops the phone into her bag, then pushes Theo toward the woman getting something out of her trunk. Ever since Michelle went on Cho's podcast, Julia's fantasized about running into Michelle in town, and going up to talk to her.

"Hi, hello?" She maneuvers Theo's carriage between Michelle's car and the one parked next to it. She can barely catch her breath. "You're Michelle, aren't you?"

The woman, the best friend, turns from the box she was about to pick up to look at Julia. "Hello," Michelle says, her voice flat. Suspicious.

Julia imagines she must get loads of people bothering her after that press conference. Julia doesn't want to be like everyone else, she wants Michelle to see that Julia is different. "I . . ." Julia can't get her words out. "You're the friend. *Lucy's* friend."

Michelle's face grows more suspicious. "Yes, I'm the friend. And?"

Julia opens her mouth, curses herself for being tongue-tied after imagining this moment so many times. People pass them on the sidewalk. They park cars, they get out, they get back in to drive away, as Julia searches for words. "I wanted to tell you . . . something . . ."

In her fantasies, this encounter goes differently: she asks questions about Lucy, she tells Michelle about her neighbor. But now there's a reward for information, and Julia's suspicions about the man suddenly seem mercenary. Not only deranged but greedy. What she most wants is for Michelle to *like* her. Besides, surely with the reward gazillions of people are calling in with clues, sightings. She'd just be yet another among the many.

Michelle is waiting for Julia to speak. "What did you want to tell me?"

Theo watches his mother. Something about his gaze breaks Julia open and she says something unexpected.

"I am Lucy too," she tells Michelle in a whisper.

Every last sharp edge in this woman's eyes disappears. This woman who Julia doesn't know, suffering her own terrible losses, reaches out a hand, weaves Julia's fingers between her own, and squeezes. Then Lucy Mendoza's best friend pulls her into a hug.

"You are not alone," Michelle whispers back.

When they pull away, Michelle glances at Theo. "Can I have your phone?"

Julia fishes for it in the bag hanging from the handlebar of Theo's carriage.

"If you ever need anything"—Michelle plucks the phone from Julia's hand, types her contact info into it—"please be in touch. I mean it."

Julia can hear that Michelle does—mean it.

"Thank you," she says, a bit shocked. "I will."

Michelle holds her gaze. "What's your name?"

Her throat tightens, eyes filling. "It's Julia," she croaks.

"It's really nice to meet you," Michelle says.

Julia nods. "I . . . I think of Lucy all the time. I hope they find your friend." As she pushes Theo's carriage away along the sidewalk, she feels Michelle watching her go.

"I hope they do too," Michelle whispers, but Julia hears.

Later on, Julia can't stop thinking about Michelle, how kind she was. She needs to do something. Instead of going to the therapy group, she puts Theo down for a nap. Paces the living room, back and forth. She owes it to Michelle to find out if Lucy is next door. She owes it most of all to Lucy. And maybe she owes it to herself to put this question to rest.

She goes upstairs, peeks into Theo's room, watches as he naps.

Then she heads into her own room and sits on her bed, cross-legged, thinking.

Glances out the window at the house next door.

Marcus won't be home until early evening.

And Theo won't wake up for at least another hour.

Her neighbor isn't home; she watched him drive away fifteen minutes ago.

Goose bumps rise across her skin.

The sun filters through the windows, landing on the bed.

Julia shifts the cross of her legs, presses her palms flat against the quilt, holds herself very still. Tries to keep herself steady. She could call Maggie back. Julia could tell her every single thing, all her fears, her failings, even her suspicions about the neighbor. She wouldn't leave a single detail out. She could even call the police if Maggie said she should. She reaches for her phone, but her hand doesn't quite make it. She turns one more time toward the neighbor's house.

What if time is running out for Lucy?

Julia gets up from the bed, goes downstairs, and opens the closet by the front door. Takes out the toolbox. Searches through it for what she wants. Before she can convince herself otherwise, before she can worry about whether this will be the moment that social services arrives to do their home check, she slips through the back door and crosses the line that divides her yard with the neighbor's for the second time. Covering Julia's hands are gardening gloves, and in one of them she holds a Phillips-head screwdriver.

It's too easy, really, for Julia to get inside Richard's house. Not long after Julia and Marcus first moved in, Julia got locked out. When Marcus came home to find his wife sitting on the front steps, shivering in the cold, he showed her a trick. If she ever got locked out again, all Julia needed to do to break into their house was take a screwdriver and remove the screws holding the door handle in place; this would cause the screws inside to fall to the ground. Then Julia could reach through the hole with her narrow fingers and pull. Their backdoor doesn't have a second lock, so once the handle is off, there's nothing to hold it shut. So easy it's chilling. And her house and Richard's are the same.

She reaches his back steps and grips the end of the screwdriver, gets to work.

Four screws hold the handle in place.

One, two, three.

Each time one comes free, Julia puts it in her pocket.

Julia goes completely still for one short beat.

She could turn around and go home right now.

Imagine if social services chose right now to do their home visit?

No. No, they won't, she decides.

She positions the tool into the grooves of the fourth screw and twists, round and round until it comes loose. She pulls it free, catches the handle as it wavers. She hears a crash inside the house, the handle on the inside falling to the tile on the kitchen floor. This one, she places on top of the steps. It lands with a quiet metal *tink* against the concrete.

She takes a breath.

Now Julia's next question will be answered. Does Richard have a second lock? Or like Julia and Marcus, did he not bother to install one? Does he implicitly trust what everyone says about this town, that it's as safe as can be, the kind of place people move when they're about to have kids? Did Richard choose it knowing he'd be the most dangerous person here?

Julia slips her fingers into the hole. Then pulls.

The door creaks open.

Before Julia does anything else, while she's still perched on Richard's steps, she reattaches the door handle, screw by screw, so when she leaves again she can go quickly. One, two, three screws back in place. Richard will never know a thing. She hopes. Julia twists the fourth one round and round until it's tight. She tries both handles.

Everything works perfectly.

She stands up. Raises her left foot and steps forward, crosses the threshold of her neighbor's house. The back door swings shut with a familiar creak. The click of the latch closing. She's in.

She immediately searches the kitchen floor for something, anything. But everything is clean—so clean. Like Richard scrubbed and buffed after she was here with the cake. Could he have done this because of Julia? Could he have known she might break in? She circles round and round looking along the baseboards, underneath the toe kick of the cabinets. But there's nothing. Not the earring, not a single suspicious object.

Did she imagine it all?

Maybe. Maybe. No. Yes.

She swallows, forces herself to keep breathing.

She should start with the basement, right?

Her head swims, dizzy with fear.

Avoids even looking at that daunting door.

She should get her bearings first, calm down, then she'll tackle it.

Julia moves slowly, eyes combing the kitchen, then the living room, the surfaces of the furniture, all the knickknacks on the shelves and tables of the ground floor. A blue glass violin that looks to be from another age, a water-stained doily stretched across a bureau of sorts, a pantry full of mac-n-cheese. She's careful to touch as little as possible. She just wants to *see*.

If anything jumps out at her. Anything unusual.

Julia's heart beats so hard she can hear it in her ears. She heads up to the second floor. It's too easy, really. The plan of Richard's house is the same as hers, but in reverse. The things on the left side of his house are on the right side in Julia's. This is why Richard's bedroom and Julia's are facing one another. What a stupid person who planned this neighborhood, setting everyone up to see into each other's private lives. Julia peeks into Richard's bathroom. His things are folded, everything in its place. A hand towel here, a bath towel on a hook there. The walls in the upstairs hallway are bare, the paint near the crown molding peeling, but everything is clean, swept. Once again she wonders: *Did Richard know I was coming?*

In the room where Theo sleeps in Julia's house, Richard has an old wooden desk pushed against the wall, a small, oval braided carpet in shades of navy blue and brown, the kind Julia's grandmother had all over the place. She checks the drawers of the desk. Aside from a few electric bills, the gas bill, and some blank paper and pens, it's nearly empty. Nothing of note. Everything in Richard's house is so typical. So normal. Sheets for the bed stacked in a closet, coats hung up in another. Doubts pop up inside Julia. They rise and burst, but more follow.

Where is *it?*

The evidence. Where is the *evidence.*

Of Lucy.

The floor downstairs creaks loudly.

Julia's skin prickles.

She stays still, heart thudding.

But there's nothing. Probably just the house settling.

Julia enters the hallway again, moves toward Richard's bedroom. With one gloved hand, she pushes the door wide, the creak of it loud. She sees a bed, and on it, a cheap, worn comforter. But the sheets are neatly tucked, the bed carefully made. The room is spartan, a single nightstand on one side with two drawers. Julia goes to it, pulls the top one open. Like the desk, the nightstand doesn't have much, but when she moves aside a notepad, she sees something interesting. A Polaroid of a baby, swaddled in white, cradled by what must be the mother. Julia raises it closer to her face, studies it. An old photo, edges curled, colors faded. The mother is smiling at the baby nestled in her arms, a bonnet on the baby's head, the mother's eyes full of love.

A keepsake from another woman Richard kidnapped?

Julia shudders. But she doesn't recognize the woman, it's certainly not Lucy. She returns the photo back where she found it, closes the drawer. Maybe it's just Richard's sibling, or Richard himself with his mother, and here Julia is, invading the man's privacy, this temple to an old man's loneliness. She reaches for the second drawer. Inside it is only one single thing: a laptop. Shiny, new, expensive-looking. So out of place with everything else. She tries to imagine Richard on it, what kinds of things he types into the search bar. She opens it, the screen lighting up. It asks for both a username and a password.

Why would a man who lives alone in a house bare of anything else, without even a television, protect his laptop with a password? What might he worry that someone else might see?

Julia's mind returns to that photo and once again she feels ashamed. *What the hell am I thinking?* She shuts the laptop, returns it to the drawer. But then as she's scanning the room one last time, her heart nearly stops.

On the floor below the window facing Julia and Marcus's bedroom is an ashtray.

Full of cigarette butts. Absolutely overflowing.

Evidence that Richard is watching Julia.

Or, just that he is smoking a lot in front of his bedroom window?

Unease zings through her entire body, rushing through her veins. She really needs to go. She needs to go home *now*. She races out of the bedroom and back down the stairs, not caring about her feet thundering across the wood. Something has turned on inside her—reason? terror? both? The house seems darker than when she entered. She reaches the ground floor and heads around the staircase and into the kitchen again because Julia is going to force herself to finally look. And there it is—the door to the basement. Just like in her house.

But also not.

"Holy shit."

Above the knob is a lock—and not just any lock.

Heavy duty, massive, thick.

Requiring a key.

Was that lock there when she was here with the cake?

Julia racks her brain, but she can't remember seeing it that day.

What's in the basement that Richard suddenly needs to protect like this?

It's out of place in such a spare house.

And it's not the kind of lock she could break into—no way.

But maybe it's not bolted?

She has to at least try to go down there, doesn't she? If only she hadn't been so afraid when she first entered. What's the point of breaking in if she leaves without seeing what, exactly, Richard is doing underneath this house? Maybe all she'll find is a workshop where he makes wooden toys and she can finally let go of this obsession. Or expensive furniture which is why he needs that lock? Then she'll know once and for all that Lucy Mendoza is not below the floor where she stands, chained to a wall.

Besides, everything is just ... so ... quiet.

If Lucy was here, wouldn't she call out for help? Wouldn't she hear Julia upstairs? Or, would she think it's Richard? Or maybe she's sleeping? Maybe Lucy no longer has any idea whether it's day or night? What if—*what if*—Lucy Mendoza really is, this very moment, right beneath Julia's feet? Cold, alone, hungry, afraid, traumatized by things Julia won't allow herself to imagine but still, they are difficult *not* to imagine? Neglected? Starving?

A strange feeling comes over her, like a heavy, warm blanket. A kind of resignation, a relinquishment of fate from her own hands to that of another. Before she can change her mind, she reaches for that basement door. Curls her hand around the knob and turns it, wondering if it will open despite the lock above it and she'll soon find Lucy curled up on the floor. But the door doesn't budge. She needs to find the key, but where? She looks around frantically, it must be somewhere in this kitchen. She moves to the other side of the island, about to start searching the drawers—when finally, she hears a sound.

The sound of an engine.

Out front.

Julia's heart lodges itself into her throat.

Richard's car arriving in the driveway.

Did he somehow guess that I'm here?

Julia races through the kitchen toward the back door, the pounding of her feet matching the pulsing in her throat. She reaches for the knob and halts, listening.

The engine goes silent outside.

She needs to go—now.

Right as Julia is pulling the door wide, she hears another one opening and slamming shut, the driver's side of Richard's car. She nearly trips over the threshold between his kitchen and the landing. Before the door can close behind her, Julia manages to catch it, shut it quietly. A knob turns, followed by the creak of another door opening at the front of Richard's house. Julia drops to a crouch, skittering down the steps and racing across the line that divides their two yards. She doesn't look back. She doesn't look sideways. To see if Richard's watching.

Soon she's up her own steps.

Into her own quiet house.

He knows, he knows, Julia thinks.

But what, exactly, does he know?

35
MICHELLE

MICHELLE IS UP in the middle of the night, thinking.

Rain pounds against the windows.

She's given up trying to sleep. She stands in the kitchen and stares out into the darkness. Alone. So alone. She shudders. Her shadow shakes violently on the wall. How long can she survive like this? Not sleeping, barely eating, responding to countless messages about Lucy, in the hopes that the world will forgive her best friend for what—struggling?

She cannot stop thinking about that journal she found in Lucy's office. Why hadn't Lucy mentioned it that night? Or any night afterward? The notion that she truly failed her friend swirls inside her. What if she doesn't have the chance to make it up to Lucy? What if... Will they never find Lucy? Will Michelle ever see Lucy again?

Her gaze travels to the ceiling as though she might see her husband through the plaster and the floorboards and the guest bed mattress between them. Is her marriage over? Was she wrong to question everything about David, even the capacity to do harm to Lucy?

An image of the woman she met downtown, Julia, appears in her brain, clear and vivid. That look on that woman's face, full of anguish. Michelle makes a bargain then, calls out to the universe, to whomever might have the power to decide Lucy's fate.

"If Lucy is found alive . . ." She speaks these words with intention—*if* Lucy's alive *then* Michelle will never fail her friend again. She will not only not fail Lucy, she will not fail other women like Julia either. *If then, if then, if then.*

"Michelle?"

She spins around.

"David?" Her voice cracks.

"Are you all right?" he asks.

"I'm praying and I never pray," Michelle answers.

He says, "Come upstairs with me?"

Despite all that these terrible days have done to them, she follows her husband, heading to the second floor and down the hall. As Michelle moves, her brain, her soul, her heart are balloons floating above her physical self, pulling her toward the heavens, toward something, somewhere. Lucy?

Lucy, is that you?

David turns into Aidan's room.

"Look," he says to his wife.

Aidan is asleep on his stomach, his little bum high in the air. His pajama top has slithered up to his shoulders, revealing all his adorable, soft pudge. This is when Michelle's heart and soul and mind fall right back into her body, *plop*. The sight of her sweet son is all it takes to knit Michelle back together, despite everything else. *What a miracle*, she thinks.

"I remember when Charlie was that small," David says.

"Me too," she sighs.

"I can never forget," he says. "I remember everything about every moment of our sons' lives. We are so lucky, Michelle."

Looking into David's face, Michelle sees the man she

married again for an instant. "David," she says, and leans into her husband's body—because he is offering, and because she needs to rest.

David's arm slips around Michelle's waist, and tightens against her.

They stand there, silent, fragile, clinging to each other among the wreckage of their lives. They watch as Aidan flops over onto his back and starts to snore. The moment pours over them, relieves and releases them, wards off the horizon that, when it comes, will see them parting ways. Michelle is in awe, amazed by how someone so small can hold back the darkness, defeat it, reminding her there is still also light in this terrible world, infusing it with love. She leans into that love and prays that maybe, against all odds, hope will prevail after all.

Thunder cracks and rumbles outside.

As Aidan sleeps below her gaze, safe and sound, she hangs on to this tiny bit of hope for dear life—for Lucy's dear life.

36
JULIA

JULIA IS UP in the middle of the night, thinking.

I broke into my neighbor's house.

From Theo's room, she peers over the edge of the windowsill, searches for movement next door, but it's difficult in this heavy rain. She's certain Richard knows Julia was there. Is she the only person who can sense the killer in him, the kidnapper lurking underneath the facade of the old-lonely-man? Or has she truly gone crazy?

Julia slides back to the floor and stares at her sketchbook. Tonight, she has drawn another portrait, this one of her neighbor and herself side by side. The caption above their heads says, "Monster & Monster." Richard's face looks back at her from the page, those sharp, empty eyes, so much like the ones she sketched on her own face. But are they really the same? Will Julia ever stop punishing herself for not loving motherhood? Is she truly a monster because of her regret?

She flips to the beginning of the sketchbook, to the first portrait she drew of herself. Then to the next, and the next. There are so many now. She grabs her phone and scrolls to Daphne's Instagram, studies it, goes all the way back to Daphne's first posted artwork. Calls up the message chain from her art school friends. What if Julia's life isn't over after all? What if she has the means to find her way up and out of this darkness, back to the woman she believed herself to be, or could become if she let herself try? What if she already knows the way?

A message pops up—yet another text from Henry.

I thought you wanted to see each other again, Julia.

She sets her phone face down on the floor. When she looks up her gaze catches on the wooden toy on the shelf near Theo's crib. She should have stopped Marcus from placing it near Theo. But Marcus would have asked what the problem was, and what would she say?

Well, honey, I'm convinced our neighbor is the psychopath holding Lucy Mendoza in his basement! Even so I brought over a cake along with our infant son and handed him to the man while I took a sharp knife and sliced our neighbor a piece of that cake. Oh, and I also may have broken into his house while Theo was napping and found a pile of cigarette butts by the window that faces our bedroom. It's good social services didn't choose this afternoon for a visit, right?

She should have taken that baby photo she found in the drawer. She should have snapped pictures of that pile of cigarette butts by his window. She should have taken that shiny laptop. She should have broken through that locked door with a hammer if she'd needed one to get down into that stupid basement.

She rises up again to peer over the windowsill.

Tonight, there are no movements next door, no glowing orange circle at the end of a cigarette to signal her neighbor is watching. No Richard coming and going with bowls, utensils, plates of cake, descending the stairs to his basement, like something awaits him. Some*one*. All kinds of thoughts fly through her mind, *Maybe he's just a night owl, maybe he's got a TV room down there, some sort of second kitchen?* If only he hadn't come home when he did, if only she could have found the key, if only she could have confirmed one way or the other: Lucy is chained to a wall, alone and afraid, or no one is there, just some boxes with Christmas ornaments. Old keepsakes.

Did Richard go on a trip? Did he take Lucy somewhere else, because he figured out someone had been in his house today? Someone like Julia?

She wonders what is really down in that basement.

37

DIANA

DIANA IS UP in the middle of the night, thinking.

About what Trey said had happened to Becca.

Susana snores softly beside her in the bed.

Trey and Becca stayed in touch for a while after Maeve and Bridget died. Then one day, out of nowhere, a letter arrived in Trey's mailbox from Becca explaining that she was leaving and promised to never forget Maeve and Bridget, that she would work to honor them for the rest of her life. Trey never heard from her again after that. At first he'd worried that by "leaving" Becca meant she planned to take her own life, that she blamed herself for Maeve and Bridget and was unable to live with her guilt any longer. Eventually Trey took comfort in the notion that Becca must have meant what she said literally: that she was leaving town and starting over somewhere new. Or that was what he'd always hoped, he told Diana. "Becca was an only child and she'd lost both her parents in college, so it wasn't as though I could go to her family and see if she'd told them the same thing."

Diana places a protective hand on her wife's back. Grateful for Susana's nearness, for the light of the lamp beside her, holding off the darkness of the night and the pound of the rain.

Her mind swirls from Maeve and Bridget and onward to Joanna D'Angelo, then to Lucy and Emma and back to Trey and Becca. She needs to find out what happened to Becca.

There's something there, but what?

Could Becca be yet another missing woman from this area, but for whom no one ever searched? Are Rebecca Abrams and Lucy Mendoza somehow connected—by the same kidnapper? Joanna as well? Yet in the parallels Diana can't stop seeing in her mind, Luca is right, Joanna seems different in all of this. Joanna isn't the same as Lucy. Not in age, not in the technicalities of their disappearances, not with respect to their children at the time and not in their attitudes toward those children. But Maeve and Bridget *are* parallels to Lucy and Emma, and Trey is to Sam. And Becca? Becca is to Michelle.

Diana is still missing something. *But what?*

As her gaze lands on a sleeping Susana a swell of love rises in her chest. She tries to imagine someone reaching into her own life to take away this person who frames her days and nights, who brings new joy to her life after she once thought all was lost. Facing a life without Clara's father is already enough grief to endure for a lifetime.

Grief.

What if *grief* is what Diana's missing? What if grief is what everyone is missing? What if Lucy's disappearance really *is* about tragedy? Loss? Regret. Remorse. Things not done, things unsaid, the kinds of things that Michelle Carvalho, Lucy's friend, has been shouting all over the place. A life cut short. A woman's life cut short.

Another woman.

But not in the way anyone's been thinking?

The different stages of grief unfurl in Diana's body and memory, the different kinds of grief she's experienced over the course of a lifetime. A woman's life cut short by becoming a mother. A woman's friendship ended because of missed signs, missed conversations, missed understandings. Isn't this at the heart of so much conversation about regret as well?

A message from Joe lights up her phone.

She reaches for it, reads the words on the screen.

You need to see this.

It's followed by a couple of photographs plus a PDF.

The pictures seem unremarkable at first. But then she opens the doc. Diana clicks the magnifying glass to make the tiny type bigger.

A tingling races across her scalp.

A rushing in her ears.

The missing piece right before her eyes.

Held in her own, trembling hands.

Diana gets up from bed and tiptoes out of the room, all the way downstairs to the first floor. Her eyes scan the screen of her phone one more time, and then she calls Joe.

He picks up immediately. "Dee."

"I know," she says. "I know."

38
JULIA

RAIN FALLS HARD to the ground this early morning, the world rumbling with storm clouds.

Julia's legs are shaking as she moves up the staircase to Naomi Bresler's office, a sleeping Theo clutched tight to her chest in his Björn. With each step she considers turning around, fleeing this house where downstairs she sits in that group. The wet soles of her shoes squeak against the wood, her hair drip, drip, drips. Julia's thoughts and fears from the night leave a murky residue all over her body. She needs to talk to someone like her life depends on it. And maybe it does.

The soft sounds of Theo's breathing are stark against the storm outside. The door at the top of the landing is ajar, but Julia knocks anyway.

"Come in."

She pushes it open.

Today, Naomi's dress is the color of red wine, the sleeves tight down her arms all the way to her wrists. "I'm so glad you called to see me again," Naomi says. "We missed you yesterday at the group. Have a seat and tell me what's going on."

Where does Julia start? With Marcus, Theo? Her neighbor? With breaking into the man's house? The messages from Henry about wanting to see her, so many they're beginning to oppress her mind? Is there something wrong with him? Then there are the self-portraits in her sketchbook, her thoughts about what she might do with them. She remembers that moment too, when she was dancing with Theo across the house, this breathing bundle against her chest. Julia wants her next move to be toward sanity. Toward new life, hope, love. She lowers herself onto the couch so as to not wake him. Reaches an arm around her baby.

Lamps are lit around the room, the glow intimate. Everything cozy and dry.

"Lucy Mendoza," is what Julia ends up saying to Naomi in a whisper, like Theo might hear and understand his mother's meaning. "Everything started with Lucy's disappearance."

The therapist changes the cross of her legs, the clogs on her feet clomping heavily against the wood floor. "What started with Lucy, Julia?"

Julia slips off her shoes, then reaches for one of the throw blankets to tuck around herself and Theo. Rain thunders outside. Lightning flashes. The world so angry. "Me, feeling like . . . like, it's only a matter of time before . . ."

Naomi's eyes are steady. "Before?"

Can Julia really trust this woman?

"I know what Lucy was going through. Her . . . regret." Julia closes her eyes, remembers how her own mother used to tell her that eventually for cuts to heal, you need to expose them. Here she is, exposing the thing that's been cutting her so deeply, hoping it might somehow heal.

"It's okay to not be okay," Naomi says over the sound of the rain. "So many women suffer after becoming mothers, and they're often afraid to express how deeply. If they use the word 'regret' to describe their suffering, they're often told that it cannot be, that they do not know their own minds. But I want you to consider something for me."

The rain falls harder beyond the window, torrential, thrashing the sides of the house.

"What?"

"Has it occurred to you that this doesn't have to be forever?" Naomi leans forward in her chair, elegant hands planted on her knees, expression searching. "You can change things. The question is, how? And what will your life look like when you do?"

A tiny bird alights on a tree branch outside Naomi's window, seeking the shelter of the awning. Tiny and lovely and perfect. A sign of life, of hope amid so much darkness. Julia plants a gentle kiss on Theo's head, lingers in his sweet smell, the fuzz of his hair. "I love my son." She looks up again, eyes seeking the bird. "But this doesn't cancel out the regret. Everyone expects me to be so happy that I had a baby. My husband is so happy we had a baby. But his life didn't change like mine." The little bird is still there and she finds this comforting. Naomi follows Julia's gaze. Together they watch the bird until it takes off in flight, back into the storm. "So I search for these distractions, anything to occupy my mind. And when I think about a future, a future I actually want, I'm not sure it's a future I'm allowed." Julia's fingers curl around the edges of the couch cushions. Her heart is racing as fast as the rain falls to the ground.

"But why wouldn't you be allowed?" Naomi asks. "Tell me the truth, Julia. Don't hold back. You are safe here, I promise."

Yet is she? It's been so long since Julia has felt safe.

"You can tell me anything," Naomi says.

Truly, anything?

Flashes of Julia moving through the neighbor's house light up her mind. Now would be the time to tell Naomi about Richard, to mention the whole ordeal, the sneaking around, the obsessive watching of the house next door, followed by those portraits of her "monsterhood." Something still holds her back. She opens her mouth, closes it. She wants an ally, and she doesn't want to squander this opportunity with Naomi. Maybe if she lets go completely, if she confesses all she's done, this chance will vanish forever like some strange, faraway dream.

But when Julia doesn't speak, Naomi does instead.

"There may be a way I can help," the therapist begins.

Then Naomi tells Julia about her own life, her own past, and how it is relevant to her now. As the therapist's words sink into Julia's body, permeate her skin, Naomi proposes a way out of her regret, or at least, a way through. All Julia has to do is take the hand Naomi offers. Then together, they will start to walk.

INTERLUDE
—

NARRAGANSETT BEACH

A BODY WASHES up onto the sand.

When the rain stops falling from the heavy gray clouds above, a local woman leaves her apartment on the Pier to walk the sea wall. First, she heads all the way to the end of it, past the Coastguard House and The Towers and all the surfers taking advantage of the big waves. Then she walks all the way back to the entrance to the beach. Steps onto the sand.

The sky is dark for daytime.

The part of the beach where the surfers ride their way into shore recedes until there's no one else but her. The waves thunder and crash, drowning out all other sound. She doesn't think much about the fact that she's alone. Why should she? She always does this walk.

The Dunes Club lies ahead to her left and she passes it, extending her walk farther, nearly as far as she can go. She pulls her sweater tight around her body. The rains left behind a chill. Fall is here, finally. She's almost all the way to the end of the beach when she sees something strange. The storm has tumbled thick patches of bright green sea lettuce, sandy piles of popweed, a brown mountain of kelp, and amid it all—a human leg?

The woman lets out a long high scream over the wind.

But no one can hear her.

She's too far down the beach.

39
MICHELLE

THE NEWS OF a body arrives when Michelle least expects it.

She hurries to the store to buy a few things for the kids. They're all out of everything—the snacks Charlie likes to eat after school, the purple carrots Aidan is obsessed with that she mashes up for him. Eggs, paper towels, yogurt. She and Melody Cho are set to do another interview—about the reward for Lucy, and to continue the conversation that has started about motherhood and regret. The story of Lucy's disappearance has ultimately become a story about women in general, Michelle realizes.

All kinds of women. Women and women and women. Women helping other women, women judging other women, women misjudging other women, women talking to and interviewing women, women defending women, women gossiping, women consoling, women regretting, women who love other women unconditionally. Women friends who will do anything for one another because that is what women long for ultimately, someone to go to bat for them, to stand up for them, to be loyal to them until the bitter end.

Michelle will be loyal to Lucy until the last breath she takes.

She races across the parking lot at the local mall. She doesn't usually come here, but there's a supermarket, and she can't bring herself to go to Belmont. Maybe she'll never shop there again.

An alert dings on her phone. Then another. And yet another.

Michelle waits for a car to pass so she can cross toward the mall's entrance. She's slightly annoyed by how slow the woman is driving. Michelle's only got an hour and a lot to accomplish during that time.

Ding. Ding!

Her phone is blowing up. She glances quickly at the screen and sees a parade of texts from all sorts of people—former colleagues she hasn't heard from in years, old friends from college, even Alejandra. She sees the time too, she'll have to read them later. But then, as she's jogging toward the entrance, a call. It's David.

She picks up. "Hi."

"Michelle."

"I'm running around. I'm outside the mall."

"I'm on my way to you," David says.

Something in his voice halts her. Instead of yanking on the heavy glass door, Michelle pulls herself to the side, stands along the cement wall of the building. "What's wrong?"

There is a pause, then, "I'll be there in five minutes."

"Please just tell me whatever it is."

David is silent, and she senses his hesitation. Fear, cold and cruel, slices through her stomach, cuts through the rest of her organs. All other thoughts—of buying carrots, of stupid paper towels, of interviews and reward money—fall to pieces there and then. Right on the sidewalk in front of this ugly strip mall. She slides down the wall to the dirty ground, right on top of a cigarette butt and the pebbles scattered everywhere. She waits for him to say it.

"They found a body down on Narragansett Beach."

40
JULIA

THE NEWS OF a body arrives when Julia least expects it.

She has just walked into the house after seeing Naomi and is busy unstrapping Theo from her chest, when there's a creak outside. A bang against Julia's house—loud, sudden.

"It's just the wind," she whispers as she sets Theo into the high chair, gets ready to feed him. "Shall we try some mashed-up bananas today?"

Theo blinks at her, waiting, watching, like always.

Julia, so absorbed in his big, wide eyes, doesn't notice the shadow that falls across the window at the side of her house. The darkness there, hovering. As she turns away from her son to peel a banana and smash it up with a fork, she fails to see how the shadow at the window shifts.

But then she hears another sound.

This time, she spins around, says out loud, "I don't think that was the wind." She goes to Theo, puts a finger to her lips like he might understand. "Shhhh. I'll be right back."

She tiptoes from the kitchen into the living room, opens the front door slowly. On the other side there is only gray light from after the rain. The cooler air prickles her skin. She crosses the porch and steps down into the soft grass of the yard. Stands there a long while, listening, looking around. There is no one that she can see.

She closes her eyes. Hears Naomi's words again, *I can help.* Imagines everything about herself, her life, returning to how it was before. Motherhood, another storm that comes, then passes, a burst followed by calm, by sun, by blue. Can she really get beyond all this regret?

Yes, Julia decides. Yes.

She opens her eyes.

Julia is no longer alone.

Richard. He stands in her yard a few feet away.

Their eyes lock.

He takes a step closer.

She inhales sharply.

"Did you hear the news?" he asks.

The way Richard looks at her, *like he knows something*, like he's always known the depths of Julia's mind. The hope of a new future vanishes. *She should have said something to someone, she should have called the police while she had the chance.* A clock is ticking down to something. Time has run out, she feels it.

Richard takes another step. "They found a body."

Cold pours through her veins. *He's come for me.* Fear covers her like a tarp. Julia thinks of Theo in the house. She backs up the porch steps.

Richard's hands reach out. "Don't you want to know who they found?"

"No," she says. This is when she turns and runs through the door, slams it, locks it. Richard's face is at the window, he bangs a hand against the wood, loud, solid. "Julia!" he yells.

Theo begins to wail.

She runs to the kitchen, scoops him up, tells him, "Shhhh." She grabs her phone, shaking so hard she almost drops it, then she runs upstairs, closes them both inside her bedroom. *Are the windows locked downstairs? Is the back door locked?*

She swipes a finger across the screen and begins to tap.

"Nine one one, what's your emergency?"

Julia goes to the bedroom window, stares outside, wonders where Richard is. She bounces Theo, talks over his cries. "I think I have some information about Lucy Mendoza's kidnapper." Julia's voice is high, shaking. "I think my neighbor took her."

"Ma'am, are you safe? Is someone with you now?"

"I think my neighbor might be breaking into my house. I don't know. I don't know!"

"Ma'am, is there a place you can hide?"

Julia hurries into the closet, shuts herself and Theo inside the darkness. "I feel like my life and my son's are in danger!"

"Help is already on the way. I'm going to stay on the phone with you, all right?"

Julia sits down on the floor among the shoes in the dark, Theo pressed to her, whimpering. "Shhhhhh."

"Ma'am?" she hears, coming from the phone. "Ma'am, are you somewhere safe?"

Her lungs heave, her mind grieves, she can't catch her breath, or stop the regret of all she's missed, the whole future she does not want to lose. She can't, she cannot. Who will Theo be one day, she wonders? Who will she be, herself? Can she really find a way through this, like Naomi says? What if she loses that chance? Yet then she looks down at her baby, his little head, this being she loves—because she does love him—and wonders how much longer she has. She sees the chance to choose on her own behalf slipping through her fingers.

"Ma'am?"

She closes her eyes and braces herself for whatever comes next.

PART 3
—
A NEW DAY

41
LUCY

A FRAMED WATERCOLOR of the ocean faces the bed.

Lucy Mendoza has been staring at it there on the wall, day after day in this shuttered room, hour upon hour, wondering why this particular image adorns this room; if it is random or intentional, if it's meant to soothe or entice, if the picture is to remind Lucy that the world is vast, that beauty still awaits her, to tempt her to reach for it and do so alone.

Does it tempt her, though?

Does beauty await? Does any future at all?

For what, really, does she long?

And what, really, does she miss?

Lucy tears her gaze from the painting, eyes sweeping the room floor to ceiling, left to right for what feels like the hundredth time. The thousandth. The thin water stain along the ceiling, the tiny tear in the gray, floral wallpaper, the small chip of wood along the edge of the dresser, the old Tiffany lamp. The books, so many books, in an otherwise meticulous space. Everything so tasteful, these small signs of wear glaring amid the monotony of Lucy's days.

How long has she been here?

Enough days to amount to a week?

Lucy thinks of Emma. Always Emma. Tiny, pudgy, smiling, gurgling, snorting, laughing, squeaking, a bundle of blinking love. A burden of regret. A thrilling future. An obstacle to happiness. The only pure joy Lucy's ever known. So many conflicting things, all of them true. Lucy thinks of Sam, of course, and of Michelle, how she misses her friend, and of the moment she started paying the price for her forbidden wishes—verboten feelings she told Michelle and only one other person. She should have stopped at telling Michelle.

So much time for Lucy to think.

A betweenness, a liminality, her whole life suspended.

A gift, a curse? Which one?

The sound of a door creaking open.

Lucy turns, draws the comforter up and over her body.

Her kidnapper stands at the entrance of the room. "It's time for you to decide."

Lucy doesn't speak, but her heart begins to pound.

With what? Hope? More regret? Both?

The kidnapper's face is shadowed beyond the door.

The decision Lucy must make hangs in the air: Which way will it be answered?

She remains still, doesn't flinch, doesn't move, just stares at this person who changed her life one sunny afternoon, who altered everything she's ever known. She's had so much time to think about what led her here—the intimacy created that made her trust this person, that lowered her guard. Who's fault was it—is it—for how she's gotten to this place? Hers, the kidnapper's, the world's, some combination? Does it even matter, in the end, whose fault it is?

Yes, Lucy decides. It does matter. It matters to her.

Naomi Bresler approaches the bed, sits down at the end of it.

Lucy often thinks back to the day she was taken, how when she heard someone behind her and turned, she opened her mouth to exclaim, "Naomi, how nice to run into you here!" Then later on, when she woke from her stupor: "I took the hardest step for you," Naomi had told her.

"You know what you should do," Naomi says now. "Your situations are nearly identical."

"But I'm not Maeve," Lucy says.

"You don't know that yet," Naomi says. "*I* don't know that yet." Her eyes drop to the comforter, hands smoothing across it. "You should take the second chance I've given you. I helped Maeve get away, then when she wanted to go back I helped her again. That was my mistake. And look what happened."

By now Lucy knows the entire tragic story of Naomi's best friend and her baby daughter, and Naomi's certainty that it was not an accident that Maeve and Bridget drowned in a stormy ocean that day. How this single event changed everything about Naomi's life forever. How she'd tried to move forward after losing them, but couldn't. The guilt was too much. So one morning, Rebecca Abrams woke up and made a vow: to start her life over completely, to devote the rest of it to providing refuge to other women like Maeve, to becoming a person with the skills and resources to save other Maeves in this life, as many as she could, to ensure that they would not be alone. Her transformation was so total that she took her second middle name, Nima, and became Naomi, using her great-grandmother's maiden name Bresler, in a rebirth of sorts. How else could she live with herself after Maeve's and Bridget's deaths?

Lucy blinks at the one other person she told her darkest secret. This woman who promised their postpartum group they would come out the other side of everything they're feeling, that when they came to the meetings they'd come to a safe space. Lucy fell for it all. All those words she allowed out of her mouth about her new baby, her struggles, they just fell from her lips and when they did, they were met with such patience, such understanding. With ancient knowing eyes, and the exact words Lucy longed to hear. "You are not alone in how you feel," Naomi had said to her. "Other women have been where you are and survived."

Finally, Lucy had thought. *Someone who knows.*

Naomi reaches inside the deep pockets of her dress and produces an envelope.

Lucy can see that it's stuffed with cash.

She places the envelope onto the bed, the keys next to it. "These are for you."

But Lucy doesn't move.

"Your heart is telling you what's right—for you and for Emma," the therapist goes on. "You and I are both aware that you could have left days ago and you haven't. You've stayed."

Guilt sloshes through Lucy, a sick feeling loose and swimming.

"Don't forget the truth of this. I might have brought you here, but you're the one who's chosen to remain."

Every day that Lucy's been here in this house, Naomi comes to visit her between clients, after groups, like Lucy is some kind of inpatient under Naomi's care. And isn't she?

Naomi said as much on Lucy's first day. "The way I think about it is this: I became worried you might do harm to yourself, so it is my professional obligation to make sure that doesn't happen. I am providing the best care I can for the very specific thing you are going through. The world doesn't offer women treatment for yet, because the world denies that women can experience it. Which is why we are here and not somewhere else."

"But I didn't ask for this," Lucy had protested.

Naomi had searched her eyes then. "Didn't you ask me for *exactly* this, Lucy?"

"Lucy?" Naomi is still waiting for her to say something, to grip the envelope, the keys, and walk out the door toward another life.

But Lucy can never seem to figure out how to go backwards to her old life or go forward into a new one. So the hours have passed, one after the other. So many hours that Lucy isn't sure any longer—whose responsibility is it that she's here in this room? Hers, Naomi's? What is all this in the end—kidnapping? Rescue? A combination of both? Does it even matter which?

Naomi slams a hand against the bed. "Lucy! Come on!"

Lucy draws her knees to her chest, curls herself away from this woman.

She doesn't move, she barely breathes.

But then she hears something else—something new.

Sirens?

"I told you time was running out," Naomi says. "You have to choose, it has to be now. You can still go!"

The high shrill sound is coming closer—and closer.

Lucy's heart thumps against her chest.

"I wanted to do the right thing," Naomi says.

"I know," Lucy says.

"Will you tell them that, when they ask?" Naomi asks. "Can you ever forgive me?"

Can anyone possibly forgive something like this?

Can Sam forgive Lucy? Can Emma?

Can Lucy forgive herself?

LUCY MENDOZA IS FOUND ALIVE

A helicopter camera caught a glimpse of Lucy Mendoza, dazed but alive, on her way into the South County Hospital's emergency wing when she was being transferred from the ambulance.

"Her family is happy to have her safe," says Michelle Carvalho, on behalf of the family, as she spoke to the press outside the hospital where Lucy is being treated.

Carvalho has been campaigning on behalf of her friend since Mendoza disappeared from the Narragansett Belmont Market parking lot six days ago.

But is Mendoza happy to be reunited with her husband and daughter again?

Police and FBI initially assumed Mendoza was the victim of a kidnapping, yet shortly after she disappeared new information came to light suggesting Mendoza may have left of her own volition. Podcasters, news commentators, reporters, and average citizens across a range of social media platforms have been debating the true nature of Lucy Mendoza's disappearance for days. The accusation that she planned her own kidnapping because she regretted becoming a mother has captured the fascination—and condemnation—of the public.

The most important question has been put to rest, however:

Was Mendoza kidnapped or not?

The answer: Yes.

Melody Cho, scholar and writer of the popular newsletter *Demystifying Motherhood*, commented that "Lucy needs time to heal," and that "whatever story Lucy has to tell, it's up to her if and when she shares it."

Until then, the world awaits Mendoza's statement.

All across social media the public has turned their talk to guessing at Mendoza's current state of mind—some constituencies expressing relief that Mendoza was found alive, their prayers answered, though many going so far as to share their disappointment. "No mother who regrets her child should be allowed to live," said one influencer.

It's rumored that Mendoza's kidnapper is a woman.

"I'm sorry but I can't comment on that," said Joe Suarez, the lead detective on the case.

Further details will be reported as they emerge.

BODY FOUND ON NARRAGANSETT BEACH

Narragansett resident Dolores Grello came upon the body of a woman that washed up on shore yesterday morning. The police and her family have identified the woman as Joanna D'Angelo, reported missing three years before by her husband, Luca D'Angelo. Details are still forthcoming.

42
MICHELLE

ON MICHELLE'S WAY into the hospital, a television on the wall of the lobby is tuned to the news. *Lucy Mendoza, Found ALIVE* reads the banner underneath the newscaster who's speaking. She can barely believe it herself. When David told her they'd found a body, she was sure it was Lucy's. But before David could pick her up at the mall, another call came up on her phone from Detective Suarez.

Michelle answered, bracing for impact. "I know, they found Lucy's body."

"No, Michelle," Detective Suarez told her. "We did find Lucy but she's alive and she's in the hospital. She's okay. Can you come?"

Michelle's heart rose to her throat; her eyes poured tears of relief. She could not believe the words she'd just heard from the detective's lips. As she stood there waiting for David to arrive outside the mall, the sun suddenly broke out over Michelle's world. She could feel its warmth, she could see its light.

She follows the hope of it now, right up to Detective Suarez, who waits for her by the hospital reception desk.

Michelle is sweating with anticipation. "Where is she?"

"Follow me." Suarez takes Michelle through a labyrinth

of hallways, winding left, right, then right again. "We're hoping she'll talk to you." He beckons her toward the end of yet another corridor. "She hasn't said a word about her kidnapper. She hasn't said a word at all."

Outside Lucy's room are two officers, standing guard.

The hallway seems overly bright, Michelle's vision shining.

Suarez stops finally, turns to her. "Ready?"

Michelle wipes the tears from her cheeks. Pulls herself together. She nods at Suarez. Then takes a deep breath, reaches for the handle on the door, turns it, and walks on through.

There is Lucy. Michelle's best friend since college, her sister in this life, staring out the hospital room window, looking thin, unmoving, the room so quiet.

"Lucy?"

Lucy Mendoza turns toward Michelle, face an expressionless mask. But then Lucy struggles in the bed, she shifts, she moves over, she pulls back the sheet.

Michelle's heart swells. She knows exactly what to do.

She always has with Lucy. As Lucy always has with her.

Michelle kicks off her shoes and climbs onto the bed to be with her friend.

43
LUCY

LUCY SITS IN yet another bed, still not speaking.

Everything seems so outside of time.

People come and go in the hospital room.

Nurses, doctors, detectives, officers.

Sam, Michelle, Michelle, Sam. Michelle, again.

"Lucy? Lucy? Can you tell us, can you?"

So many people asking questions, saying her name, whispering like they're afraid to disturb the air with words, like she's a bird they might scare away. Everyone wanting answers. Meanwhile, Lucy searches for the doorway back into her life, the threshold that will take her there, from this liminal space onward into the world that is solid, real, hers again.

"I'm here, Lucy, I'm here," Sam keeps saying when he visits, waiting for her to tell the story about her captivity, whatever it may be.

Sam has yet to bring Emma.

Deep down, Lucy knows why.

So she stays silent. She has not yet found her tongue for this, whatever this is which turned her life into a before and an after, that revealed her deepest, most shameful secrets to the world. When she does speak, what she says must be specific, well thought out; she knows it will be recorded, regarded, replayed over and over as people search to find some kind of meaning in Lucy's story, her kidnapping, and in all that unfolded as a result of her disappearance.

Other people find plenty of words for Lucy, though.

As the days and nights bleed one into the next and because she has no phone, Lucy watches the television from her hospital bed, the talking heads debating her character now that she's been found.

Is Lucy Mendoza ultimately good?

Is Lucy Mendoza ultimately a monster?

Should Lucy Mendoza be allowed to mother now that she's back?

Is Emma safe with a mother like *that*?

How could she, what did she, can you just imagine, a woman thinking such things, saying such things, trying to come back from such things? How, who, when, why?

Innocent, guilty, cowardly, heroic?

Victim, perpetrator?

Lucky, awful, deserving of *what she got*?

So many names, so many theories, so many ideas, so much opinion, Lucy now a thing to dissect, a source on which to heap everyone's anger, dismay, hope, grief, theories about women, mothers, second chances, redemption, hope, god's existence, all because she disappeared and then returned, all because she isn't there to speak for herself, all because it's so easy for everyone else to say things, because it isn't *them*. Lucy, a marvelous distraction, a source of gossip, a symbol, an opportunity for conversation and debate.

People debate Naomi Bresler too.

The airwaves turn to her with a kind of religious fervor.

Her former clients, her current clients.

Was this therapist ultimately trying to do good?

Was this woman ultimately still a monster?

Are these two women—the woman who was kidnapped, and the woman who was the kidnapper—ultimately somehow the same?

Lucy isn't sure, herself.

Retired Detective Diana González visits Lucy again, this woman Lucy has learned is the person who figured out Naomi Bresler had her. Diana's wavy gray hair is long and loose today.

"I wondered if you were feeling up to talking?" she asks.

The requests for Lucy to speak of her ordeal always begin the same way: so and so was wondering when Lucy would be feeling up to talking, when she'll be ready to speak, when she's feeling better and wants to share. When, when, when and if. Michelle is usually the one to go through the list of them, carefully organized, vetted, ordered most important to least.

Does Lucy plan to write a book?

Would she like to write a book?

Would she be willing to go on a podcast?

Would she be willing to do her own podcast?

Offers from agents, of all kinds.

Made for TV movies, made for TV specials.

Interview upon interview upon interview.

Lucy knows she will do none of these, that she will speak only to the people who matter. To Michelle, to Sam, to Sam's mother. To Melody Cho, who defended her—eventually Lucy will speak to her. But maybe only to Cho.

"Lucy?" Diana presses.

Lucy shakes her head.

Diana holds out a notebook and pen in her hands. "This might help."

Their eyes meet—Lucy takes what Diana offers.

She immediately starts to write.

Diana drags a chair to the side of the bed and sits. She reads Lucy's words out loud: "Can I see her?" Diana looks at Lucy, brow furrowed. "Can you see who—your daughter?"

Lucy shakes her head.

"Michelle?" Diana tries again.

Lucy picks up the pen, scribbles something else, a name: *Naomi Bresler.*

Detective González exhales with her whole body. "I don't know, Lucy. That's not typical."

Lucy grips the pen in her hand harder, angling it over the page. *Please.*

"Let me see what I can do with Detective Suarez," Diana says.

One morning Lucy hears the hospital room door open.

She expects the nurse.

But she hears a cry.

There is Emma, cradled in Sam's arms, looking straight into her mother's eyes.

Lucy calls out, "Emma!"

If only everyone could be born again, she thinks, if only every single person on this earth could choose their new first words so carefully, and with such total intention.

Sam's face fills with relief. "I wasn't sure if you were ready."

She looks at her husband very hard, wonders if he was really thinking, *I wasn't sure if Emma would be safe with you.*

Lucy reaches out both arms. "Let me hold her?"

A question.

Her heart pounds.

Sam walks over to the bed and carefully passes Emma to Lucy.

Lucy looks down at her wiggling, pudgy baby.

Emma looks up at her mother.

So many thoughts flash in Lucy's mind, and she experiences a truth bigger than any other she's ever known: that if she has any regrets right now, it is not that she had Emma. But something else. Something that might have happened but that, in the end, did not:

To never see her daughter again, to never have the chance to witness Emma grow up and become a girl and then a young woman.

As Emma snuggles into her body, Lucy is acutely aware of how these days outside of time have altered her thinking. That her regret is real, that it's still in her, but that regret can also fade—that it *is* fading. That she can get through it to the other side and make peace with the choices she's made and the life she still has.

Because Lucy still has this life.

Miraculously. After everything.

After coming so close to doing something so drastic.

She kisses the top of Emma's head, breathes in her familiar scent.

A second chance, and she takes it.

44

JULIA

JULIA IS LYING in bed, still not speaking.

Marcus is sitting next to her, working from home. At her beck and call, taking care of her every need. At Theo's beck and call, taking care of his every need. Finally. All it took was finding out a murdering psychopath lived next door to make Marcus finally spend some time helping out his wife.

He leans over, tilts his laptop in her direction. "Look at this headline, Julia."

LOCAL MOTHER CATCHES KILLER.

"They're calling you a hero," Marcus says.

Julia studies those words, and how they identify her—not as a "local woman" but as a "local mother," and she bristles. Even when people think she's done something brave and important she is first and foremost a mother. Why is the world this way? The headline would never be: LOCAL FATHER CATCHES KILLER, for example. They'd just say "local man."

Marcus shifts his laptop in front of him again. "I can't believe that all this time we had some psychopath next door, keeping a woman in his basement. How awful. And how lucky that you called 911 when you did. I could never have lived with myself if you and Theo had been hurt somehow. It's tragic about that woman, though, that she ended up dead."

Julia's gut swims.

She turns over in the bed, toward the window where their neighbor used to watch her. She wonders how long the FBI will be there, cordoning off the yard, searching every nook and dusty corner of it. Yes, it *is* tragic, Julia thinks. It's the worst possible outcome and she feels responsible. So she doesn't want to think of Joanna D'Angelo and what she suffered under that house, only a few yards away. And yet she can't stop thinking of the woman. She lies in bed and tries to sleep but sleep never comes. Only thoughts of Joanna D'Angelo, so many and so vividly that she's filled an entire sketchbook about it all. Speaking of monsters. The regret she's felt about becoming a mother seems small now in comparison to what this woman must have been through, and only to wind up dead. If only Julia had called the police sooner, maybe Joanna D'Angelo would still be alive. If only she had broken into the basement, smashed through that door. If only she hadn't been so caught up in her own mind, her own misery. If only, if only, is the refrain of her existence now. And if only Naomi Bresler, the first—the only?—person who truly gave Julia hope for the future was not also in jail for having kidnapped Lucy Mendoza.

What were the chances?

When Julia saw the headlines about Naomi, she nearly laughed and cried at once.

She shuts her eyes tight against it all, her house, her husband, her own thoughts. The day the police found Lucy was the same day Julia called 911 and then hid herself and Theo in the closet on the floor among Marcus's work shoes, the heels she used to wear but does no longer, a pair of stray woolen socks. Theo curled up against his mother's skin, napping peacefully through one of the most terrifying moments of her life.

After what felt like hours but was only maybe twenty minutes, Julia heard talking outside the door. Followed by a knock.

"Ma'am, are you all right?" came the muffled voice of a woman.

Heart pounding, she'd reached around Theo's little body, twisted the knob and peeked out. Then she pushed the door wide.

"Ma'am," said a man in a police uniform. "You can come out. It's lucky you called us. We've got your neighbor in custody. He's not going to hurt anyone else. You're safe now."

A dizziness came over her, and she wondered if she might pass out. She tried to comprehend his words. "But Lucy—"

The woman next to him, clearly a medic, crouched onto the floor outside the closet. She reached out her hands. "We're going to take care of you. It's going to be all right. That's all that matters."

"But—" Julia tried again.

"Ma'am, can you hand me the baby?"

Her teeth were chattering. She didn't answer.

She squeezed Theo tighter to her chest.

"Ma'am?"

"Theo! Julia!" She heard Marcus's voice crying out.

Then he was at the door, reaching for their son.

She let Theo go.

"I'm here, I'm here. You can come out. I'm so glad you both are okay."

A police officer was talking to Marcus. "You should have seen what we found in the basement . . . might be related to that dead body that washed up—" Then the officer clammed up as if catching himself speaking things he should not.

Julia heard the conversation above her head as though from far away, eyes returning to her son. She blocked out the words swirling around her. Something stirred in her as she watched Theo during those moments. As she saw her husband nuzzling his soft baby cheek.

Love. It was definitely love.

But it was also regret. Both.

An impossible equation.

Julia gripped this love as hard as she could, she held on to it with all her might and tried to allow it to overpower everything else.

She got up off the floor and went to her husband and son.

"Mama's here," she told Theo.

But she knew it wasn't enough. Not for her, not for Theo, not for Marcus. It became clear right then that she would both love Theo with all her heart, and also never be an ordinary mother. That she would always want different things for herself, for Theo, for Marcus. A different life. In those moments in her bedroom on that terrible day, Julia realized the best way she could love Theo, the best way she could give Theo and therefore Marcus the future they needed, was to do the hardest thing a mother could ever do.

Let them go.

45
DIANA

DIANA HAS BEEN doing a lot of thinking.

As she sips her coffee in her kitchen at home, Naomi Bresler's words repeat in her mind. *Becca's* words, the words of this woman Diana knew from a previous life.

"I wanted to help Lucy," Becca Abrams had said to Diana when they saw each other for the first time in decades. "I never intended to hurt her. Of all people, you must understand why."

They sat across from one another at a table down at the precinct, in a small, quiet room that Joe arranged for them to speak.

"You saw what happened to Maeve and Bridget," Becca went on. "You were there. That's why I had to protect Lucy and Emma. I did it the best way I knew how. I devoted my life to preventing deaths like theirs from happening again. Someone needs to stop silencing women."

Diana resisted a reply. She could tell Becca wanted to say something more.

Becca closed her tired eyes. "I wish I'd convinced Maeve not to return home. That I'd done for her what I tried to do for Lucy. But I didn't and I failed her. I failed Maeve *and* Bridget."

As these confessions have echoed inside Diana, she's tried

to decide what she thinks of Becca's attempts to give Lucy what she thought Lucy needed, how she believed she was saving Lucy's life. How the day Maeve and Bridget were lost to the waves and the stormy ocean, Becca had been lost as well. As the press and the public dissect this therapist's motives, as her former patients condemn her and defend her, some claiming that without Bresler they would not be alive today, people are also fascinated that Lucy's kidnapper was not a man, but a woman. A woman who heard Lucy's secret and believed it was true. Enough to risk her own life and career to save Lucy's. And for this, some women are calling Naomi Bresler a hero.

Diana's gaze shifts past the stools along the kitchen island to the coffee table in the living room, and the puzzle of the sky still on top of it. Susana finished it—alone.

Diana wonders what she wants from the rest of her life, her retirement years with her wife. About how she couldn't help but get involved in a case that wasn't her own. But then, she's glad she did—she always will be. Just as she will always be upset by how she and Joe and everyone else on their force failed Joanna D'Angelo and her poor husband and daughter.

She can't get Luca out of her mind, how certain he was that someone had taken his wife.

And he'd been right.

His worst fears—Diana's too—confirmed.

Susana takes a seat on the other side of the island. "Do you want to talk about it?"

Diana looks up from her coffee. She's been sitting at the table, staring into its milky depths, her mind full of Naomi Bresler, Lucy, and now Joanna, Luca, Franny, Joanna again, the man who held her captive for nearly three years. "I'm not sure you'd want me to."

Susana reaches across the island for Diana's hand.

Her beautiful wife. How lucky Diana is to have Susana.

"I can handle it," Susana says. "It might help to tell me."

So Diana does. She tells her wife how Joanna had been shopping in Walmart and—much like Lucy Mendoza—was snatched from the parking lot. How everyone claimed Joanna likely fled her marriage, or that it was her husband's fault because of his family's connections, yet the worst had been true. About how some women get all the police and FBI resources and some just fall through the cracks. When Diana gets to the part about Joanna being held in not just one but two different basements—because over the last three years, her kidnapper had moved from one house to the other and taken her with him—she trails off.

"Diana?" Susana prompts. "You can say whatever it is."

She shakes her head. "Another time."

"What do the police know about this guy?"

She takes a sip of her cold coffee. "I don't know much yet. I'm sure Joe will tell me eventually."

"Have you gotten ahold of Luca?"

"No." Diana's called, she's texted. She even drove down to Jo's Clam Shack again, to see if she could catch him there but the place was boarded up.

"One day he'll reach out," Susana says.

"Maybe."

"Mi amor, don't forget the part about how you figured out where Lucy Mendoza was being held. And that's good news."

Diana gives Susana a small smile. "I know. It is good news."

But she can't stop thinking about Joanna. One woman

saved, another sacrificed. But as with Trey and all the other loved ones of the women lost over the years, kidnapped, murdered, taken from their lives by the world we live in and the men within it, she hopes Luca will find a way forward from this, and Franny too.

She won't ask Luca to forgive the unforgiveable, however.

Diana didn't find Joanna, in the end.

Another woman—failed.

She knows too: there will always be *another woman*.

And another.

For this, she'll never forgive herself.

No one should.

"Hello, Diana. Joe."

Diana looks up and sees Lucy Mendoza standing there, amid the bustle of the precinct.

Joe scrambles to his feet, the chair by his messy desk squeaking again as he does. "Lucy, so nice to see you! How are you feeling?"

The officers around them are trying hard not to stare at this woman who's still a media sensation—unfortunately for her and her family. But Diana thinks Lucy looks good. Better. Her hair is pulled into a high ponytail, her attire is simple, a plain silk blouse and loose pants, pointed flats, her cheeks fuller, brighter now. Her eyes have lost their dark circles, her face is not so drawn. "Just taking things day by day."

"That's all anyone can do," Joe says.

Diana smiles as she gets up. "You are looking well," she says. She reaches out to shake Lucy's hand and is surprised when the woman pulls Diana into a long hug.

"Thank you for everything, especially your patience," she whispers to Diana. And then, after Lucy pulls back, she looks Diana in the eyes. "I'm ready if you are."

Joe grabs his keys. "All right, let's go."

The three of them head down the long hallway to the private visitor's room of the precinct. After a lot of string-pulling, Joe and Diana managed to fulfill Lucy's request to speak with the therapist she knows as Naomi Bresler. Diana wonders what Lucy wants to say. They come to a stop at the door.

"Are you ready?" Diana asks.

Lucy reaches up, tightens her ponytail. Then she nods.

The three of them enter the room.

Becca Abrams is at the table, hair tucked neatly behind her ears. Lucy's therapist looks up at her former captive, this woman who turned Lucy into a household name, a cautionary tale, a hero and a role model to some, a villain to so many others, and who changed Lucy's life forever.

"Hi, Lucy," she says.

"Hello," Lucy says, voice steady. "Naomi. Rebecca?"

Diana gestures for Lucy to sit, and she does.

The two women look into each other's eyes a long time.

Then Lucy speaks. "You'd wanted to know if I could ever forgive you."

The therapist nods.

Lucy leans forward, stretches one arm across the table. She places a hand on top of Naomi's. Without breaking eye contact, she says, "I wanted to tell you that I do forgive you. That it's already done. I understand why you did what you did. I really do."

Naomi's eyes fill with tears, they overflow down her cheeks. "But you didn't take the second chance I gave you."

Lucy squeezes Naomi's hand, these two women connected by grief, regret, by loss, for better and for worse. "But I did," she says, "I used it to choose a life with my family. Despite everything, you did help me see that this was what I wanted. And I'll always be grateful." She meets Naomi's gaze. "So thank you. In a way, you did save my life. The one I thought I didn't want, but in the end, I did. I do."

POSTSCRIPT
—
FIVE YEARS LATER

46
JULIA

JULIA STARES AT the wall of the gallery, reads the title on it in big block letters.

MONSTERHOOD: Portraits of an Unmothering

Drawings by A. Silva.

A for Anne.

She looks around the beautiful bright space, at all the artworks hung side by side, three big rooms full of framed sketches. Her art. Well, A. Silva's art, the pseudonym Julia chose for the Instagram she created so long ago now. It's been over four years since she posted that first sketch. For two of those years, no one really noticed A. Silva's work, which was fine with Julia. She'd used it as an outlet for her grief, her shame, her regret, her isolation, her loneliness. Her rage at herself for not calling the police in time to save Joanna D'Angelo, her nightmares about the man next door. But then some influencer found the account. After that, it didn't take long for A. Silva to blow up, for Melody Cho to find her too, for the invitations to speak on podcasts and write articles that talk about her work and all that it represents.

A. Silva who "speaks the unspeakable," as one critic wrote.

Galleries fought to house this show. Julia needs to pinch herself sometimes. She nearly can't believe how her life and work have changed. Thank god she used a pseudonym from the beginning. She'd never want Theo to be associated with this show. She's glad to shield him from it all, and wonders whether one day she might tell him the truth about her art. But becoming Anne Silva has allowed Julia a public space to talk openly about her experiences of motherhood. About her regret. It was her art that saved her in the end, that pulled her from the dark.

The gallerist, Mia, returns from the other room and fusses with the white wine bottles chilling in a metal bucket full of ice. Then she rearranges the bottles of red on the table and re-straightens the glasses. She looks up at Julia and smiles. "People should be here soon. Are you ready, Anne?"

Is Anne ready? Is Julia? But in the art world Julia Gallo *is* Anne Silva now. As though she slipped into another life after all, just like she longed to back during those early days after Theo was born. She wonders if some time in the future she'll own the truth of her real name in relation to her art. But for now, Anne will do.

"I think so," she says.

"We're expecting quite a crowd," Mia says.

"We'll see, I suppose." Julia—Anne—walks to the center of the room and turns toward the door. It's nearly dark. She wonders if Daphne will be here tonight. She's invited all her old art school friends. They're in touch again and they know the truth about A. Silva's identity.

But someone who will not be here is Marcus.

On some nights when Julia's trying to sleep, she can't help but think of that first year with Theo, how her marriage to Marcus ended that same year. Sometimes this part of her life seems far away, yet there are others when the memories pour over her torrentially, soaking Julia like it's all still happening. During those nights, her regret seems as big and looming as it was in the beginning. Most of the time though, it's tiny, just one small voice amid the many others in Julia's life and amid the things that have grown much bigger. Her career of course, but also the love she feels for her son, the fun she has with him when they're together on vacations and visits a few weeks each year. She's glad Theo is still part of her life—that he always will be.

It's not perfect.

But she's glad she left. By leaving she found a way back to herself. To something like happiness, a place where she's unearthed her own way into motherhood however cursory, a passageway she worked hard to locate, however unusual it may be to others. She wishes it hadn't been so hard, especially not so hard on Marcus. She laments her bumpy path, the way it seemed like so much stumbling in the dark. But no one woman—no one mother—is the same. This is a fact that Julia has worked hard to accept.

Though A. Silva doesn't have quite so much trouble as Julia.

A woman enters the gallery.

She looks around, then her eyes land on Julia. "Am I the first one here?"

"So far," Julia says. "But I hope there'll be more. I know Melody Cho will be here, and she posted about it." Julia walks up to the woman, extends her hand. "I'm Anne Silva."

The woman takes it. "I follow your account. It's meant a lot to me."

"It means a lot to me to hear you say that," Julia says. "Thank you for coming. I hope you enjoy the event this evening."

She watches as the woman walks up to the wall with the show's title and the paragraph etched below it that describes what the artworks represent about motherhood—the motherhood that will always be a part of Julia's identity no matter what, whether people call her Julia Gallo or A. Silva or some other pseudonymous person, as yet unnamed.

There is never any going back.

47
LUCY

LUCY SMILES AND raises her glass. She glances at Sam next to her and says, "I'd like to make a toast."

Michelle looks toward the ceiling, at the thumping upstairs, the kids thundering down the hall. Aidan, Charlie, Emma. The bigger they get, the louder their footsteps.

Lucy likes the pounding above, it's reassuring, like they are tethered tight to the earth, like they are making impressions that will last.

Michelle leans toward Lucy. "Should I go and check on them?"

Lucy shakes her head. "Let them be. I hear fun happening up there."

Sam laughs. "We wouldn't want to interrupt any fun."

The three friends extend their glasses toward the center of the table, above the remains of pasta and salad and homemade bread in a basket, the aftermath of a delicious storm of eating. Everyone a little bit tipsy, a little bit drowsy, a whole lot stuffed with food and conversation.

"Your toast," Michelle prompts Lucy.

She leans forward, glass suspended. "To my favorite people who are also my family." Her voice grows hoarse. "I'll always need you."

Michelle bites her lip and Lucy knows she's trying not to cry. "To makeshift family."

They clink glasses, and Michelle and Lucy take a sip, Sam's so big a gulp that it streams down to his chin.

Lucy dabs a napkin there.

Sam gets up to clear the plates. "To the kitchen I go."

The two women take their wine and conversation into the other room, settling in on the couch. Michelle looks at Lucy, and Lucy returns the stare.

"You okay?" Michelle asks, in that way she always does after all that happened.

"I am," Lucy says. "Really."

Michelle places a hand on Lucy's arm. "You know you can tell me anything."

Lucy leans into her friend. "I know. I promise I do."

"I love you, Lucy, I always will," Michelle says.

This time it's Lucy who bites her lip, trying not to cry. Sometimes Lucy needs to pinch herself, convince herself that everything is real, her life, each day, the people in it. It wasn't that long ago when Lucy wondered if she would ever see her friend again, if she would ever see anyone she loved again, so she knows not to take a single thing for granted.

"I love you back. I always will too."

Emma's ice cream drips down her hand. She brings it to her mouth, licks it and laughs.

Lucy gives her daughter a napkin. "You're supposed to eat the ice cream, not wear it."

"Maybe I'd rather wear it," Emma says, like this should be obvious, as the mother and daughter walk around the Pier. Emma's hair flows all the way down her back.

Lucy takes in this growing girl she and Sam created, marveling at the swing of her arm, the bounce of her step as she bobs along the sidewalk. Emma has no idea how beautiful she is.

"But Mom, if I *was* going to wear it," Emma is saying, "I'd want it to be mint chocolate chip, not peanut butter, because I love the color green and I also love polka dots, and I don't want to wear the color of peanut butter."

"That all seems very reasonable," Lucy says, and steers them toward a bench.

The two of them sit, licking their ice cream, the only sound between them an occasional slurp, or the birds chirping in the trees, or the sounds of people laughing as they wander the shops on this nice summer day.

Emma licks all the way to the cone, then takes a big bite. "So Mom," she says, mouth full and crunching. She swallows before speaking again. "I have this question."

Every Wednesday, Lucy takes time off work to pick Emma up from school or from camp, depending on the season, to take her somewhere. Sometimes to a diner for pancakes, sometimes to a museum, sometimes they go shopping. Sometimes they head to the beach with towels and pails and shovels and go for a swim. Sometimes they just take a walk through town and get themselves an ice cream, on a lovely sunny day like this one.

And they talk. About all kinds of things, whatever Emma would like to discuss. School, her friends, her favorite teachers, her less than favorite ones. Her latest interests, her newest obsessions, which lately involve astronomy, which is also why they often end up at the planetarium on their outings. Sam got Emma a telescope and the two of them spend clear evenings looking through it, searching for the constellations Emma wants to find. Lucy got Emma glow stars for her ceiling, and the three of them spent one entire afternoon mapping the night sky above Emma's bed, so when she goes to sleep, it shines above her.

Lucy slurps her own ice cream, lavender honey. "Yes, Emma?"

Melted peanut butter ice cream is rolling down her daughter's arm. "Are you ever going to tell people the story of what really happened when you went away?"

One of Emma's favorite questions lately.

Lucy turns to her daughter, sees the delicate lashes fanning her eyelids, the soft silk of hair down her back, the knob of her knees, every precious angle of her limbs. "What you really mean is am I ever going to tell *you* that story."

A bird comes to rest on a nearby branch, cocking its head, watching.

Emma considers her mother's statement. "Maybe," she says.

"One day, I will tell you everything. But all you need to know right now is that I only thought about you the whole time I was gone." Lucy places a palm over her heart. "You were in here with me." Then Lucy takes her hand and presses it against Emma's heart. "And I was in there with you too, even if you couldn't see me." Lucy looks at Emma, looks her daughter straight in the eyes and says, "No matter what anyone says, my little Emma, your mother loves you. She loves you very much."

Emma nods, her expression serious. "I know that. But Mom, I'm not so little anymore."

Lucy laughs, then wipes her eyes. "It's true. You're not. You are growing right up. So fast." The bird starts to sing. "And your mother is so proud of you."

Then, ice creams both finished, Lucy and Emma stand up and make their way home.

AUTHOR'S NOTE

NEARLY TWENTY YEARS ago—around 2005 or 2006, early in my career as a writer—someone in publishing told me I should never write about a woman who doesn't want children; that nobody wants to read about "her." I remember feeling crushed and ashamed and admonished. I desperately wanted to write about *that woman*—I am that woman. But I banished the idea, and the advice was burned into my brain. I already knew what it was to be hated and villainized for not wanting children and I'd learned to keep my mouth shut about it.

Over a decade later—and after years of being pressured to have a child I'd never wanted, insistently and constantly told I was going regret it if I did not have one—I decided: To hell with this, I'm writing a book about a woman who doesn't want children, despite the probability that this book will never see the light of day. I still wanted to see "that woman" on the page.

This was how my last novel, *The Nine Lives of Rose Napolitano*, came into existence. It involves nine different versions of a woman who doesn't want children but whose marriage has come to rest on whether she will change her mind. I was shocked when that novel was bought. That comment made to me all those years ago was still vivid in my mind.

I loved writing *Rose*. But I learned things from publishing her: namely, that if a woman doesn't want a baby, she needs a good reason. Money issues? Problems in childhood? Career necessities? Why, exactly, doesn't Rose want a baby, especially since she seems to love her own mother? I was tasked with accounting for this why. I remember feeling stumped. Couldn't it simply be that *Rose just doesn't want one*? Isn't lack of desire a good enough reason? My own why has always been simple, and has nothing to do with money or climate change or anything else—I've just never wanted a baby. Period.

I'm so happy that Rose was published. But there was one very important version of Rose's story I longed to tell yet didn't dare: the one where Rose regrets her baby.

During the end of my twenties and throughout my thirties, when I was being pressured on all sides to have a baby that everyone knew I didn't want, I agonized about what would happen if I went ahead and had one. My biggest fear was regret. I'd have the baby and regret that I did for the rest of my life, and it would be a disaster for everyone, for me, for my husband, and most of all for the child. I was terrified this would become my fate. I knew deep down to my bones that motherhood was not for me, yet everyone kept implying that my self-knowledge didn't matter, that once I had the baby, I'd see that motherhood was the best thing to ever happen to me.

Yet inside me, this question kept percolating: *But what if it isn't? What then?*

People freely insisted if I didn't have a baby I would regret this for the rest of my life, but not a single person worried about the opposite: that if I had the baby, I might actually regret the *baby* for the rest of my life. That I might actually regret *the motherhood*.

And I'd think to myself: *Watch me have a baby and then run.* I'd lie in bed at night and fantasize about how regretting a baby was so unspeakable I'd not only have to leave my family but also change my name and never come back. I'd imagine how I'd plan my own disappearance. This seemed like the only way out of motherhood-regret in my mind.

So, *Her One Regret* is the story I was too afraid to tell in *The Nine Lives of Rose Napolitano*. It's a version of the fantasy that would unfold in my mind again and again as I agonized over the baby question in my own life.

I will never know what would have happened if I'd had a baby, but I do know this for sure: I have no regrets about not having children. I wish someone had told me back then during those years of terrible pressure to do something I knew I shouldn't, that there also existed a possible future where I didn't have children and was completely happy about it. But no one did.

And I feel like I need to add here, so we're clear: There are so many wonderful mothers in my life. I have nothing but respect for women who become mothers and motherhood as a life's goal. But I can love and respect mothers and motherhood and also not want to become a mother myself. Both things can be true and are.

A few notes about some of the content in this novel:

Julia's turn toward sketching about herself as a Monster-Mother was inspired by my discovery of Abigail E. Penner's artwork, which takes up the topic of punishing self-images, exhaustion, and sadness. I became fascinated with the blatant vulnerability and ruthless self-revelation in Penner's sketches, and began wishing for Julia to find an outlet like this for herself in this story.

Melody Cho's character is inspired by the real-life Emily Oster, who is a brilliant scholar, writer, and professor. She has truly become the guru of all things parenting and motherhood, and is an overall champion of all kinds of women in all kinds of ways.

Finally, and perhaps most importantly: All the comments from women speaking about regret from Melody Cho's "survey" that Cho reads during her podcast are real. They are direct quotations from the important and heartbreaking book *Regretting Motherhood: A Study* (pp. 60-7), which is based on the unparalleled research about mothers who regret conducted by the scholar and researcher Orna Donath.

In the introduction to *Regretting Motherhood* (pp. xvii-xviii), Donath writes: "I am not interested in simply acknowledging the existence of regretting motherhood. This lets society off the hook: if we personalize regret as a failure of some women to adapt to motherhood (and therefore suggesting that these specific mothers should try harder), then we stay oblivious to the way numerous Western societies vehemently push women not only into motherhood but into the subsequent loneliness of dealing with the consequences of this persuasion . . . If we think of emotions as a means to demonstrate against systems of power, then regret is an alarm bell that not only should alert societies that we need to make it easier for mothers to be mothers, but that invites us to rethink the politics of reproduction and the very obligation to become mothers at all. As regret marks the "road not taken," regretting motherhood indicates that there are other roads that society forbids women from taking, by *a priori* erasing alternative paths, such as nonmotherhood. As regret bridges between the past and the present and between the tangible and the recalled, regretting motherhood also clarifies what women are being asked to remember and what to forget without looking back."

ACKNOWLEDGMENTS

AS WITH ANY book, there are many people who stand behind it, helping it along and to eventually exist. Thank you to everyone who read the different drafts of this novel: Caitlin Wahrer, Rebecca Stead, Marie Rutkoski, Molly Millwood, Emily Oster, and Miriam Altshuler. Most especially, I want to thank my editor at Soho Crime, Juliet Grames, who believed in this book from the beginning, and who pushed me past my lingering fears of writing about this subject in each subsequent draft. I am so grateful to you, Juliet, for your intelligence, kindness, courage, honesty, and incredible editing. I am so happy that editors like you still exist.